For my son

Matthew

the real writer in the family

I don't have a favourite,
but if I did . . .

Prologue

'No nannies,' I pant, as the newspaper vendor spreads copies of *The Times* across the pavement behind his kiosk. 'We made that decision before we got pregnant.'

A freezing gust of wind slaps my wet skirts against my legs.

I grope clumsily for his stool. 'My brother and I were brought up by nannies. Davina says I'm mad to contemplate twins without help, but what's the point of having children if you're not going to look after them yourself? There's a nice Montessori – ohhh – near us that takes them from six months, and until then I'll work from home.'

For nine months, I've fondly imagined sitting at the kitchen table with my notebooks and laptop, sifting through pictures of orchids and peonies, Bach playing on the iPod, the twins gurgling happily in baby gyms at my feet.

'It's going to take a little bit of adjustment, I know that, but lots of women do it, don't they? Juggle work and children. It just takes organization. No different from running a company. If I can do that, I'm sure I can – *ohhhhh.*'

'Hold on, love,' the vendor soothes anxiously. 'The ambulance is on its way.'

'Don't worry. My husband will be here soon. I've got hours to go yet—'

I'm assaulted by another vicious wave of pain, and feel

the first stirrings of panic. The contractions are barely a minute apart. I'm not going to have time to get to a hospital. I'm not even going to make it to the ambulance.

This can't be happening. Not to *me*. I don't do drama. I'm not the kind of person who gets caught out. I have it all planned. Where's my private room, my soft music, my TENS machine, the solicitous hands rubbing my back and warming my feet? Where's my expensive obstetrician? Where's my *husband*?

As if from a distance, I watch myself slide from the stool and crouch like an animal on all fours on the cold, filthy pavement behind the newspaper stand. The vendor shouts at curious passers-by to fuck off, this ain't a peep-show, can't they see the lady needs some air?

A passing collie strains his leash and licks my cheek. I lift my head. It's Christmas Eve. Fairy lights glitter like stars in the trees around Sloane Square. 'Hark the Herald' blares from the Tube-station speakers behind me. All we need now are three wise men and some sheep.

This isn't the way I planned to bring a child into the world.

It's going wrong already.

St Jane's School for Girls

MAGDALEN AVENUE, OXFORD 0X5 2DY

SCHOOL REPORT

Summer Term 1982

NAME   Sterling, C. P.
YEAR   Junior IV
AGE   10 yrs 7 months

GENERAL COMMENTS

Clare is a responsible and hard-working member of the class. She has put effort into her studies, and her excellent examination results reflect this. Clare is an extremely organised student, but does not always cope well with sudden change. She needs to learn flexibility if she is to achieve her full potential. She would also benefit from expanding her interests beyond the classroom. If she could be encouraged to engage in sports or other extra-curricular activities, she might find it easier to make friends.

    Overall, we are very pleased with Clare's progress and look forward to welcoming her to the Senior School in September.

Anne Marsh
Headmistress

1

Clare

Orgasms are so tricky, aren't they? You need just the right mood and atmosphere; one false note and it's all over, however diligently your husband tongues your clitoris. I've never really enjoyed oral sex at all, actually, but I didn't like to say so when we first met in case it made me seem dull. And then you get stuck with it, don't you? You can hardly tell your husband after seven years that he's barking up the wrong tree.

I knew I was too tense from the start, of course; but when I put something on my List, I like to get it done.

'Darling,' Marc says, looking up from between my labia, 'is something wrong?'

Not that sex is ever a *chore*. I put facials and reflexology on my List too. How else could I run seven boutique flower shops in seven different parts of London and still keeps things ticking over smoothly at home without being ruthlessly organized? It may not seem very romantic, but if more wives put sex on their lists, there'd be fewer divorces. Though I don't think Marc would see it quite that way.

Poor Marc. He wasn't really in the mood tonight either: he wanted, rather keenly, to watch the ice hockey on cable (his home team, the Montreal Canadiens, were playing); but of course it's never difficult to change a man's mind. They don't need warm baths, soft music, candlelight and forty minutes of foreplay. Or even a flesh-and-blood woman, come to that.

He returns conscientiously to his task, but I'm tired and we both have to be up in five hours, so I ... well, I exaggerate things a bit. We all tell little white lies from time to time; imagine the scene on Christmas morning if we all said what we really thought of that hideous nest of flesh-coloured Tupperware boxes. Sometimes faking pleasure is the only polite thing to do.

After a brief interval, Marc slides comfortably inside me. I hold him close so he doesn't pull out too soon and waste our efforts.

Three months isn't very long to try for a baby; but I'm already thirty-seven years old. I work very hard to make sure my handsome, charming husband forgets he's nearly a decade younger than me; but I don't forget.

Not for a moment.

Sex with Marc is usually very nice. So it's unfortunate I conceive during one of our more pedestrian encounters.

My pregnancy is textbook; I know, because I read fourteen of them. They give different, and frequently conflicting, advice, but when in doubt I err on the side of caution. As I explain to Marc (crossing my fingers behind my back):

it isn't that I've gone off sex, but neither of us wants to take any risks with the baby.

And then, at the thirteen-week nuchal fold scan, we discover it's bab*ies*, plural.

Marc is delighted, of course, at this sign of his exceptional virility. Once I get over my initial shock, I quickly see the practical advantages. Two babies are scarcely more work than one; it's just a question of organization. Doubling up on the home-made apple purée, that sort of thing. It's taken five years of marriage and a great deal of careful planning to create a window in our schedules, and finances, for this pregnancy. At least now I won't have to take time off from PetalPushers again. Marc may have wanted six children (he has five older sisters), but two has always been my limit.

'Darling! *Twins*?' my mother ventures when I break the news. 'Clare, are you quite sure that's wise?'

'A little late now,' I say drily. 'Davina, I manage nineteen staff and seven shops. I think I can take care of two small infants. I've researched it thoroughly.'

'I'm sure you could write a marvellous thesis on child-rearing,' Davina says, gathering her summer furs, 'but it's not quite the same thing as actually *doing* it.'

Kettles and pots come to mind, but I let it pass. My mother has never pretended to enjoy motherhood; possessed of a maternal instinct that would make one tremble for a pet rabbit, she made a point of not taking the slightest interest in me or my younger brother, Xan, until we were legally adults. Growing up, I understood 'mother' to mean a remote, impatient figure who brushed away hugs – 'Darling! Sticky fingers!' – and punctured the small accomplishments of her children with verbal stilettos: 'Sweet that you came top in Biology, but, darling, there *are* only twenty-two of you in the class.' I was quite sure she loved us; and just as certain she'd never have had us at all had my father not made it clear her duty – and his fortune – required the provision of an heir.

I've never blamed her for palming us off on a series of nannies, of course; but from the start I was determined to do things differently.

It never occurs to me that my childcare plans are at best vague, at worst steeped in denial.

By the time I'm seven months pregnant, I'm completely prepared. Everything on my Baby List has been satisfyingly crossed off. Stair gates are installed in our Chelsea townhouse – 'The rug-rats aren't even here yet and you're corralling them,' Marc grumbles good-naturedly – and plastic safety covers fitted to every electricity outlet. The nursery is decorated a gender-neutral pale green with child-friendly non-toxic paints; an artist friend stencils primroses (signifying hope and youth), daisies (innocence) and asters (tiny beginnings from which great things proceed) around the door and windows. I spend weeks researching travel systems that incorporate the maximum number of safety features whilst providing ultimate comfort to the infant(s). The obstetrician I select (having interviewed four) dissuades me, against my better judgement, from the sleep-apnoea monitor, but I have Marc mount a state-of-the-art video system throughout the house so I can keep an eye on the twins wherever I am.

Craig, my VP, is primed to take over the reins at PetalPushers at a moment's notice. I finish all my Christmas shopping by November so I won't have to rush around with two newborns should they arrive before their due date (New Year's Eve). My overnight bag is packed and all set to go. I'm ready.

The twins, it seems, are not.

I try to rest, as the books suggest, but I've never been much good at waiting. I prefer to make things *happen*. If I wasn't so determined to have a natural birth (I've read that drugs cross the placenta, making the baby drowsy and less eager to feed in those first vital bonding hours after birth) I'd seriously consider an elective caesarean. It's so hard to plan ahead when you don't know your schedule.

And then on Christmas Eve my waters break as I travel the District & Circle Line, my arms filled with a massed ball of mistletoe for one of my most important clients.

I double up as a belt of white pain tightens around my abdomen. It's so much worse than I thought it'd be. Why doesn't anyone *tell* you?

The newspaper vendor puts his thick padded jacket around my shoulders. My teeth chatter. I can't seem to get warm. I want it to stop. I want this to be over. *I want my husband—*

'Clare!'

'Marc!' I sob, clutching his hand.

Voices fade in and out:

'We need to get her into a taxi—'

'Too late for that, mate—'

Someone is talking to me. I want them to go away. I'm so tired. I could bear the pain if they'd just let me *sleep* first. If only I could rest, and come back to this tomorrow—

'Clare, *stay with me*,' Marc demands. 'When I tell you to push, give it all you've got.'

'But my private room! My TENS! Everything's arranged—'

'Darling, our babies are coming! Isn't this exciting?'

'You fucking try it!' I yell.

Marc, *sotto voce*: 'Christ, it must be bad. My wife *never* swears.'

'You might want to let that pass for now, mate.'

'I could see the baby's head during that contraction, Clare. When the next one comes, I want you to push—'

'Just get this thing out of me!'

Suddenly I have a desperate need to bear down, as impossible to ignore or control as the urge to vomit. It feels like a huge iron fist is trying to punch its way through my rectum. *It can't be the babies*, I think stupidly, *it's in the wrong place, I'm going to shit myself, everyone will see but I can't help it, I can't stop it*, I have to push—

I feel a burning, tearing sensation, as if I'm splitting open like a ripe melon.

'One more push . . .'

This isn't right, it can't be, I'm not big enough, something is wrong—

'The baby's beautiful, Clare, beautiful. *Push!*'

'I *am* fucking pushing!' I scream.

There's a sudden rush and slither, and the pressure has gone.

'Open your eyes,' Marc whispers.

My baby is placed in my arms. He isn't crying. I open my eyes and look directly into his, deep blue like mine and already questioning. His skin and hair are still waxy with vernix.

Minutes later, his twin sister is born. She yells her fury at the indignity of her arrival immediately. Dimly I register that my son still hasn't drawn his first breath.

I hear the sound of sirens, and a paramedic thrusts her way towards us.

'Tell them not to worry, I think I'm getting the hang of this,' I say; and promptly black out.

Our daughter, Poppy (named for the qualities I see in her: pleasure, consolation and peace), takes after Marc. A vital, vigorous baby you want to devour, with smooth honeyed skin, thick dark hair and lashes like Dusty Springfield's.

Rowan is pale and blond like me. I hope that, by giving him a name associated with potency and magic, it will somehow keep him safe.

For two weeks Marc shuttles heroically between home, where Poppy is thriving, and the NICU of the Princess Eugenie Hospital, where Rowan clings precariously to life. Meanwhile, in a different hospital on the other side of London, their hormonal, humiliated and exhausted mother is confined to bed by a virulent infection picked up giving birth in the streets like a gin-soaked whore in a Hogarth print.

Davina doesn't visit, of course. I didn't expect her to.

I'm astonished by the apparent ease with which Marc has taken to fatherhood. I'm the one biologically pro-grammed to bond with my young; and yet, as I struggle to adjust to the idea that I'm now *a mother*, he's the one who seems to find it as natural as breathing.

Marc Elias was not promising parenthood – or marriage – material when we ran into one another at four o'clock one foggy February morning nearly seven years ago. Literally: I didn't even see his grey BMW until it slammed into the side of my van.

'I'm *so* sorry,' I apologized, as only women do when they're clearly in the right. 'But it's one-way.'

The driver buzzed down his window. 'You didn't signal—'

'As I said,' I repeated, rather less politely, 'it *is* one-way.'

'Look, it's only a dent. You'll be able to—'

If there's one thing I can't stand, it's a man who won't take responsibility. I held up my hand to silence him. 'That really isn't good enough,' I said coolly, 'is it?'

It didn't occur to me to be nervous till he got out. At five-ten, I'm tall, but he towered over me. It was still dark, and the streets of New Covent Garden were deserted; most stallholders and early-bird wholesale buyers like me were already inside the covered market, out of the wind and sleet. No one would hear me scream.

I stood my ground and wondered if my knee would even reach his groin.

He caught me completely off guard.

'How about lunch?' he said.

Later, as I sat at the Oyster Bar and toyed with my shellfish, I wondered what he wanted. I hadn't been fool enough to think he'd been mesmerized by my beauty. I'm no oil painting at the best of times, and seven years ago, my life was as far from the best of times as it was possible to be. I'd foolishly over-extended myself buying up shop leases across London as if I was playing Monopoly, regularly putting in twenty-hour days just to keep PetalPushers afloat. I was running on empty, and it showed.

With the benefit of daylight, I could see that Marc, on

the other hand, looked good enough to eat. Skin the colour of caramel, eyes like bitter chocolate. (I learned later he owed those smouldering Omar Sharif looks to his Lebanese father, who'd emigrated with the family to Canada when Marc was four.) He was witty, charming and well read; he even had a sexy foreign accent, somewhere between French and North American, thanks to his upbringing in Montreal.

He was also, at twenty-three, eight years younger than me.

He asked me out to lunch again; I said no. As if following a woo-by-numbers rulebook, he sent me books of poetry, chocolates shaped like lilies, tickets to *Madame Butterfly*; I thanked him and went with my brother, Xan. Of course I didn't take Marc seriously; despite the millions he traded daily at a Canadian bank in the City, as far as I was concerned he was still barely out of short trousers. I was thirty-one; I needed an older man, an equal, someone I could look up to (metaphorically rather than literally).

But despite – or perhaps because of – his youth, he continued to pursue me with a level of ardour and persistence I'd never experienced before. Most men were put off once they discovered I had a First from Oxford and earned well into six figures. Marc was different. He wasn't fazed by any of it. I put it down to the fact that he was so much younger; maybe this generation of New Men really *did* see women as equal.

Even so, I might never have returned his calls, had he not found my website and started emailing me.

At first, his emails were the kind of casual notes you'd send a friend; I'd thought (with a surprising pang) that he'd given up on the romance idea. He sounded off about global warming (ah! his age was showing *there*) and debated the wisdom of remaking classic movies. Then gradually he started to tell me about his life; he discussed his five older sisters in such detail I felt as if I'd stepped into an Austen novel. He told me how he'd felt when his best friend shot himself in the head at the age of seventeen, and wondered if he'd ever have a marriage as strong as his parents'. It was less what he said, of course, but that he said it at all: for a woman used to dating emotionally constipated toxic bachelors, nothing could have been more seductive than a man who told me, without asking, what he was thinking. For six months he emailed me pieces of his life, and before I knew it, he was a part of mine.

When he asked me to marry him, a year after we met, I still had no idea what he saw in me. I sucked in my stomach as I gazed up at the shining young knight standing beside me at the altar, and prayed he loved me for my mind.

'Tell me,' my mother, Davina, said, 'has he ever asked you what *you're* thinking?'

It is Marc who brings my newborn daughter to stay with me every day, so I can feed her, not my mother. I've read about the difficulties of breastfeeding and latching on, of course, but nothing has prepared me for the reality of the two hot, painful, misshapen bombs strapped to my chest. The slightest brush against them is torture. Poppy's suckling isn't the tranquil, bonding experience I'd imagined, but a violent wrestling match with an incubus I can never satisfy.

'She's doing it wrong!' I wail, as Poppy squirms and screams, red-faced and hungry, in my arms. 'She's got to open her mouth more!'

'Clare, you need to relax. The more upset you get, the more you upset her.'

'She's not getting anything! She'll starve! Davina was right, I'm going to be a terrible mother, I can't even feed my own baby . . .'

Marc perches on the hospital bed and reaches around me, cradling us both in his arms. 'She's just getting used to it, same as you. Look, stroke her cheek, so she turns her face towards you. There, you see?'

'I'm the one with the breasts,' I sob. 'How is it you know what to do?'

'I have five sisters, and seventeen nieces and nephews. You pick up a few things.'

'I should be able to do it. Why can't I do it?'

'You *are* doing it,' he soothes.

As Marc promised, Poppy soon gets the hang of it, but by now my nipples are cracked and bleeding. If only I could ask my mother what to do; and if wishes were horses, beggars would ride.

On the advice of one of the nurses, Marc brings in cold cabbage leaves for me to score and place against my engorged breasts, but nothing helps. Every time Poppy latches on, I want to scream with agony.

But at least I'm managing to feed my daughter, however painfully. I haven't even seen my son, fighting for life in a hospital the other side of London, since he was born. Marc takes dozens of photos on his mobile phone, but I ache to hold him. He looks so tiny, though he's putting on weight faster than Poppy. A nurse with a bottle is nurturing my son better than I can nourish my own daughter.

I can't seem to get it together. I burst into tears all the time, and forget things I *know* I know. My hair falls out in clumps, my stomach is stretch-marked and pouchy, and I'm bleeding so heavily I have to wear a huge pad like a mattress between my legs. I have eight stitches in my perineum and haemorrhoids the size of grapes. Even my toenail polish is chipped. I've been a mother less than a fortnight, and already I'm letting myself go.

In the second week of January, Rowan is unexpectedly discharged from the NICU, a healthy six pounds, and Marc is finally told he can take me home too.

'I'm not ready,' I panic, 'I can't, not yet—'

'You'll be fine,' Marc smiles, strapping the twins into the back of the Range Rover. 'You'll feel much better when you get home and everything goes back to normal.'

Normal? I think. *Nothing will ever be normal again.*

If I could just get a good night's sleep. Gather my resources. But the first night home, the twins wake at midnight, at two, at three, three-thirty, four-thirty. Poppy feeds hungrily, but Rowan struggles in my arms, red-faced and frantic, wanting the familiar rubber teat of a bottle in his mouth, not this strange, warm nipple. I'm used to Poppy in my arms; when I cradle Rowan, I feel as if I'm holding someone else's baby.

Marc sleeps through it all. At 6 a.m., he leans over the bed and kisses me on the cheek. His jaw is smooth and freshly shaven.

Blearily, I push myself up on one elbow. 'You're going to work?'

'I have to, Clare. I've already taken too much time off looking after Poppy. There's a major deal going through in the European—'

To my shame, I start to cry.

'Oh, darling. You're going to be fine.' He sits on the

edge of the bed and thumbs the tears from my cheek. He looks as handsome and carefree as ever. 'You've just got to get into the swing of things. It's not that hard once you establish a routine. Fran said she'd pop over later this morning. She's done this herself three times, remember. She knows what it's like.'

'But nothing's organized, we need more nappies, food—'

'Sweetheart, you've been organized for months,' Marc laughs. 'By the way, can you get me some more razor blades? I forgot to buy some, and I'm out.'

The moment the front door shuts behind him, Poppy wakes. Her imperious cries disturb her brother. Rowan's sobs are anguished and desperate. I agitate beside their cots, not knowing who to pick up first. I've never been alone with my son before. I don't know what he wants. I don't know how to please him.

Feeling guilty, I choose Poppy.

'I can't,' I plead with my son. 'I can't feed both of you together.'

I wrestle with the buttons on my maternity nightdress and unhook my nursing bra with one hand, fumbling in my haste, petrified I'm going to drop Poppy.

Rowan's cries redouble. He sucks in a breath, but doesn't exhale, mouth open and eyes screwed shut in a silent scream. His face and lips turn blue. I tug Poppy off the breast, ignoring her indignant yells. Holding her under one arm, I scoop up Rowan with the other, then stand there with two screaming infants, unable to satisfy either one. Tears stream down my own cheeks. I don't know what to do. I don't know which mouth to feed.

Somehow, I prop us all in the nursing chair, using two

of the ridiculous oversized soft toys the twins have been given to protect their heads from its beautifully carved flame-cherrywood arms. (Why didn't I pick the cheap padded rocking chair? What use is *carving* to a baby?)

I wedge them on each side of me, trapping their small hot bodies against the chair. I push one small face – none too gently – towards each fat brown nipple. Snuffling like a little animal, Poppy latches on immediately. Rowan twists his face away, searching again for the bottle. I yelp with frustration, and rub my milky nipple hard against his mouth. Finally, he starts to suck. I close my eyes. For the first time in my life, I feel a flicker of sympathy for my mother.

Fran is late. Fran is always late, which usually drives me wild – honestly, it's just a question of planning ahead – but today I'm relieved at the reprieve. It's midday, and I've barely managed to get dressed. How do other mothers do it? How do they even find time to go to the bathroom?

'Sorry I'm late,' Fran says, kissing my cheek. 'I caught Kirsty smoking on the nanny-cam, the little cow. I'd fire her, only she might go running to Rod, and this divorce is bloody enough as it is.' She unwinds her scarf and throws it over the banister. 'Darling, you look marvellous! So *thin*! Where are the twins? I've been dying to see Rowan—'

'Upstairs. Sleeping.'

'I'll be quiet as a mouse!'

She's upstairs before I can stop her. Reluctantly, I follow her into our bedroom, where the twins are top-to-tail in the very heavy, old-fashioned pram that Marc and I lugged upstairs last night, since they refuse to settle in the expensive matching Simon Horne cots in their newly decorated nursery. The only way I can get them to sleep is by rocking the pram until my arm aches.

Fran leans over them, and I flinch as the oak floorboards squeak. *Don't wake don't wake don't wake.*

'Oh, Clare. They're adorable,' she breathes.

'They are now.'

'Oh, dear. I remember that feeling,' Fran sighs. 'I know it takes a bit of getting used to, especially with twins, but you'll soon get the hang of it. And think of the benefits of getting the whole baby thing out of the way in one go, two for the price of one. Perhaps if Rod and I had done that—'

'It took me four hours to get us all ready this morning,' I say bleakly. 'First I had to feed the twins, and then they needed changing. I put them back down for five minutes to have a shower, but Rowan screamed and screamed until he was sick all over the sheets and his clean clothes, so I had to strip the pram and change him for a second time, by which time Poppy wanted feeding again. I just can't seem to catch up. You've no idea how hard it is to feed two babies at once. Rowan keeps refusing the breast, I practically have to *force* him—'

I break into sudden sobs, and clamp my hand over my mouth to keep from waking the twins.

Fran pulls me into a sympathetic hug. 'Clare, sweetheart, you're doing a *won*derful job,' she says firmly. '*Every*one feels like this at first. You should have seen me when Hector was born. Every time he had a temperature, I was rushing off to Casualty, convinced it was meningitis or worse.'

'I feel – I feel so *hope*less . . .'

'You're not hopeless,' Fran says, misunderstanding. 'Darling, you've had a terribly rough start. I can't believe how marvellously you've coped with it all. First having the babies in the *street* – I still can't believe it! – and then getting so ill, and not even being able to *see* poor Rowan for two weeks.'

'I don't think,' I say slowly, 'he likes me. He cries every time I pick him up.'

'Of course he *likes* you! He's just getting used to you, that's all. Look,' she adds, steering me back downstairs, into the sitting room, and handing me a tissue, 'would you like to borrow Kirsty to help out for a few hours a day, just till you find your feet? Now Imogen's at kindergarten she's got time on her hands, and as long as you frisk her for cigarettes on the way in, she's marvellously organized. You could have her for a couple of hours after she's done the school run—'

'That's very sweet of you, but we'll be fine,' I say quickly. 'You're right. We just need to get ourselves into a routine.'

'If you change your mind—'

'I won't,' I say firmly.

But, over the next weeks, there are times I long to swallow my pride and take Fran up on her offer. I'd crawl over broken glass and stick shards in my eyeballs for a single good night's sleep.

Rowan never takes milk from me without a fight. He twists and turns in my arms, arching his back and kicking his legs as if he's trying to get away from me. Poppy nurses contentedly till she falls asleep with a smile on her milky lips. Rowan is sick after every feed; my clothes and hair permanently smell of vomit. I'm ashamed to admit it, even to myself, but there are times when I find it very difficult to summon even a shred of affection for my son.

Then, when he's three weeks old, he develops colic.

I've read about it, of course, but the first time Rowan shrieks in agony, cramps twisting his tiny stomach, his little legs pulled up tight against his frail body, I have no idea what is wrong. Marc and I are frantic with worry, imagining twisted bowels, peritonitis or worse. When the paediatrician tells us the next day it's colic – 'Hundred-day colic,' he says cheerfully, 'never lasts longer than that' – I cry again, this time with relief.

But that night, Rowan screams solidly from eleven till four. I give him his useless medicine, rub his back, massage his tummy, stroke his bare toes. He doesn't stop screaming. I take him downstairs so he doesn't keep Poppy and Marc awake too; we eventually collapse into an exhausted sleep on the sofa together, both of us cried out. I never even hear Marc leave for work the next morning. The following night, at Fran's suggestion, Marc takes him for a drive; Rowan falls asleep when the car is moving, and wakes up the second Marc steps back inside.

Marc and I are both shattered, but, as he says, he has a full-time job to hold down. One mistake could cost his company billions. I tell him to sleep in the spare room to get some rest, and then resent him furiously when he agrees.

By the time the twins are six weeks old, I'm a zombie. I'm dizzy from lack of sleep and weak from having no time to eat. I cry all the time. All I care about is the next pocket of time in the day when I can snatch a few moments of sleep. The second the twins close their eyes, I close mine. I wake when they wake. I have no life outside their needs.

There's no one I can talk to. Everyone thinks I'm coping marvellously; they've no idea that inside I'm falling apart at the seams. Marc's mother had six children in seven years; how can I admit to him I can't handle two? Fran's sympathetic, but she's got her own life. I can't burden her with my problems.

I could manage, if it was just Poppy. She sleeps through the night already. If it was just Poppy, I wouldn't be so tired; I could catch up with things, pick up the reins at work (Craig's stopped bothering to leave messages, since I never return them). I'd be a better mother, a good mother: the kind of mother who plays peek-a-boo with her new baby and blows raspberries on her tummy, instead of slumming around the house in a stained nightdress at three in the afternoon. If I didn't have Rowan, I could enjoy Poppy. She's such an easy baby. She goes four hours between feeds; she gurgles with pleasure whenever I walk into the room. But I'm so tired and anxious, I'm a nervous wreck. I'm short-changing them both.

If something should – *happen* – to Rowan . . .

Not that I'd ever want it to. He's my son. *Of course* I don't want anything to happen to him. But . . . but if it did . . .

For a brief moment, as I pace the floor in the soulless small hours one night with my screaming son, shivering with tiredness, I give in and allow myself to picture life without him. Just me and Marc and Poppy, a perfect little family. Going on outings, feeding the ducks, walking in the park. Simple, ordinary things that are beyond us now.

Poppy deserves better. It's not that I don't care about Rowan. But I have to think of what's best for Poppy. It's only because I love her so much I'm thinking such unnatural, terrible thoughts.

The clock in the hall chimes twice. I stare at the wailing

infant in my arms with curious detachment. I feel nothing: sadness or pleasure, grief or anger. I'm at the bottom of an abyss deep below the dark ocean. Nothing reaches me. I sit on the sofa and place him carefully next to me, wedging a cushion on either side of him so that he doesn't fall. I know even as I do it that it's pointless. Unless I pace with him in my arms, he'll scream himself sick.

Within seconds, his cries are deafening.

Instead of picking him up, I sit and watch him scream, his face scarlet and shiny with tears. If I left him, would he literally cry himself to death? Or would he realize it was hopeless and give up?

He'll wake Marc and Poppy. They need their sleep.

You wouldn't think his lungs were big enough to make this much noise.

The streetlight outside casts orange Hallowe'en shadows across the floor. It's never truly dark in the city. Never truly quiet.

The room is filled with screaming. My head vibrates with sound, the way it does when a car has stopped next to you at a traffic light, the bass so loud you feel rather than hear it. My knuckles are white from gripping the arm of the sofa, but I can't feel my hands.

'I'm sorry,' I say calmly. 'I can't do this any more. It's too much. It's not fair to Poppy. You do understand, don't you? It's not fair to Poppy.'

And then I pick up a cushion to smother my son.

114 Essex Road, Islington,

London N1 8LX

(0207) 714 7885

1st March 2009

Mrs C Elias
97 Cheyne Walk
Chelsea
London SW3 5TS

Dear Mrs Elias,

I confirm that Jenna Kemeny worked for our family as a nanny for two years, until her <u>abrupt</u> departure last month, with sole responsibility for our two children, Tatiana, 2, and Galen, 3. She fulfilled her general duties adequately for the most part, although she was <u>not</u> as flexible in her hours as we would have liked. She also took a rather relaxed attitude towards punctuality. The children's immediate physical needs were usually met, but Jenna did not always grasp the additional demands required when caring for <u>gifted</u> <u>children</u>. She struggled to cope without imposing rigid, structured routines in the nursery. She also demonstrated a rather uncompromising streak and ignored our requests to let the children express their creativity in their own way. As a qualified psychologist, I can tell you that cars may, after all, be repainted, but a child's imagination, once caged, will never soar again.

I believe Jenna would prove an adequate babysitter for your child. However, if you require a more <u>nurturing</u> environment for your baby, you may wish to broaden your search.

If you have any further questions, please do not hesitate to contact me.

Yours sincerely,

Margaret Hasselbach, PhD

2

Jenna

Best cure for a bad hangover is a good fuck.

Looks like I'm in for a monster headache, then.

I curl against Jamie, wrapping my arms around his stiff back. I know better than to tell him it doesn't matter.

He prises my fingers away. 'You're going to be late for work.'

'Jamie . . .'

'Try to get home on time.'

The room swims when I get out of bed. I lean my forehead against the cool bathroom tile, wondering queasily if I'm going to puke again. Maybe I'd feel better if I did. I'm certainly in no fit state to take on two spoiled brats whose fucked-up parents should never have been allowed to reproduce.

When I finish my shower, Jamie has gone.

I sweep up the shards of his coffee mug – still warm – and run my finger lightly over the new dent in the bedroom wall. It's been two months now. He's got to talk to somebody who knows how to help him. I'm not sure how much longer I can cope with this on my own.

Maggie is standing on the doorstep when I arrive at the Hasselbachs'. She thrusts Tatiana into my arms with a glare. The two-year-old promptly spits in my face.

'Well, you can't blame her,' Maggie snaps. 'You're late.'

Yeah, *three minutes*. I watch Maggie stalk down the front steps. Should I tell her she's got her executive skirt tucked into her tights?

Tatiana spits at me again.

Screw it.

Three-year-old Galen is slumped on the floor of the living room, transfixed by *Spongebob*. I turn the TV off ('Please understand, Jenna, the children are *not* permitted to watch television. We believe it Rots Young Minds'). Galen yells and turns it on again. I turn it off. Galen kicks my leg and lunges for the remote. I put Tatiana down, take the remote away and put it on a shelf out of his reach. The little sod pulls his sister's hair, upends the Lego table and throws himself on the floor in a tantrum. So far, so normal.

In the kitchen, Maggie has left her usual list (heavily underlined) weighted to the hand-hewn butcher's block with an empty bottle of avocado oil: her subtle way of telling me to buy a new one.

I skim my errands for the day. 'Collect dry cleaning. Tati haircut (remember we are <u>growing out her fringe</u>). Galen needs new shoes, <u>not</u> leather.'

Christ. That'll mean a trip to the fancy vegan shoe store on the other side of town.

'Birthday present for Lottie's party (<u>nothing</u> made in China.) Toilet roll. Crushed garlic. Organic salmon fillets x2 (<u>fresh</u>). Pick up tile sample from Bathstore. NB dishwasher

Tess Stimson

man coming 2 p.m. Do <u>not</u>' (triple underlined) 'let him leave without fixing problem <u>under any circs.</u>'

'D'you think she expects me to sleep with him?' I idly ask my BFF Kirsty later.

'Would it help?'

'Not unless he's into necrophilia. I look like death.' I jam the phone beneath my chin and rip open my second packet of Resolve. 'I shouldn't have let you talk me into that last tequila. I'm too old for this shit.'

'Stick the kids in front of the TV and sack out for a couple of hours.'

'I can't. Maggie's left me a list of jobs a mile long.'

'So? She doesn't pay you to organize her entire life. You're a nanny, not a bloody slave. You need to put your foot down. If I was you, I'd – Hector, leave that alone! You know Mummy doesn't let you— Oh, fuck. Hang on, Jen.'

I knock back the Resolve and root around in Maggie's cupboard for the expensive shortbread biscuits she always hides at the back. Upstairs, Galen and Tatiana are battling it out in the playroom. It's my policy not to intervene till there's blood on the floor.

'Little bastard,' Kirsty pants, picking up the phone again. 'He broke that vase on purpose. If Fran tries to knock it off my wages, I'll quit.'

'Yeah, as *if*. You'll never get a job this good again. She didn't even fire you when she caught you smoking on the nanny-cam.'

'Only because she knows I'd go to Rod and she'd get fucked in the divorce.'

'Maggie's got no idea what a pain it is dragging two kids all over town,' I mumble through a mouthful of shortbread. 'You need a bloody Physics degree to get them

28

in and out of those fancy car seats of hers. It's not fair on the kids, either. No wonder they're so bratty, they're bored shitless. She might as well – oh fuck. She's on call waiting. I'd better go.'

'Who were you talking to?' Maggie demands.

'Cold caller—'

'Yes, well, never mind that. You need to take the children to get new ski outfits this afternoon,' she snaps. 'We've decided to go to Val d'Isère at half-term after all. And you'll have to buy yourself a decent jacket, the one you wore last year was *totally* inadequate.'

Yeah. That would be the one you made me pay for myself, Maggie.

It suddenly registers. 'Actually, Maggie, I'm off that week.'

'So? You can have the week after off instead.'

'But I'm going to Malaga with Jamie. We discussed it months ago—'

'I can't be expected to recall every little conversation, Jenna.'

'I've already booked the flights!'

'Well, you'll have to change them. I can't *possibly* go skiing without a nanny.'

Has she got any idea how up her own arse she is?

'Perhaps Jan and Curran's au pair could—'

'Oh yes, that reminds me. We're doubling up this year to save money, so you'll be looking after their three boys too. You've got to go with Galen and Tati to ski school anyway, so it's not as if it'll put you out.'

'Maggie, I really can't,' I say desperately.

'Jenna, there isn't much point me having a nanny if she's not going to be there when I need her,' Maggie says pointedly. 'Most girls would be *thrilled* at the idea of a holiday in France, *especially* when someone else is paying for it.'

The threat hangs in the air. We both know how much I need to keep this job with Jamie not working. I'm two months behind on the rent already, and my credit cards are maxed out.

'Yes, Maggie,' I say dully.

'I'll make it up to you,' Maggie promises, now she knows she's won.

Sometimes I really hate her. How many times have I heard that line before? 'Sorry I was three hours late and you missed your mother's birthday dinner, but I'll make it up to you.' 'I know I said you could have Christmas off this year, but this trip is really important, I'll make it up to you.' 'We can't afford to give you a pay rise this summer, but don't worry, we'll make it up to you.'

I've no idea how I'll break it to Jamie. He's been pinning everything on this break.

I'm exhausted by the time Maggie gets home – late, as usual. The children have been absolute fuckers; dragged from pillar to post on Maggie's errands, they're fractious and overtired. As soon as she walks in the door, they fling themselves dramatically at her, clinging on to her legs like tree-frogs, and she glares at me accusingly. *What, you think I've kept them locked in the coal cellar and fed them stale bread and water?* Suddenly I'm not sorry I gave the kids chocolate biscuits and Coke as a treat after tea. They'll be bouncing off the walls all evening.

When I pull up forty minutes later outside our block, I see Jamie has every light in the flat blazing. I sigh inwardly. He can't bear the dark these days.

'Jamie?' I throw my keys on the hall table. 'Sorry I'm so late. Maggie was an hour late because of some meeting, and then—'

I never even see the punch coming.

'Live-in,' I say casually.

Annabel looks surprised. 'I understood you've always preferred live-out?'

'I need some . . . personal space.'

Her eyes flick towards my bruised cheekbone, then back to her screen. 'I haven't had a chance to go through your file properly yet. Remind me, how long is it since Caroline placed you with the Hasselbachs?'

'Two years.'

She gives me a beady look. 'The salary's pretty good. What's the problem?'

'Nothing really,' I fib. 'I think the relationship's just gone stale. You know how it is. We both need to find someone else.'

'Before this, you were with the Corcorans for just over a year.' Annabel scrolls down, tapping her red nails on the screen. 'Two boys, eight months and a year and a half. But just one other family before that, I see?'

'The Martindales were my first nannying job. Maeve, their little girl, was on my county swimming team. When she was about eight her mum got sick, and they asked me to look after her full-time,' I say, thinking that, actually, it was Anna Martindale who rescued *me*, 'and, well, it sort of went from there.'

'I hadn't realized you were on the county team. We should put it on your CV.'

'I was in the nationals. I had to quit when I got knocked off my bicycle and broke my shoulder, so I started coaching instead.'

She looks pitying. There's no need. I was gutted at the time, of course, but I'm over it now. It's been nine years, after all. You can't keep thinking, *What if*?

'We'd be able to get you a much better placement and salary if you had a CACHE diploma or some other child-care qualifications,' Annabel muses. 'Parents can often be funny like that. They'd rather have an eighteen-year-old with a bit of paper than someone experienced like you.'

'I didn't exactly plan this as a career,' I say mildly. 'It just sort of happened.'

'Well, your references from the Corcorans and Martin-dales are fantastic, and I'm sure Mrs Hasselbach will give you a glowing one too. I've got at least three lovely families on my books I think will suit you; let me make a few calls. When can you start?'

'As soon as you can find me a job,' I say.

Jamie and I were in trouble before The Accident (he insists on referring to it like that, as if he'd been hit by a car, or slipped and fallen down a flight of stairs). We've been together too long; we aren't the same people any more. Six years is a long time. I'm twenty-seven now, not twenty-one. People change.

When we met, Jamie was the weekend rugby captain at the South London Sports Centre where I coached part-time after taking the job with the Martindales; I fancied the arse off him, and he knew it. A couple of years older than me, he was a real Jack-the-lad, everybody's friend: laughing loudest and drinking heaviest. He could stop a tank with one massive fist, and lift me on to the bar without breaking into a sweat. I was the club princess, everybody's sweetheart (people say I look like a younger Sandra Bullock, only with green eyes); most of the rugby team fancied the pants off me, and I knew it, too. Of course we ended up together. We were the Homecoming King and Queen of Stockwell.

Friday nights to Monday mornings were just one long party. Sometimes I wished we could spend more time alone together, just the two of us, but, as Jamie said, you're only young once. Plenty of time to stay in and watch TV when we're collecting our pensions.

I don't know when Jamie's drinking tipped from sociable last-man-standing into a serious problem, because it happened so gradually I didn't notice. Or told myself I didn't notice. But around a year ago people began to take me aside and ask if something was wrong at home. (There wasn't; unless you count a chronic reluctance to grow up.) Jamie started missing rugby practice, turning up late to games, or not turning up at all. Most nights, he fell asleep on the sofa in front of the TV, a dozen empty beer cans on the floor at his feet. I tried to speak to him, but of course he brushed it off. Eventually, the club had no choice but to drop him from the team. I felt sorry for him, of course, even though it was self-inflicted; I knew exactly what he was going through, after all. But Jamie couldn't pull himself out of it. He just sat around feeling depressed and sorry for himself. I still cared about him, but it got harder and harder not to lose my patience.

I was pretty sure he was building up to ask me to marry him on Christmas Day; he'd turned thirty in November, his plumbing business was doing really well despite his drinking, and his mum was dropping heavy hints about grandkids. I couldn't let it drift on any longer. I had to end it. I was just waiting for the right moment.

And then he had his 'accident', and everything changed.

I don't know what Annabel's idea of a 'lovely family' is, but I think their surname might be Addams.

The first family live in a huge fuck-off McMansion in Notting Hill. I'm mentally doubling my salary as I sit in a lounge the size of my parents' semi, and wondering if I should go for a car too (Kirsty has the use of a brand-new Mini Cooper) when they offer to show me round. 'My' room turns out to be a single bed in the corner of their two-year-old daughter's nursery.

'We have a lot of guests,' the mother says brazenly. 'We can't afford to tie up a good bedroom on a permanent basis.'

The second family live in Wimbledon, near the tennis club. The house isn't that big, but I'd get the whole of the attic floor to myself, including a small kitchen. The wages are a bit more than I'm getting now, and best of all, I'll have eight weeks off every summer when my charge, a seven-year-old boy, goes to California to stay with his dad.

Then I meet the kid.

'He's a fucking psycho!' I yell to Annabel later. 'His mother left the room to answer the phone, and the bastard stapled the cat's tail to the rug! He just grinned when he saw me watching – I swear, that little bastard's another Ted Bundy. Why did his last nanny leave?'

'Personal reasons,' Annabel says uncomfortably.

'How much did the mother pay her to keep quiet?'

'She had a very generous severance package—'

'I'll bet. How many nannies has he had so far?'

A pause. 'You'd have been the eighth.'

'*Annabel* . . .'

'You'll love the next family,' she promises quickly. 'Two little girls aged four and six, BUPA, great salary . . .'

I take to the mother immediately, and the little girls are sweet too. My own room, a car at weekends, decent wages. It's a bit too near home – I don't want to run into Jamie at the supermarket – but other than that, it seems ideal. Until the father puts his hand on my bum as he shows me round and tells me he and his wife are very comfortable with nudity.

'You said no babies,' Annabel retorts, when I complain. 'That rules out an awful lot of nice families.'

'It's too hard,' I sigh. 'I fall in love with them. It's going to break my heart to leave Tati. There must be *some*thing else.'

'Are you quite sure you actually *want* to leave Maggie, Jenna?'

I hesitate. Maggie pays good money, and the children are OK really; I could probably limp on in this job for another year, till Galen's at kindergarten. But the situation with Jamie won't wait. I can't give up on him completely, after what happened to him. But I'm not going to stick around to be his punch-bag. I have to move out now, ease him gently into the idea of us splitting up.

Fuck it. 'OK, what the hell,' I tell Annabel. 'Give me babies.'

*

35

'One baby, Annabel,' I mutter, staring up at the smart Chelsea townhouse with its shiny black front door and gold door-knocker. 'No need to go overboard.'

I'm tempted to keep right on walking. Not just because it's twins ('Oh, didn't I tell you?' Annabel said innocently, after I'd already agreed to the interview. 'Never mind, if you split your focus, you won't get so attached'), but because I know people who live in Cheyne Walk are never going to hire someone common like me. The leafy street is lined with Bentleys and Jags; as I skulk on the front steps, an old woman with more bling than Elizabeth Taylor walks past, giving me a dirty look and the kind of wide berth you reserve for dogshit. These people can afford a posh Norland Nanny in a cap and uniform who knows the difference between napkins and serviettes. Forget it. Even if they give me the job, I don't want to spend my life being treated like a bloody serf.

'Are you – are you Jenna?'

I turn back. A tall, fragile woman is peering around the shiny door, one infant cradled awkwardly in her thin arms, another strapped to her chest in a filthy baby sling. Her fine blond hair needs a good wash, and her pale face is etched with tiredness. Baby puke stains both shoulders of her cashmere sweater, and she's barefoot, despite the freezing February weather.

'Mrs Elias?'

'Oh, thank God!' she cries, and bursts into tears.

In one swift motion I shoo her into the house, take the baby she's holding, unfasten the other infant from her chest and settle us all on settees in the lounge, nudging a box of tissues towards her with my elbow.

'I'm so sorry,' she sobs. 'You must think I'm a complete

disaster. I'm just so *tired* – two of them – never sleep – no idea how much *work* – hungry *all* the time . . .'

I let her cry it out, not understanding most of what she says, rocking the babies in my arms. The Corcorans' two boys were only eleven months apart, so I've had a bit of practice handling two wrigglers at the same time. I dip my head to them. God, I'd forgotten how *yummy* babies smell.

The twins stare up at me with the intense, old-soul gaze of very young infants. They don't look a bit alike. The girl (dressed in the kind of pink-and-white smocked top only posh people who've never had babies buy) is dark and plump and the colour of honeycomb, with eyes like Maltesers; the boy (in a navy sailor suit you know will run in the wash) is more of a Milky Bar kid, all pale angles and ashy hair and velvet-grey eyes. Neither of them cries. I love them already.

Their mother blows her nose, and leaps up. 'I'm a terrible hostess. What must you think? Did you have a good journey? Can I get you a cup of tea?'

'I'm fine, thank you, Mrs Elias—'

'Please, call me Clare. You must be thirsty. Or hungry. Are you hungry? I've got some lovely—'

'Mrs – Clare – it's OK. Really. I'm sure you've got lots of questions you want—'

'The other girls were so dreadful,' she blurts suddenly, plonking back down, 'and you look so nice and *normal*. I was beginning to despair; you've no idea. The first girl we interviewed sounded pleasant on the phone, and then she turned up in spiky red heels and a skirt so short you could see her knickers. I'm sure she was very sweet, but *really* . . . And then the next girl was a vegan, which doesn't matter at all, of course, but she was so *thin*, I just couldn't see how she was going to manage, not with all our stairs, and Marc said even with his bonus we couldn't afford to feed her special organic beans and things, and she had this *dread*ful cold . . .'

I add another hundred a week to my asking salary.

'. . . Then there was a girl who didn't speak a word of English and couldn't drive, and a Russian girl who spent the whole interview making eyes at my husband—'

'Clare,' I prompt gently. 'Was there anything you wanted to know about *me*?'

She stares blankly, shredding a tissue. I don't get it. I already know from Annabel that Clare Elias is a mega-successful businesswoman who owns a load of fancy flower shops, and yet it's like she's gone about the most important decision of her life absolutely blind, jotting down names from hand-scrawled ads pinned up on gym bulletin boards next to notices for second-hand treadmills and unwanted gerbils.

It's obvious she hasn't a clue what to ask me, so I give her a brief history of my previous jobs, while the babies magically – alleluia! – fall asleep in my arms.

Thankfully she doesn't have the experience to enquire why I'm leaving my previous job, or get into any of the sticky issues that always cause trouble, like whether I believe in dummies (better than thumbs) or smacking (yes, but only to stop small hands from getting burned on stoves). Clearly I've already scored highly on the Bonding With Baby section of our show. I usually hate it when the children are brought out and I'm expected to demonstrate some amazing facility with kids. It's like a bizarre mating ritual, where two animals are thrown together: interested parties gather round to watch, wondering if they'll take to each other.

'Would you like me to put the twins down in the nursery?' I ask. 'Perhaps you could show me my room afterwards.'

'Your room?'

Oh, fuck.

'I understood this was a live-in position,' I say carefully.

'That's not – we didn't – I'm sure I told the girl at the agency . . .'

I'll kill Annabel. She's totally set me up.

Clare wrings her hands. 'I don't suppose you'd consider . . .'

'I'm sorry,' I say truthfully. 'I really do need a live-in job.'

'No, no, I understand.' She hesitates. 'Maybe we can sort something out. The house is certainly big enough. We've got five bedrooms. It's just – well, my husband wasn't too keen on the whole nanny thing, to be honest. I'd planned to work from home for six months, then maybe send the twins to the Montessori . . .'

Christ. Poor cow. She really doesn't have the faintest what she's let herself in for.

I've met so many new mothers like Clare. Intelligent, successful women who've handled their entire lives brilliantly up to now. They make lists and schedules, they run vast research projects and orchestrate multi-million-pound deals over the phone. They write their Christmas cards by the end of August, and have inheritance tax plans and private pensions and pre-nups. When they get pregnant, they put their foetuses down for posh private schools and spend hours online researching Bugaboos and organic baby food. They think broken nights won't bother them, because they've 'pulled all-nighters' at work dozens of times before. They expect to sail through pregnancy, pop out a baby and pick up the threads of their lives with a cute new accessory as if nothing more significant has happened to them than the purchase of a new car.

Then the baby arrives.

Clare looks shattered and bewildered, like a disaster victim. She can't believe what's happened to her. She isn't turning out to be the sort of mother she thought she'd be, and she's panicking. She's petrified she'll fuck it up. And she probably will. Some women just aren't meant to be mothers.

'Please, Jenna, please take the job,' she begs. 'You can live in, whatever you want. And I'll – I'll double whatever you're earning now!'

'Clare,' I say. 'When would you like me to start?'

Two weeks later, I'm given the kind of reception my mother would reserve for visiting royalty. Clare's made some disgusting fancy tea that tastes of cigarettes (I don't have the heart to tell her I'm a PG Tips kind of girl) and set out an array of expensive biscuits on a plate. The twins are nowhere to be seen – 'Marc's taken them for a morning walk, I thought you'd like a chance to settle in first' – so Clare shows me to my room, then tactfully withdraws so I can sort myself out in peace. There are fresh flowers on the windowsill (perk of her job, I guess) and a basket of Lush toiletries on the chest of drawers. She's even fanned the latest issues of a selection of magazines on the bedside table. I'm surprised she hasn't had the fluffy white bathrobe in my en-suite shower monogrammed with my initials.

I plunk on the edge of my double bed – crisp white linen, still with knife-edge creases from the cellophane – and struggle with the lump in my throat. I'd almost rather I'd been thrown in the deep end with the twins, to take my mind off my misery.

They say you don't know someone till you divorce them. First Maggie begged me to stay, 'for the sake of the children'; then, when I admitted I'd already found someone else, she dropped all pretence at friendship.

'You selfish *bitch*!' she screamed. 'How can you do this to me? After everything I've done for you! What's this woman got that I haven't?'

'It's not you, Maggie. It's me—'

'Don't expect a reference! I don't want you in my house another minute! Get out! Go on, *get out*!'

She wouldn't even let me say goodbye to Galen and Tati. Never mind the countless times I've bailed her out, working overtime for free and cancelling my arrangements to fit in with hers. I've loved and cared for her kids for two years, and she bins me like an old coat. I can't bear the children to think I abandoned them without a word. I sent them both goodbye presents, but I've no way of knowing if Maggie has passed them on.

Leaving Jamie this morning was gut-wrenching too, in a different, unhealthy, way.

'I can't cope without you,' he pleaded, as I packed my suitcase. 'Please, don't leave.'

'I'll be back at weekends,' I said uncomfortably.

'It's not the same. I don't want to be on my own. If you love me, Jenna, you'll stay.'

I hefted my bag on to the floor, hating how impatient his neediness made me feel. 'It's because I care about you that I'm leaving.'

There's a tentative knock now at my bedroom door. Clare nervously puts her head around the jamb. 'Marc's back. I wondered if you'd like to come and say hi.'

I'd have preferred to meet the husband before I took the job, but I wasn't exactly in a position to be picky. If he turns out to be a groper, I'll just have to deal with it. At the end of the day, it's Clare I'll really be working with. You barely see the father, as a rule.

Marc Elias looks up from his *FT* and smiles politely. 'You must be Jenna.'

'Darling, don't be rude,' Clare murmurs, throwing me an apologetic smile. 'Come on, get up and say hello to Jenna properly.'

'I wasn't being rude,' her husband says irritably.

'Please, Mr Elias, there's no need—'

'I'm late for work anyway,' he mutters, tossing his paper aside.

Fuck, he's tall. And *young*: more my age than Clare's. I glance at her with new respect. Props to her. He's not at all what I expected. I thought she'd be married to some bald rich banker, not a hot stud muffin like this. I can certainly see where Poppy gets her gorgeous Italian colouring.

He doesn't give me a second glance as he stalks out of the room.

'Sorry about Marc.' She twitches as the front door slams. 'He stayed late specially this morning to see you, but he's normally at work by seven-thirty and he gets a bit—'

'It doesn't matter, really. Where are the twins?'

'Down for a nap. Why don't you get unpacked, and I'll make us both a cup of tea. Do you take sugar? Milk? I bought some digestives, but if you'd prefer something else, Hobnobs or—'

'Please, Clare,' I laugh. 'I'm here to help *you*. A cup of tea would be great, but after that, I'll take over, OK?'

'Yes, yes, sorry, I didn't mean to interfere.'

'You're not interfering,' I reassure her.

I unpack my clothes – jeans, T-shirts, fleeces: nothing that will be ruined by baby puke and frequent washing – and join Clare in the large, airy kitchen at the back of the house. It looks like a spread from a lifestyle magazine, with its limestone floors, maple cabinets and glowing granite work surfaces. Vases of fresh flowers are scattered along the counters, and gleaming copper saucepans hang above the kitchen island. A couple of big, squishy red armchairs look out on to the small paved garden. Clare is sitting in one of them, the twins playing happily in their bouncers at her feet.

'We look like we belong in a magazine,' Clare acknowledges ruefully. 'Trust me, this isn't par for the course.'

'You don't seem to need me at all,' I smile.

'We do, we do – oh, Jenna, please don't change your mind—'

'I was just teasing. Hey, Rowan,' I add, reaching forward as the baby squirms in his rocker, 'how are we doing? Is the sun in your eyes?'

Clare reaches for her son at the same time. In that moment, both of us stretching towards the baby, my left sleeve slides back.

She stares at my scars, while I stare carefully at the baby.

'This pot of tea is getting cold,' she says, standing up. 'I need to add more hot water.'

Later, when I tell Clare I'm taking the babies for an afternoon walk, she asks if she can come with us. 'They might get upset,' she explains. 'They haven't really had a chance to get used to you yet.'

There's a little tussle over the pram when we get outside.

'Sorry,' Clare says, embarrassed, 'force of habit. You push.'

We walk side by side in careful silence towards Sloane Square. I can't tell if she's nervous about trusting me, or just can't bring herself to hand over her babies yet. She wouldn't be the first new mother to feel guilty about wanting to rush back to work. If they were mine, there's no way I'd let another woman take my place.

The twins are both fast asleep by the time we reach Peter Jones.

I touch Clare's hand as it rests possessively on the hood of the pram. 'I think we'll be fine from here,' I tell her gently.

She hesitates. I smile encouragement, and she reluctantly lets go. With a brief wave, I turn and push the twins towards the King's Road.

I feel her watching me until we're swallowed up by the crowd.

I'd planned to go out with Kirsty this evening to let off steam and sink a few vodka-tonics, but while I was taking the twins for their walk Clare whipped up a four-course gourmet meal in the kitchen 'to celebrate your first day'. She lays the dining table for two: 'Marc's working late; I'll leave him something in the oven.'

'Be careful,' Kirsty warns, when I call to cancel. 'Boundaries, remember.'

'It's just this once,' I whisper back. 'I can't turn her down now she's gone to so much trouble.'

'What's the husband like?'

'Haven't you met him?'

'No, only Clare. I can't be*lieve* you're working for Fran's best friend! Talk about small world.'

'Yeah, well, I guess it's not really that surprising. These rich women with nannies all know each other.' I put on a Princess Anne voice. 'Oh, yah, dahling, we must meet up at Ascot. Got to dash, the Palace is on the other line. Mwah! Mwah!'

'You sound just like Fran,' Kirsty giggles. 'So, what's he like then?'

'Mr Elias? Grumpy. Cute. Young. Just my type, actually.'

'Jenna . . .'

'Oh, relax,' I say crossly. 'What do you take me for? You know that's not my style.'

I have a thing about married men. As in: *not ever*. Partly for the sisterhood, partly out of common sense: a man who cheats with you is bound to cheat on you, sooner or later. Leopards and spots and all that.

'Reckon he's a player?' Kirsty asks, reading my mind.

I remember my first impression: despite allowing for Marc's bad mood, they just don't seem to belong together. It's not even an attraction of opposites; they simply don't *fit*.

'I don't know. He must be at least ten years younger than her. What d'you think?'

'I think you need to be careful,' she says again.

Clare relaxes over dinner, and not just because of the wine. She acts like a weight's been taken off her shoulders by my mere presence. It never fails to amaze me that women who can manage a hundred staff without blinking an eye can be totally thrown by one small baby (or in this case, two). What *is* it they find so scary?

Her husband's still not home by the time I go to bed. I crawl beneath the 400-count Egyptian sheets, wondering if he's really working late. I hope to God he's not having an affair. I don't want to get caught in the crossfire. I've known friends who were nannies for couples who split, and it's not pretty. You end up part surrogate spouse, part therapist and part whipping-boy, and you're paid for none of them. Both sides expect you to choose their corner, when all you really care about is the kids.

I'm woken several hours later by the sound of a baby crying. I bolt upright, listening alertly, but the house is now silent. I wait several minutes, and hear nothing but the radiator muttering in the corner. I relax against the pillows. Clare must have got up to see to the twins herself.

Suddenly I'm aware of someone else in the room.

A hand covers my mouth.

'Don't say another word,' he hisses.

Daily News Friday 2 May 1968

Society lothario commits suicide

HUGO FOSTER-JONES, the former Olympic gold medallist and celebrated playboy, has been found dead at his home in Oxfordshire.

Mr Foster-Jones, 53, who won Eventing gold in the 1948 Games and once owned a property portfolio worth millions, died from a single gunshot wound to the head. Police are not seeking anyone else in connection with the incident.

His body was found in the early hours of yesterday morning by his daughter, Davina, 17. She is being comforted at home by friends.

It's the latest in a series of tragedies to strike the family. In 1953, Mr Foster-Jones' wife, Rebecca, was killed in a private plane crash while on a family holiday to Kenya. Mr Foster-Jones was also injured, putting an end to his promising career. Their daughter, then two, was unharmed.

Mr Foster-Jones went on to build a successful business in property development. At the height of his success in the mid-Sixties, he was reportedly worth £15,000,000. More recently, however, he suffered severe financial difficulties, losing much of his fortune.

The funeral will be held at the Brompton Oratory in London on Thursday, 8th May.

3

Davina

Silly girl. The nanny is a wonderful idea, of course – attempting twins alone was madness – but what possessed her to get such a pretty one?

As Clare is fond of reminding me, I know very little about business and spreadsheets and flow-charts; but I do know *men*. They have needs: especially *young* men. Bringing a highly attractive girl into the house at a time when – to be frank – one is hardly looking one's best is a recipe for disaster. Particularly when the young lady in question is also keeping the man's house and cooking his meals and looking after his babies. One never wants a husband to question what, precisely, his wife is *for*.

Clare springs out of the Range Rover as Marc parks and runs up the front steps.

'Davina, you look marvellous! So brown! Have you been away?'

'Not really, darling.' I kiss her cheek. 'Just a long weekend in Nevis, nothing special.'

'Oh, Davina! I'd *kill* for a few days in the Caribbean. I hate England in March, it's so dreary.'

'Darling, you should have said. The Bartholomews would have loved to see you—'

'You know that's not an option.' She turns and ushers the pretty girl forward. 'This is our new nanny, Jenna. I thought it might be fun if she joined us this weekend, and got to know the family.'

'Lovely to meet you, dear,' I say. 'Welcome to Long Meadow.'

The girl gazes up at the house with awe. 'This is all yours?'

How *sweet*. One forgets.

Marc struggles up the steps with the twins, a plastic baby-seat swinging from each hand, like Jack and his pails of water. Two quilted bags are slung across his chest. He looks cross and out of sorts, as usual.

I lead the way into the orangery, where, despite the dull weather, Mrs Lampard has set the table for lunch. Clare insists on a place being added for Jenna – 'She can't eat in the kitchen, Davina, she's part of the family, not a servant!' – and, worse still, brings the twins to the table when they start squalling.

'I'm sure Jenna wouldn't mind,' I murmur discreetly.

The girl leaps up. 'Of course—'

'Jenna, sit down,' Clare says. 'It's Saturday, it's your day off. I invited you to Long Meadow as our *guest*.'

'I don't mind, honestly.'

At least *some*body knows her place. How Clare runs a successful business mystifies me. One has to maintain a certain reserve with staff, and Clare has always worn her egalitarian heart on her sleeve.

Other children bring home stray kittens and litter runts; as a child, Clare used to turn up with vagabonds from the local council estate that she'd picked up in the village and invited back to tea. Mrs Lampard would fill them with toast and pound cake in the kitchen, and then Lampard would return them to their miserable high-rise dwellings (having frisked them for teaspoons first). Clare was always devastated not to receive a return invitation.

She thinks me a dreadful snob, I know; but it never occurred to her how unfair she was being, giving these children a glimpse of privilege they could never share.

Jenna seems a perfectly nice girl, if a little common (gold hoop earrings and rather cheap shoes), but one doesn't make friends with servants. Although Clare does seem a little more like her old self again now she's finally seen sense and hired some help. I knew she wouldn't take well to motherhood. She's more like me than she thinks. I did *tell* her.

'Darling, you really don't have to breastfeed,' I reprove her gently as Clare whips out a huge, blue-veined bosom, 'it's terribly nouveau. Very *Guardian*. Formula is quite acceptable these days.'

'Just because *you* didn't want to,' Clare retorts.

I make no apologies for my failure to enjoy child-rearing. There is a dreadful amount of sentimental hoop-la about babies. With few exceptions, they are *not* beautiful; most infants resemble Churchill in his far-from-finest hour. They bawl, squirm, vomit on one's clothing, and are generally as appealing at the dinner table as a sandwich full of maggots.

Nor, in my opinion, do they improve with age. Once mobile, they leave a slimy trail of stickiness wherever they go, like snails. The moment they master the rudiments of communication, they use them to demand the repetition of the same mind-numbing games and stories until you want to scream with boredom. How many times must the wheels of the bus go round before they are satisfied?

I never wanted children; but unfortunately the issue of an heir was somewhat of a deal-breaker for my first husband.

I married Manon Sterling for love. Admittedly, he was also obscenely rich, but I find that a very attractive quality in a man.

For years, Manon had been a dedicated playboy who adroitly side-stepped any talk of marriage. But at fifty-one he was starting to feel the first cold intimations of his own mortality. He wanted a pretty, nubile wife to make him feel young again, and an heir to inherit his vast fortune. I was twenty, a virgin and extremely beautiful; but destitute, since my father, who'd given me a taste for the finer things in life, had then gambled away any means to enjoy them.

Manon and I were a perfect match. He enjoyed doting on me; I enjoyed being doted upon. Sex with my new husband was pleasant, and undemanding. I fell pregnant with Clare within weeks.

I had no choice but to go through with it. It was the most appalling experience of my life. Manon – utterly in love with every aspect of my pregnancy – proclaimed me glowing, but all I saw was *fat*. I shuddered every time I caught sight of my swollen body in the mirror (oh, my twenty-three-inch waist!). The only thought that sustained me throughout the entire nightmarish nine months was that I would never, *ever* have to do this again.

Clare was born by Caesarean section; nothing would

have induced me to endure the indignity of a 'natural' birth (and I refuse to believe that anything, once stretched to ten times its normal size, is *ever* the same again).

I might have warmed to her a little more had it not been made clear in advance that an heir – *n.* (male) – was expected. I had nightmares I'd be forced to endure pregnancy after pregnancy, like some medieval brood-mare, until I was delivered of a son. My relief at the birth of Alexander four years later can only be imagined.

I felt nothing in particular for either child. Oh, I didn't wish anything dreadful to happen to them, of course; I actually became quite fond once they went off to school. But there was nothing *visceral*; none of that tigress maternal instinct one reads so much about. I was perfectly happy to cede day-to-day care to a series of nannies until the children grew up and became recognizably human. (My own mother had died when I was two, and nannies clearly hadn't done *me* any harm.)

No, Manon was the one who spent hours in the nursery, lavishing love and attention on Clare, with whom he was besotted. It was particularly unfortunate, then, that he had a stroke and died when she was seven and Alexander not quite three.

I had liked my husband (better, after all, to be an old man's darling than a young man's slave), and was in no rush to marry again. However, it appeared Manon was no longer quite as obscenely rich as everyone thought. In fact, he'd lost rather a lot of money in the past couple of years. A series of bad investments, heavy stock-market losses and a staggering unpaid tax bill meant that, once his debts were paid, very little, beyond our house in Pimlico, was left. Without his life insurance (ring-fenced from the bailiffs), the children and I would have found ourselves on the street.

It's easy for Clare to take the moral high ground, but she should try poverty for a while. I wasn't brought up to work. I could throw a dinner party for twenty at the drop of a hat or organize a charity ball in my sleep, but I hadn't the faintest idea how to earn my own living.

Clare never liked Guy. She didn't rebel (that wasn't Clare's style), but it was quite obvious, despite her scrupulous politeness, that she detested her stepfather. Where Clare led, Alexander followed.

Thank God Guy could afford good boarding schools.

Mrs Lampard serves lunch: cold roast chicken and new potatoes for Marc and Jenna, egg-white omelettes for Clare and me. Clare pulls a face, but she'll thank me for it one day. She's ballooned to a size eight since her pregnancy, and the nanny really is a very pretty girl.

I watch Jenna use the edge of her fork to cut her roast chicken. I grimace inwardly, and then realize it's not from ignorance; she appears to have sprained her wrist.

I lean forward and tap her hand. 'How did that happen?'

'She fell over the coffee table last weekend when she went home,' Clare answers. 'I *told* her she should go to hospital and get it X-rayed, just in case, but she wouldn't listen.'

'Do you live with your parents?'

'My boyfriend,' Jenna says.

'And what does he do?'

'He's a plumber—'

Clare interrupts. 'He has his own business, Davina. Plumbers earn a fortune these days. Ours went to the Maldives for a fortnight last year! *We* can't afford to go to the Maldives—'

'Yes, thank you, Clare. I do know the value of a good plumber,' I retort tartly. 'He doesn't mind, your boyfriend, that you've taken a position where you're required to live in?'

'Oh, but she wasn't required to—'

'He doesn't mind,' Jenna says.

She doesn't quite meet my eye. Hmm. I know what that means.

'And your parents?' I ask. 'What did you say your father does?'

'Davina.' Clare laughs self-consciously. 'Stop giving her the third degree.'

I dread to think how my daughter found this girl. A poster on a lamp post, perhaps? Did she not think to check what kind of family the girl comes from? Knowing Clare, she'll have considered it 'judgemental' to investigate her background. I wonder how much effort she put into researching the purchase of each of her flower shops, and checking the references of those she employed there. And how much time, in contrast, she spent finding the woman who will be shaping her children's characters, moulding their minds.

Clare has no idea. A nanny affects the way your child sees the world, and sets the defaults in their nature. 'Give me a child until he is seven, and I will show you the man.'

I blame Nanny Frieda in no small measure for the way Clare has turned out. She was the one who encouraged Clare to mess about with pots in the greenhouse. It was amusing at first; and Clare certainly had an eye for colour and detail. By the time she was twelve, everyone wanted her to do their flowers. It was rather sweet to have her go to friends' houses and throw a few roses prettily in a vase. Reflected rather nicely. But I never expected her to pursue it as a *career*. First the business degree – I know university is all the rage these days, and it can be a good way to find a husband if you choose the right sort of place; but Clare spent her entire time studying, *such* a bluestocking. Then came the obsession with setting up her own company. She ran herself ragged financing it all herself, buying up bits of land to grow things, wouldn't take a penny from Guy or use any of the spare acreage at Long Meadow. I was rather relieved when she finally said she'd met a man. She was thirty-one, after all. If she'd left it any longer she'd have missed the boat.

'I suppose you'll go back to work now,' I sigh, passing Marc the devilled eggs. 'I'm sure the children will miss you.'

'It's only part-time to begin with, Davina. The twins will be fine with Jenna; it'll be like having three parents living at home, instead of two.'

'I've told Clare she really doesn't have to—'

'I *want* to, Marc.'

Trouble in Paradise. I thought as much.

All this fuss about careers. Men may tolerate a working wife, if needs must; they've been bludgeoned into accepting it as a necessary evil, these days. But that doesn't mean they *like* it. They just want a nice house and a pretty wife and children to come home to, whatever they might tell you. Men are simple. Women have to understand that, if they expect to be truly happy with their husbands. A good man is hard to find, not keep. All one has to do is give them good food, respect, appreciation and plenty of sex. Lots of sex and no nagging. It isn't hard.

To paraphrase that marvellous American president (*dear* Jackie: now there was a woman who knew what men want): girls these days get married thinking about what their husband can do for them, not what they can do for their husband. Is it any wonder so many of them run off with the *au pair*?

I push my omelette around the plate. 'Darling,' I suggest, 'now you've got a spare pair of hands, why don't you spend a bit of time on yourself? Get back in shape, buy a few pretty clothes. I know your shops kept you busy when you had time on your hands, but there's really no need to—'

'Davina, I run a *business*. I'm not on a rota for church flowers!'

'Yes, dear, I understand that. But surely the whole point of being the boss is that you don't have to go in every day. You can manage things from home. It'd be a shame to miss out on—'

'You just can't help yourself, can you?' Clare cries. 'It's bad enough when you correct the way I fold a napkin, but if you think I'm going to sit here and listen to *you*, of all people, tell me how to raise a family—'

'You're upsetting the babies, Clare.'

Marc picks Rowan up and puts him against his shoulder. 'You know I'm behind you a hundred per cent,' he adds firmly, 'but your mother's right. I don't want you pushing yourself too hard. It's been a really tough few months, and now that we've got Jenna, you should take a break and relax while you can.'

Clare looks on the verge of tears. 'If I'm worrying about PetalPushers, I can't relax. You know how much the company means to me.'

'Don't bite your nails, darling,' I murmur. 'Ugly habit.'

'It'd be different if you needed to work, Clare. But I'm earning enough now, we could manage for a bit—'

'I need to work for *me*,' Clare pleads.

I really don't understand my daughter at all.

'Oh, Christ,' Marc laughs, leaping up. 'He's puked all over me! Jenna, would you mind holding him for a moment?'

'But that's a new shirt,' Clare complains. 'It cost a fortune.'

'It doesn't matter. I just need to sponge it out, it'll be fine.'

He disappears to clean up. I don't miss Clare's sour expression as she glances Rowan's way. How ironic, that Marc should take so naturally to fatherhood. It must be his Arab genes. They're very big on family in that part of the world, I understand. At least as far as boys are concerned.

I knew as soon as Clare brought Marc home that it was going to be a disaster. Oh, he's definitely very charming. Good at handling women – that's five older sisters for you. But not the one for Clare. Absolutely the wrong choice.

Have you noticed how certain sorts of girls – Italians, for example – bloom early? By the time they're twenty-eight, no matter how pretty they were at fifteen, they're overblown and spent, already turning into their mothers. Genetics, you see. Some young men seem so liberal and open-minded at twenty; but by thirty their genes have won out and they've reverted to type. Just like their fathers and grandfathers before them, they expect dinner on the table when they get home and a wife who runs around picking up their socks. Marc may adore his children, but I have a feeling he won't expect to do the dirty work – the *women's* work – involved in actually raising them.

Nothing wrong with that, of course. Except that Clare was never the type to play Jane to his Tarzan. The gulf between them is widening every day. Opposites may attract, but they seldom last.

Clare wouldn't listen, of course. Kept insisting it was his age and family background that bothered me. (Well, I wasn't *thrilled*, especially after I had a private detective do a little digging, but that's not the point.) It's a question of compatibility. There are reasons we do better when we stick to our own sort.

I don't hold Marc's family against him; I don't have a racist bone in my body, and he is Christian, at least. But he comes from a very different culture. Marc may have grown up in Canada himself, and he's perfectly civilized. But when push comes to shove, blood will out. Clare's simply storing up trouble for herself.

Jenna stands up now, cradling Rowan affectionately. 'Why don't I go and give him a bottle?' she asks Clare. 'It'll give you a chance to get Poppy settled.'

'But it's your day off.'

'Clare,' Jenna says firmly, 'this isn't the kind of job where you watch a clock. I'm sure there'll be times things will work the other way. Now please stop worrying. I'll settle him down, and everything will be fine.'

It's quite clear who's in charge in *this* relationship.

It's easily done. Far too many new mothers make the mistake of not clearly laying out their expectations of

Nanny in the beginning. They're so desperate to be *liked*. But a relationship that is tentative and ill-defined only leads to trouble. You can't undo familiarity.

'You can't let her take over like that,' I tell Clare. 'I realize she's only trying to help, but that's not the point. She needs to know who's boss.'

'Davina, this isn't *Upstairs, Downstairs*. It's the twenty-first century. Jenna and I are a team—'

'She *works* for you,' I correct. 'She isn't here out of the goodness of her heart, or because she wants to help you. She may love your children, but it's a mercenary kind of love, and it certainly doesn't mean she loves *you*. She's not your friend. She's here because you're *paying* her.'

Clare looks hurt. 'It's not like that. Things are different these days. I've told you, we're a *team*. And anyway, I'm quite used to dealing with staff, thank you, Davina. As I've told you. I've been running a very successful business for years.'

'Hardly the same thing, darling. You must admit you have a tendency to fraternize with domestics—'

' "*Fraternize*"? God, Davina. How very Orwellian of you.'

I pin Clare with a hard look. 'How much do you really know about this girl? Those scars on her arms, for instance. The sprained wrist. If she's involved in an unsuitable relationship, you don't want the chaos spilling over into your life. And you need to consider Marc in all of this.'

'What do you mean?'

'He seems very quiet, Clare. And he looks very tense. It can't be easy for him, having to get used to a stranger living in his home. It doesn't give him much privacy. Men like to retreat from the world. Their home is their castle, don't forget. You want to be very careful he doesn't start to feel left out. It's hard enough to get used to sharing you with the twins—'

'He wanted a baby as much as I did!'

'Rather more, I suspect.'

'And whose fault's that?' She shoves back her chair; I wince as it scrapes against the antique tiled floor. 'I've had to learn everything about being a mother from scratch, out of books, because I certainly haven't been able to learn from *your* example! All you've ever done is undermine and criticize me, and that's on the odd occasion you're not ignoring me altogether! Yes,' she shrieks, as I point tactfully towards Poppy, 'I can see my daughter is crying! I have eyes in my head, Davina! I may not be a perfect mother, I may in fact turn out to be an utterly dreadful one, but unlike you, at least I am *trying*!'

I stare at her in astonishment. I can only assume it's her hormones. I wasn't a 'hands-on' mother, as they say these days – such an appalling expression – but I love both my children, naturally; as adults, as *individuals*. One would have thought that far more satisfactory than a reflexive emotion based on animal instinct and shared DNA.

I pour myself a glass of water, pleased to note that my hand doesn't tremble. 'Really, Clare. I don't know where *that* came from.'

She sucks in a breath. 'No,' she says tightly. 'I don't suppose you do.'

'What *is* that dreadful noise outside? Mrs Lampard really should see to it. And some more tea, I think—'

The door opens. 'Excuse me, Lady Eastman—'

'Please, Jenna, no need for that. "Davina" is perfectly fine—'

'Oh, don't go all democratic now,' a voice drawls behind me. 'Not after you've had Guy pony up millions for that title.'

'Alexander,' I say, proffering a cheek without turning. 'How lovely.'

'Hello, Mother,' says Alexander.

If Clare takes after her father, then I suppose I must claim Alexander as mine.

Women love him; in the beginning. By the time it ends, as it inevitably does – whether 'it' is a few days (sometimes), a few weeks (usually) or a few months (once) – they have run the full gamut of Shakespearean emotion, from infatuation, through devotion, obsession and jealousy, to end in hatred and despair. One poor child threw herself, like Ophelia, into the river; taking her homage to the Bard a little too far, I feel.

Alexander knows the lethal effect he has on women. With disingenuous insouciance, he washes his hands. 'I never lie,' he protests. 'I always *tell* them I'll leave.'

Which is precisely the attraction, of course.

I rather admire his amorality. He is at least honest. I despise hypocrisy; to my mind, the greatest sinners are those who affect to be saints. Alexander parlays his charm into success both in bed and in business without pretending to do good for anyone but himself. Not that he intentionally sets out to do harm either; sheer idleness, if nothing else, keeps him neutral. He is the consummate survivor in every respect – and yet somehow I can't imagine him growing old.

'I didn't expect you this weekend,' I reprove, as Alexander flings himself into a chair.

'What can I say? I felt the need to nestle in the bosom of my family.'

He's staring intently at the nanny. It's an expression I'm familiar with.

'Have you met Jenna?' I ask, watching him carefully. 'Your sister's new nanny.'

'A pleasure,' he says blandly.

The girl blushes furiously. Alexander has been on the premises a matter of minutes; such a response is quite an achievement, even for him.

Oh, but he is charming, my son. A fallen angel. Long-limbed, graceful, careless, with thick dark hair and ice-blue eyes as glittering, and warm, as diamonds. That he is so clearly damaged seems merely to draw the moths closer.

'Lady – um, I mean, Davina . . .' she flusters.

'Be careful, dear,' I tell the girl lightly. 'He's every bit as dangerous as he looks.'

Alexander reaches inside his jacket for the silver hip-flask he inherited from his father. He's already quite drunk, although only those closest to him would know it. The slight shake of his hand and the glaze in those blue eyes betray him.

The drinking started when he was fourteen. At first, he confined it to school holidays and exeat weekends; within a year, we were receiving letters from the school. There was an ugly incident with another pupil when he was sixteen, a broken nose and allegations of assault; with typical care-lessness, Alexander merely said the boy had had it coming. Guy visited the school and made a substantial donation to the library, and the matter was quietly dropped.

The drunkenness could be overlooked; the drugs were taken more seriously. Guy's money exculpated Alexander from the joints he was caught smoking, but nothing could excuse the cocaine he was discovered selling the week after his seventeenth birthday.

After some persuasion, the school agreed not to make it a police matter, but Alexander was immediately expelled. Guy cut off his allowance and refused to reinstate it unless Alexander sorted himself out. To our lasting surprise, he responded by going out and getting himself a (legitimate) job.

ShopTV could have been founded with Alexander in mind. Everything he touched turned to gold. By the time he was twenty-five, he was head of marketing; now, at thirty-three, he's running the network with one hand tied behind his back.

Which leaves the other free for all sorts of mischief.

'Where's hubby?' he asks me, never taking his eyes off Jenna.

'Guy had business in London,' I say shortly.

'Of course. Big sister wouldn't be here otherwise.'

'Xan . . .' Clare says warningly.

'You're a guest in my house, Alexander. Kindly remember – oh dear God, will someone *please* tell me what all that noise is?'

'I've been trying to,' Jenna sighs.

I fling open the french windows on to the terrace. Mrs Lampard is running across the croquet lawn with an athleticism I'd thought decades behind her. In the distance, Lampard and two of the groundsmen are yodelling as if at a rodeo. Bellowing animal grunts sound from behind the topiary, and there is enough splashing from the pool to drown a herd of elephants.

'*Alexander,*' I demand.

'Bit of an altercation with a tree,' he says, tipping his head back to drain his flask.

I sweep outside. As I round the corner of the house, I see Alexander's imported red Mustang wrapped around the ancient oak tree at the bottom of the drive. The force of the impact has knocked down the adjoining split-rail fence; the old five-bar gate swings crazily from its hinges.

Of the bull normally in the field behind it, there is no sign.

Mrs Lampard picks up her skirts and runs past me. Behind me, Alexander laughs.

I will kill him, I think grimly as I stalk towards the pool. *That animal is worth a fortune. If it has to be turned into rump steak, I will personally see to it that Alexander is barred from every pub and bar in Oxfordshire.*

Marc, shirtless and muscular, is in the swimming pool, up to his waist in floating shit. The bull is flailing in the deep end, panic having loosened its bowels to devastating effect. The stench is overpowering. Marc has managed to catch hold of its rope halter, and is attempting to lead it towards the shallows. I remember he grew up in Quebec: farmboy country. Lampard and the groundsmen yell support, and I realize my first impression was correct: this *is* a rodeo.

Clare pushes me out of the way. 'Lampard, go to the far end and make as much noise as you can,' she yells. 'Drive it towards the steps.'

Marc clearly has the situation under control, but Clare kicks off her pumps and throws her husband another rope, yelling instructions. Marc ignores her and patiently draws the bull towards the shallows, doing his best to calm it. The groundsmen whip its flanks, and with another mighty bellow the bull finally lurches up the steps and on to dry land.

'Make sure that car is moved before my husband gets home,' I tell Lampard, and once more go in search of my son.

The nanny is in the orangery, the twins asleep in their baby seats at her feet. 'Is everything all right?' she asks, rocking gently.

'Naturally. My daughter is at her commanding best. Where's Alexander?'

'Alexander?'

'My son,' I say impatiently.

'I think he left.'

She's lying. Oh, Alexander may have disappeared, leaving, like the Cheshire cat, just his grin; but she's lying about something. I can always tell.

Something about this girl doesn't quite add up. Clare won't have noticed: she's never learned to judge books by their covers. No doubt my daughter is paying the girl far too much, but even so, how can a nanny afford a (genuine: I know these things) Cartier watch? And I realize some women delight in caring for small children, immune to the dribble and soul-destroying tedium, but conscientious though Jenna clearly is – one can tell from the professional way she handles the babies – I don't pick up the burning need to nurture that one might expect to find in a girl who's chosen proxy mothering as a career. She's too bright to be satisfied with a life of building Lego and wiping small bottoms.

And then there's the way she looked at Alexander. I have the distinct feeling there is a story here.

So I'm not altogether surprised when Clare rings me four days later from Chelsea police station and tells me that Jenna's vanished, and has taken the twins with her.

Clare Elias

97 Cheyne Walk, Chelsea, London SW3 5TS

Guy

I believe I have made it clear to you on a number of occasions that I don't wish to accept anything from you. I've kept my silence for my mother's sake, not yours. No amount of money can make up for what you've done. Please stop trying to buy me off. I'm quite capable of paying my own mortgage, and if you attempt to discharge it again, I will have no choice but to instruct my lawyer.

Please do not contact me again

Clare

4

Clare

'Jesus Christ! The woman's a bitch!' Marc explodes as we drive out of Long Meadow.

'Marc!' I exclaim. '*Pas devant les enfants!*'

'If you have to talk like a stuck-up snob, at least try to get your accent right.'

I bite back a sharp retort. Marc's always like this after we've been to see Davina, and I can't blame him. She treats him like a foreigner, a second-class citizen. The only consolation I can give him is that she's just as brutal with me.

There's no point getting upset about it. Davina is never going to change. Wanting her to be a different sort of mother from the one she is will only lead to disappointment and heartbreak. I know she loves me, in her own way. She doesn't mean to be so hurtful. I shouldn't have lost my temper with her. I just have to let it go.

But how can she be so ... so *cold*? Now that I'm a mother myself, I understand for the first time that Davina never has been one in any meaningful sense of the word.

She spent my entire childhood training me to do without her. By the time I was six, I could get the bus back from my private primary school, walk the fifteen yards from the stop and let myself into our Pimlico flat. At nine, when she sent me off to boarding school, I had my own bank account.

'Is she – is she always like that?' Jenna asks from the back, where she's squashed between the twins' car seats.

'Yes,' Marc snarls, 'she is. How you turned out even part-way decent with a mother like that is beyond me, Clare. No wonder Xan drinks.'

'*Marc.*'

'Excuse me,' Jenna says, 'but Marc, do you think you could open a window?'

'Oh, fuck. I smell, don't I?'

'A bit,' she giggles.

He's wearing just his white T-shirt and boxers (roomy and concealing, thankfully), the rest of his wet clothes wrapped in a plastic bag in the boot. His bare thighs ripple as he floors the accelerator and the Range Rover bounces out of Davina's rutted drive on to the main road. I'd forgotten quite how much I fancy him. It's been so long since we had sex, I've got spiderwebs between my thighs.

'How in God's name did that bloody bull get in the pool, anyway?' he demands.

'Xan knocked down the gate to its field when he crashed his car.'

'Knowing him, he did it on purpose to piss off your mother.'

'Do you have any siblings?' I ask Jenna over my shoulder.

'Nope. Just me.'

'I can't imagine being an only child. Do you get on well with your parents?'

'Once a month,' Jenna says drily.

'Davina should never have been allowed to breed at all, never mind twice,' Marc says darkly. 'No offence, darling – I'm glad she did, of course – but the woman has as much maternal instinct as a vampire.'

'I suppose that's where I get it from,' I sigh.

'You're not like her at all!' Jenna bursts out. She blushes furiously. 'Sorry, I didn't mean it to come out quite like that. But you're wonderful with the twins. I can see how much you love them.'

I'm engulfed by the familiar rush of guilt. I love both my children, of course I do. But with Poppy it's effortless, as automatic as breathing. I have to choose to love Rowan every single day.

'I never know why they're crying,' I tell Jenna. 'You seem to have a sixth sense . . .'

'I've been doing this a lot longer than you, that's all. Don't be so hard on yourself. It'll be much easier next time round.'

'Sounds like an idea,' Marc murmurs, putting his hand on my thigh.

I remove it, my ardour rapidly cooling. 'Not in my lifetime.'

'I know we said that two – Christ almighty!'

He yanks on the steering wheel as a figure stumbles out of the hedgerow, and the Range Rover swerves towards the middle of the road. A car coming in the opposite direction mounts the grass verge to avoid us, horn blaring angrily. Marc slams on the brakes and pulls over to the side of the road, his face white with anger. I twist in my seat and watch Xan stagger towards us, oblivious to the near-accident he has just caused, shirt-tails flapping, laughing as if this is all a huge joke.

Marc buzzes down his window. 'What the fuck d'you think you're playing at?'

'Needed a lift, mate,' Xan grins.

'Don't "mate" me. If you think I'm taking you anywhere after that—'

'Please, Marc,' I mutter. 'He'll get himself killed if we leave him here.'

Marc's jaw tightens. He nods tersely towards the back of the car. 'You'll have to get in the boot. There's no room in the back.'

'Nice one.'

I climb out and wait for my brother to haul himself into one of the flip-down seats in the rear of the car, making sure he puts his seatbelt on. Within minutes, he's passed out. I glance at him in the rear-view mirror. He looks about twelve years old.

I can cope with the careless way Davina behaves towards me; it stings sometimes, but I'm used to it. I try to remember that her own mother died when she was two; instead of sending her to school, her father kept her at home with him and an army of servants who waited on her hand and foot. Davina is shallow and irresponsible and utterly selfish, but is it any wonder? I can't find it in me to hate her; if anything, I feel sorry for her.

But I'll never forgive her for what she's done to Xan.

No one who's ever seen *Sophie's Choice* could forget it. That harrowing moment on the railway platform at Auschwitz, when Sophie is forced by the Nazi concentration camp commandant to choose life for one of her two small children, and death for the other.

'Don't make me choose,' Sophie begs, clutching her children, 'I *can't* choose!' But then, when a young Nazi is told to take them both to the death camp, she releases her daughter, shouting, 'Take my little girl!' and has to watch helplessly as the screaming child is carried away to die.

I was only nineteen or twenty when the film came out, motherhood a distant glimmer on the horizon, but the scene haunted my sleep for weeks. How could any mother choose between her two children? How would the ensuing grief and guilt not drive you insane?

Except . . . except that I *would* be able to choose.

'Do you find Poppy . . . easier?' I ask Marc tentatively one Monday morning.

Marc finishes knotting his tie. 'Rowan can't help having colic. It's not his fault.'

'Oh, I know,' I say quickly. 'I'm not blaming him. Just, you know. Saying.'

'He's had a tougher start than Poppy. It's bound to take him a while to settle down.'

He's four months old, I think.

Marc reaches for his jacket. 'Look, it'd be nice if Rowan calmed down, sure, but he'll grow out of it, the physician said so. Until then, we'll manage.' He smiles. 'We've done OK so far, haven't we?'

No one knows what I nearly did that night. Sometimes, even I manage to forget. I tell myself I'd never *really* have pressed that cushion into Rowan's face; that even if Marc hadn't come downstairs with Poppy – hiccuping and tearful, woken yet again by her brother's screaming – I'd still have thrown the cushion aside and scooped him into my arms and covered him with kisses, soothing his frantic cries like a good mother. It was just a moment of madness, that's all. A split-second impulse.

Yet I'm afraid to be alone again with my son. I adore him, but I'm terrified of what I might do, what I'm capable of. How do I know I won't have that . . . *impulse* . . . again?

I've read about baby blues, post-natal depression, sleep deprivation; I know what they can do to you. Of course I don't really want to suffocate my baby! I love Rowan! I'd never *want* to hurt him.

But I can't be trusted.

Rowan doesn't bother to cry as I reach into the pram for Poppy. He knows I won't pick him up until his sister is fed.

'It's a shame you gave up breastfeeding with Rowan,' Marc says as I settle into the rocking chair and unhook my nursing bra. 'You never know, it might've helped.'

'He didn't want me. He only liked his bottle.'

'*You* only liked his bottle.'

'Come on, Marc. You make it sound like I put him off on purpose.' I swaddle Poppy more tightly in her blanket. 'You know how much I like breastfeeding Poppy now. I tried my best with Rowan, but he got too used to the bottle in hospital—'

'Well, you'd have pulled the plug on it anyway, wouldn't you?'

'I haven't pulled the plug with Poppy,' I say, surprised by his tone. 'And I express milk for Rowan every day—'

Marc shuts the wardrobe door with a little more vigour than necessary. 'I still don't see why you had to rush back to work. You're the boss, you set the rules. It's not like you don't get paid if you're not there. Anyone would think you didn't *want* to spend time with your own children.'

I stare at him. First the outburst at Davina's, and now this. Marc used to be so supportive of my job! He knows how much it means to me; and we both need PetalPushers to do well if we're to pay our massive new mortgage. For years we've put in long hours building our respective careers, working weekends and evenings, rarely taking holidays, so we could get to where we are now. It's meant we've had less time together than we'd have liked, but neither of us has ever complained. We accepted it as the price we had to pay for our joint success. We discussed having a baby for years, planning when and how to organize it so that it didn't disrupt our lives or affect us financially. So why is Marc suddenly coming over all Neanderthal on me?

'Fine,' I say shortly. 'Why don't *you* stay home and look after them, and I'll work? I'm talking twenty-four/seven care, Marc, not a cuddle for thirty minutes before bed when they're all clean and sleepy, and a walk in the park for an hour or two at weekends. Let's see how *you* like surviving on three hours' sleep—'

'You're not the only one kept awake all night, Clare.'

'I'm the only one actually *up*, though, aren't I?'

'I'd give my fucking eye-teeth to stay at home with the kids instead of slaving away in an office all day,' Marc says bitterly. 'Women don't know how damn lucky they are to have the choice.'

'*Choice?*' I demand, livid. 'Is *that* what you call it?'

We glare at each other over Poppy's head. It feels as if

the ground is shifting beneath my feet. I've never heard Marc talk like this before. Since when did we become one of those strung-out couples who bicker over whose turn it is to take out the rubbish and indulge in I'm-more-tired-than-you competitiveness?

Since we had children and our lives as we knew them ceased.

The truth is that, even though he agreed to it in the end, Marc hasn't forgiven me for hiring Jenna. I've tried to explain how desperate I was, how fretful and anxious, that every time the babies cried it felt like a slap in the face. I tried to describe the endlessness of it, the relentless demands and chaos and incessant neediness. 'You said you wanted this,' Marc responded, confused. 'You wanted a baby, you *wanted* to stay at home for a while.'

The dreadful thing is, he's right: this *is* what I wanted. I just had no idea what it really meant. I wanted children, yes; but when I pictured motherhood, what I saw in my head was the baby, not me *with* the baby. I had no idea how much work one child would be, never mind two. But even more than the sleeplessness, the relentless routine, the effort required just to get through the day, I hate being needed. I hate the repetitiveness, the mind-numbing *boredom*. My mother's right. I can't do it. Usually unflappable, I've been flapping away like a dodo trying to take flight since the birth of the twins. I've done everything recommended in all the books, I've approached child-rearing like I have everything else in my life, by reading and studying and becoming an expert; and instead of the success that has always rewarded my efforts until now, I've failed. *I've failed*.

There was only one thing I could do to put things right:

hire someone who *was* an expert, someone who could succeed where I had fallen short. Marc's a professional, a businessman. Surely he can understand that?

'Look, I'm sorry,' Marc says unexpectedly, rubbing his hand over his face. 'I didn't mean to bite your head off. I'm just stressed out. I've had a bitch of a time at the bank. Of course you should work if that's what you want.'

'It's only a few days a week . . .'

'I know. I'll see you tonight.'

He leaves without kissing me, though he drops a butterfly kiss on Poppy's forehead, and ruffles Rowan's pale halo of white curls on his way out.

Five minutes later, Jenna's head appears round the door. 'Marc didn't look too happy,' she says, rolling her eyes. 'He had a face on him like a slapped arse. Oh, Rowan, baby, are you still waiting for breakfast? You must be starving!'

'I'm just finishing with Poppy—'

She picks up my son. 'Don't worry, I'll sort out his bottle. Everything OK?'

'Yes, fine.' I hesitate. 'Well. Actually, Marc and I had words.'

'Yeah, me and Jamie had a few over the weekend . . .'

'He doesn't want me to go back to work.'

She snorts. 'I'd like to see him giving up the expense accounts and company car to change shitty nappies.'

Instantly I regret my impulsive confidence. I've got no right to criticize my husband in front of the nanny.

'He's under a lot of pressure,' I say quickly, 'this recession – the bank—'

'Jamie's the same. All macho,' Jenna says, kissing Rowan's bare toes.

I feel a pang of something bittersweet as I watch my son gurgle and reach for her; it hurts my chest, my breasts. I'm glad that my children love her, I *want* them to; and yet.

And yet.

She lifts his soft vest and blows a raspberry on his round belly. 'Jamie thinks the man should be the provider, though he doesn't mind spending my money now he's screwed up his business.'

'Oh, but that's the thing,' I confide. 'Marc's never been like that. He's always been really proud of what I do, I've heard him boast about it to his friends. He's got five older sisters, he really respects women. Although,' I add thoughtfully, 'none of his sisters has worked since they had kids.'

'So you're going to fire me and stay home after all?'

'Heavens, no. No! I'd go mad if I couldn't work.'

'He's just going to have to deal with it then, isn't he?'

'I suppose he is,' I smile.

'You need to make it clear nothing's changed, Clare. I see it all the time: men marry a really successful woman, then she has kids, and suddenly he expects her to stay home and turn into a perfect housewife. But if she does, he gets bored with her and fucks off with the au pair.'

Her language is a bit – well – colourful, but she does cheer me up.

'Maybe I *should* fire you if you're going to run off with my husband.'

'Yeah, but then you'll be stuck with him for ever.'

I laugh. 'Oh, Jenna. What would I do without you?'

'I'll remind you of that next time I want a pay rise.'

She thinks I'm joking, but what *would* I do without her?

I listen to her chatter to Rowan as she takes him downstairs. He never laughs like that with me. Jenna is a lifesaver;

my rock. Already, after just two months, she's become the lynchpin of the family.

That first morning, as I waited for her to arrive, I was literally sick with nerves, racing off to the lavatory twice to throw up. Maybe I shouldn't have hired her, I panicked; maybe I shouldn't have hired *any*one. I'd made a dreadful mistake. What was I thinking, opening my home to a complete stranger, handing my babies over to someone I barely knew?

I'd rushed around the house with jugs of flowers and scented candles, laying out plates of hand-made biscuits, wanting her to feel welcome, pleased to be here. *Love me, love my babies*, I pleaded with my magazines and my body creams and my Lapsang Souchong, *help us, fix us, make it better*.

And then she arrived, calm and reassuring, radiating competence. I watched Rowan turn to her, like a flower towards the sun, and knew I'd made the right decision.

Jenna imposed order. She had the twins sleeping in their expensive cots in the nursery within a week (though Marc and I still lapse sometimes at weekends and put them in the pram in our room). The nursery looks like a spread from a parenting magazine: the stuffed animals lined up with artful carelessness, babygros folded just so, cot sheets so crisp you could bounce a coin off them. No matter how closely I try (and I took a photograph one Friday night after she'd left for the weekend, so I could copy it precisely) I can never make it look quite the same.

With Jenna in the nursery, I've been able to take back control of the rest of my life. I've had my hair cut, the leak in the roof has been fixed, I've fired the cleaner (who spent all her time drinking my expensive coffee and calling Brazil on my phone) and hired someone who actually knows where the mop is. Craig biked over the accounts for PetalPushers, and I've caught up with my emails, all 407 of them. I know that when I go to work this morning, the twins will be happy and cared for and organized without me.

The real surprise, though, is how much I enjoy Jenna's company. We come from different worlds, of course. I don't expect us to be real friends. But I've never had a sister, and Davina and I are hardly close. It's so nice to have a girl around.

Poppy disengages milkily from my breast, and I button my nightdress and take her down to the kitchen. A month ago I'd have cringed at the very idea of allowing a virtual stranger to see me half naked and without my make-up, but it's as if Jenna and I have signed an unspoken pact, and entered a partnership that's already intimate. A partnership, I acknowledge, that excludes Marc.

I put Poppy in her pink Bumbo seat and pour myself a glass of orange juice.

'Jenna!' I exclaim suddenly, noticing her bruised cheek. 'How did you get that?'

'Cupboard door swung back and caught me,' she says, too quickly.

I watch as she takes apart Rowan's bottle and puts it in the sterilizer. Last week, she caught her hand in the car door. The week before, she burned her arm on the iron.

'You seem very accident-prone,' I say carefully, 'when you go home.'

She laughs. 'Too many vodkas, that's all.'

'Jenna—'

'Better get going. The twins need their bath.'

I can't force her to confide in me. And I could be wrong,

of course. Maybe she *is* just partying hard at weekends, getting drunk, falling over. She knows so much about my life, but I still know next to nothing about hers.

You've never asked.

I suddenly feel ashamed. For the past few weeks, Marc's worked late at the office most evenings, so Jenna and I have fallen into a comfortable routine. She goes through my cookery books for a recipe she fancies, and washes and chops everything ready for when I get home. I throw it together – she can't cook, it seems, apart from nursery food – while she opens a cheap bottle of wine for the two of us. It's so nice chatting over dinner. I hadn't realized how much I'd missed having someone to talk to.

But I haven't given a second thought to what *she* might have to say. Guiltily, I resolve to make more effort to draw her out in future. I want her to feel she can tell me anything. I want us to be friends.

Before I leave for work, I run upstairs to kiss the twins goodbye.

'I haven't seen these outfits before,' I say, surprised. 'Where did they come from?'

She looks pleased. 'I went shopping at the weekend, and saw them. I couldn't resist.'

Oh dear. I rather wish she had. She's dressed Poppy in a hideous outfit emblazoned with Hannah Montana stencils, and Rowan in some sort of faux-tartan waistcoat and black jeans. I hope she doesn't take them out anywhere. People might think I'd dressed them like this.

Don't be such a snob, I tell myself. *You're as bad as Davina. It was a lovely gesture.*

'You shouldn't have,' I scold, 'you must let me pay you back—'

'No, please. I wanted to. I like buying them things.'

'As long as you don't make a habit of it.'

She turns away. 'I like buying things,' she says again.

'*Sex and the City* is on in two minutes,' Jenna calls from the sitting room.

I put the roasting tin into the sink to soak, and load the dishwasher. 'Would you like a cup of rooibos tea?'

'Why don't we just finish the Pinot?'

Help. I'm not used to drinking this much, but I don't like to say no.

'Marc hates this programme,' I say, curling up on the sofa.

'So does every straight man on the planet. That's the whole point.'

A key rattles in the front door. There's a thump as Marc flings his briefcase on to the hall table. 'Christ,' he exclaims. 'I've had the most fucked-up day.'

I listen as he walks through to the kitchen and mixes his usual (whisky, a dash of water, no ice). 'This credit crunch is killing us,' he calls. 'Another two of the big US banks just wrote down huge losses. We can forget about bonuses again this— Oh. Jenna. I didn't realize you were here.'

'Hi, Marc.'

I swing my legs down to make room for him next to me on the settee. He doesn't sit down.

'I need to talk to you,' he says curtly.

'What about?'

'Do you mind if we go upstairs and discuss it?'

'We're watching *Sex and the City*,' Jenna says.

Marc scowls. I put down my glass. 'It's OK, Jenna. I'll see you in the morning.'

'Doesn't she know to take a hint?' Marc hisses furiously as we go upstairs. 'It's after ten o'clock! When do we get to spend any time alone?'

'Sssh! She'll hear you. Be fair, Marc. You've only just got home. She was keeping me company.'

'Well, she needs to learn when to give us some privacy.'

Emboldened by the wine, I slide my arms round his waist. 'Why,' I murmur, 'would we need privacy?'

He stiffens. I'm quite sure he's about to push me away; and then, suddenly, the tension leaches out of him and he pulls me close. 'Mrs Elias,' he whispers thickly into my hair, 'you've no idea how much I've missed you.'

I've missed you too.

Suddenly, unexpectedly, the warm haziness of the wine gives way to a sharp, greedy hunger. I grab his face between my palms and kiss him: a hot, grinding kiss that crushes his lips against his teeth. *I want my husband inside me*, that kiss says. *I want him to fuck me* now.

Marc falls backwards on to the bed, pulling me on top of him. His answering erection presses into my stomach. He yanks up my skirt and tugs aside my knickers, fingers probing roughly between my legs. I grope for his belt buckle, freeing his penis. He's pulling my T-shirt over my head, scooping my heavy breasts from my bra. My nipples tingle, and a few drops of milk leak on to his chest. He catches one swaying breast, sucking hungrily.

Slipperiness gushes between my thighs. I guide him inside me and ride him hard, rearing back to take him in even deeper.

Moments later, Marc flips me abruptly over on to my

back, and thrusts furiously. My orgasm breaks over me with such speed, I'm gasping for air. He comes within seconds and collapses against my chest. He hasn't even taken off his shirt.

By the time I remember to ask what he wanted to talk about, he's already asleep.

I smile secretively as I go downstairs for breakfast, raw and throbbing in all the right places.

Jenna is feeding the twins their morning gruel: baby rice mixed with expressed breast milk. She glances up as I come into the kitchen, but doesn't smile. She looks tired and rather fed up.

I put on a pot of coffee, as Jenna seems to have forgotten this morning. 'You're up early.'

'It's eight-fifteen,' Jenna says tightly.

I flush guiltily. 'I didn't realize. Marc must have turned the baby monitor off when he got up for work. Jenna, I'm really, really sorry.' I reach for the breakfast bowl. 'Let me do that—'

She snatches it away. 'We're up now.'

'I'll pay you overtime,' I promise. 'Or you can take some time off instead if you like?'

She finishes feeding the twins and makes a big production out of scraping the bowl into the waste disposal. She's really annoyed with me. It can't just be the early start, can it? Oh, God. I don't want her to take it out on the twins. Or supposing she quits and hands in her notice? I can't manage without her, I can't go back to—

'Actually, Clare,' Jenna says suddenly, turning round, 'I'm going out tonight, so I will finish early and take some time off, if that's OK. About five? It'll give me time to get ready and do my hair.'

I'd meant to stay late at PetalPushers, to go over the books with Craig and see if we can get to the bottom of the discrepancies.

For heaven's sake. *You offered her the extra time off, even if you didn't mean her to take you up on it quite so soon. But that's not her fault. She wasn't to know. And she can't be expected to work morning, noon and night, can she?*

'Yes, yes, of course, that's fine. Are you going anywhere nice?'

'There's a new club opened in Stockwell, thought I'd give it a go.'

'Sounds . . . fun.'

'I'll be back to start at seven tomorrow, usual time. Don't worry if I don't come home before then, though.'

I smile awkwardly. 'I don't know how you can stay up all night and then work all day. I don't think I could do it.'

'Guess it's easier when you're young,' Jenna shrugs. 'Right, I'd better get on. I don't want to end up behind today.'

Ouch. I've been thinking of myself as more or less Jenna's age, but of course she doesn't. I suppose thirty-seven seems ancient to her.

Davina is right, as usual. We're never going to be friends.

'Do I look old to you?' I ask Craig.

He hefts a bucket of early pink cherry blossom out of the way of the fire door. 'Darling girl, when you get to my age, Elizabeth Taylor seems young.'

'That's not terribly helpful,' I sigh.

'Sweets, you're ageless. Helen of Troy. If I didn't bat for the other side, I'd have put the moves on you long ago. Why the mirror-mirror soul-searching now?'

I've never quite figured out why Craig affects an outrageously camp persona at work, when he's actually happily married with three gorgeous daughters and another baby on the way. Perhaps he thinks it's expected of a man who works with flowers, like hairdressers.

'Oh, I don't know,' I say disconsolately. 'Just feeling a bit sorry for myself.'

'You saw Davina last week?'

'Well, yes—'

'And your nanny is young, free and single?'

'Not quite single, but yes—'

'There you are, then. Asked and answered.'

I've never been a great one for nightclubs and parties. I'm not very good at dancing, and I hate getting drunk and out of control. I can't think of anything worse than schlepping across London to some cold warehouse playing music that makes my head hurt, and then having to get up the next day to work. I'd hate to be back in the dating pond, kissing toads. I love being married, being settled. There's absolutely no reason to feel jealous of Jenna—

'Craig,' I say, suddenly distracted, 'is that baby's-breath over there?'

He dodges in front of a bench of bleeding hearts. 'No.'

'Yes it is – wait. Are those *ferns*?'

'Of course not— Oh all right. Yes.' He flings his arms wide in dramatic fashion. 'Yes, I bought in baby's-breath and leather-leaf ferns, I've bulk-ordered forced roses, I've been selling 'mums, I've sinned, *mea culpa*, shoot me now!'

I gape in astonishment. 'Craig, what on earth is going on?'

He deflates and plops on to the ripped stool behind the till. 'Look, darling, I know it's blasphemy, it goes against everything we believe in, but we've been losing money hand over fist recently. It's not just the odd discrepancy, it's by the bucket. I didn't want to worry you while you were on leave, so I've been cutting the odd teeny corner here and there.'

'What kind of corner?' I demand.

'Chartreuse flowers and ornamental amaranths are divine, of course, but it's such a niche market. People *like* baby's-breath and ferns and roses—'

'The niche market is what we *do*!' I exclaim. 'Craig, you *know* that.'

We've never built our inventory around workhorses like carnations and 'mums. We have an aesthetic; either our customer base buys in to that, or they go elsewhere.

I glance around the shop. This is where PetalPushers started; of all my shops, this tiny Fulham one is my favourite. Little more than a grown-up kiosk, it's filled with interesting, quirky, old-fashioned flowers dancing in buckets that spill on to the pavement outside. Right from the beginning, I was determined to keep things organic. No forced flowers from Sun Valley growers or truckloads of Dutch tulips. Instead, I saddled myself with a terrifying bank loan, bought a few acres of land and, with the last of my seed money, planted my favourite flowers and rented this shop. I sold what I grew, and bought from other small gardeners like me. I kept my inventory seasonal: larkspur and poppies in spring, mistletoe and holly in winter. It's taken twelve years and a lot of hard work, but I've earned my reputation as a high-end, boutique florist. It's all about the flowers. White callas, deep purple hyacinths, parrot tulips, all crammed into crystal vases, their stems cut short to focus on the blooms. Our signature bouquets are monochromatic and simple, using no more than one or two varieties of flowers. I've never gone after the mass market. I wanted to play to the high-net-worths. Our arrangements are expensive, but worth it.

I don't understand the reluctance to spend money on flowers 'because they're only going to die'. How long will a fancy meal last? One of my bouquets will bloom for ten days and lift your spirits every time you see it. There's beauty even in a decaying rose.

'Why are we in such trouble?' I ask Craig suddenly. 'The last quarter's accounts were healthy enough.'

'We're in a major recession. It's hurting everyone—'

'We cater to the high end of the market. Our clients aren't hurting that much.'

'We've got a lot of competition. Another supermarket opened just round the corner last month—'

'We're not competing with inexpensive mass-market flowers. We've never chased pennies on a bloom. It can't have made that much difference—'

'I don't know,' Craig shrugs crossly. 'I just look at the bottom line.'

I shush him as a customer enters. Normally I'd let Molly, the Fulham manager, serve him, but I like to spend a few hours every week or so working on the floor at one or other of my shops. It keeps me grounded and in touch with my client base.

'How can I help?'

'Flowers,' he says shortly.

Too angry for a funeral. Or a lover, unless he plans to beat her to death with the calla lilies. His brooding, bitter intensity fills the room like smoke.

I hesitate, and then move towards a bank of glorious pink peonies.

'Not those. She has enough secrets.'

I glance up in surprise. Not many people know the Victorian language of flowers; certainly not – I hate to sound like Davina – an American. From the Deep South, judging by his mellow accent.

'Yellow tulips?' I hazard.

'Hopeless love and devotion? Hardly. Nor abandonment,' he says drily, as I reach for a small crystal bowl of anemones.

Craig is agog. 'What did you have in mind?' he asks breathlessly.

For a long moment, the bitter American says nothing.

'Lilies,' he says finally. 'Lilies and jasmine.'

Innocence and good luck. Somehow, I don't think he means it as a compliment.

Under his sardonic gaze, I deftly pull together a bouquet, weaving the jasmine through the lilies in a tight, crisp arrangement. *This* is why I love my shop, my job. These flowers won't be thrust into someone's hand, sniffed cursorily, jammed into a vase and forgotten. They will become part of someone's story.

I watch the American curiously as he pays and leaves without another word.

I feel sorry for her, whoever she is.

*

It's ten to six by the time I get home, thanks to a security alert on the Circle Line. I expect Jenna to be champing at the bit, wanting to get ready, so I'm slightly surprised to find the house in near-darkness. She must have popped out for a minute.

I hesitate by the drinks cupboard in the kitchen, then pour myself a very small gin and tonic. I've never really liked drinking alone. It feels . . . sordid, somehow.

I kick off my shoes and tuck my feet up under me in a squishy armchair by the unlit fire. I'm exhausted, but it's a satisfying weariness, born of hard work rather than quiet desperation. I don't know how I ever thought I could look after the twins myself. I'm just not cut out to be a hands-on mother. That doesn't mean I love them any less, does it?

I pull a folder out of my leather satchel and flip it open. I don't know why our profits are suddenly down, but I refuse to sell out to the fern-and-carnations brigade who'd be just as happy with a cellophaned bunch of weeds from the garage forecourt. Craig means well, but I created my business for customers who understand the importance of working *with* nature, who know that stepping out of season, forcing flowers, goes against the order of things; customers who know that flowers mean so much *more*, like that strange, angry American.

I must have fallen asleep, because I'm startled by a car alarm sounding outside in the street. I jolt awake, knocking the file on to the floor, and glance at the clock. Eight-fifteen! Where on earth is Jenna? And the twins?

I stem an instant gut surge of panic. She's probably gone to see a friend, lost track of the time, the traffic—

She doesn't answer her mobile. I call four times, growing

more and more concerned. Davina is right. How much *do* I know about this girl? She's only been here a few months. *Any*thing could have happened—

Don't be ridiculous. This is Jenna.

I ring Fran, suddenly remembering that Jenna knows her nanny, Kirsty. They could have gone off together, forgotten to call.

Except that Kirsty hasn't heard from Jenna, even though they were supposed to be meeting an hour ago.

'It's nearly nine,' Fran says carefully. 'I'm sure everything's fine, Clare, but maybe you should call Marc if she's not home soon. She's a responsible girl, but something could have happened—'

'Like what?'

'Well. She might have got lost—'

'Of course she isn't lost! This is London, not the Black Forest! Why isn't she answering her phone? Something's wrong, Fran. I'm going to call the police.'

'Maybe you should,' Fran admits.

Marc's left the office, and his mobile goes straight to voicemail. He's probably stuck on the bloody Tube himself. And Jenna still isn't answering.

I grab my keys and run out to the car. I'm not calling the police to be fobbed off with a patronizing pat on the head. I'm going down to the station in person. I'll *make* them pay attention.

To my surprise, the police take me seriously straight away, which alarms me even more. Fighting tears, I tell them everything I know: it's pathetically little. Jenna could describe the intimate details of my life: she's met my friends, my family, she could tell you a thousand things about me, down to the perfume I like and the kind of knickers I wear; but I still know next to nothing about her. The policewoman assigned to interview me seems pleasant, but I don't miss the flash of exasperation when I admit I don't know the address of Jenna's flat. I don't even know if that's her real name. She could vanish off the face of the earth with my children, and I've got no way of tracing her.

I ring my mother, just in case, but of course Jenna's not there. 'I told you,' she says tartly. 'I warned you. She's probably run off to Morocco with your husband. He's a lot nearer her age than yours, it does happen—'

'Marc hates hot weather.'

'He's *Arab*,' Davina retorts, 'of course he—'

I hang up. In thirty-seven years, I've never put the phone down on my mother, but for once I refuse to listen to her ugly nonsense.

There's a commotion from somewhere within the station. I look up, and Jenna is there, struggling to get a double buggy I've never seen before through the gap next to the sergeant's desk.

I swoop on my children, lifting them bodily within the push-chair. I'm sick and sobbing with relief. There's no room for anger or questions right now.

Xan wanders through behind Jenna, answering most of them by the mere fact of his presence. I should have known he'd be involved in this; whatever *this* is.

He's drunk, of course.

He staggers slightly, and a policeman behind him catches his arm. I realize, without real surprise, that he's in handcuffs.

'Hi, Clare,' he calls cheerily. 'Did you know Marc's cheating—'

And passes out on the floor.

PRIVATE & CONFIDENTIAL

PATIENT REPORT

Date   14/12/00
Patient   Jenna Kemeny, d.o.b. 10/10/82
NI   NH882282C

Jenna's physical injuries are now well healed. However, there is some concern with regard to her mental and emotional well-being. She is still only eighteen, and does not yet seem to have come to terms with the significance of her shoulder injury. When she does, there is a danger her mood will crash, bringing on a prolonged bout of anger and depression.

There is little by way of a support network. Her relationship with her parents appears affectionate, but reading between the lines, the parents, to whom Jenna was born late in life, are very much occupied with each other and their business (corporate hospitality). They are a somewhat distant presence in their daughter's life. Jenna is currently living with a group of other young people in rented accommodation in Stockwell.

At her most recent visit (13/12/00), she presented with a number of partially healed minor lacerations to the forearms. She claimed to have had an accident with a glass platter, but self-harm must be a consideration.

Our next appointment is scheduled in the New Year, and I will follow up then.

Caroline Johnson

Caroline Johnson
Consulting Psychiatrist

5

Jenna

'Marry me,' Xan says.

'Don't be ridiculous.'

He leans out of the window and slows the car to my pace. 'Come on a date with me, or I'll drive into that tree.'

I ignore him and keep walking towards the house, switching Rowan to the other hip. Behind me, Xan revs the engine of his stupid red American sports car. I give Rowan a clean dummy. I'm not playing Xan's silly games. I learned a long time ago: you don't shit on your own doorstep.

I nearly drop the baby at the deafening crunch of metal behind me.

I whirl around. Xan's Mustang is wrapped around the base of a large oak tree at the bottom of the drive. I scream as a branch snaps and falls on to the bonnet, spearing the broken windscreen and missing him by inches.

In the next field, a bull bellows.

He kicks open his door and staggers from the car. 'Damn, it's so much easier when they say yes.'

'Fucking psycho,' I gasp.

The bull bellows again, and lurches towards the broken gate. Xan leans against the wreck of his car and calmly lights a cigarette, laughing as I back nervously towards the house. I want to run, but I'm terrified the bull will chase us. Shit, I wish I hadn't put Rowan in red this morning.

I run into the conservatory where we had lunch. 'Excuse me, Lady Eastman—'

Clare jumps. Her face is white and tense; clearly she and her mother have been getting into it while I've been gone.

'Please, Jenna, no need for that. "Davina" is perfectly fine—'

Xan abruptly breezes past me, blowing me a kiss over his mother's head. 'Oh, don't go all democratic now,' he tells her, his eyes on mine as he brushes his lips against her cheek. 'Not after you've had Guy pony up millions for that title.'

'Alexander. How lovely.'

'Hello, Mother.'

He throws himself carelessly into a chair, staring pointedly at me. I blush furiously, wishing he'd stop. Someone will notice.

Davina pours him a cup of tea, which he ignores. 'I didn't expect you this weekend.'

'What can I say? I felt the need to nestle in the bosom of my family.'

'Have you met Jenna?' Davina asks. 'Your sister's new nanny.'

'A pleasure.'

There's the alarmed sound of shouting outside. Shit. The bloody bull. 'Lady – um, I mean, Davina . . .'

She fixes her cold blue gaze on mine. 'Be careful, dear. He's every bit as dangerous as he looks.'

You could cut the air in here with a knife. I listen to them bicker. Mum and Dad sometimes have blazing rows, and I've been known to add my fair share of drama, but we never fight like this. As if we actually *hate* each other. What a fucked-up family.

'. . . dear God, will someone *please* tell me what all that noise is?' Davina exclaims.

'I've been trying to,' I mutter.

Davina flings open the french doors. The bull's bellows echo across the lawn, accompanied by shouts and the sound of splashing. Fuck, I hope it doesn't come charging in here.

Clare thrusts Poppy at me and storms off after her mother. I juggle the two babies, wondering what the hell is going on.

Xan opens a cupboard and pulls out a bottle of whisky hidden at the back, then refills his silver hipflask. He settles himself back in his chair, lifting his feet on to his mother's crisp linen tablecloth.

'You don't seem very happy to see me,' he observes.

'You don't exactly set out to make yourself welcome.'

Xan laughs. 'You didn't seem to mind making me welcome last time we met.'

'I didn't get much choice, did I?' I flash back.

My cheeks flame. Every time I think about the night Xan sneaked into my room, I burn with embarrassment.

God knows why I didn't just scream and throw him out. *Some guy climbs in your bedroom window in the middle of the night, Jenna, puts his hand over your mouth, climbs into bed next to you, and you just* let *him?*

But there are mitigating circumstances. One, I was so relieved it wasn't Marc trying to get a leg over, I forgot to be scared. Two, I recognized him immediately as Clare's brother from the photos in the sitting room. And three ... three, he's fucking *gorgeous*. I mean, would *you* throw Daniel Craig and Ashton Kutcher's love child out of bed?

So instead of yelling my head off and crying rape, I tugged the duvet up to my chin so he couldn't see the crappy old T-shirt I was wearing (and, more importantly, what I wasn't wearing underneath) and moved over to make room for him.

'Why the fuck don't you just ring the doorbell and come up the stairs like a normal person?' I demanded.

'It's three in the morning,' he pointed out.

'He*llo*?'

'Look, I had a bit of a run-in with Marc last time I was here. He found my stash under the bed – just a few Es, no big deal ... Anyway, it seemed easier all round just to climb in the bedroom window and lie low till he'd left for work in the morning.'

'*My* window,' I hissed.

'OK, OK. I'm sorry. I didn't mean to freak you out. My ride let me down, I didn't have any cash on me, and I didn't feel like walking five miles home to Fulham. I thought I'd crash here.' He smiled ruefully. 'I'd forgotten Clare'd hired a nanny. Nice of her to give you the best guest room.'

'I don't mean to be rude,' I said stiffly, getting out of bed and opening the door, 'but I think you should go now. This is my first day and I'm sure you're very nice but if you don't mind, I'd rather not get sacked or spend the rest of my life in Holloway. I'm sure you can see yourself out—'

'I do *love* that T-shirt.'

I clapped my hands in front of my bush, flushing scarlet. 'Please go.'

Clare's brother unfolded himself lazily from my bed and headed towards the door. At the last moment he stopped, so close to me I could feel the heat radiating from his skin.

His hand slid between my thighs. My eyes widened with shock as he shoved his fingers inside me. His other hand found my breast, pinching my nipple hard enough to hurt.

His eyes never left mine as he found my clitoris with his thumb. I gasped as a hot bolt of lust zipped from my groin to the tips of my fingers and toes. If he'd wanted to throw me back on to the bed and fuck me there and then, I'd have let him. And he knew it, too.

With a dark smile, he released me, and licked his fingers. Then he was gone.

The memory triggers a sudden heat between my legs now. I bend to put the twins in their baby seats, hiding my blushes behind my hair. I'm not going to let the cocky bastard win. If he thinks he can humiliate me again, he's got another think coming.

I jump as Davina stalks into the conservatory. Of Xan, there's suddenly no sign.

'Is everything all right?' I ask nervously.

'Naturally. My daughter is at her commanding best. Where's Alexander?'

'Alexander?'

'My son.'

'I think he left.'

Five minutes later, Marc and Clare come back in. Clare looks OK, but you'd think Marc's been dragged through a hedge backwards. He's just wearing a tight white T-shirt and a clingy pair of boxers, and I have to force myself not to check out his lunchbox. He's nowhere near as cute as Xan, but he's still pretty ripped. I don't want Clare thinking I fancy her bloody husband. I need this job.

Davina doesn't come back to say goodbye. Marc's still steaming when he roars out of the drive, and nearly runs Xan down as he staggers across the road.

Clearly Marc would be happy to reverse over him, but Clare makes him stop, then leaps out and helps Xan into the back of the car. She totally mothers Xan, but having met Davina, I can kind of see why. The woman has all the maternal instinct of a flesh-eating virus. Clare may not be the perfect mother herself, but at least her heart's in the right place.

I study Xan, passed out in the boot. It's just as well he's not really interested in me. It'd never work. Never mind the whole money and class thing; the boy's a total fuck-up.

Gently, I tuck my sweater around him.

Fuck. This is the trouble with living in. It's like sleeping at the bloody office.

I roll over and glance at the luminous green dials. Six-ten. Jesus. I hope Clare gets up to see to them soon. I'm knackered.

I clamp the pillow over my ears. I can tell it's Rowan. Poppy's cries are cross, but Rowan always sounds so *lonely*.

It's obvious to anyone with half a brain their mother favours Poppy. I don't think Clare really dislikes Rowan; it's more that she doesn't seem to know how to handle him. It's a shame; now he's over the colic, he's actually a real sweetheart. He'll lie for hours peacefully gurgling at his mobile. Poppy's adorable, too, of course, but she's got a temper on her. She always seems to be thirsty. When she's awake, she demands your undivided attention.

Shit. I can't just lie here listening to Rowan scream.

I throw back the covers and pull on my sweats. Clare's probably still lying dead to the world in a cloud of post-coital bliss, I think crossly. These walls are paper-thin. It's almost as bad as listening to your parents getting jiggy.

I'm not jealous or anything. I could get laid too, if I wanted to. It just really pisses me off when girls drop you like a snotty tissue the moment a man shows up.

This is why I've never lived in before. I'm never quite sure when I'm off duty. Clare loves all this girly togetherness, the two of us cooking in the kitchen, watching chick flicks like we're at some sort of sleepover, but she's not, like, my best friend. I don't want to spend every night with her. I *work* for her. Who wants to spend all their time off with their boss?

I shuffle into the nursery and pick Rowan up. *Fuck.* He's got the shits again; bright yellow crap has leaked through his nappy all over his sheets.

Poppy pushes herself up on her tummy when she sees me, and starts to wail.

'Sorry, Poppy, you'll have to wait,' I say tersely.

I can't put Rowan down anywhere while he's covered in shit, so I've no choice but to hold him while the bath runs. Now I'm covered with shit too. I bet it bloody stains.

I love my job. I love my job. I love my job.

I bath Rowan, dress him in this gorgeous tartan outfit I bought last weekend, and then sort out his sister. I have to bath her too, which means emptying out the dirty water, cleaning off the lumps of shit ringing the bath, and running it again. Finally, we're ready to go downstairs. I feel as if I've run a marathon already.

I'm halfway through feeding them breakfast (baby rice and formula; I'm supposed to mix it with breast milk, but Rowan won't eat it, so let's not tell Clare) when she finally comes down, looking smug.

'You're up early,' she says brightly.

Poppy smacks her hand in her bowl, splattering me with baby rice. 'It's eight-fifteen,' I snarl, wiping cereal off my face.

Her smile fades. 'I didn't realize. Marc must have turned the baby monitor off when he got up for work. Jenna, I'm really, really sorry. Let me do that—'

I snatch the bowl away. 'We're up now.'

'I'll pay you overtime. Or you can take some time off instead if you like?'

I scrape the twins' bowls into the waste disposal. Clare's nice, she's nowhere near as bad as Maggie Hasselbach, but she still doesn't know how good she's got it. She wasn't much older than me when she met Marc, and look at her now: gorgeous toy-boy husband, two beautiful babies, this amazing house – must be worth millions – not to mention the sixty-grand car parked outside. It's not fair. I'd love to get my hair done every month at Nicky Clarke, or have enough clothes to fill a whole spare bedroom. *And* she owns her own business. She can pull a sickie whenever she bloody feels like it.

Meanwhile I clear up her kids' shit, chop her onions, do what I'm told. You could fit everything I own into a couple of holdalls. My boyfriend's a total loser, and I can hardly even afford our rent. In three years I'll be thirty, and I've got nothing to show for it.

The only thing I've got that she hasn't is freedom. I'm bloody well going to make the most of it while I still can.

I swing round. 'Actually, Clare, I'm going out tonight, so I will finish early and take some time off, if that's OK.' I don't give her a chance to change her mind. 'About five? It'll give me time to get ready and do my hair.'

'Yes, yes, of course, that's fine. Are you going anywhere nice?'

'There's a new club opened in Stockwell, thought I'd give it a go.'

'Sounds . . . fun.'

'I'll be back to start at seven tomorrow, usual time,' I add, rubbing it in. 'Don't worry if I don't come home before then, though.'

She's gone by the time I come back downstairs. I call Kirsty, and then raid the larder for something edible. This is easier said than done, since Clare is the sort of person who keeps wheatgrass smoothies and tofu in her fridge, whereas I'm more your Red Bull and frozen pizza kind of girl. But eventually I locate some doughnuts she pity-bought last week from the hospital fundraiser, and settle down with a cup of tea in front of Jeremy Kyle. MY SISTER STOLE MY LOVER – AND NOW SHE WANTS A THREESOME! Perfect.

The doorbell goes just as two bleach-blonde slappers lay claim to a bald lardarse with hair coming out of his ears.

'I like the cinnamon frosting,' Xan says, thumbing sugar from my top lip; 'adds a nice touch.'

A bolt of lust shoots straight to my groin.

Xan saunters past me into the sitting room and sits down. 'Hope you didn't overdo the doughnuts, though. I thought we'd do lunch.'

I blink. 'Don't be stupid. I've got the twins—'

'Bring them.'

'No. I've got a thousand things to do, and anyway, I don't think Clare would like it.' I go back into the hall and pointedly open the front door. 'No. Absolutely not.'

'Come on. You know you want to.'

'I told you, I can't.'

'I promise I won't tell.'

'As if I'd believe *you*.'

Xan laughs and pushes the chocolate lava cake towards me. 'You'd have a lot more fun if you just did what I told you.'

'Yeah, and I'd end up getting arrested.'

I give in and reach for the cake fork, but before I can take a bite Xan catches my hand and turns my forearm over. Carefully, he fits his fingertips to the livid pattern of bruises circling my wrist. 'He's got a firm grip,' he comments, 'your boyfriend.'

I pull my arm away. 'He just doesn't know his own strength.'

'Oh, I think he does.'

I open my mouth to deny it. 'The cupboard door swung back and hit me.' 'The phone distracted me when I was ironing.' 'I caught my hand in the car door.' I've got so used to making excuses for Jamie, the lies automatically trip off my tongue. Last weekend, Mum remarked on a half-moon scar on my knee, and instantly I rushed to explain it away: I was carrying some wine bottles out to the recycling bin, I slipped on some wet leaves, must have fallen awkwardly—

'You did that when you were seven,' Mum said, looking at me strangely. 'You fell over the campfire at Brownies, don't you remember?'

I busy myself with the twins now, wiping noses and cleaning hands. It's not Jamie's fault. I know every sad bitch who's ever had her eye blacked by her boyfriend says that, but in my case it's really true. Jamie's got PTSD, the counsellor said so. Like those soldiers in Iraq and Afghanistan. He really *doesn't* know what he's doing when he gets into these blind rages. I don't think he even sees me: I just happen to be there.

That doesn't make it OK, of course – but actually, it kind of *does*. What am I going to do, kick him when he's down?

Xan tips his chair back on two legs. 'He'll break something next,' he says laconically. 'Your wrist, your ribs. Your neck.'

'You'll break something if you don't stop tilting your chair.'

He smiles mockingly. 'Sorry, Nanny.'

Who the fuck does he think he is? Just because Mummy lives in a bloody castle and he went to a posh school. If I'm so beneath him, what's he doing here? *He's* the one who came to *me*. If he's that bothered, he can go back to guzzling champagne with the Honourable La-di-dah Horse-Face, instead of slumming it at Pizza Express with the staff. Arrogant fucking arsehole.

I shove back from the table. 'It's time I got the twins home.'

'Wait. Don't go.' He thumps his chair back down. 'Look, no more bullshit, Jenna, I promise. It just pisses me off, that's all. I don't know why anyone would want to rough up a gorgeous girl like you, but it's your business. Just tell me one thing. Forgive the cliché, but do you love him?'

Gorgeous girl.

Oh, get over yourself, Jenna. It's a line.

'I can't leave Jamie,' I say tightly. 'You don't understand.'

Slightly to my surprise, he doesn't press the point.

Instead he stands up, grabs the twins' push-chair and throws four twenties on the table. 'Let's go.'

As soon as we're outside, he flags down a taxi and hefts the stroller into it.

'What are you doing?' I demand. 'We can walk home from here—'

'You need to chill out,' Xan says. 'And I know just the place.'

Thirty minutes later, London lies spread beneath us. A murky haze blankets the city, the last of the day's bleached sunshine glinting off the sluggish brown river. Viewed from the sky, far from the traffic and crowds and noise, it all seems so much more peaceful and gracious than at ground level. London suddenly looks like the print Clare has over her fireplace by one of those Impressionist painters: Manet, Monet, something like that. Kind of elegant and timeless.

'The London Eye,' I sigh, as the huge Ferris wheel slowly turns, revealing slices of the horizon by degrees. 'You are seriously sad.'

'Come on. You're loving it.'

I try, and fail, to suppress a smile. He's right. I am.

I hold Rowan up against the curved glass so he can get a clear view of the river. He gazes owlishly at me, refusing to look anywhere but at my face.

'Rowan, look! Look at the pretty boats! No, you dope, not at me, down *there!*'

'I know which view I'd rather look at,' Xan says.

Poppy squirms unhappily in his arms, and he knuckles his forefinger and rubs it gently against her pink gums. 'Teething.'

'What would you know about teething?'

'You'd be surprised what I know.' He shrugs his left shoulder. 'Here. Reach into my back pocket.'

I slide my palm into his jeans. My pulse quickens at the intimate contact.

'Don't worry, I'm just going to rub it on her gums,' he snorts as I ease the silver hip-flask out and hesitate. 'I'm not going to get her drunk. She *is* my niece.'

Poppy screws up her eyes, splutters, then opens her mouth wide for more. Just like her uncle, in fact.

The wheel slowly brings us back down to earth. I check my watch as we leave the glass pod, shocked to see it's already quarter to five. Shit. I made such a big deal about Clare letting me off early today, and now I'm going to be late home myself. She'll have a fit.

I jiggle Rowan more comfortably against my hip, and make for the bank of push-chairs and strollers parked near the ticket booth, searching for Clare's fancy Bugaboo. If we can find a taxi, we might not be that late—

Xan's arm is suddenly tight around my waist. 'Keep walking,' he hisses.

'*What?*'

'Keep going. Don't stop, and don't turn round.'

'What are you talking about? I need the twins' push-chair—'

'Christ, Jenna! Pick another one! That one,' he says, pointing to a cheap fold-up double stroller at the end of the row. 'Clare's is worth ten times that, right?'

'Yes, but you can't—'

Xan is already pulling it out of the stroller line-up and strapping Poppy into one of its seats. Too bemused to argue, I follow suit with Rowan.

'Stop looking around,' Xan mutters. 'Shit, could you *be* more obvious?'

A Hispanic man with earrings through his eyebrow and lower lip is staring hard at Xan from a nearby doorway. For a moment, I think he's the one we're trying to dodge; and then I spot the cops. Four single men in cheap business suits, heads swivelling, thread their way through the tourists and young families. They stick out like sore thumbs.

Xan ducks his head into the push-chair, hiding his face, and fusses with the twins' blankets as I start to walk the stroller away from the crowded square.

'Not too fast,' he whispers tersely.

'Did the cops *follow* you?' I demand, *sotto voce*. 'Fuck, Xan, what have you done?'

'Mistaken identity. Keep walking.'

We reach a narrow side street without being spotted. Xan risks a glance over his shoulder. No one shouts or raises the alarm.

'Jesus,' Xan says, straightening up. I'm still too shocked to speak.

We round the corner to the main street just as a taxi with a lit sign crests the hill like the cavalry. Xan jumps recklessly into the middle of the road, his arm raised. The taxi pulls neatly in to the kerb and switches off its light. I start to unfasten the twins from the strange push-chair, and realize my hands are trembling.

'Excuse me, miss,' a voice says behind us.

I can't believe Clare doesn't fire me on the spot.

I *so* would, if I were her. But when she finds us at the police station she doesn't say a single word to me. She organizes a cab to take Xan back to his flat in Fulham and then drives the twins and me home, without even glancing in my direction. I sit huddled in the passenger seat, too ashamed to speak. Technically, it's not my fault Xan was arrested, but if someone entrusted with my children had just wound up in a police cell for four hours, I'd want to rip them a new arsehole.

'I am so, *so* sorry—' I choke out as we pull into a parking bay near the house.

'Jenna. I'm really tired. I'm sure you are too. We'll talk about this in the morning.'

She reaches into the back of the Range Rover, releases Poppy's car seat and carefully carries the sleeping baby up the front steps. Silently, I pick up Rowan.

The house is in darkness. Marc obviously isn't home yet, despite the fact that it's now well after ten.

'Did you know Marc's cheating—'

I put the twins to bed, unable to get Xan's drunken parting shot out of my head. God knows what Clare must be going through right now. She must be devastated. Unless . . . unless she already knew, of course. She didn't act like someone who'd just found out her husband was screwing around. Maybe they're one of those couples who have an open marriage. They're not exactly warm and fuzzy together; I know they have sex, but I never see them holding hands or kissing. Still, I can't see Clare tolerating him having an affair. It doesn't seem quite her style.

'If you wouldn't mind making sure I don't oversleep,' Clare says briskly when I come downstairs. 'I don't do well with late nights, and I have an important appointment with my lawyer in the morning. My *forensic* lawyer,' she adds drily. 'I'll be spending the next two days at work, going over the accounts.'

I flush. I swear she can read minds.

'And Jenna?' She stands and turns off the light. 'If I were you, I'd stay away from Xan,' she says.

Two weeks later, and I *still* haven't worked out what's going on with Marc and Clare. She leaves for work every day looking immaculate, her blond hair smoothed back neatly, fingers manicured into perfect pale pink ovals, not a stray hair or wrinkle marring her usual work uniform of boring grey or black trousers and pastel cashmere T-shirts. (When Annabel first told me she was sending me for an interview with a woman who ran a flower shop, I'd pictured this hippy, earth-mother type, with mad spirals of dark hair, long flowing skirts, wellies and broken finger-nails. Clare is *so* not my idea of a green-fingered goddess.)

Clare's great at keeping up appearances, but it's hard to hide everything when you live with someone. I never actually hear them row, she's far too discreet for that, but I can't help noticing that when Marc comes home now, later than ever, she doesn't smile or get up to greet him like she used to. She won't bother to cook him dinner if he gets home after we've eaten. There are no fresh flowers around the house any more. I can't remember the last time I was woken by the sound of bedsprings on the other side of the wall.

Talk about caught between a rock and a hard place. I'm not sure which is worse: weekends with Jamie, or Monday-to-Friday here. I'd go home to Mum and Dad, but they converted my old room into an art studio for Mum about a minute after I left home. They're always pleased to see me, of course, but after about three days on the fold-away I can tell I've outstayed my welcome. It's the way she hoovers round me.

I'm feeding the twins breakfast when Marc comes down one morning, his expression tense. Clare follows him, looking tired and distracted, as if she hasn't slept. I can tell they've had another of their 'discussions'.

Marc pours himself a coffee. 'Would you like one?' he asks Clare stiffly.

'Thank you.'

'Milk?'

'Black, if you don't mind.'

They're *polite* to each other, I realize. Like total strangers.

I spoon baby rice into the twins as fast as they can swallow, desperate to escape the atmosphere in the kitchen. The taut silence is deafening. *For God's sake, someone* say *something.*

'Can you sign a permission slip for the doctor?' I ask Clare. 'They're due for their next lot of jabs this morning.'

She glances quickly at Marc, pretending to be absorbed in his *Financial Times*. 'You won't need it. I'll come with you.'

'I thought you had to go to work early?'

'Nothing that won't wait.'

Marc snaps his paper derisively, but says nothing.

Clare looks close to tears. My heart goes out to her. Whatever's going on, I hope they sort it out soon, for the sake of the kids. And not to be mean or anything, but it's not exactly a picnic for me either. It's like being at a dinner party where the couple giving it have had a screaming match seconds before you got there. Only, in my case, you get to stay behind afterwards and live it twenty-four/seven.

Clare doesn't speak on the way to the health clinic, except to mutter cryptically into her mobile – 'I'll be at the bank by eleven; no, he's got no idea' – and fret about the heavy traffic. I don't know why she's come.

As usual, the surgery is running late. Clare neurotically paces the waiting room while I try to placate Poppy, who's uncharacteristically fretful and difficult. I think Xan's right; she must be teething. If Clare wasn't here, I'd pull my usual trick and dip her dummy in a packet of sugar. I've never known a baby with such a sweet tooth.

We're finally ushered into a chilly exam room, where the twins are stripped to their Pampers, weighed, measured and prodded. Finally a skinny, purse-lipped nurse takes off their nappies and sticks a thermometer up their bums. Unsurprisingly, both babies bawl in protest.

'They're very fussy,' she sniffs.

'You try having a pole stuck up your arse,' I mutter. 'Oh, I see you already have.'

Clare stifles a smile.

Moments later a fit, clean-shaven doctor of about fifty bounces excitedly into the room.

'Wonderful lungs!' he shouts over the screams. 'Good job, Mum!'

'Thank you,' Clare says faintly.

'So, are we weaned? Eating solids?'

He addresses Clare, but she turns helplessly to me.

'We started them off a few weeks ago,' I say. 'They're eating most things now, but they still like their milk in the morning and at bedtime.'

'How many dirty nappies a day?'

Again, he looks at Clare. Again, she looks at me.

'About six each, I think.'

'Sleeping through the night?'

'Yes,' I say, feeling like a ventriloquist's dummy. 'Rowan's over the colic now.'

'Good, good. Well, Mum, you've done an excellent job. Love and care, that's all most babies need. They don't want Mum in the boardroom or running the country, do they? They want her at home, isn't that right?'

Oh, for fuck's sake.

'Do you have children, doctor?' I ask sweetly.

'Yes, four.'

'How lovely. You must be very proud. Tell me,' I add, 'you must work such long hours here. Weekends and evenings too. It must take a lot of commitment.'

'Always on call,' he says brightly.

I stop smiling. 'So how many bloody sports days did *you* turn up to?' I demand. 'Or was Daddy always too busy saving the world? I'm sure your kids must have found that a *great* consolation.'

'Jenna,' Clare says quietly.

'Well, don't talk to me about love and care,' I say

defiantly. 'No one could love these babies more than Clare does.'

She shoots me a grateful look. The doctor coughs, and picks up his syringe.

Poppy doesn't put up any resistance, but Rowan's already arching and squirming when I pick him up. The doctor preps his arm with a Medi-swab, but as he gives him the injection, Rowan moves. The needle jabs deeper than the doctor intended, and Rowan screams in pain.

In a second, Clare has crossed the room and pulled him from my arms, her eyes dark with distress. She paces up and down, rubbing his tiny back and murmuring gently in his ear.

As he gradually stops hiccuping, she turns and looks at me, an expression of surprise and delight on her face so genuine it makes my heart turn over. 'I can't bear him to be hurt,' she whispers.

'I know,' I murmur back.

It isn't that Clare didn't love Rowan; she just didn't *know* it. I've watched her pick up Poppy and experience a glorious rush of natural, uncomplicated love; and then seen that smile falter and fade, drowned by her guilt at not feeling the same for Rowan. She was convinced she was going to turn into another Davina. I kept telling her mothers often take time to bond with their babies; people talk a load of shit about it, but the truth is, motherhood's different for every woman. Clare wouldn't listen. She's been beating herself up for months.

But in one single, simple moment, everything's changed. She could no more choose between the twins now than split the moon in two. I can see it in her eyes.

The Cradle Snatcher

There's an unexpected lump in my throat. Lost for words, I give Clare a clumsy hug, trying to let her know: I get it. 'You're going to be fine,' I tell her. 'You and Rowan and Poppy.'

We leave the surgery with the bashful, tearful-but-happy expressions you see on women as they walk out of tearjerker chick-flicks. *We had A Moment*, I think. I wish I was close enough to Mum to ring and tell her.

As we struggle down the steps to the street, two grannies step aside and wait for us to manoeuvre the push-chair past them.

'Oh, twins!' one exclaims. 'Look, Joan. Aren't they beautiful?'

The other peers into the stroller, and then smiles at Clare, instantly identifying her as their mother, even though I'm the one pushing the pram. 'You must be so proud!'

Clare pinks with pleasure, and squeezes my shoulder. 'We are.'

Tears threaten again. She didn't have to include me like that. The old biddies probably think we're a couple of dykes, but I don't care. For the first time, I realize Clare actually means it when she says we're a team.

Except . . . except the twins still aren't mine, are they?

I feed them, I wipe up their shit and vomit, I play mind-numbing games with soft balls and sing them endless dumb nursery rhymes. I schlep around in hideous sweats and trainers so it doesn't matter if they're sick on me, and have short, stubby nails so I don't scratch them by mistake. I'm putting in all the hard work, and at the end of the day I'll have nothing to show for it.

But that's the deal. The twins aren't mine, will never be

mine. They'll never even remember me. It's like pouring all your money into renting a flat, when you could buy one and keep it for ever.

At times like this, I wonder how much longer I can keep working as a nanny. Every time I say goodbye to one of 'my' babies, a little piece of me goes with them. One day, there'll be nothing left.

We reach the car, and strap the twins into their car seats. Together we wrestle to fold the cheap stroller I stole at the London Eye, which has the perverse personality of a seaside deckchair. It's already taken the skin off my knuckles several times.

'I must remember to get a new push-chair,' Clare pants, as she slams the boot. 'This thing is driving me crazy.'

'It's my fault we lost the Bugaboo. I'll pay for it—'

'Don't be ridiculous. They cost a fortune. If anyone's going to pay for it, it's Xan.'

Silence makes a sudden space between us.

I swallow. 'Clare. You know what Xan said that night at the police station. About Marc cheating. I'm . . . I'm sure it wasn't true. He was drunk, he didn't mean it. Marc would never have an affair—'

'Oh, Jenna. Of course he wouldn't.' She starts the car, and turns to me, her eyes as flat and cold and hard as blue pebbles. 'I'm afraid it's much, *much* worse than that.'

Coares

PRIVATE & CONFIDENTIAL

COARES & CO.
220 STRAND
LONDON
WC2R 0QS
T: 020 7753 3000
www.coares.com

Mr Marc Elias
97 Cheyne Walk
London
SW3 5TS

2 March 2009

Dear Mr Elias

I write with reference to your letter dated 28 February 2009.

We would be prepared to provide a short-term loan for a period of one year in the amount you requested, £750,000, using your wife's portfolio with us as collateral. I enclose the necessary paperwork, which both you and your wife will be required to sign.

I can confirm there will be no arrangement fee for this facility. Our interest charges are 6% above the Bank's Funding Rate, currently 4.25% per annum (subject to variation from time to time).

I look forward to receiving your completed application in due course. In the meantime, if you have any questions please contact me on 020 7597 2638.

Yours sincerely

Joanna Yeates

Joanna Yeates
Private Banker

Calls may be recorded

6

Marc

'Screwed her yet?' Felix asks.

The screen turns red. 'Wait till it hits two hundred!' I yell into the phone. 'Fuck you,' I tell Felix amiably.

'Don't tell me: the nanny turned you down—'

'She didn't fucking turn me down. I said two hundred!'

'You sad bastard.' Felix shakes his head and swivels back to his desk. 'Wife's got you bloody pussy-whipped, Elias.'

I tune him out, watching the screen intently. It's another bloodbath in the markets, but so far Voyage is holding up. Health and pensions are where it's at these days. Straightforward demographics. Even in a bear market, you can still walk away with a shitload of money if you keep your nerve—

'Jesus Christ!' I shout, leaping out of my seat. 'What the *fuck*?'

'What's up, mate?'

I slam my phone shut, abruptly cutting off my broker.

'Voyage!' I yell, pointing at the screen. 'What the shit is happening to Voyage?'

Felix grabs his keyboard and types furiously. 'Class action in Mississippi. Just hit the wires. Some cholesterol drug causing seizures—'

'Can't be. Voyage doesn't do pharmaceuticals. They're strictly insurance.'

'Says here they bought out GITA, the Indian drug company, last summer. Used a shell to make the deal.'

I collapse into my chair. The price has steadied, but I'm already out four hundred thou. I just lost *four hundred thousand pounds*.

'Mate? You're not exposed, are you?'

'Four hundred.'

'Peanuts, mate. Hamish lost three mill last Friday—'

I laugh shakily. 'Not the bank. Personal.'

Felix whistles. 'Nasty.'

'It was a done deal,' I plead, running my hand through my hair. 'Voyage has been steady as a rock for years. I had a couple bad trades, I was counting on my bonus to put things right, but after the crash last year it never bloody happened, did it? I needed to get a foot back on the ladder, so I ran a spread bet. Voyage seemed like a safe haven. It was a done deal,' I repeat.

'You can probably go back in and pick it up on the turn. What are you out for, total?'

'One point eight.'

'Christ, Marc!' Felix exclaims. 'One point eight *million*?'

'It's been a fucking rollercoaster this year,' I snap. 'We've all taken a hit.'

'Yeah, with someone else's money. This is a fucking

lousy market to take a punt on, mate. What were you thinking?'

'It's no big deal,' I bluster. 'You win some, you lose some, right?'

Felix slaps my shoulder. 'Yeah, sure. At least you've got the wife to bail you out if it all goes south. Looks like you better keep on giving the nanny a wide berth for the time being.'

'Tits like fried eggs,' I lie.

'That's the spirit.' He hesitates. 'Look, mate. It's Lyle's stag do tonight at Spearmint Rhino. Why don't you change your mind and come? Reckon you could do with drowning your sorrows.'

'Yeah. Yeah, why not? Might as well live it up while I still can. It'll give my brilliant wife the chance to earn a few more million before I get home,' I add bitterly.

One point eight million. Felix is right. What the fuck was I *thinking*?

I stare into my whisky glass. None of this would've happened if it wasn't for Clare. I just wanted to prove I could bring something to the table too.

It started when I got this hot tip last summer. Clare was newly pregnant, and we'd just squeezed under the wire with a huge mortgage on the new house before the credit crunch hit. Cash-flow was a bit tight. We weren't desperate, but some extra money could certainly come in handy. The tip was a shoo-in. My source was solid as a rock, I'd done business with him a thousand times. Legally, I was sailing a little close to the wind – the bank has a strict zero-tolerance policy on insider trading – but he reckoned I could make a 100 per cent return in six months. I had a couple hundred thou in bonds set aside from my last bonus. I knew Clare would never OK it, she's anal about anything she calls 'shady', but I'd double my money and put it back before she even knew about it. On the strength of the deal, I even blew eighty grand on a top-of-the-line new Range Rover.

Then the company filed for Chapter Eleven, another victim of the sub-prime fallout. My source was mortified, but the damage was done. Two hundred twenty thousand, down the drain.

I couldn't tell Clare. The twins were only a few weeks old, her hormones were all over the place, and anyway, I wasn't going to run to Mummy like a naughty schoolboy and admit I'd put my hand in the cookie jar and got caught out. She's not a risk taker, she wouldn't understand. Hell, she could have a hundred flower shops up and down the country by now if she'd listened to me.

I play the markets all day for a living. I'm head of pan-European equity sales, I manage a team of forty people, I have CEOs and major hedge-fund managers on speed-dial! I generate a huge amount of business for the bank. I knew I could make back a measly couple hundred grand in no time. But I needed seed money. With annual bonuses off the table again this year, courtesy of the recession, and short-selling newly outlawed, I was screwed. Clare had her own portfolio with Coares, of course, but I couldn't borrow against it without her signature and agreement. The house, though, was in my name; Clare's idea, to protect us from creditors if PetalPushers ever went belly-up.

I pulled in a few favours, finagled a second mortgage –

punitive fucking rates, but what choice did I have? – and got straight back on the horse. I made everything back in the first few trades. I was riding high. I was going to give Clare a cheque for a million on her birthday. She wasn't the only entrepreneur in this family.

So, I lost a few deals again. That's the nature of the beast. It's why you need balls to stay in this business. You don't see many women on the trading floor.

Fucking Voyage! I'd be free and clear if they'd come through.

I knock back my drink, my head pounding in time with the music. *One point eight. One point eight.* If I don't get out and settle the bet now, it could get much worse, but how the hell am I supposed to explain that to Clare?

A woman's arms slide round my shoulders, bringing with them the stench of cheap perfume and stale sweat.

'Baby, you look like a man who needs to relax,' she purrs in my ear. 'Feel those knots. You're so tense, baby. I know how to fix that.' Sharp fingers knead my shoulders, then slide down the sides of my ribcage and reach towards my groin.

I push her away and lean across to Felix. 'I'm out of here,' I yell over the music.

'Don't be an old woman, Elias,' Felix yells back, his eyes on the hooker. 'I've already paid her. I want my money's worth.'

The girl puts her hands on her knees and bends over, treating me to a peek-a-boo glimpse of her slit. Felix leans forward and puts another bill in her G-string, and she gyrates over to him. He buries his face in her silicone cleavage. Her eyes meet mine, flat and dead.

I stand up abruptly, pushing my way through the

crowds towards the door. I've sunk a bottle of champagne and Christ knows how many shots, and it hasn't even begun to take the edge off.

I only did it for Clare. For *us*.

It takes for ever to find a taxi. I'm surprised the lights are still on when I get home, and then glance at my watch and see it's not yet ten. It seemed much later at the club.

I dump my briefcase in the hall. Maybe if I can just explain it to Clare properly, I can get her to see where I'm coming from. She could bail me out, easy. A couple of million is back-pocket change to her family.

'Christ, I've had the most fucked-up day,' I call to Clare as I go into the kitchen. I pour myself a stiff drink. This is one conversation I really don't want to have.

Suck it up. There's nowhere else to run.

I tug off my tie as I walk into the sitting room. 'This credit crunch is killing us. Another two of the big US banks just wrote down huge losses. We can forget about bonuses again this—'

Fuck. Fuck fuck fuck.

'Oh. Jenna. I didn't realize you were here.'

'Hi, Marc.'

I wait for her to get up and make herself scarce, but she just sits there and carries on watching television. I seethe. I should never have agreed to the girl moving in. I've got no damn privacy any more. If I want a glass of water in the night, I have to get dressed in case I run into her in the hallway. It's like have a permanent house-guest. Clare and I are reduced to whispered conversations through rictus smiles and gritted teeth. We can't have a row and clear the air like we used to.

'I need to talk to you,' I tell Clare, nerves making my tone sharper than I'd intended.

She frowns. 'What about?'

'Do you mind if we go upstairs and discuss it?'

'We're watching *Sex and the City*,' Jenna says.

Is it really asking too much to come home after a *fucking* hard day and expect a few minutes' conversation in private with my wife?

Strike that. What I *really* need is another Scotch and thirty minutes on my own, no phones, no interruptions. No one climbing up my ass and wanting things done yesterday. All I need is some bloody peace and quiet to unwind.

What I don't need is to get in and find my wife glued to some subversive anti-men American shit on TV, while the bloody nanny sits there in *my* chair, drinking *my* wine and acting like she owns the place.

Clare finally throws me a bone and puts down her glass. 'It's OK, Jenna. I'll see you in the morning.'

Don't do me any fucking favours.

'Doesn't she know to take a hint?' I demand. 'It's after ten o'clock! When do we get to spend time alone in our own house?'

Clare pushes me up the stairs. 'Sssh! She'll hear you. Be fair, Marc. You've only just got home. She was keeping me company.'

'Well, she needs to learn when to give us some privacy.'

Clare winds her arms around me. I'm uncomfortably reminded of the girl in the strip club. 'Why,' she murmurs, 'would we need privacy?'

I want to tell her where to stick her drunken come-on, but despite my mood, the Scotch and 'one point eight' going round and round in my head, my cock jerks painfully against my pants. Can't help it. She's a bit scrawny since she had the twins, but Clare still knows how to get me hot.

It was her voice that suckered me in first. When she leaped out of that crappy old van at four in the morning and started bitching at me, all I could hear was her accent. So fucking *classy*.

I'd never met a woman like Clare Sterling. At the time I'd only been in the UK for two years; having graduated *magna cum laude* from Toronto Business School with a profitable sideline brokering trades for my classmates, I'd blagged my way into a job as the new hot-shot *Wunderkind* with Canada Central Bank, and been sent straight to their London office to shake things up. I was greener than a new-mown lawn. I hadn't left Canada since moving to Montreal when I was four. My parents had fled Lebanon when I was a kid so that Dad wouldn't get drafted into the civil war, and had been too paranoid to let any of us leave the country since. I spoke fluent French, Arabic and English, but when it came to women I wasn't quite as worldly-wise as I made out. My previous girlfriends had all been straightforward, wholesome farm girls from rural Quebec with pink cheeks and shiny pony-tails. They put out on the fifth date, gagged on my cock, and invited me home at Christmas to meet their parents.

London girls were different. They drank beer, threw up in the street, forgot to wear knickers and bought their own condoms. I dated a bunch of them at the same time; none of them seemed to care. Marriage and babies were the furthest thing from their minds.

Clare was in another league. I knew that straight away. The accent, the clothes – she dressed nice, but not cookie-cutter preppy – the gold signet ring on her pinkie. I'd worked with enough London bankers by then to know that ring meant 'family'. I nearly peed myself when she told me her mom was a Lady, even if, as she pointed out, her stepdad had bought the title by shelling out enough cash in donations to the right government fixer. My grandfather had been a fisherman in Tyre; he'd lived and died in a one-room shack.

Dating Clare catapulted me into the same elite club as Felix and Hamish and the rest of them. In an instant, I was One of Us. And – the icing on the cake – I genuinely *liked* her. She had a plan. She was ambitious, she knew what she wanted out of life and how to get it. We had that in common at least.

The age thing didn't bother me one way or the other. Sure, I got a kick out of hooking an older woman, but I didn't have this whole sugar-mommy complex. She'll be pushing eighty when I'm seventy: so what? I grew up with five older sisters; I don't see it as a big deal. At least, I didn't use to. These days, the whole Clare-knows-best routine is starting to grate. It was fine having her take charge when I was twenty-three, but I'm fucking thirty years old in a few months. She needs to let go the reins a little.

She pulls my head down now and crushes my lips beneath hers, hot and demanding. I can't remember the last time she was this horny. I put the money out of my mind. I'm not going to ask my bloody wife for it. I'll figure it out myself.

I press my face into her hair, wishing, just for a moment, it was the two of us again.

'Mrs Elias, you've no idea how much I've missed you,' I whisper fiercely.

I yank up her skirt and shove her knickers aside, jamming my fingers roughly inside her. She squeals; I ignore her, throwing her down on the bed beside me. She unzips my pants and I pull her astride my cock, ripping her T-shirt over her head. Her titties leak milk, and I latch on and lap it up. I love her being pregnant, feeding my kids. I loved her walking around with her huge belly: *I've been fucked*.

She starts riding my cock, taking over again, so I flip her on to her back and drill my dick hard into her. The bedroom's the one place I'm in charge, and I know she fucking likes it that way.

I come inside her, hoping she's had enough wine to forget she's not back on the Pill yet. I want her pregnant again soon. If I had my way, she'd give me a dozen kids.

After, she curls happily in the crook of my arm. I guess she came too, then.

'Marc? What was it you wanted to talk about?'

Christ. Why do women always want to talk *after* sex? It's doing things ass-backwards, like putting your socks on over your shoes.

I pretend I don't hear her. Pretty soon she's asleep, and I stare at the luminous green figures on the clock next to my bed, knowing I have to be up again in a few hours, but unable to switch off. Sex tonight was fine, yes, but it hasn't wiped the slate the way it usually does for me. If anything, I feel even more pissy. Clare's changed since she had the twins, and not in a good way. I've watched five sisters have kids, and it softened all of them, even Rania, the wild child of the bunch – Christ, you should have seen her at sixteen. Jailbait. My father was all for sending her back to Lebanon to knock her back into line. Then she met Antoine and had the boys, and she's blossomed.

Clare's always been controlling (Mom reckons she's a bitch on wheels: she's never approved of women who work), but it never really bothered me before. She couldn't have achieved what she has if she didn't have a tough, steely streak. I know she could be a great mother: you can see it in the way she fusses over her flowers. I always figured she'd relax once we had a family. You have to go with the flow where kids are concerned. Life gets messy. Rania's three are in and out of the ER with one minor emergency after another.

But Clare didn't even try to make it work. She simply passed the ball and brought a sub in off the bench. She's paying someone to mother her own babies. There are times I think she cares more about her business than me or Rowan and Poppy.

I ease my arm from beneath her head, the muscles tingling painfully as blood flows back into them. A wisp of hair falls across her face and flutters as she breathes.

PetalPushers is her real family.

For two weeks, I try to find a way out of the nightmare, but come up empty. I can't borrow any more from the bank, I've already taken out a second mortgage on the house, and no one will give me a loan this size in the current economic climate. Scared shitless, I drink myself stupid, trying to block it all out, but all it earns me is a monster hangover and a slap-down from Clare when I make the mistake of trying it on with her.

In the end, I run out of time. When the trading floor gives you a margin call, you pay up or you're screwed. I have twenty-four hours to find the cash, so I do what

I have to, and take it from Clare again. Where else was I supposed to get it?

It's not like I'm having an affair, for God's sake. She'll never even know. I can make it back with a couple of good trades. I swear, once this is all over, I'll never stick my neck out like that again. I'll settle the bet and walk away from the table once and for all.

For once I come home sober, putting my game face on as I let myself into the house. I've never lied to Clare, even by omission. Every night when I come home, I'm terrified she'll see it in my eyes.

I needn't have worried. She doesn't even bother to look up.

Instead, she holds out her wineglass to Jenna, who tops it up. Acid burns in my gut as I watch them from the doorway. They've been thick as thieves since that business with Xan a couple weeks ago. I should've punched the bastard's fucking lights out. Nobody puts my kids in danger. And as usual, Clare stuck up for him. 'Silly misunderstanding', my ass. If I'd been in charge, I'd have locked him up and thrown away the key.

I pour myself a drink in the kitchen. The remnants of dinner are in the sink. I check the oven. Cold. Nothing left for me, as usual. The fucking cat gets treated better than I do.

I hear them giggling in front of that damn show like a pair of teenagers. I want to slap the pair of them. They've even started to look alike, Clare in jeans – I didn't know she owned any – and the nanny with her hair tied back in a prissy knot like my wife's; for God's sake, the girl's even wearing a pair of bloody pearl earrings.

'I'm going to take a shower,' I say tightly.

'Fine,' Clare says.

I run the water as hot as I can bear it, and stand under it until I feel the tension start to drain away. A year ago, my life was pretty much perfect. I was making money hand over fist; I had a beautiful, attentive wife, two babies on the way, a fantastic new house: life was sweet. I thought when the twins arrived there'd be no looking back. Instead, ever since that fucking cuckoo moved in, my life's been falling apart. I feel like a third wheel in my own home. I could lose my job and the roof over our heads if I don't dig myself out of this hole. And if Clare finds out I've borrowed against her company, I'll lose her.

I'm towelling myself dry in our dressing room when Clare comes upstairs.

'You didn't have to be so rude to Jenna,' she snaps. 'A "hello" would have done.'

'Jesus. Do we have to talk about the nanny now?'

'I'm helping her put some sort of monthly budget together,' Clare adds, as if I haven't spoken. 'She hasn't got the first idea how to manage her finances. That Cartier watch cost her six months' salary.'

I throw my damp towel into the laundry basket. 'Why d'you have to get involved? It's none of our business how Jenna spends her money.'

'She's part of the family, Marc. She looks after our children.'

'Your choice,' I mutter.

Clare stares at me like I'm shit on the sole of her shoe. For fuck's sake, what does she want from me? Who gives a damn about the nanny's overdraft? I've got enough problems worrying about my own.

'It's none of your business, Clare.' I pull on a pair of

boxers and climb into bed. 'I know it makes you feel better to think of her as part of the family, but she's not. She's an employee, the same as Molly and Craig and anyone else you pay to work for you. *You* decided you wanted a nanny. Don't try to reason your guilt away by dressing the relationship up and making it something it isn't.'

'*I* have nothing to feel guilty about,' she says sharply.

'Whatever.'

'I just want Jenna to be happy, so Poppy and Rowan are happy—'

'You want the children to be happy? Fantastic. Fire the nanny and look after them yourself.'

Clare spends longer than usual finishing up in the bathroom. When she gets into bed, I feel the covers tremble, and realize she's crying.

I want to comfort her, but something holds me back.

I'm glad to see the invincible Clare Elias rendered vulnerable, like everybody else.

For the next few days, Clare leaves the house before my alarm has even gone off. I thoughtfully regard my reflection in the mirror the third morning after I wake to find my bed empty. Something isn't right. Clare hasn't been herself for weeks. It's not just the girly bonding with Jenna and chucking my dinner in the bin. I've been married to Clare long enough to recognize when she's using politeness as a weapon. She consulted me about the summer holidays, she takes my suits to the dry-cleaners and hands me my cufflinks; but when I've tried to talk to her properly, she courteously shuts me down. On the couple of occasions she's given in and we've fucked, I can tell she's faking. *I've got to know if she knows.*

'Jenna,' I muse, as I walk into the kitchen, 'is everything all right with Clare?'

She lifts Rowan out of his seat and puts him in the playpen with Poppy. 'What do you mean?'

I spoon coffee into the percolator. I really don't want the nanny involved, but I have to find out what's eating Clare. If she's found out about the money, who knows what she might do? I don't want to come home one evening and find she's changed the locks on me.

'She's just been a bit ... distracted ... lately,' I say carefully. 'Like she's got something on her mind. I thought she might have mentioned something to you.'

'Such as?'

Christ, she's not making this easy. 'I don't know. Girl stuff.'

'Oh. *Girl stuff.*'

'Is she worried about something? At work, maybe?'

'Not that I know of,' Jenna says, wiping down the twins' high-chairs. She straightens up, and looks me dead in the eye. 'Is something on your mind, Marc?'

I blink first.

'I know I've been a bit preoccupied lately,' I say evasively. 'I haven't spent as much time with Clare or the twins as I'd have liked ...'

'They've hardly seen you.'

Fucking bitch. 'Look, Jenna. I love my kids. I love my wife. I'd like nothing more than to come home at five and hang out with them at bathtime. I'd kill to take the kids to the park or the zoo today, instead of going into work.'

'So take the day off.'

'It's not that simple.'

I'm suddenly tired; I don't have the energy to keep fighting with her. 'Jenna, in my business, taking time off is seen as a sign of weakness. It's a young man's game, and there's no room for passengers. Particularly with the economy the way it is. You can't imagine the pressure I'm under. Every day I go into work, I wonder if I'll be clearing out my desk by lunchtime. You're only as good as your last trade. The first sign of blood in the water, and the sharks move in. They fire you on Friday, so you don't depress everyone. By the time Monday rolls around, they've forgotten you even existed.'

It's such a relief to finally tell someone. To admit how fucking terrified I am. I could never talk to Clare like this. She despises me enough as it is.

'Why don't you quit and do something else?'

I laugh shortly. 'Like what?'

'I don't know. Work in an ordinary bank, or something?'

'Behind a counter? Filling ATMs?'

'Well, couldn't you manage a branch? With all your experience—'

'And earn fifty grand a year before tax? It wouldn't even cover the basics.'

There's an awkward pause. I get up and pour my coffee. Fifty grand must seem like winning the lottery to Jenna. What would she say if she knew I owed almost *two million*? It sounds like Monopoly money, even to me.

Jenna picks Poppy up from the playpen. 'I'm sure Clare just wants you to be happy,' she says uncertainly.

'Clare's got no idea what it feels like to fail. She couldn't begin to understand. She's never made a mistake in her life.'

'D'you ever feel a bit – well . . .' Jenna hesitates.

'Inadequate? Pathetic?'

'No, no, of course not. I just meant . . . you must wish she didn't have to work so hard.'

Poppy squirms fretfully in Jenna's arms, her long dark lashes spiked with tears, and the nanny gently rubs her back. 'Is she OK?' I ask. 'Her cheeks are a bit red.'

'I think she's teething again, that's all. She's been really thirsty, and that's always a sign. She'll be fine by tomorrow.'

'Clare should have stayed home—'

'Marc, it's fine. Babies are always teething or getting a cold. You can't take a day off every time. Anyway, looking after them is what *she* pays me for.'

I don't miss the snide emphasis. She couldn't make her position any clearer: *I work for Clare, not you.* Well, she may be Clare's new best friend, but I'm still her husband. If Jenna doesn't want to find herself out of a job, she'd better mend her fucking attitude.

'I'd rather my children were cared for by their own mother,' I say tersely. 'They'll be going to nursery in a year or two. The damn flowers will still be there then.'

Jenna bites her lip. I drain my coffee, feeling slightly guilty. I shouldn't have thrown Clare under the bus like that. I don't want this conversation coming back to bite me on the ass one day. But these are *my* kids too, a fact both Clare and Jenna tend to forget.

Screw it. It felt good to finally say what's on my mind.

I grab my briefcase and head into the office. For once, Lady Luck is on my side; I have a better day than I have done for months. Several potentially risky trades come off, and by the closing bell I've earned several million for the bank, and 220 against my personal debt. If I can hold the line, I may – just *may* – survive this.

I emerge from the Tube a little earlier than usual into one of those rare, warm May evenings. Everyone is spilling on to the pavements from cafés and restaurants, eager to grab the first real summer warmth of the year.

My mood lifts. I mull over my conversation this morning with Jenna as I walk home, and realize I've been more than a little unfair to Clare. Aside from the fact that I shouldn't have sold her out to the nanny, much of what I said wasn't even true. Clare always made it clear she wouldn't give up work – although she did say she'd stay at home for the first six months – and it's me who moved the goalposts, not her. I was the one who secretly hoped she'd change once the babies came. It's not her fault she didn't.

I've got to come clean, and tell Clare what I've done. Our marriage is in serious trouble otherwise. I can't live with the guilt and worry any longer.

A siren shatters the calm of the evening. An ambulance roars past, jumping a red light, and I nearly get my toes run over by a van pulling onto the kerb out of its way. I don't know how I'm going to break it to her. I know Clare: she'll want to close the bet now. But if we do that, we'll have to sell the house to pay off our debts. Even then, it'll take us a long time to recover financially. It'll mean living somewhere smaller, in a less upscale neighbourhood. We'll have to let Jenna go, too. We can forget Eton for Rowan. Oh Christ. What a fucking mess.

As soon as I see the ambulance parked outside the house, I know it's bad.

Subject: Poppy Elias (Confidential)
Date: 26/05/2009 11:24:36 A.M.
From: <fsharpe@princesseugenie.co.uk>
To: <hcarter@princesseugenie.co.uk>

Harry

Clare Elias was officially hospitalized with a post-partum infection following the twins' birth five months ago, but her medical notes suggest borderline post-natal depression may have been a strong factor in the length of her stay. Dr Johnson is currently away, so I am unable to verify, but according to the midwife's report, the mother struggled to breastfeed and became agitated when left alone with the child. Under the circumstances, I fear the hospital must err on the side of caution. I would not rule out the nanny as the culprit, but the girl's manner, while naturally concerned for her charge, did not present as overly anxious or distressed as one might expect. I consider the mother to be a far more likely candidate for Munchausen's by proxy, and we should proceed under this assumption.

I would suggest that you refer this to Diane, and strongly recommend the involvement of Social Services without delay.

Frances

7

Clare

'Did you know Marc's cheating you?'

Not cheating *on* you. Cheating you. Funny how I heard the difference straight away, and understood instantly what it meant.

Once Xan had sobered up, he came round and gave me the whole story. A friend of his at one of the big investment houses had heard about Marc's losses at the bank. It's common knowledge in the City, apparently. And then suddenly the debt was settled. Xan had a hunch, and got one of his contacts at the Fraud Office to do a bit of after-hours checking. He didn't know how to break it to me, so he went out and got drunk.

Jenna's still young enough to think an affair is the worst thing that can happen. I almost wish Marc had been unfaithful. At least I could rationalize that: *He's so much younger than me, men are easily tempted, it didn't mean anything, it was just a fling*.

He's been draining money from my company for

months. I think I knew it had to be Marc, even before I sat down with my forensic lawyer and went through the books. He hadn't really tried to cover his tracks. He'd wiped out a year's profit in less than two months. I didn't know, but I could guess, why he needed it: in another life, Marc would have been one of those desperate men crowding the bookies, grey-faced, living on hope and the never-never.

Bad enough that he'd stolen from me, but then, when I dug deeper, I discovered the second, usurious mortgage, when we're struggling with the first. The roof over our children's heads. How could he think I wouldn't find out?

Until Xan came to me, I'd had no idea of the scale of the debt. One million eight hundred and thirty thousand pounds. It's almost inconceivable.

I nearly left him, there and then. I felt so betrayed that he could risk everything we've built up over the years like this. But at the end of the day, it's *our* money, after all. We're not one of those couples with separate accounts, who go on holiday together and then split the bills fifty-fifty. How can you promise to share your lives with each other until death parts you if you can't even share a bank account?

So I decided to swallow it and say nothing. Marc would come to me in his own time and own up. And in the meantime – well, in the meantime, I quietly moved the company's investment funds and capital assets out of his reach.

It's just . . . I'm so *angry* with him. I can hardly bear to look at him, much less sleep with him. I want to forgive him. I just don't know if I can.

I startle when Craig nudges my elbow. 'It's *him*,' he whispers.

The angry American, Cooper Garrett. Craig says he's

come in three times a week for nearly a month to send flowers to the same woman. Lilies, usually. Sometimes roses, once tulips; and always white.

We've had customers who've done this sort of thing before: men who've sent flowers daily, an extravagant, look-at-me gesture. But whatever is going on between the American and this woman – her name is Ella Stuart – it isn't your typical romance. I watch him prowl the shop, briefly diverted from my own preoccupations. I can see the anger seething below his harsh, set features; grief too, I think. Passion, certainly. How many of us ever inspire that? I know Marc loves me, in his way: as his wife, the mother of his children. I don't doubt his sincerity, even now; but was it a *coup de foudre* when we met, for him? Attraction, yes, interest, desire, I know he felt all of those – but not passion. Lucky Ella, whoever she is.

'You're back,' the American says, turning abruptly.

I put aside the pale green pods of a vine called love-in-a-puff that have just arrived from South America. Such a beautiful, delicate flower, so hard to grow in a cold climate. Like love, I think, and then laugh inwardly at my own cliché.

'I don't work on the shop floor very often,' I say. 'I have an office. But sometimes, I—'

'Need to.'

Again, this strange man who knows the meaning of flowers catches me off guard. The anger and hostility I saw in him last time have faded, leaving a melancholy that's almost worse. His blue eyes are midnight with sadness. What has he lost, to fill him with such despair?

He looks at a point somewhere to the left of my head. 'For me, it's the piano.'

Instinctively I glance down at his hands, resting on the counter. Strong, square, with the blunt, callused tips of a man used to hard manual labour; and yet there's an elegance to the spread of his long fingers on the wood surface. I can see them coaxing plangent music from piano keys yellowed with age. He's a man of contradictions, this Cooper Garrett. He dresses like a plains farmer, with his faded jeans and the worn leather duster reaching almost to the floor; but the Breitling on his wrist is expensive, his boots soft, supple leather. I'd put him in his late forties, though at first sight he looks older. The deep grooves bracketing his wide mouth and furrowing his forehead add years, and dull otherwise classic square-jawed good looks. This isn't a man who smiles often.

But there's something about him that invites confidences, and trust. *A safe pair of hands*, I think.

Tentatively, I smile. To my surprise, he returns it. He's transformed. His blue eyes are suddenly as bright and warm and clear as the Caribbean. Something unknown tugs at me. I want to talk to this man more. I want to know his story. I want to make him smile again.

Craig feigns a breathy little squeak of excitement. His nonsense slaps me awake like a bucket of cold water.

I flush and turn to the bank of flowers. 'How can I help today, Mr Garrett?'

There's a brief silence. Then, 'The white tuberoses, please,' he says coolly. 'Same details as before. Your colleague has the address.'

'The Princess Eugenie Hospital,' Craig puts in.

'She's in hospital?' I ask, surprised.

'She's in a coma,' Craig sighs. 'She was hit by a car trying to save her daughter.'

'Stepdaughter,' the American scowls.

I pull together a neat bouquet on automatic pilot, more curious than ever. What's his relationship to this woman? No wedding ring – I noticed that earlier – though that doesn't necessarily mean anything. Mind you, if they were married to each other, he wouldn't be sending flowers three times a week. Where does the child, the almost-stepdaughter, fit into the picture? And what is the cause of the grief that hangs around his broad shoulders, as tangible as his travel-stained coat?

Cooper Garrett glances briefly at his flowers, and leaves without more than a curt nod in my direction.

'Oh, be still my beating heart,' Craig sighs. 'That man is wasted on a woman. Who do you think she really is?'

One of these days, Craig is going to bite off more than he can chew with his camp Graham Norton act.

'I've no idea. How do you know so much about him, anyway?'

'I *ask*, darling.'

I tidy the tuberose stems and discarded twists of raffia. 'Can you make sure the flowers get to the hospital before five?'

'Will do. Are you ready to go over the quarterly accounts now? I've got the paperwork from Price—'

'Can't. I had to postpone the meeting with the accountants so that I could go with Jenna to the doctor's. I'll deal with it next week.'

'I can handle it if you—'

'No,' I say sharply.

Craig looks surprised. 'No,' I say again, forcing my voice to sound normal. 'It's fine. It can wait. I'm sure you're right, anyway. The recession's hurting everyone. Things will probably pick up in their own time. No point worrying unnecessarily.'

Humiliating enough to have my husband leach money from the company accounts without my knowledge. I shouldn't have told Jenna, and there's certainly no need for Craig to know too.

'Actually, I think I'll go home,' I say, surprising myself. 'I want to spend some time with the twins. I miss them,' I add.

Surely this is so much better than resentful foot-nailed-to-the-floor mothering? I've found my babies someone who can look after them with pleasure, while I'm free simply to love them, to give them the best of me, the real quality time. Not only is nothing lost by my going back to work; my children are better off than if I were at home. It's almost as if they've got three parents, instead of two.

Jenna is just about to give the twins a bath when I walk in around six. 'The chocolate pudding went well,' she says drily.

'I can see that,' I say, regarding my Cadbury-coated infants. 'Look, I'll bath them.'

'It's fine, I can—'

'I'd like to,' I say.

Jenna hovers in the bathroom, handing me the baby soap and sponges as I need them, laughing as the babies, sitting up toe to toe, kick each other's feet. Poppy's cheeks are a little red again as she sucks her sponge, but other than that neither twin seems the worse for wear.

'Marc doesn't know what he's missing,' I sigh.

I scoop Rowan out of the bath and bury my face in his neck, inhaling the sweet, milky scent of my child. Oh, how I love him: every bit as much as I love his sister. I couldn't make Sophie's choice after all. Thank God. I'm not a freak, an unnatural mother. It just took a little time, that's all.

'I thought Marc was coming home early tonight?' Jenna says, bundling Poppy in a towel.

'He called and left a message on my mobile. Apparently he has a meeting.'

'And you're going to let him get away with that?'

'What's done is done,' I say heavily. 'I have to give him the chance to try and put it right.'

'How can you say that? After he stole money from your company—'

'No one's perfect, Jenna. We all compromise with those we love, don't we?'

Reflexively she touches the latest bruise on her jaw, acknowledging the point with a blush. 'But how can he complain about you working?' she adds after a moment. 'You'd think he'd be grateful for what you earn.'

I shrug non-committally. I may agree with her, but I've already confided too much. Sometimes I forget Jenna's not actually family.

She empties the bath and picks up the rubber ducks and plastic fish. 'If my dad told Mum she couldn't work, she'd flip.'

I bundle Rowan in his soft blue hippo towel and take him into the nursery. Jenna follows with Poppy wrapped in her pink polar bear, and we lay them on opposite sides of the changing island, top to tail. Together we put on Sudocrem, Pampers, vests, babygros. It's Monday: Jenna fans out four tiny hands while I cut twenty miniature fingernails. I hold their heads steady, and she gives each some Calpol for their teething. We're the perfect team: synchronized mothers. If only it were an Olympic sport.

'Marc's so old-fashioned,' Jenna says as we settle in the cheap sofa I bought to replace the ridiculous carved rocking chair, and give the twins their bedtime bottles. 'He's worse than my dad.'

'His mother stayed home and raised six children. I suppose he's just reverting to type.' I stroke Poppy's cheek as she gulps noisily. 'It's not that I don't want to look after the twins, Jenna. I adore them. But I love my job too. I couldn't bear to give it up. Every time I walk out of the house, I feel torn in two. Marc has none of that guilt,' I add resentfully. 'He's not conflicted at all. No one expects him to quit work and stay home with the baby. It's all so straightforward for men.'

By the time my husband comes home, Jenna and I have eaten, and I'm already in bed. I listen to him stumble around downstairs, cursing as he smashes into something. I hear glass breaking, and feel a spurt of anger. Isn't it enough that he's been playing Russian roulette with our home, without turning into a bloody drunk as well?

He finally lurches upstairs and clambers into bed. Whisky fumes roil my way as he leans over me and runs a sweaty hand over my haunch. I lie still, hoping he'll think I'm asleep and give up.

'Clare?' he whispers loudly. 'Are you awake?'

I keep my breathing slow and even.

He clumsily grabs my breast. 'Ow!' I yelp, slapping his hand away.

'Are you awake?'

'What do you think?'

'I missed you,' he slurs. 'You're my best friend, Clarey, do you know that?'

'Yes,' I sigh, pushing him away.

His hands are more insistent now. 'I love you. I just want a cuddle, tha's all. Not too much to ask, is it? At th'end of a very long day.'

'Marc, I'm really not feeling very sexy right now—'

'You've never looked more beautiful,' Marc pants.

Men always say that, don't they? When what they mean is: *I really*, really *want sex right now*, and frankly, who looks at the mantelpiece when they're poking the fire?

I'm a conscientious wife. I make sure Marc and I have sex every weekend, even if I'm not in the mood (and find me a woman with young children who wouldn't prefer an extra hour of sleep). If I'm feeling reckless, I'll even throw in a quickie in the shower on Sunday morning. It's usually enough to keep him sweet the rest of the week, but on the odd occasion Marc asks for snacks between meals, I never say no. Once we get going, I enjoy it (Marc is a skilled and thoughtful lover) – although, if I'm honest, not quite as much as the latest *Times* best-seller. Sex just isn't the driving force it used to be. It's not Marc; it's a woman thing.

But right now, even if my husband weren't breathing sour fumes in my face, or fumbling my nipples like they're volume controls, or prodding an unappetizing semi-flaccid penis against my thigh, I wouldn't feel particularly inclined to accommodate him. Right now, I'm too angry even to fake pleasure.

'No, thank you, Marc. Sweet of you to offer,' I add politely, 'but actually, I'd rather not.'

I have a meeting with a grower in Islington at seven the next morning. I leave home before anyone is up, relieved not to have to face Marc over the breakfast table. It's becoming a strain coming up with things to talk about without invoking the pink elephant in the room. I keep waiting for him to come and tell me what he's done, but his solution to the problem seems to be to go out and get roaring drunk, then come home and make a move on me.

He's such a child sometimes. He reminds me so much of Xan. I remember when Xan was about five: he cut off all the heads of Davina's roses, and then panicked and tried to sellotape them back on. Marc was just trying to put things right the only way he could think of. He's a fool, not a bastard. If I didn't truly believe that, I would have left him.

I race home to see the twins at lunchtime, but to my disappointment, they're sleeping. 'Stop worrying,' says Jenna, 'they haven't forgotten who you are. Go and get your highlights done, we'll be fine, really.'

So I go to Nicky Clarke and sit reading *Harper's Bazaar* and drinking cappuccino and feeling dreadfully guilty for paying someone to look after my babies while I go off and do something so frivolous. A nanny is almost excusable when I'm working flat out to save us from bankruptcy, but how can I justify this?

Though my hair does look *great*, I think as I hand over my credit card (trying not to notice the total), and in my business, like any other these days, image is everything.

I put my wallet back in my bag and notice I've a missed call on my mobile.

Four of them.

'She was fine until about an hour ago,' Jenna says. 'I put them both down for their naps, and went back when I heard Rowan crying. Poppy was just lying there, like this.'

My baby is limp in Jenna's arms, her eyes half-closed and rolled back in her head. She's so pale she looks carved from wax. I want to be the one to hold her, but I'm terrified to touch her (*Bad mother*, a voice says inside my head) in case I make things worse.

'Is it the vaccinations?' I demand. 'All that publicity about the MMR—'

'They haven't had MMR yet. This was just their third dose of DTP. Neither of them has had any reaction to the first two.'

I didn't know that. I even went with them to their last appointment and I've no idea what vaccinations the doctor gave my babies.

Ever since the twins were born, all I've done is wish them away. 'Please stop crying, so I can get some sleep.' 'Can you take them, Jenna, I have to work.' How could sleep or work be more important than spending time with my children? It's not as if this pregnancy was unwanted or unplanned. I *chose* to have a baby. I love the twins. What's wrong with me, that I spend all my time trying to escape them?

I deserve to lose a child. It's karma. I wished one of them dead, and now . . .

'Where's the damn ambulance?' I pace towards the window. 'It's taking too long. I think we should drive her to the hospital ourselves—'

'We have to wait for the ambulance, Clare, we can't risk getting stuck in traffic.'

'She could have died, while I was off getting my hair done. I should have been here. I didn't even hear the phone—'

'She's not dying, Clare,' Jenna says firmly. 'I know this is hard, but you need to calm down. She's going to be fine.'

'And you *know* that, do you?' I shout.

'Yes,' Jenna says stoutly.

She's pale, but composed. I force myself to take my cue from her.

'I can hear sirens,' Jenna says suddenly.

I pick up Rowan and we run down the front steps as the ambulance double-parks outside, squeezing between parked cars with the babies held aloft like precious bundles above floodwaters. Jenna passes Poppy to the paramedics, who whisk her into the back of the ambulance out of sight.

I don't even notice Marc standing on the pavement in shock until he grabs my arm.

'Clare! What the hell is happening?'

'It's Poppy,' I say, shaking him off. 'She's sick, we don't know what's wrong with her, we've got to get her to hospital. Thank God you're home, you can look after Rowan. He seems fine now, but if he starts to—'

'No!' Marc roars. 'For God's sake, Clare, *Jenna* can stay home and look after Rowan! Poppy's my daughter too! I'm coming with you!'

I don't have time to argue. I give Rowan to Jenna, and clamber into the back of the ambulance. My heart constricts at the sight of my precious baby on the stretcher, a miniature oxygen mask already strapped to her pale face. It actually *hurts* my chest. I can't lose her. I can't. I close my eyes and pray to what I hope is a forgiving God. *I'll be a better mother, I'll spend every minute with them. Please don't take her.*

One of the paramedics reaches across me to shut the

door. 'Sir,' he tells Marc, 'if you wouldn't mind following behind in your car—'

'Like hell,' Marc snarls, and forces his way in after me.

I'm sick with fear, but the paramedic smiles pleasantly at me as if we're off on a sightseeing tour. His zip catches on a blanket; he swears as he nips his finger freeing it. A phone number is scrawled in biro on the back of his freckled hand.

I watch him pull out a clipboard and laboriously start to fill in details. His pen runs out, and he scratches it in the margin, then shakes it several times, and tries again. It still won't write, so he begins a painfully slow search of his pockets for another pen. I want to scream at him to hurry, *hurry!* My baby could be dying, and he's looking for a biro!

Finally, he finds a pen tucked into the seat pocket beside him, and starts to ask me questions. Is she on medication? Any allergies? Any history of seizures? I tell him about the vaccinations, wishing Jenna was here. I don't know if Poppy's been off her food the last few days. I don't know if her nappies have been normal recently. I don't know what normal *is.*

'I don't know,' I say again, close to tears, when he asks me how long Poppy's lips have been cracked like this. I hadn't even noticed. *How could I not have noticed?*

'Why don't you know?' Marc demands suddenly.

'I'm sorry. Jenna didn't mention—'

'You're her mother! *You* should know!'

We arrive at Accident & Emergency, and I answer the same questions again for the triage nurse. Poppy is whisked to a cubicle, and once more I go through the same question-and-answer routine with the junior doctor who examines her. By the fifth time of repetition, to another more senior doctor and then a paediatric consultant, I'm struggling to hide my frustration. I don't want to upset anyone. I want them to think I'm a good mother. I want them to approve of me, even though my five-month-old daughter is lying semi-conscious on the bed with – how did I not notice this before? – small but definite bruises on her neck and arms.

It's Marc who erupts again, leaping up from his metal chair and kicking it across the cubicle. 'Enough with the fucking questions!' he yells. 'When is somebody going to *do* something?'

'Marc,' I soothe, glancing nervously towards the cluster of doctors outside the curtains, 'I'm sure they're doing their best—'

'Don't you read the damn newspapers?' he shouts. 'I'm not having my daughter turn into another damn statistic! This bunch of quacks need to get off their sweet asses and figure out what's wrong with her, or there's gonna be a few more patients around here!'

Fury boils in my chest. How does this stupid, macho posturing help? Marc should be calming *me* down, reassuring me and telling me everything's going to be OK. Instead, he's behaving like a frightened teenager and adding to the chaos and confusion. If I have to look after him, who is left to look after me?

I tug his arm. 'Marc, please. You're making things worse.'

'Worse? How can they be any fucking *worse*?'

One of the doctors detaches from the group. 'Mr Elias. Mrs Elias,' he says firmly. 'We can't treat your daughter until we know what's wrong with her, so we're doing some tests to find out. Believe me, we want to help her get better as much as you do—'

'She's got a fucking name!' Marc bellows. 'She's called Poppy! *Poppy!*'

'What tests?' I ask.

'Everything we can think of until we come up with an answer. I realize this is a very difficult time, Mrs Elias, but if you could try to bear with us,' he adds, as a nurse gently takes my shoulder. 'We just need to get a few more details from you. Don't worry, we'll come and get you as soon as we know anything. Mr Elias, you can stay with me.'

I look uncertainly at Marc. 'Go on,' he snaps. 'I'll look after her.'

'Can I get you a cup of tea?' the nurse asks, leading me to a small, private waiting room with worn brown and orange carpet tiles and hard, utilitarian plastic seats. Torn posters peeling from the walls exhort vigilance against meningitis and flu.

'No. Thank you,' I add politely.

The questions are the same, but this time there's a subtext I can't quite read. It's almost as if she's trying to catch me out.

'So,' she says finally, 'your daughter was with your nanny today, is that right?'

'Jenna,' I supplement.

'Jenna. How long has she been with you?'

'Since the twins were eight weeks old, so about three months.'

'And you haven't had any problems with her?'

'What sort of problems?'

The nurse taps her pen against her notepad. 'Anything unusual you might have noticed about her behaviour. Mood swings, emotional outbursts, that sort of thing.'

'No . . .'

'Drinking? Drugs?'

'Of course not! Look, what is—'

'Any sign of cutting or self-harming? Bulimia, anorexia, anything like that?'

I push away the image of the faded scars criss-crossing Jenna's arms. 'No, nothing. She's wonderful, the twins adore her. I checked all her references. I'd trust her with my life.' My voice rises. 'What exactly are you trying to say?'

'Just routine, Mrs Elias. Nothing to get upset about. So, apart from the nanny, Jenna, only you and your husband have had access to your daughter?'

'Yes. Well, Marc's at work most of the time, he only really sees them at weekends—'

'I see.' She scribbles something else down on her pad, and gets to her feet. 'Are you sure I can't get you that cup of tea?'

'Please, can I just see Poppy now?'

'Let me find out how she's doing. Someone will be in to see you shortly.'

I shred a tissue in my lap. I know what the nurse was getting at; I read the papers. It's called Munchausen's by proxy: when someone gets attention through a sick child. They think Poppy's ill because someone is deliberately making her sick. It's got to be the mother or the nanny, that's what they're thinking.

Jenna would never hurt the twins, and obviously I didn't.

But I've been so tired recently – so worn down – sometimes I can't remember what I had for breakfast. Supposing I had . . . an *impulse* . . .

151

The door opens. I throw myself into Marc's arms, desperate for reassurance. He strokes my hair awkwardly, and then holds me away from him. 'Come on, Clare. Pull yourself together. This isn't going to help anyone.'

The senior doctor who spoke to us before follows Marc into the room. He gestures to us to sit down, but doesn't take a seat himself. DR GARDNER is embroidered in navy thread over his left breast.

'Your daughter's doing much better,' he says, without preamble. 'She's regained consciousness, though we're keeping her sedated for the moment. Obviously we're admitting her to Intensive Care for the time being. She's on an IV drip, and she's being closely monitored. As soon as we find out anything more, we'll let you know.'

'So what happened? Did she have a fit, or something?' Marc demands.

'We don't think so. She was extremely dehydrated, which can—'

'Dehydrated?' I ask in surprise.

'It's when there's an insufficient volume of water to keep the body—'

'Yes, I know what it means,' I say tightly. 'How can she be dehydrated? She drinks plenty of milk, she loves water and juice. Is something wrong with her kidneys? Is she not processing liquid properly?'

'That's what we're trying to establish,' Dr Gardner says smoothly.

'Is she going to be OK?'

'We're doing our best to—'

'What about long-term effects? Is she going to—'

'Mrs Elias, we really don't know any more than we've already told you,' he says, slightly impatiently. 'I understand your anxiety, but we have to wait and see. The good news is that she's responding well to treatment so far.'

I stand up. 'Can we see her now?'

'Yes, of course. If you'd like to wait here, someone will take you up to Intensive Care in just a moment. Your daughter is out of immediate danger for now. You and your husband can return home when you've seen her and we'll call you as soon as we—'

'I'm not leaving,' I say stubbornly.

'Of course. Well. If you'll excuse me.'

We wait in tense silence until the same nurse returns and escorts us up to Intensive Care. I grip the rails of the tiny bed containing our daughter, more afraid than I've ever been in my life.

'I don't understand,' I whisper numbly. 'Is it the vaccinations? Remember all those children who got sick after they had the MMR jab – maybe Rowan's going to get sick too . . .'

'I thought you said he was fine?'

'Yes, but Poppy was fine too, until this afternoon,' I sob. 'Oh, Marc. Look at her. She's so tiny and helpless.'

Finally, he reaches out to me. He looks like a lost, scared child himself. I grip his outstretched hand across the bed, my heart aching. This stupid fuss about money has been needlessly driving us apart for weeks. I know he didn't mean any harm. He was just trying to be a good husband and father, to provide for his family. Set against what we stand to lose now, what on earth does it matter?

The nurse leads us back to the viewing gallery overlooking Intensive Care. I press my face to the glass, watching doctors prod and poke my baby with their needles and tubes.

Tess Stimson

'I know about the mortgage,' I say quietly, without turning round.

I feel, rather than hear, his sharp intake of breath.

'I've known for a few weeks,' I continue. 'And about the money you "borrowed" from PetalPushers. I'm guessing you needed it to clear some sort of deal that went wrong.'

'I wanted to tell you,' Marc says hoarsely. 'I tried.'

'I know. It's my fault, too. I've been too busy and too angry to listen.'

'I didn't mean to go behind your back, Clare. I kept trying to work up courage to come to you, but—'

'How much do you owe?'

'I've had a couple of good trades,' he says quickly. 'It's below a million now. I'm sure I can make the rest back if—'

'Close the bet,' I say.

'But if I close it, we'll lose the rest!'

'Then I'll go to Coares, and liquidate my portfolio. If I clear the second mortgage, and pay off the rest of what you owe, we can just about manage. It's going to be tight, but if needs be,' I grimace, 'I'll talk to Davina. We'll get through this, Marc. It's only money.'

'I – I don't know what to say.'

I turn round, and look him in the eye for the first time. 'Promise me you'll never, ever put us all at risk like this again. If you need to gamble, go and buy a lottery ticket.'

'Of course, I promise, never—'

'No more lies, Marc. Don't ever touch my company again.'

'I swear.'

I'm aware I sound like a controlling bitch, but I need

154

him to understand. I have to be able to trust him. I can't keep cleaning up his messes.

'Stay away from Felix, Hamish, all of them. They don't have families to think about. Maybe you should think about finding a different job, something a bit more reliable. A bit safer.'

'But I love what I do—'

'It's too tempting. You can't handle it, Marc.'

Marc nods tightly. 'Clare, I'm so sorry. It all got so out of hand, I didn't know what to do. I thought you'd leave me if you found out.'

'Am I really that much of an ogre?'

'I didn't want to disappoint you,' Marc mumbles.

He sounds like a small boy. The thought occurs to me: *Do I really want to be married to a child?*

The doors behind us whoosh open, and the nurse bustles in.

'I'm afraid we've got triplets on the way up. We'll need you to wait downstairs for a bit. I'll come and find you as soon as I can.'

'I think we should go home,' Marc says. 'Poppy's in good hands, and I want to check on Rowan. I'd be happier if he slept with us tonight, so we can keep an eye on him.'

'You go. I'll stay with Poppy—'

'Clare, we can be here in less than ten minutes. Come home.'

Later, I lie in bed wide-eyed and sleepless, listening to the sound of my husband and my son breathing on either side of me. I have to consciously relax my hands, and loosen my grip on the coverlet. At any moment, I'm afraid the phone will ring and tell me my daughter—

I can't even think it.

Eventually I drift into a troubled sleep, in which I'm running down endless corridors, searching for Poppy and Rowan. Something nameless and terrifying is pursuing me, and the faster I run, the faster it comes after me. I can't find my children anywhere. And then Marc is there, standing on the other side of an unbridgeable crevasse, holding the twins and laughing—

I'm woken by the sound of banging on the front door. I push myself up on one elbow. It's still dark; the clock on the dresser says 5.16. Marc stumbles out of bed, knotting his dressing gown. 'This better not be your damn brother again.'

I tuck Rowan safely in the centre of the bed, and get up and pull on my own robe. I dismiss my first panicked thought – *the hospital* – realizing they'd phone, not send someone round. Voices rumble downstairs. I lean over the banisters. I can't make out what they're saying, but a pit of unease opens in my stomach.

Marc comes to the foot of the stairs. 'Clare, it's the police. You'd better come down.'

'The police? But Xan's not here—'

'It's not Xan they want,' Marc says, his voice strangely hard. 'It's you.'

BERRELL DEBT RECOVERY
7A BALFOUR ROAD, HOUNSLOW, TW3 1JX
020 8570 7901

Mrs J Kemeny
69 Binfield Road
Stockwell SW9 9EA

31 May 2009

Account No.: 4587 3217 5924 2488

Dear Mrs J Kemeny,

We have been appointed to act for GE Capital Credit concerning
the outstanding monies due on the above-referenced account(s).
As of 29 May 2009, this total stands at £7,031.42. We understand
from a recent telephone conversation with your daughter that you
are currently travelling in Argentina and are not expected to return
to the UK for three months. Your daughter was unable to pass on a
forwarding address or contact details.

We must inform you that unless the minimum payment of £351.57
is received within the next seven days, we will commence legal
proceedings to recover the debt. Failure to comply may result in
confiscation of property, fines, and/or a criminal record.

If you have already made payment(s), please ignore this letter.

If you have any questions, you may reach us at 020 8570 7901,
Monday to Friday from 8.a.m. to 12 midnight, or on Saturday from
9.a.m. to 8.p.m. Our associates are ready to assist you.

Sincerely,

Delinquent Account Manager
Debt Recovery Department

Enclosures

8

Jenna

'*Salt* poisoning?' I exclaim. 'How on earth could that happen?'

'It's complicated,' Marc says evasively. 'The doctors say her sodium levels are off the chart, but they don't know why. Her kidneys are functioning fine, but she's got way too much salt in her body. Basically, she's really dehydrated.'

'I don't get it. Poppy drinks loads, she's always thirsty—'

'That's one of the signs, apparently.'

I slide Rowan into his high-chair and put on his bib. 'I still don't understand. Signs of *what*?'

'They're still trying to figure that out.'

'So, it's like some kind of illness?'

'Not really.'

'Well, what then?' I say impatiently. 'Everything Clare buys is fresh and organic, no additives, nothing, she's totally anal about it – sorry, Marc, but she is. There's no way Poppy could get salt poisoning from her food—'

'They don't think she did.'

The penny drops.

'You mean ... they think someone gave salt to her *on purpose*?'

'The concentration in her body was the same as you'd find in seawater,' Marc says. 'It's as if she'd swallowed four whole teaspoons of salt. No one could accidentally give a baby that much.'

'That's insane.'

Marc says nothing.

'Who'd want to make Poppy sick? It's not me, Marc, I swear, I love the twins, I'd never do anything to hurt them, I—'

'No one thinks it's you.'

'But she's never out of our sight! Clare or me are with her all the time—'

'Exactly,' Marc says.

I feel queasy. I know he and Clare have been having a few problems over money, but he can't believe she'd hurt her own baby like this. That's *sick*.

'Where is she?' I ask suddenly.

'The police wanted to talk to her,' he says reluctantly. 'They came round early this morning. She's still with them.'

'They *arrested* her?'

'She hasn't actually been charged. They just want to ask her a few questions.'

'Marc, there's obviously been a mistake!' I cry. 'The doctors are wrong. Clare would never hurt Poppy, you know that. She adores her!'

'She hasn't been herself lately,' Marc mutters.

'But she'd never hurt the twins. You told them that, right?'

He shifts uncomfortably. 'Clare never really took to the

whole motherhood thing. It's a miracle she survived her own childhood, given her own bloody mother. I thought she'd get used to it, but . . .'

He trails off, unable to look me in the eye.

I can't believe this. The spineless little shit! He's her husband! How can he believe this *crap*? What the fuck is the matter with him?

I'm only Clare's nanny, but I *know* she didn't do it. Working with kids gives you a kind of sixth sense about people. I can walk into a class full of four-year-olds and know right away which little suck-up is going to be teacher's pet and which kid is the charming bastard who'll cause nothing but trouble. Clare's neurotic and a total control freak, but she's not the type of woman to suffocate her baby with a pillow because it won't stop crying. She's far too sorted. I wish I could be a bit more like her. I might not have backed myself into a corner with Jamie if I was.

'Lots of women take a while to adjust after they've had a baby,' I snap. 'They don't all rush out and stock up on table salt.'

'She's never really bonded with Rowan. And look at the way she went off and hired you the moment she came home from the hospital. She couldn't wait to get shot of them—'

I slam Rowan's breakfast bowl on the table. 'Oh, don't be so fucking ridiculous! Are you telling me every woman who goes back to work after she's had a baby is secretly a homicidal maniac? Get real, Marc! This is the twenty-first century. Women have careers too, or hadn't you heard?'

For a frozen moment, you could hear a pin drop. Marc steps forward and pushes his face into mine.

'Who the *fuck*,' he hisses, 'do you think you are?'

I flinch. Perhaps I may have stepped over the line a little. Frankly, I don't give a shit about my job right now, but the last thing Clare needs is to come home and have to deal with everything on her own, particularly with Poppy still so sick.

'I'm sorry,' I say quickly. 'I didn't mean that. I'm just a bit stressed out . . .'

He looks like he wants to hit me. 'You fucking women. You all stick together, don't you? For all I know, you're in on this with her.'

'That's not fair! I'm just trying to—'

Upset by the raised voices, Rowan starts to wail. Marc picks up his bowl and shoves it at me. 'Why don't you do what you're paid to do, and look after my son, instead of interfering in something that's none of your fucking business?'

'But what about Clare? Did you get her a lawyer? You can't just leave her at the—'

'I'll deal with Clare,' he says grimly. 'She's my wife, and this is my family. It has nothing to do with you. Stay out of it.' He picks up his briefcase, and turns in the doorway. 'And if you ever . . . *ever* . . . speak to me like that again, I'll make sure you're thrown out so fast your feet don't even touch the ground.'

'Marc's been amazing,' Clare sighs. 'I'd never have got through this without him. He's been so supportive.'

The bastard shifts uncomfortably on the sofa. At least he has the grace not to catch my eye.

I realize I've made a permanent and dangerous enemy.

The first chance he gets, he'll find an excuse that forces Clare to fire me.

Well, screw him. Clare pays me, not him. She's the one in charge. It took me a while to figure it out, but I finally twigged why he was so quick to believe the worst of her. He *wanted* to. He wants her to be in the wrong, so he can feel better about what he's done.

'Such a pity Marc couldn't go down to the police station with you,' I say sweetly.

'I was a bit upset at first. But that's all forgotten now, darling,' she adds quickly. 'As you said, someone had to stay home to organize things. And Davina's lawyer did a brilliant job. I'm so glad Marc called her. She can be a bit difficult, I know, but she's marvellous in a crisis.'

Marc called her? Excuse me, *I* was the one who picked up the bloody telephone.

Clare squeezes his hand. 'I'm so relieved it's all over. Honestly, Jenna, they'd got me to the point where I didn't know which way was up. I was almost ready to believe I *had* given poor Poppy that salt.' She shudders. 'The important thing is, she's well enough to come home tomorrow. That's what we have to focus on now.'

'That's fantastic news! Oh, Clare, I'm so relieved. What *was* it?'

'They don't actually know yet,' she says awkwardly. 'But my lawyer made it clear that unless they can prove I had anything to do with it, they've got no reason not to let Poppy come home. I suppose they're hoping I'll be too scared of being caught to try anything again.'

Poor cow. She's far from a perfect mother, but she doesn't deserve to be policed like this. In future, every time one of the twins falls out of a tree or off a skateboard, they'll pull up Poppy's case notes and treat Clare like a criminal. She'll never be free of it.

As it is, she's lucky they haven't taken this any further. If she wasn't Lady Eastman's daughter, with a godfather in the House of Commons, and a big-shot lawyer, she'd probably be slopping out with a bunch of tattooed lesbians right now, and the kids would be in care.

'Jenna, can you come into the kitchen with me a minute?' Clare says. 'Marc wants to have a little party on Saturday to celebrate Poppy coming home, and I've got a thousand things to organize.'

She smiles brightly, but the weariness in her eyes tells a different story. This is the last thing she fucking needs. What the hell is he playing at now?

Moments later, as the front door slams behind him, I discover his game.

'I was hoping to get into work this afternoon, but I don't think I'll have time now,' Clare confides. 'It's very sweet of Marc, but I wish he'd waited until I'd got everything sorted out at the shop. It's going to be days before I get a chance to go in now and catch up.'

'Look, just tell me what you need me to do. I can hold the fort for a couple of hours.'

'Oh, Jenna, that would be wonderful,' she says gratefully. She pulls out an emerald Smythson diary – I'd kill for one of those – and flicks through it. 'I'm not sure who'll be able to make it at such short notice. I know Marc wants to push the boat out, but I was thinking something a little informal would be better; that pretty black and white dress you wore to Davina's would be perfect. Actually, we could make it a black-and-white theme – what do you think?'

I think Marc would shoot me on sight if I crash his party.

'It's really sweet of you, Clare, but I'll be going home. I babysat last weekend, and—'

'We *did* pay you overtime,' she says, slightly huffily.

'It's not that. It's just . . . I promised my boyfriend . . .'

'I realize Saturday is your day off, but obviously you won't have to work this time, Jenna, you'll be our guest.'

Sure. And you'll treat me just the same as Lady Horseface.

'The thing is, Jamie hasn't been well recently, and—'

'I'm sure he'll understand, after everything that's happened. And it'll give you a chance to meet our friends, and get to know everyone. We haven't had a party for ages.' She smiles persuasively. 'Go on, it'll be fun.'

Fun? I know exactly what it'll be like, and 'fun' isn't the word I'd choose. The women will patronize me or not speak to me at all; the men will talk to my cleavage and pinch my bum. Halfway through the evening, Clare will forget I'm a 'guest' and ask me to pass round a tray of hors d'oeuvres. One of the twins will start wailing upstairs, and I'll spend my precious Saturday night pacing the hallway and changing shitty nappies. Sometime around midnight, after everyone's left, she'll decide it'll be much better if 'we' clean up now rather than wait till morning, and I'll be on my hands and knees getting red-wine stains out of her Persian carpet at 3 a.m. Oh, yes. It really sounds like a riot.

'You can tell me all about it on Monday,' I say firmly.

Not that my weekend at home is likely to be a barrel of laughs either, I think wearily on Friday. I get the Tube home and walk back from the station, my feet dragging slower with every step. I'm exhausted from organizing Clare's party; all I really want to do is sleep. And I still haven't figured out what to say to Jamie. Easing out of this relationship gently is proving harder than I thought. He keeps guilting me into promising things I don't mean. I'm going to end up walking down the bloody aisle still wondering how to dump him.

I let myself into our flat. Every light is blazing, as usual, but I can't hear the television, which means Jamie's out. I hope he's not down the pub. He can get really violent when he drinks.

The door jams on a heap of mail. I skim it quickly for anything interesting. Oh joy: a magazine from the Jehovah's Witnesses, and a special offer for a Stannah stairlift. All the others are credit-card bills and ominous brown envelopes.

I shove them in a kitchen drawer already overflowing with unopened mail, and dump my overnight bag in the lounge. The room is a fucking tip. The floor is carpeted with pizza boxes, balled-up dirty socks, beer cans and empty takeaway containers. Newspapers are strewn across the couch. A copy of *Playboy* is open on the coffee table, surrounded by stiff wads of used tissues. Marc may be a loser, but at least Clare's got him house-trained.

I kick a pair of cheesy trainers out of the way and unhook a brand new Wii system that wasn't here last time I came home – God knows how much *that* cost – before I trip over the trailing cables and break my neck. There isn't room to swing a cat in here. You could fit our entire flat into Clare's dining room.

I turn off the lights and go to the bedroom, trying not to notice the mould in the bathroom and the black pubes stuck to the cheap supermarket soap. Funny how none of it bothered me before I moved in with Clare. I hate this shower. You could spit faster. My power shower at home –

I mean, at Clare's – is amazing. It has jets from the side as well as the ceiling, and a sauna setting, so you can steam yourself clean if you feel like it. The toilet flushes first time, too, and there are no turds floating in the bowl. God, men are pigs.

I'm towelling my hair in the cold bedroom when I hear a strange mewing coming from the airing cupboard.

I wrap the thin, bleach-stained towel around me and storm on to the landing. Don't tell me he's got a bloody cat. I love animals, don't get me wrong, but I don't have time for this right now. Jamie will get bored of looking after it in a few weeks, and I'll be the one left with the vet bills.

Where is he, anyway? It's nearly eleven. There's not much point me making the effort to come home if he's not even going to be here.

I wrench open the airing cupboard, and scream.

'But I *need* you,' Clare protests. 'It's really important I go into work today. Please, Jenna. I'm sure your boyfriend can't be *that* sick—'

'Clare, he is. I'm sorry, but there's no one else to look after him.'

'Can't you just dose him up with something and put him to bed? I'll send a taxi to come and get you. You don't have to stay overnight, I'll be home by six—'

'I'm sorry, Clare, I really *can't*.'

'There must be something you can do,' she insists.

Oh, God. I need a break; from Clare *and* Jamie.

'There's really nothing—'

'You don't understand. You can't let me down like this. I *have* to get to work. What am I supposed to *do*?'

'Look, I'm not doing this on purpose,' I say tightly. 'I didn't *ask* him to get sick.'

She sighs. 'Well, I suppose it can't be helped. Will you be back tomorrow? You *are* coming back, aren't you?'

'Yes, I'm coming back,' I mutter.

It'd be nice if, just once, she spared a thought for *me*. She hasn't acknowledged how stressful the last few days have been for me too. For God's sake, Poppy nearly died, and then my employer was arrested! Obviously it was far worse for Clare, but she still managed to throw a cocktail party for fifty on Saturday. I'm sure she can deal with looking after her own children for a day or two. Her flowers will still be there when I get back.

I promise to call her in the morning, and shut my phone. I wasn't snowing her. If I had any choice at all, I'd much rather be looking after the twins.

Jamie's still sitting in the armchair nearest the television, dressed in the same filthy blue sweats he's been wearing since I found him crouched in the airing cupboard on Friday. I was on the verge of calling an ambulance for the second time in a week, until I managed to persuade him to crawl out and get into bed. He's been like a bloody zombie all weekend. How can I leave him like this? I'm tempted to call his shrink, but once people get in the system, it's a bitch to get out of it again. If he's sent to the loony bin, it'll be on his medical records every time he goes for a job, or applies for a mortgage, for the rest of his life. Even after everything he's done to me, I can't do that to him.

The scars on my inner forearms itch, and I run my fingers down the ladder of criss-crossing fine lines. I understand exactly what Jamie's going through.

In the months after my accident, I wanted to crawl

into a dark cupboard and hide, too. One stupid woman
fiddling with the car radio when she should have been
concentrating on driving, a split-second swerve into the
bicycle lane, and at eighteen years old my whole life was
screwed. I only started coaching at the club because I
couldn't think what else to do. I couldn't bear to give up
the swimming life entirely; but then I found myself resent-
ing everyone who still had what I'd lost. I hated the woman
who'd ruined my life, hated the poor girl who'd taken my
place on the team, hated everyone who dared to feel sorry
for me; and most of all, I hated myself for turning into such
a bitch.

Cutting was my way of making it feel better. I still don't
know why I started, really. I'd seen this movie: *Girl, Inter-
rupted*. Only Angelina Jolie could make being psychotic
seem sexy. I don't suppose the filmmakers meant to inspire
me, but I was curious. And when I drew the paring knife
across my arm and watched lovely scarlet ribbons appear,
somehow it *did* make the knot of pain and misery inside
me dissolve, for a while.

Anna Martindale, the mother of the youngest swimmer
on the team, found me one evening. I'd forgotten to lock
the changing-room door and didn't cover my arms in time.
She didn't say anything at first; she just sat down on the
bench next to me.

'I have leukaemia,' she said quietly. She waited while I
took that in. 'Cancer of the blood,' she added.

I think she meant to make me feel guilty for being so
careless with mine.

'Anna—'

'I'm only telling you because I need someone to look
after Maeve,' she said. 'She's only eight. The chemo is going

to be pretty tough, and I'm not going to be able to give her the care and attention she needs.'

I couldn't say anything. I just stared at my feet.

She squeezed my fingers. 'Maeve loves you. You'd be perfect. And I think you need a change of scene,' she added gently, 'till you feel yourself again.'

If Anna hadn't rescued me, I don't know where I'd have ended up. She didn't have to take a chance on me, especially with her own life thrown into chaos, literally hanging in the balance. But she cast me a lifeline. Maeve needed me, and I didn't have time to feel sorry for myself. It just takes one person.

I reach out and touch Jamie's shoulder. 'Please. Come upstairs. You can have a shower, put on some clean clothes. We'll spend the day together, just you and me—'

He shakes me off, burying his head in his chest with a sullen growl.

I sigh. I don't want this responsibility, but there's no one else. If only he had some family in this country. His father's dead, and God only knows where his mother is. He does have an older brother in New Zealand, but—

The phone rings, and without thinking I answer it.

'Jenna Kemeny?'

'Yes—'

'Ms Kemeny, we act for GE Capital Credit. We'd like to talk to you about an outstanding debt of seven thousand four hundred and—'

'You want my mother,' I fib quickly.

'This *is* Jenna Kemeny?'

'We, um, have the same name.'

'I see. Well, do you happen to know when *Mrs* Kemeny will be back?'

'She's gone on holiday,' I gabble. 'To Argentina. She won't be back for three months.'

I say a quick prayer that my eminently prudent and sensible mother, who has never been in debt in her life and is happily running a wine bar with my father in Barnes, never finds out about this conversation, and hang up.

Shit. Seven grand! How did that happen? I had no idea it was so much. Mind you, I haven't actually opened a statement for months. It's too depressing. Seven hundred, seven thousand: I haven't got a hope in hell of paying it either way. If they can't get hold of me, they'll just give up in the end, won't they? I mean, seven thousand is nothing to Visa. They'll just write it off.

Still. It's not very nice, having people chasing you for money. Clare never has debt collectors ringing *her*. Marc could embezzle millions from her company, and she'd never even—

I scream as a dead weight slams into me, knocking me to the floor. An iron band tightens round my throat. Within seconds, I'm struggling for breath. I claw at my neck, gasping and choking.

'Who is he?' Jamie hisses in my ear.

I can't speak. I can't breathe. My vision blurs.

'Who was on the phone?'

He's twisting the phone cord round my neck like a garrotte. *Should have got the hands-free, Jenna.*

'No . . . one,' I pant. 'Just the . . . bank . . .'

His grip relaxes slightly. I suck in oxygen, spluttering like a landed fish. Jamie kneels astride me, crushing me, the cord still wrapped around my windpipe. 'You love me,' he repeats. 'Say it.'

'I love . . . you.'

'Promise you'll never leave me.'

'Promise.'

Suddenly, the pressure's gone. Jamie slumps down against the wall, pulling me into his arms and stroking my hair. Tears stream down my cheeks and snot bubbles from my nose. 'I can't cope without you, you know that,' he murmurs into my hair. 'Why do you make me do these things to you? Why do you make me so jealous?'

'Didn't mean—'

'Show me how much you love me,' he whispers.

I twist round. Jamie pulls down his filthy blue sweats and boxers, and looks proudly down at his erection. Violence always turns him on. My stomach lurches. Oh God, I don't think I can do this.

His eyes narrow. 'Come on, then.'

'Let's just . . . take our time,' I prevaricate. 'Why don't we go upstairs, and you can have a shower and—'

'I thought you said you loved me?'

'I do, but—'

He grabs my hair, and shoves my head down between his legs. He smells rank and sour. I gag as he thrusts his cock in my mouth. If I throw up, I think he'll actually kill me. He's gone way too far this time. He hasn't just crossed the line: it's a little dot receding into the distance.

I give him what he wants, trying not to inhale his stench. I know it's not all his fault. He's sick. He doesn't mean it.

Clare wouldn't put up with this, I think suddenly. Marc would never dare treat her this way. She has his respect, albeit grudging, because she *demands* it.

What kind of fucking masochistic idiot am I? Instead of

feeling sorry for Jamie and making endless excuses for him, I should have walked out the first time he hit me, and never looked back.

Abruptly, Jamie stiffens, then pulls out at the last moment and deliberately squirts his cum into my face and hair. I wipe it out of my eyes, feeling dirty and humiliated. He laughs nastily, then gets to his feet, lazily tucking his spent dick into his pants.

My scars tingle. I'm not sure who I hate most: Jamie for doing this, or me for letting him.

'Everybody, this is Jenna,' Clare announces.

'Hello, Jenna,' everyone choruses.

Half a dozen groomed, no-make-up-made-up faces smile politely at me. Pearl earrings, Chanel suits, Patrick Cox driving shoes and the obligatory discreet Tiffany bling, almost to a woman. Clare's International Crises charity committee. What do they do, distribute designer handbags to the unfortunates of Darfur?

Clare takes my arm. 'Come on, I want to introduce you properly.'

'I really should see to the twins' lunch,' I hedge.

'It's OK, Jenna, they're still asleep, and the intercom's on. Now, Fran you already know, but this is Olivia, Poppy—'

'The original,' Poppy laughs.

'Candida, Georgiana – you want to be *very* nice to her, Jenna, she has a *gorgeous* younger half-brother, Fergus, and his father's an earl,' Clare teases. 'Play your cards right and you could be Countess Jenna one day.'

More laughter. Because it's just so *hilarious* that the nanny could end up married to one of them.

'So you're the famous Jenna,' one of the women – Marina? Sabrina? – drawls coolly. 'We've heard *so* much about you.'

'Clare says you've saved her life,' Poppy (the original) adds. I think she's smiling, but she's so Botoxed up, it's hard to tell.

'Well. The twins are wonderful to look after.'

'You can't imagine what I've been through finding a decent nanny,' a skinny blonde comments. 'Especially one who speaks *English*.'

'Did Olivia tell you what happened with her last girl, Clare? Went out to get the dry-cleaning one morning, and never came back. Just left you in the lurch, didn't she, darling?'

'*Night*mare,' the blonde confirms. 'Tarka and I were supposed to be going to Nevis the following week, and of course we couldn't find anyone to look after the boys at such short notice. Can you imagine!'

Clearly these women define an International Crisis as having to take your own children on holiday with you.

Poppy winks at me, and leans conspiratorially towards Clare. 'You're lucky, darling. I wish I could find someone like Jenna to come and work for me.'

'Oh, Jenna doesn't work *for* me,' Clare says hastily. 'She works *with* me. We're a team.'

I know she means well, but I wish she'd stop trying to pretend we're friends. It's embarrassing for both of us.

Candida opens a sandwich, takes out the wafer-thin slices of cucumber and puts the bread aside. 'But English girls are so *expensive*. Once I've paid Vicky, put petrol in her car and added in overtime and health insurance and all the rest of it, she makes more than I do. You have to give them endless holidays, too, and sick days. It's ridiculous.'

'Candida! You can't say that!' Clare says, clearly embarrassed. 'Nannies aren't slave labour. Anyway, I'm sure poor Jenna thinks all this is very boring. I hate to think what our nannies would say about us if they got together—'

'Do you know,' Candida says, ignoring her, 'the other day I caught Vicky on the phone to Georgiana's girl discussing her *salary*!'

'Be fair,' Clare protests. 'You can't tell me you don't talk about your income to the other lawyers in your chambers. It's just harmless gossip—'

'If that's all it was, it wouldn't be so bad. But it turns out,' Candida pauses for dramatic effect, 'Charlotte Hughes-Foster had *tried to steal her*!'

Shocked gasps all round.

'But Horatio and Alfie are in the same class at Ludgrove!' Clare exclaims.

'She came to my wedding,' Candida says indignantly. 'I thought I could trust her. If she'd had an affair with my husband, I might have been able to forgive her. The man's an alleycat anyway. But my *nanny*! We've been together for years! How *could* she?'

'What did you do?' Poppy demands.

'Well, Vicky and I sat down and had a long heart-to-heart. We've been taking each other for granted, I think we both realize that now. We'd grown apart and stopped really communicating. So we've decided to really work at things from now on,' she adds earnestly. 'We've set aside one night a week to spend together, so we can concentrate on each other. I think this whole affair might be the making of our relationship.'

A loud wail emanates from the twins' intercom. I breathe a sigh of relief and leap to my feet. No one even seems to notice me pick up the intercom and leave.

I'm tempted to spit in the organic lemonade as I pass. None of these spoiled, rich, self-obsessed women cares about the nameless girls they entrust with their precious children. Clare's nice, but even she forgets I have a life of my own. She hasn't once asked how Jamie is since I came back. I don't just walk offstage when I leave her house, and vanish into thin air.

I'm upstairs changing Rowan's nappy when the nursery door shuts quietly behind me. I jump.

'Please, don't let me disturb you,' Olivia says, waving her hand.

'The bathroom's just along the hall—'

'Actually, darling, I'm glad I've got you alone. I wanted to have a quiet word.'

Casually she picks up a pair of pink bootees from the changing table. 'So sweet. Mine are both boys. I do so *long* for a little girl. The thing is, Jenna,' she says, briskly changing tack, 'my current nanny isn't really working out. I need to find a new one, and I was wondering if you could help.'

'Well, I could ask around,' I say doubtfully. 'Maybe a friend of mine—'

'Oh, no, darling,' trills Olivia, 'it's *you* I want.'

I hesitate, wondering if I've misunderstood. 'But I work for Clare.'

'Obviously. And I love Clare, sweetie, I really do, but I'm absolutely desperate. I know it's a little bit naughty, and Clare probably won't be on speakers with me when she finds out, but she's done nothing but sing your praises since you joined her. You're smart and presentable, and your accent isn't *too* bad—'

'I couldn't possibly, I'm sorry,' I say firmly. *My* accent? Cheeky bitch. At least I don't sound like I've swallowed a bucket of marbles.

'How much is she paying you, darling? Two thousand? Two and a half?'

'I really can't—'

'I'll pay you four. And I'll buy you a car; you can keep it if you stay a year.'

Four? Four thousand pounds a month?

'Don't worry, darling. My boys are very sweet, I'm not paying you silly money because they're monsters. *I'm* the difficult one, as if you hadn't guessed. As long as you keep me happy, we'll be fine.'

I think fast. I love the twins, and I like Clare, a lot; I can even tolerate Marc. This woman clearly has the moral scruples of a blood-sucking leech. She'd be a total bitch to work for, and she might easily change her mind and sack me after a week, and then I'd be fucked.

Four thousand a month. I could clear my debts, pay Jamie off: if he has enough start-up cash to find his own place, he might leave mine.

Put that way, it's a no-brainer.

Dr Jerrold P Sloffin MD MRCP
17a Munster Road
Fulham SW6 5AF
020 7336 5478

11/06/09

Vincent

Sorry not to have got back to you earlier about Wimbledon;
Laura says yes please!, so count us in. Let's hope we still have
some home-grown talent to cheer by the time we get
to the second week!

Need to ask a favour. I'd like you to see a terminal patient
of mine, Alexander Sterling. He's exactly the type who fights
shy of "trick-cyclists" but I suspect you might fare rather
better than most with him, if I can persuade him to see you.
He's in more need of a sympathetic ear than he thinks. Very
bright lad; and very much aware of the magician's sleight of
hand. Involve him in the process and you might just crack it.
At the very least, he could do with someone to fight his corner.
From what I gather, apart from a sister who has her own
young family to worry about, the family aren't much use.
Such a shame, all in all. Terrible waste.

Do pass my love on to Joanna and the boys.

Best

Jerry

9

Xan

If there were any justice in this world, I'd wake with a splitting headache and a mean coke hangover: depression, lethargy, and the Monday-morning blues on a Thursday. Not to mention a couple of remorseful, teary women and an angry husband/father (I'm still not quite sure how old they are) at the door.

Thankfully, the Devil has all the best tunes.

I hold out my hand to check: not even shaking.

Flipping back the duvet, I chivvy the two girls who picked me up at Mahiki last night out of bed. They totter home happily; neither asks for my number, or offers me hers. This is the beauty of letting women make the moves: no guilt, no grief, no strings. Everybody's happy.

By seven-thirty, I'm behind my desk in my huge new fuck-off corner office at ShopTV, bright-eyed and bushy-tailed. I spend the morning checking yesterday's sales figures, chairing the daily review meeting and touching base with the presenters and guest reps from suppliers going on air. We're doing a big push on pearls this week, tying it in with the launch of a major new skincare range – pearls have to be worn against the skin to keep their lustre, blah, blah. Our sales figures on the segments are down on last year, but only slightly; given the depth of the economic shit we're all in, I'm still in my happy place. Most people think when a recession hits it's the luxuries women cut back on, but surprisingly, our homeware lines suffer most. If she can't afford a new frock, a woman cheers herself up with a nice pair of shiny earrings, and sod the saucepans.

I toss the viewing figures across my desk. I can sell anything to anyone, but it helps when I have a decent product.

My mobile rings; I check the ID, and grin. 'I take it I'm forgiven?'

'You don't deserve to be,' my sister says crisply.

'C'mon, CP. Even you can't sulk for ever.'

'Don't call me that. You know I hate it.'

Our dear departed father was Catholic. He chose Clare's first name, but graciously permitted Davina to pick her middle one – on condition it featured in Butler's *Lives of the Saints*. She spent hours combing through all six thick, leather-bound volumes for the most irritating one she could find. Clare Perpetua it was.

'So, am I off the hook?' I ask.

'Just because they didn't charge you, it doesn't mean you weren't guilty,' Clare says tightly.

'Oh, absolutely. Our boys in blue never make a mistake, do they?'

A low blow on my part; but irresistible. My sister is the kind of civic-minded person who picks up other people's litter; I've never seen her jump an amber light, never mind a red one. She certainly didn't deserve to be hauled off in the middle of the night by some Plod. As if Clare would harm her own kid! She's more wholesome than organic apple pie. Whereas I definitely deserve to have my collar felt. I am a reprobate, a sinner, a man without qualm or conscience. Or, may I point out, a criminal record, thanks to a talent for low cunning and a well-connected stepfather with a guilty conscience.

Fortunately for me, Clare, fair girl that she is, doesn't distinguish between her innocence (genuine) and mine (the thorny question of proof). I'm constantly amazed, given her level of integrity, that she ever makes any money at all.

'Well, never mind all that now,' she says briskly. 'I called to invite you over to supper, but if you're going to be difficult—'

'I'm the soul of amenability. But I have to ask: am I liable to have my nose punched by your charming husband?'

'Don't be ridiculous.'

'He threatened to, and I quote, "beat me three ways to Sunday" if I darkened his doors again.'

'You were smoking marijuana in our drawing room!'

Clare must be the only person under forty who calls it 'marijuana'.

'I told you, I'm sorry. It was a misunderstanding. I thought they were menthol—'

'Oh, for heaven's sake, Xan. I wasn't born yesterday. Frankly, I don't care what you smoke, as long as you don't bring it into my house or involve my family and staff.'

'Darling, I didn't mean to involve Jenna. I had no idea I was being tailed by the police. Though I must admit, I've rather gone up in my own estimation as a result.'

'Next time they arrest you, I'm *not* bailing you out.'

'Fair enough.' I put my feet up on my desk, and flick an elastic band across my office. 'Just for the record, am I to take it the small matter of your devoted spouse embezzling your fortune has all blown over?'

'It was just a . . . misunderstanding. I don't want to talk about it. And I don't want you to talk about it either, Xan, or you can forget supper.'

'We're a very misunderstood family,' I muse. 'Don't worry. "Discretion" is my middle name.'

'And there was me thinking it was "Trouble",' Clare says waspishly, and rings off.

My arm twitches as I slide my phone back in my pocket, and I drop it. I try to pick it up, but the muscles of my right hand won't seem to work properly. Cursing, I kick the phone, and it skitters out of reach beneath my desk. I leave it there and pull open the bottom drawer with my left hand. My fingers close around the silver hip-flask. Who gives a damn if it's not yet noon? I need a shot of the hard stuff if I'm going to get through the rest of the day.

I'm nicely mellowed by the time I reach Clare's around seven. I stumble slightly on the steps, just as she opens the front door.

'Xan, are you drunk?'

I grab the railings. 'Just warming up, CP.'

'Sometimes,' Clare says through gritted teeth, 'you're enough to try the patience of a saint.'

'Marc home yet?'

'Not yet, no.'

I follow her into the kitchen, where the twins are playing happily in the playpen, steadily throwing all the bricks out on to the limestone floor. Debussy is on the iPod, and I smell jasmine and saffron. I sniff the air like the Bisto Kid. 'Shrimp curry?'

'Your favourite.'

I sweep her into a clumsy hug. '*You* are my favourite.'

'It'd be nice if you'd remember that sometimes, and stop drinking yourself into an early grave. You know how much I worry about you—'

'Jenna!' I exclaim, as the woman who's haunted my erotic dreams for the past three months comes downstairs. 'Have you missed me, darling?'

'I'm working on my aim.'

'You don't have to pretend with me. I know how you really feel.'

'That'd explain your Kevlar vest.'

Fuck, she's sexy.

'Jenna,' Clare says, 'can you give Poppy her sippy cup?'

'It's a bit full,' Jenna says, taking it.

'She'll be fine.'

'Shall I empty some of the juice out first?'

'Jenna, I *said* she'll be fine.'

I eye my sister in surprise. She usually treats staff like visiting royalty, to prove she doesn't think she's better than they are. It's the rest of us she bosses around like serfs.

Poppy holds her cup in two fat fists, and drinks without spilling. I'm impressed. It's more than I can manage these days.

Clare throws Jenna a triumphant look. *Now* I get it. This is a turf war. Clare may believe she's a crap mother, but she's still going to make sure Jenna knows who's in charge. To be honest, I'm kind of surprised she ever let another woman in on her territory in the first place. Davina is to motherhood as Cruella de Vil is to animal rights, but I always figured Clare would be the Ultimate Soccer Mom. Home-made birthday cakes, hand-sewn party dresses, the whole Suzy Homemaker shebang. Whatever she does, it's always a success. There are times (few, admittedly) when I feel quite sorry for Marc.

Talk of the Devil. As a key scrapes in the front door, Jenna scoops the kids out of the playpen and takes them off for their baths. I admire her arse in her tight jeans as she climbs the stairs.

Marc goes straight to the drinks cabinet in the corner of the kitchen, nodding curtly at me. 'Can I get you anything?'

Clare grinds pepper over a saucepan. 'I think he's had enough.'

Cluck, cluck, mother hen.

'Scotch works for me,' I say.

Marc hands me a generous glass. I realize this is what passes for an apology from my brother-in-law. Fair enough. I *was* smoking weed on his sofa.

'Good day?' Clare asks her husband.

'Hectic.'

'Did you call Michael Peters? He said they couldn't hold the job open for long—'

'Christ, Clare. Let me get through the door before you start in, would you?'

Her lips tighten. She turns back to the simmering pan, her back rigid with righteous indignation. I love my sister to death, but she's a hard act for us sinners to follow. Marc must get sick of eating shit while she pitches her tent on the moral high ground. Yeah, he's been an arse, but I reckon he's a good bloke underneath. He loves his kids, loves his wife. He just doesn't have a clue what makes her tick.

You'd think a man with five older sisters would *get* women. Superficially, he's OK: he's great at birthday presents – Clare's got a box full of the kind of hard-to-find, one-off pieces of jewellery women love – and I'm guessing he doesn't just roll over and go to sleep after a shag, but he's fucking useless when it comes to the hard stuff. He had six mothers fussing over him for most of his life. He's used to dumping his problems in a woman's lap and having her unravel them for him. Clare's always got him wrong. She thinks because he lets her take charge of things he doesn't mind that she earns four times his salary and makes all the big decisions. She's never figured out he's actually an old-fashioned boy who just likes Mummy running round looking after things.

Dinner is a tense affair. Clare chatters brightly about nothing, her hostess-with-the-mostest mask firmly in place. Jenna keeps her head down, literally (though on the plus side, at least this presents me with an unchallenged view of her impressive cleavage). Marc grunts monosyllabically. If you ask me, we could all do with a few 'shrooms in the stew to lighten things up.

'By the way, I called Hurst's,' Clare tells Marc, passing me the garlic naan. 'You can take the Range Rover in on Thursday. Once they've had a look at it, we can—'

'What did you do that for?' Marc snaps.

'We agreed we don't need a four-by-four in London. It's too expensive, and we could save—'

'And I told you I'd handle it, Clare. Let me sort it out in my own time.'

'Every month it's sitting outside, it's depreciating—'

'For God's sake! Fine! I'll take it in on Thursday!'

I wink at Jenna over the salad bowl. I can see why she fucked off the moment she heard Marc's key in the door.

She pushes back her chair. 'I'll put on some coffee.'

'I'll help you clear the table,' I offer quickly.

We clatter plates noisily in the kitchen. 'Is it always like this?' I whisper.

'Pretty much,' Jenna whispers back.

Fuck it. Divorce is the last thing I'd wish on Clare. I hate to say it, but Davina's right. Marc's a decent bloke, but he's all wrong for my sister. Even a spoiled Mummy's boy wants to grow up sometime. Clare's too used to doing everything for him. It's one thing mothering me (and fuck knows, with Davina as my default option I needed it), but you can't keep treating your husband like one of the kids. He needs to start taking some responsibility – and she needs to *let* him.

Poor cow. She's always had shit luck with men. First Dad dying when she was seven (any shrink will tell you that fucks a girl up for life) and then there was Guy. Dirty old bastard. I don't know all the ins and outs, but something happened the summer she turned fifteen. As far as I can make out, he tried it on, she slapped him down, threatened to tell Davina everything if it ever happened again. She's a girl of her word, our Clare. He knew she meant it.

I remember when she went to Oxford. She spent most of her three years there with a skinny asexual Indian guy who thought his legs were too thin and wore two pairs of jeans to hide them. After he finally dumped her (for a cute blond boy), she worked her way through a succession of second-rate losers she utterly intimidated. Smart women have a knack for attracting arseholes who make it their life's work to demean them. Clare was so used to taking on challenges and winning, she simply didn't know how to quit while she was ahead. She's programmed to succeed. Instead of cutting her losses and walking away at the first sign of trouble in a relationship, she always fought harder to make things work.

Clare slams the salad bowl down on the counter behind us, making us both jump. 'Jenna, don't put tomato-based sauces in Tupperware. I've told you before, they stain the plastic.'

'Sorry, I forgot—'

'Do I have to do everything myself to make sure it's done right?'

'Give her a break, Clare,' I say softly.

Clare looks like she's about to spit out another sharp retort, but instead she deflates against the counter.

'You're right. I'm sorry, Jenna. It's not you I'm upset with, you know that. It's Marc. He needles me all the time. It's so unfair. He's the one who screwed up.'

I shoot my sister a sharp glance. Clearly Jenna is familiar with all the dirty laundry in this house: literal and figurative. I sympathize with my sister, but Clare shouldn't be telling the nanny this stuff. It's not fair on either of them. If there's anyone she should be talking to, it's her husband.

Jenna smiles neutrally, and takes the cafetière into the dining room. Smart girl. See no evil, hear no evil, speak no evil. At least, not until you know who's going to win.

I pick up the tray of cups and saucers to follow her. My leg gives way, and I stumble drunkenly against the kitchen island. If it wasn't for Clare's quick reaction, I'd have dropped the lot.

'Please, Xan,' she says in a low voice. 'Don't drive home tonight. You've had too much to drink. You can stay in the spare room.'

'Don't worry. I'll have a coffee and I'll be fine—'

'You're *drunk*,' she snaps.

Maybe, I think, as she stalks into the dining room. *But in the morning I will be sober, and you'll still have a resentful, inadequate husband you can't handle.*

'For God's sake,' I hear her exclaim. 'That tablecloth was from Brussels, Marc!'

'It's not like I spilled the bloody wine on purpose—'

'It never is, is it?'

Clare is mopping ineffectually at a spreading stain with a paper napkin as I walk in. Marc rolls his eyes. 'Clearly my wife thinks I'm conducting a one-man war of attrition against the lacemakers of Belgium.'

'Clearly my husband thinks we're made of money.'

'Clearly the two of you belong in the nursery,' I retort.

'I have a headache,' Clare cries, throwing the dirty napkin on the table. 'I'm going to bed.'

'I'll be in my office,' Marc says, shoving his chair back from the table.

Jenna and I stare at each other across the balled-up napkins, empty wineglasses and cooling coffee.

'And they wonder why I'm still single,' I say.

Jenna sighs. 'It's like living in Baghdad. Only not as much fun.'

'How come you don't just quit?' I ask as we clear the table.

'I love your sibling loyalty,' Jenna says acidly.

'I'm not saying you should.' I pour coffee dregs down the sink and rinse the cafetière. 'I guess I'm impressed you've stuck around, that's all.'

'I'm planning to cash in and sell my story to the *News of the World*.'

I laugh. 'Seriously, though. The way I understand it, it's easier to find a rich husband than a good nanny. I bet any one of her friends would write you a blank cheque.'

Jenna is suddenly very busy putting glasses into the dishwasher.

I narrow my eyes. 'Someone already has, haven't they? Don't tell me. They offered to double your money and you loyally turned them down.'

She hesitates.

'Oh, come on. I'm not going to drop you in it. Look. Fuck the dishes. Grab a bottle of wine from the fridge and I'll get the glasses.'

I lurch slightly as I reach up. Jenna quickly puts the wine down and steadies my elbow.

'Guess that last Scotch went to my head,' I grimace.

'Guess that last *four* did.'

I open the wine, and follow her into the sitting room. 'So. Are you going to tell me about it?'

'You won't tell Clare?'

'Of course I bloody won't. What do you take me for?'

'One of her friends offered me a job. Like, a *lot* more money. She's been divorced for a few years—'

'So no getting caught in the marital crossfire.'

Jenna curls up at one end of Clare's ridiculously expensive overstuffed sofa, and I settle down at the other. Our toes are touching. She really is lovely. Like a young Sandra

Bullock: girl-next-door wholesome, but with that subtle, and unmistakable, hint of dirty-in-bed. I like the way she's toned down the make-up and cheap jewellery since she's been around Clare, too. She looks younger; classier. Though there's nothing she can do to minimize the enormous tits. Thank God.

She holds out her glass and I pour. 'I really like Clare, and I love the twins. But I'm fed up playing pig-in-the-middle. And I could *really* use the extra money.'

'Who's the so-called friend who's trying to poach you?'

'Olivia Coddington.'

'Christ. That woman's a real piece of work.'

Jenna sips her wine. 'She made me promise to give her an answer by Monday.'

I think for a moment. 'Look, why don't you try asking Clare for a raise?' I suggest. 'Tell her the truth. Say you've had a better offer, and you don't want to leave, but you can't afford to work for her unless she ups your salary.'

'Suppose she fires me?'

'She won't. But if she does, as soon as her friends find out, you'll have half a dozen job offers before you've even packed your suitcase.'

Jenna smiles, and suddenly I've got a hard-on the size of Nelson's Column. As she shifts on the sofa, her T-shirt rides up, exposing a tanned, rounded belly and a cool starburst tattoo around her navel. Her nips are like organ stops. It's not cold in here, so I know she fancies me too. Which only makes it worse. She's holding me off, keeping her distance, even though I know she wants to fuck as much as I do. She's the one in control of what happens next. It's a novel feeling.

'So what's going on at home?' I ask suddenly. 'Why all the drama?'

'There's no drama—'

'Give me a break.'

She drops her gaze. 'Really, it's no big deal.'

I lean forward, and run my thumb gently down the side of her neck. Looks like the bastard tried to strangle her. 'I'd call those bruises a big deal.'

'He didn't mean—'

'Bullshit.'

'What the fuck do you know?' she cries. 'You arrogant shit! Who do you think you are? You have no idea what you're talking about! You haven't got a clue what Jamie's been through!'

'OK. Why don't you tell me what he's been through, and then we can work out if I know what I'm talking about or not.'

'He was attacked, all right? Three men jumped him when he took a short-cut across the park on Christmas Eve. He was trying to get home in time to take me to a carol concert. They raped him. OK? They *raped* him!'

She stares at me, waiting for me to rush to apologize, to back down: *I didn't know, how awful, God, I'm so sorry.*

'And that makes it OK for him to take it out on you?' I say evenly.

'Did you hear what I just said?'

'Yes. Did you hear what *I* just said?'

'You've got no right to judge him! You don't know the first thing about it!'

'He was raped. I get it. It sucks, but it happens, Jenna.'

'Easy to say when it hasn't happened to you!'

'Ah, but it has.'

She falters. 'You're lying. You're just saying that so—'

'My mother sent me to boarding school when I was six.

I was buggered for years, by every boy big enough and strong enough to yank down my trousers. It only stopped when I figured out they liked my drugs better than my arse.' I shrug. 'Did I enjoy it? Not particularly. Did it fuck me up? Probably, but no more than thousands of other public schoolboys. Did I start thumping women to feel better about myself? Of course not.'

For a long moment, Jenna says nothing.

'He's – he's so scared,' she whispers. 'Of the dark, of crowds, everything. He thinks what happened to him makes him less of a man. I don't know how to help him.'

'The only thing that makes him less of a man is hitting a woman.'

She suddenly starts to cry, choking, ugly sobs. I hesitate a moment, then pull her into my arms, trying not to notice the softness of her breasts against my chest, the clean, citrus smell of her hair as it brushes my neck. I rub her back, struggling to channel brotherly and supportive thoughts. A little difficult to do when you've got a hard-on like a tent pole.

After a moment, she turns in my arms. She has the most extraordinary eyes: a vivid Irish green, shot through with hazel and gold lights. Her dark lashes are spiky with tears. I can feel her heart beating fast beneath her thin, tight T-shirt.

Her lips part slightly. I know when a woman is waiting to be kissed.

'Jenna?' a voice calls down the stairs.

We leap apart as if spring-loaded.

Clare comes down to the half-landing. 'Jenna, you have to be up early tomorrow with the twins. Don't you think you should get to bed?'

I grab my jacket. 'Look, I'd better go. I'll catch you later.'

'Aren't you staying over?'

'Not a good idea,' I say ruefully.

I take the steps two at a time. Only as my feet hit the pavement do I start to breathe a little easier. I suck in a lungful of crisp night air. Normally I wouldn't hesitate, but there's something about this girl. I can't believe I'm saying this, but I don't want to fuck her up. It's not like it could ever be a permanent thing.

I head towards the Tube station, leaving my car parked at Clare's house. Jenna's got enough problems. The last thing she needs is to get tangled up with me.

'It's getting worse,' the doctor tells me two days later.

'Sugar-coat it, why don't you,' I say, fumbling with the buttons on my shirt.

'I'm sorry, Alexander. I wish I had different news for you. I had hoped we'd have a little more time. As you know, once symptoms start to accelerate, there is a very definite degenerative rate—'

'Got it,' I say.

A couple of years ago, when I first started tripping and stumbling, when I had trouble fitting the key in the lock and problems zipping my jacket, I put it down to too many late nights, too much booze, too much charlie; *too much*. Then I started slurring words even when I wasn't drunk. The muscles in my legs and arms twitched and cramped. One night I woke up choking and gasping for breath. I told myself I'd just pushed my body too far, that all I needed was to take it easy for a bit, but deep down I knew it was something more.

ALS is a process of elimination. Basically, if you haven't got Huntington's, motor neurone, MS or Alzheimer's, you've probably got amyotrophic lateral sclerosis. Sometimes it's random, a genetic mutation; but Davina says her father – my grandfather – was clumsy and often slurred his words, though she claims she never saw him drink. He blew his brains out when she was eighteen. I think it's a fair bet that he and I share the same fucked-up genes.

It seems I'm in good company. My nemesis is also known as Lou Gehrig's disease, after the famous Major League baseball player. David Niven died from it. Stephen Hawking has it too.

Did I mention there's no cure?

But I've got lots to look forward to. Eventually, I won't be able to stand or walk, to get in or out of bed on my own, or to use my hands and arms. In the later stages, I'll have difficulty breathing as the muscles of my respiratory system weaken. Most people with ALS choke to death, usually within three to five years of the onset of symptoms. I probably have another couple of years, if I'm lucky.

'I'd like you to see somebody,' the doc says, scribbling on his pad.

'A shrink, you mean?' I stand up. 'Thanks, but I'm fine.'

'You're thirty-four, Alexander. No young man is fine with something like this. You need to talk to someone—'

Hello, vodka, this is Xan.

I take the piece of paper, since it means so much to him. As soon as I leave the surgery, I crumple it and throw it into the footwell of my car. (How much longer will I be able to drive?)

But I wasn't lying. For some reason, I *am* fine with this. I wasn't ever meant to grow old. Can you see me settling down with 2.4 kids and a pension plan?

The only person I really feel sorry for is Clare. It'll break her heart. I haven't told her; I haven't told anyone. No need for her to find out before she has to. I don't drink nearly as much as everyone thinks I do. Alcohol isn't the *reason* I trip and stumble and slur; it's my *excuse*.

I'm sorry about Jenna, too. She's the first girl I'd have liked to give things a shot with. Fortunately, since I've always been such a fuck-up with women, there'll be no distraught widow or fatherless babes left to mourn. Looks like my complete inability to form a lasting or meaningful relationship has done everyone a favour.

I don't plan to go quietly into the night. I'm not going to end up a prisoner in my own body, unable to walk or talk or piss or breathe on my own.

The car jolts as I take a sleeping policeman a little too fast. Underneath my jacket on the back seat, my grandfather's shotgun rattles.

STAR HOUSE
24 DUNCANNON ST
LONDON WC2N 4NP
T 020 7798 9485
F 020 7798 9480
E robert@stoppardandco.uk

STOPPARD AND CO.
CHARTERED ACCOUNTANTS

RMS/pjr/CE39   1 June 2009

Mrs Clare Elias
97 Cheyne Walk
London
SW3 5TS

Dear Clare,

It's not good news, I'm afraid. Even allowing for the
suspension of your plans for the new Hyde Park and
Clapham shops, the company outgoings still significantly
exceed current receipts. Your husband withdrew a
substantial amount from your capital account earlier
this year, in addition to numerous monthly current
account withdrawals. The funds you injected from your
portfolio last month have covered the overdraft, and all
creditors have now been paid. In addition, now that
Mr Elias's bank loan has been settled, the financial drag
should lessen somewhat.

However, I am still deeply concerned. Your cash reserves
are negligible, and should there be any further downturn
in cashflow, you have very little room to manoeuvre.

With the economy continuing to weaken, I must advise you that you are extremely vulnerable. Your level of borrowing is high, and if property prices fall further, you will find it difficult to offload the shops, should the need arise. I would strongly advise you to take pre-emptive action, and consider putting one or more on the market now. The Fulham and Kensington properties are the least profitable in cost/income terms, and would probably be the easiest to sell.

I realize this is not what you want to hear. I know how hard you have worked to build your company, and I am loath to suggest you sell any part of it. However, I am even more reluctant to see you lose everything, and can see no other realistic solution given the scale of your husband's borrowing.

Please give me a call any time, and we can discuss this further.

Kind regards,

10

Clare

'Craig, please. Won't you reconsider? This is such a bad time—'

'That's why I have to leave,' Craig says firmly. 'I'm sorry to break it to you over the phone, Clare, but you've hardly been here for the past few weeks—'

'My daughter was ill!'

'And before that, Rowan had colic, and before that, you were on maternity leave.' He sighs. 'What's happened to you, Clare? PetalPushers used to be the most important thing in your life. These days, even when you're here, your mind's not on the job. I keep telling you we're losing money hand over fist, and you just bury your head in the sand. I grant you, it's been much better this past month or so, but we still need to branch out if we're going to survive. A recession is a bad time to cater to a niche market, but you won't—'

'We've been through this,' I interrupt tersely. 'I'm not selling out. PetalPushers will come through this. We'll put the expansion plans on hold for a bit, tighten our belts, ride out the storm.'

'It's not going to be enough,' Craig says. 'Look, Clare. I'm sorry to do this to you, but to be honest, you could do with saving my salary right now anyway. KaBloom! has offered me limited partnership, and free creative rein. They're very interested in some of my marketing ideas.'

I pace the kitchen, twisting the phone cord around my fingers. 'Craig, I need you,' I plead. 'I can't be everywhere at once, not with seven shops. You've been with me since the beginning. No one else knows the business as well as you. I realize we have very different ideas about where PetalPushers should be heading in the future, but maybe there's room for compromise. I'd hate to lose you. If it's a question of money—'

'You can't afford to pay me any more.'

I suppress a flare of anger. This is *my* company. I know it better than I know my own children. Craig isn't privy to everything that goes on; he has no idea of the real cause of our financial problems. How *dare* he tell me what I can and can't afford?

Because he's got me over a barrel, that's why.

'I know what I can allow. Look, Craig. Let's sit down and talk this through, see if we can work something out.'

'I've already accepted the job.'

'Have you signed a contract?'

'Not yet, but—'

'I'm coming in.' I glance at the kitchen clock. Jenna's running late today: she's usually here by seven-thirty on Monday mornings, and it's ten to eight now. 'I'll be there in an hour. Don't do anything until I get there. Will you promise me that, Craig?'

'Well...'

'At least hear me out. Surely I deserve that much, after twelve years?'

He sighs. 'I promised to go and sign everything this afternoon. You've got until then.'

I hang the phone back on the wall and mollify the twins with a bowl of Cheerios. Rowan stuffs them in his face with two fat fingers, but Poppy seems more interested in seeing how many she can work beneath the waistband of her nappy. She beams happily at me, the picture of health. You'd never guess how ill she was just a week ago.

I feel sick every time I think about it. In my wildest nightmares, I never thought such a thing could happen to me. My baby lying sick in hospital, maybe even dying, while I'm dragged out of bed in the middle of the night and hauled down to the police station to be asked dozens of stupid, pointless questions – 'Do you ever feel jealous of your daughter, Mrs Elias? How did you feel when your father died?' – and all the time, all I could think of was Poppy, Poppy alone and wondering why her mother wasn't there.

Marc should have come with me. He didn't stay behind because he needed to marshal the troops and call Davina. He stayed because *he wanted it to be true.*

I've forgiven him for stealing from my company, remortgaging the house, putting the whole family in jeopardy. But I'm not sure I can forgive him for this.

I barely hear the eight o'clock news, anxiously listening for Jenna's key in the lock. I really need to get going; it'll take me thirty minutes to drive to the shop in Fulham. I can't let Craig leave now, not with everything else up in the air. If Marc and I ... if we ... if I can't learn to live with this ... I need work to stay settled. I can't cope with the business *and* the children on my own. Thank God I have Jenna. As long as she's here, I can deal with everything else.

Damn it, where *is* she? She's never been late before. I hope the wretched Tube isn't out; the whole of London will grind to a halt and I'll never—

The phone rings, and I grab it off the wall with one hand, liberating the ketchup bottle from Poppy's curious reach with the other. 'Yes?'

'Clare, it's Jenna—'

'Where are you? Is it the Tube? How long do you—'

'I can't make it in today, I'm sorry. Jamie's sick, I need to stay with him. I know it's short notice, but you said you weren't planning to go into the office today—'

'But I *need* you,' I exclaim. 'It's really important I go into work today. Please, Jenna. I'm sure your boyfriend can't be *that* sick—'

'Clare, he is. I'm sorry, but there's no one else to look after him.'

No. She can't do this to me. Not today, not now.

'Can't you just dose him up with something and put him to bed? I'll send a taxi to come and get you. You don't have to stay overnight, I'll be home by six—'

'I'm sorry, Clare, I really *can't.*'

For a moment, I almost hate her. She has no idea what she's just done. What does she know about real life? She swans around, partying and having fun, with no responsibilities or obligations or worries to speak of. A little credit card debt! She should try my life for five minutes.

'There must be something you can do,' I say, suddenly near to tears.

'There's really nothing—'

'You don't understand. You can't let me down like this. I *have* to get to work. What am I supposed to *do*?'

Her tone turns stroppy. 'Look, I'm not doing this on purpose. I didn't *ask* him to get sick.'

My mind races, seeking a way out of this trap like a rat in a maze. Marc's at the office, Davina's two hours' drive away, Candida, Poppy and Fran will be at work. Fran! Maybe I can borrow Kirsty.

I want to scream. Of all the times for Jenna to leave me in the lurch! For all I know, her boyfriend's not sick at all, and they're both going back to bed to shag all afternoon at my expense.

With an effort, I hold on to my temper. I can't afford to have her quit either.

'Well, I suppose it can't be helped. Will you be back tomorrow?'

A chill thought strikes me. Suppose she's seen through my little sweetness-and-light routine with Marc? If she's guessed things are going off the rails, she won't want to be caught in the middle. For all I know, she's got another job lined up already. 'You *are* coming back, aren't you?'

'Yes, I'm coming back. I'll call you tomorrow,' Jenna says shortly, and rings off.

Fran's phone is engaged, so I bundle the twins into their playsuits and jackets, and jump in the car. I just hope she doesn't leave home before I reach her.

I could strangle Jenna. She has no idea how complicated my life is. All she has to do is turn up to work on time, and look after two babies. She doesn't spend sleepless nights wondering how she's going to hold it all together: work, marriage, family. She doesn't have to feel guilty about short-changing all three. She has no mortgage to pay, no company to steer through increasingly choppy economic waters, no husband to soothe and keep happy while she decides if she even wants to stay married to him.

Deep down, I realize I'm being unfair. I want the impossible: a patient, uncomplaining nanny who'll love my children as her own, look up to me, think of us as her family rather than her job, never give anything less than 100 per cent – and make sure that the twins never love her more than they love me.

But I am so *tired* of picking up the pieces.

I leave the twins with a startled but willing (once I brandish a fistful of twenty-pound notes) Kirsty, and race to the Fulham shop, where I coax Craig, by dint of a crippling, unaffordable pay rise and the promise of free rein with some of his new ideas, into staying. Then I give him the rest of the afternoon off, and send Molly home early too. I need some time alone. I need to be with my flowers. I'm worn out. So many people wanting a piece of me, pulling me in different directions. It's never bothered me before – I'm used to organizing everything – but for once, I wish there was someone who could share the load. Just for five minutes.

I'm in the back, sorting through some vivid blue lobelia, and wondering how to use them. With a twist of hedera ivy, they could look wonderful. I imagine a June bride walking down the aisle with these, a splash of tropical colour against her white gown. I had ivy in my bouquet, ivy and mistletoe and white calla lilies—

The bell signals a customer. I walk out to the shop floor, unbraiding a twist of raffia from my wrist.

'Cooper,' I smile. 'How is Ella this week?'

'Recovering at home.'

'Oh, I'm so pleased.'

He nods shortly. 'Zinnias. Please,' he adds, as an after-thought.

Zinnias. I glance at him sharply. The Victorian meaning of zinnias was absence, as well as the emotional correlation, sorrow.

Maybe he has to travel again. Over the past weeks, each time he's come into the shop to order flowers for his girl-friend, I've gleaned a few more piecemeal details about his life. He's a journalist; well, a writer, really. 'Journalist' makes him sound like an inky-fingered hack. Cooper Garrett freelances for some serious magazines like *Newsweek* and *Time* (Craig elicited those particular details; like getting blood out of a stone, he said) and does some travel writing too. But what I find more interesting is the unpaid work he does for several high-profile NGOs, like the Red Cross and its sister arm in the Middle East, the Red Crescent. Cooper is the one who writes those emotive, wrenching colour pieces that drum up donations. He's so silent and taciturn in person; you'd never know how articulate, how eloquent, he can be on the written page. I've looked up and read his pieces online, of course. Everything I can get my hands on.

I scoop a bunch of stunning zinnias out of a water bucket. They're deep orange at the centre, radiating to hot pink and then bright yellow. Not my favourite flowers; but certainly cheerful, and they work well mixed against the late pussy-willow.

'No need to deliver this time,' he says. 'I'll take them myself.'

I can't imagine Cooper abandoning his wife in a police station in the middle of the night. Or getting himself into a financial mess and leaving it to Ella to sort out. Oh, I'm sure she gets stuck with his dry-cleaning when he gets back from a trip, but I bet she doesn't have to rush around making sure his life runs smoothly, as if he were a third child. From the first, he's struck me as the kind of man you can rely on in a crisis. Even if he is a little rough around the edges.

'How's your daughter?' he asks suddenly. 'Poppy, isn't it?'

I start. 'She's much better,' I say. 'How did you—'

'Your colleague. Craig.'

'How kind of you to remember. She had us terribly worried for a few days, but she seems over it now.' My voice cracks. 'She had so much salt in her body, they thought I must have given it to her. The police came . . . it was so dreadful—'

Tears spill suddenly down my cheeks. I dash them away, hopelessly embarrassed.

'Of course it wasn't you,' Cooper says, his matter-of-fact conviction an unexpected balm to my lacerated self-esteem.

'They can't seem to find another explanation,' I say helplessly.

'Then they're idiots,' he snaps. He stares intently at me, then spins on his heel. 'I'm sorry. Something – I have to go.'

He picks up his zinnias and bolts for the door, leaving me open-mouthed. He really is the most extraordinary man. It must be quite a challenge for Ella Stuart to sustain a full-length conversation with him. Still, he seems devoted to her. He's been in here every other day for weeks now.

In seven years, Marc has never once bought me flowers.

'Did you have to be so rude to me in front of Xan?'

Marc tosses his jacket on the end of the bed. 'Give me a break. The man's a drunk.'

'He's my brother! At least you could have—'

'You're the one who stormed upstairs over a spilt glass of wine,' Marc snaps.

'I had a headache.'

'You *are* a headache.'

I wrap my arms defensively around my chest. 'How can you say that?'

'Christ. All you ever do is bitch,' Marc sneers. He balls up his socks and throws them in the direction of the laundry bin, his voice taking on a mocking falsetto. '"Get another job. Sell the car." Have you heard yourself lately?'

'I'm not the one who got us into this mess.'

'Yeah, yeah. Save it, Clare. I'm not in the mood.'

He climbs into bed and turns his back to me. I switch off the bedside light and stare miserably into the darkness. I can't seem to do anything right any more. Marc blames me for everything. How *could* he believe I'd ever hurt Poppy? He must really . . . he must really *hate* me, I realize, with a spurt of shock. He's lived with me for seven years, he knows me better than anyone except Xan. To believe the worst of me like that . . . to *want* to believe it . . . how much resentment has he been harbouring, for how many years?

I'm bewildered by the speed at which we've fallen apart.

I can't remember the last time he kissed me, never mind the last time we made love. But we were fine until we had the twins. Weren't we? Or ... or was I just too busy with PetalPushers to notice?

Was I so wrong, to expect the same from marriage as Marc? A partner who was my lover and my friend; a career; a family. Is that really asking too much?

I push myself up on my elbow, but Marc's light snores tell me he's already asleep. *How can he?* My own stomach churns with anxiety. How can he *sleep* when our marriage is in crisis?

I throw myself restlessly back on my pillows. I haven't heard Jenna or Xan come upstairs yet. I'm very fond of Jenna, of course. It's not that I don't think she's good enough for Xan, obviously. But if they got together, it would ... complicate ... things too much. He'll break her heart, and I'll be the one left picking up the pieces.

Sliding out of bed, I reach for my robe and tiptoe out on to the landing. There's a soft murmur of voices below me, and then, as I stand and listen, a long, pregnant silence. Suddenly, the thought of Jenna stealing kisses from my brother – *my* brother: the one man whose loyalty and love I can still count on – fills me with a dark, ugly jealousy.

'Jenna?' I call sharply. I descend to the half-landing. 'Jenna, you have to be up early tomorrow with the twins. Don't you think you should get to bed?'

Moments later, the front door slams. Instantly, I feel ashamed of my pettiness. I didn't mean for Xan to drive home. He's in no fit state.

I slink upstairs and climb back under the cold covers. Next to me, Marc is stiff and unyielding, even in sleep.

I doze fitfully, haunted by dreams in which my life and

Jenna's are entangled and confused. At one point, I reach for Marc, only to have him turn into a wild-eyed Jenna, laughing manically as she brandishes a salt cellar in each hand.

I wake disorientated and exhausted. Marc's side of the bed is empty. The two of us are getting up earlier and earlier in our attempts to avoid each other.

Downstairs, I find Jenna in the utility room, loading the washing machine. Elbow deep in our dirty laundry: literally and metaphorically.

'Thank you so much for clearing up the kitchen last night,' I say nervously. 'I really appreciate it. I didn't mean you to get caught up in—'

'Forget it.'

She slams the washing-machine door shut and twists the knob. I follow her back to the kitchen, cowed. Jenna has a way of giving you the cold shoulder, making you feel in the wrong even when you don't know exactly why. After all, I certainly pay her enough to clean up a few coffee cups now and then. And Xan was here to help. It's not like I'm using her for slave labour.

Jenna picks up the kitchen sponge and, ignoring me, wipes down the counter-top. I hover uselessly. It's like being back at school. I never quite grasped the unwritten playground rules. I couldn't work out why I would be cast out of my small circle of friends for no apparent reason, and would spend tearful hours trying to discover what I'd done wrong, until I was suddenly admitted back into favour without explanation. I hated it then, and I hate it now.

'Was Xan . . . was he OK to drive when he left?' I ask tentatively.

'He got the Tube. He said he'll come round to pick up his car in a day or two.'

She's obviously in one of her moods. I decide to ignore it and hope she gets over it. 'Did the twins sleep through?'

'They woke up at seven.'

She clears away Rowan and Poppy's breakfast bowls, hands each of them a Farley's Rusk, and then starts briskly to sponge the already gleaming kitchen table.

'You haven't forgotten about their play date at Olivia's?' I venture. 'It's not far from here, but if it rains you need to get a taxi. I don't want to risk Poppy catching cold.'

'I haven't forgotten,' she says coolly.

I move out of the way as she starts on the Viking range. 'I could help you get the twins ready if you like. I don't have to go into work until later today,' I add, suddenly wondering as I say it why I have to go into work at all. I could spend the afternoon lazing in Olivia's back garden, the children playing on a picnic rug at our feet, enjoying the gentle June sunshine on my face, a glass of crisp Pinot Grigio in my hand and the feeling of grass between my bare toes.

I lift Poppy out of her high-chair, inhaling her warm, milky smell. She's growing up so fast, and I'm missing it.

Poppy squirms, and reaches towards Jenna. 'Ma! Ma! Ma!'

It's like a knife in my stomach.

'She says that to everyone,' Jenna says.

'She wants you,' I say, handing her to Jenna.

'Cupboard love.' Jenna smiles at Poppy. 'She knows where the biscuits come from.'

Forcing a smile, I go upstairs and get ready for work. When I come back down, the twins are playing on the floor of the sitting room. She's dressed Poppy in one of the hideous starched, frilled dresses I hate, and Rowan in a loathsome pair of black jeans and a miniature bomber jacket. Why does she keep buying them this dreadful stuff? Why can't she let them look like babies? They're only six months old, for heaven's sake! I don't want them going round to Olivia's looking like this. They're not *Jenna's* children.

'Look, do you mind if I change them?' I say suddenly. 'I'd rather they wore something more comfortable.'

Deliberately ignoring her outraged expression, I take them back upstairs. My hands tremble with anger as I lay each of them on the changing table and take off the scratchy, cheap synthetic outfits. I pull out their soft, worn sweats and T-shirts, in pale, faded colours: lavender, mint, robin's-egg blue. It's like Jenna's trying to take over. Imposing what she wants against my wishes. She needs to remember she's just here to do a job. They're *my* babies.

She's sitting at the kitchen table when I bring the twins back down, her arms folded. I don't have to be a mind reader to see trouble coming.

Instantly I regret my childish power play. It's not fair to take out my foul mood on her. And Jenna's the last person I need to alienate at the moment.

'I'm sorry, I didn't mean to be so picky,' I apologize. 'It's just that the twins will be crawling around Olivia's back garden, and I'd hate it if they ruined the lovely clothes you bought them. They should be kept for best—'

'Look, Clare. We need to talk.'

Words you never – as employer or lover – want to hear. I sit warily opposite her.

'It's not about the clothes,' she says quickly.

She hesitates, rubbing the palm of her hand up and down her inner arm as if she's cold. I've noticed it's something she does when she's nervous or unsure.

'I've been offered another job,' she blurts. 'It's a lot more money, and the hours would be shorter too. You know how much I love the twins, and I'd hate to leave you, but . . . well . . .'

She trails off. I simultaneously want to kill her and throw myself at her feet and beg her to stay.

'I didn't realize you were looking for another job,' I say carefully.

'Oh, I wasn't. I'm really happy here. It's just—'

'Clearly you're *not* really happy here, if you're considering leaving.'

She flushes. 'It's not that. Something just came up and . . . and, well, I thought I should talk to you about it before I did anything.'

I smooth my hands outwards against the surface of the tabletop. 'I can't see why,' I say evenly. 'If you want to leave us, there's nothing I can do to stop you.'

'But I don't!'

'I'm sorry, Jenna. I don't quite understand. If you don't want to leave, why are you telling me you've been offered another job?'

'I'm in so much debt, Clare,' she pleads. 'I don't know how I'm ever going to pay it off. I can't even afford the minimums on my credit cards. I'm months behind with the rent, and now Jamie and I have split up, he's refusing to let me break the lease, and I can't do it unless he agrees because we both signed it and—'

'You've split up with your boyfriend?'

She nods unhappily.

I sigh. No wonder she's so upset. At her age, breaking up seems like the end of the world. 'I didn't realize. When did *that* happen?'

'The weekend before last. When I had to take a couple of days off.'

'Two weeks ago? Where did you stay last weekend?'

'With Kirsty, at Fran's.'

'Oh, Jenna. You could have stayed here. Why didn't you tell me?'

'You've had so much else to worry about—'

'But you're part of the family, I keep telling you that.'

'I know, and I really don't want to leave you, but—'

'Look, I'm sure we can work something out.' I rub my eyes wearily. First Craig, and now Jenna. I don't know how I'm going to afford any of this, but I don't seem to have a choice. I can't lose either of them. Jenna rubs me raw sometimes, and she can be a bit bossy, shoving my nose in my inexperience; but when it comes to babies, she *is* the one who knows best. I'd be lost without her.

Maybe I could pay off her debt for her. It can't be that much. 'What do you owe?'

'About . . . well, about sixteen thousand all together.'

'Sixteen *thousand*?'

She bites her lip. I'm not surprised she's embarrassed. How on earth can she have racked up a debt of £16,000? What has she been buying, Picassos?

'Jenna, who offered you this job?' I demand. 'It's someone you've met here, isn't it? One of my so-called friends – wait. We had that charity meeting last week. It was one of them, wasn't it?'

She looks uncomfortable.

'Who, Jenna?'

'Olivia,' Jenna mutters.

'Olivia Coddington? My *friend* Olivia?'

'I shouldn't have said anything . . .'

'I'm glad you did,' I say tightly. Once the rest of the committee find out what she's done, her name will be mud. And if she thinks I'm going to sponsor her membership of the Hurlingham after this, she's got another think coming. 'I don't know how much she's offered you, Jenna, but I have to tell you, you'll earn every penny. Olivia's last two nannies haven't lasted three months between them.'

'I know. I don't want to leave you, but I really need the money. Is there . . . could you . . . I hate to ask, but . . .'

More money. Of course. Jenna already earns more than most of my friends' nannies, because of the extra work involved in looking after twins. And she's only been with us a few months; hardly time for a pay rise.

I need her, of course I do, the last thing I want is to lose my nanny now; but I feel like I'm being held to ransom. If I give in this time, am I going to be facing the same scenario in another few months?

'Let me think about it over the weekend,' I say finally.

I spend the rest of the day at work fretting about nothing else. Maybe I *should* let Jenna go. I can't afford to match the kind of salary Olivia can offer, and if Jenna's heart isn't in it, I don't want her looking after my babies.

Perhaps I could take care of them myself, I think wildly. It'd certainly please Marc; and I've been surprised how much I've missed spending time with them, too. I never intended to be this sort of mother. Maybe I could give Craig a bit more of the independence he craves, and take on a part-time role myself. Enrol the twins in a nursery. I could juggle things somehow—

I'd never cope. Who am I fooling? Look how I went to pieces last time.

But they're older now. In eighteen months, they'll be ready for nursery school. I don't want Poppy calling Jenna, or anyone else, Mummy. *I* want to be there for her first steps, her first word. What's the point of having children if I'm going to hand over my mothering to someone else?

At the end of a long, difficult day – Craig, bristling with ideas and self-importance, has been in and out of my office every five minutes; and then my Islington manager, Wendy, broke the news that she's four months pregnant – I'm relieved to get home, and say goodbye to Jenna for the weekend. I've had about as much of staff problems as I can stand for one week. I'm looking forward to spending a couple of hours simply enjoying my children.

Rowan and Poppy, however, have other ideas. They scream, spit out their food, squirm and cry in the bath, and throw up twice each over their clean babygros. It's as if they're picking up my anxiety and amplifying it a thousandfold. By seven-thirty, they're bouncing off the walls, and I want to tear my hair out with frustration. What on earth was I thinking? I can't do this. I could *never* do this. Motherhood is 99 per cent slog, grind and mind-numbing boredom. It's not worth going through that for the one moment when they smile at you or say your name. I'm sorry, it's just not. I'll pay Jenna anything she wants if she'll just stay.

I'm cleaning up a bottle of milk Poppy has thrown against the stove door when Marc gets home. In my rush to mop up the mess, I've forgotten to cage Rowan in the playpen; as Marc enters the kitchen, he grabs hold of the plastic tablecloth and attempts to pull himself upright. A bowl of chocolate mousse – for Fran's barbecue tomorrow – catapults off the table and spills all over my cream linen Jigsaw skirt.

'For God's sake, Rowan!' I scream.

'You don't have to shout at him,' Marc says coldly. He picks up his son and soothes him with exaggerated patience. 'He's only a baby. He didn't mean to do it.'

'I've been dealing with them on my own for the past four hours!' I cry. 'I've put in a full day at work too, Marc! The last thing I need is to come home and clear up after these two monsters!'

'*Monsters*?'

All the frustrations of the day spill over. 'They've been absolute horrors! As soon as I get one settled, the other one starts. It's a total nightmare—'

'Can't you control two small babies for five minutes?'

'It's not that easy—'

'My mother had six children under eight,' Marc says. '*She* managed.'

'She didn't work!'

He shrugs. 'Your choice.'

'If I didn't have the company, we'd be on the streets right now,' I flare.

He pushes his face into mine. 'Has it ever occurred to you that you *drove* me to take chances? Flaunting how much more money you earn, how successful you are. Too successful to look after your own children—'

'You try it!' I start to sob. 'It's impossible. *They're* impossible. They hate me. They've been fine all day with Jenna. It's *me* they can't stand. I'm a terrible mother. I should never have had them. They'd be better off without me.'

I wait for Marc to tell me I'm being ridiculous. Of course I'm a good mother, of course my children love me. I've just had a bad day, it'll be better tomorrow.

My husband levels a cool look at me.

'Yes,' he says. 'Maybe we would.'

P G G H

6/13/08

Ella,

I'm glad you liked the peonies. Please don't feel you have to call and thank me every time. Consider it understood.

I don't have your new number, and need to ask an urgent favor. Not for me; but for the creator of these arrangements we both so admire.

I'd rather explain in person. Let me know what time suits.

Best,

Cooper

PARSONS GREEN GUEST HOUSE
21 Langthorne Street, SW6 5RT
Reservations: 020 7334 5809
reservations@parsonsgreenguesthouse.co.uk

11

Jenna

All right, I know. The sugar-water and chocolate biscuits were a mean trick. I do feel a bit bad about it now. The twins were probably bouncing off the walls after I left last night. But the last thing I need is Clare thinking she can manage without me. I don't want to have to quit and work for Olivia What's-her-face. It's just that I'm *so fucking broke*. I've *got* to find more money somehow. Clare can afford it. If she really wants to.

I knock back my cocktail, wondering where the fuck Kirsty's got to. I'm starting to feel slightly sick from the heat and the tequila and the smell of sweaty, unwashed bodies. My head pounds in time with the music. I wish she'd get a move on. She's supposed to be going to the loo, not having a flipping baby.

To be honest, I shouldn't have come out tonight. I know she's only trying to cheer me up because I've left Jamie, but I'm really not in the mood to meet anyone new yet. I still feel really crap about the way things finished. Six years is a long time to be with someone, even if it did totally suck by the end. At least I should've had the guts to end it in person, instead of leaving a pathetic message on the answer-machine. I know Jamie's been a bit psycho recently, but it was still a shitty thing to do. I don't really blame him for changing the locks on me. The trouble is, I'm still paying rent on the flat, and now I've got nowhere to stay at weekends. Kirsty's been great, but I can't doss on her floor for ever.

I glance around the heaving club. If I *was* looking for someone new, it wouldn't be anyone here. I still can't stop thinking about Xan. Bloody Clare. Why'd she have to interrupt us the other night? All her 'we're friends and equals' crap. Yeah, sure; until it looks like I might end up her sister-in-law.

You know, she can be a right cow sometimes. Like with that shit yesterday over the twins' clothes. They looked *great* in those outfits I bought them. She only changed them into those boring sweatpants so she could get one over on me. She's always pulling rank when it suits her. Telling me what the twins can and can't drink, what they can and can't wear, what time they should go down for their naps. Like, if you're such a bloody good mother, why are you bothering to employ *me*?

She could easily give me a pay rise if she really wanted to. She's got tons of money. But no, she has to make me grovel. 'I'm sorry, Jenna. I don't quite understand. If you don't want to leave, why are you telling me you've been offered another job?' It was really embarrassing having to tell her how much I owe. And then she gets this face on, like I'm the first person on the planet to max out their credit cards. Everyone's in debt these days. She's worse than my mother. I mean, what business is it of hers anyway?

I grope in my bag for my mobile. If Kirsty doesn't come back soon, I'm out of here—

'I've met these really cute guys,' Kirsty giggles, emerging from the mass of pulsating bodies. She nods towards a couple of stud muffins who look like they live at the gym. 'Whaddya think?'

I shrug. They're OK. Just not my type.

'Don't be such a stroppy tart,' Kirsty hisses. 'Forget Jamie. He's a fucking loser.'

If she knew what he'd done to me that night, she'd go round and cut off his balls with a breadknife. But here am I, feeling guilty for dumping him! I don't even *like* him! It's not like I'll miss him. Why am I always so bloody *feeble*?

It's never going to happen with Xan. Seriously, what do we have in common? My life sucks, but I'm not that fucking sad. He's only out for one thing; but I've never slept around, and I'm not starting now. Clare doesn't know how lucky she's got it, going home to a regular shag every night. Everyone bitches about how miserable it is to be married, but they should try single for a change.

Kirsty shoves a Bacardi Breezer in my hand. 'Here. Have another drink.'

'I don't want another drink.'

'Would you lighten up already?'

I hesitate, then tilt the bottle to my lips. 'One more,' I scowl. 'And then we're leaving.'

Some bastard's riding a jackhammer in my head. I can't even open my eyes, it hurts too much. My mouth tastes of cigarettes and puke. I don't remember how many times I threw up last night, but put it this way: my stomach's still inside-out. I hate Kirsty. I am never, ever going to drink again.

A grating warble next to my ear makes my teeth rattle.

'Yours,' Kirsty mumbles.

I pull the pillow over my aching head.

'For fuck's sake, answer it!'

I snake out a hand and fumble for my phone, knocking a glass and several books off Kirsty's bedside table. Without opening my eyes, I flip it open.

'I think I can do another five hundred pounds a month,' Clare says breathlessly. 'I know it's probably not enough, but things are terribly tight right now. If you can wait until Christmas, I might be able to do a bit more then, it depends how things go with the—'

'What time is it?' I grunt.

'What time—? Oh. About nine-thirty, I think. Yes, nine-thirty-five.'

On a Sunday? Is she fucking *insane*? 'I don't mean to be rude, Clare, but can't this wait till tomorrow?'

'Yes, of course—'

'Great. Bye.'

'Wait! Do you think you'll say yes or no?'

I flop over on to my back, and wait for the room to stop tilting. I'm never going to get rid of her till I sort this out. Screw it. I didn't want to work for that stupid Olivia bitch anyway. And five hundred quid is five hundred quid. 'OK. Yes.'

'That's fantastic! Oh, Jenna, thank you so much. You won't regret it. I know things have been a bit, well, difficult lately, but—'

The Cradle Snatcher

'Forget it.'

'Well, if you—'

I shut the phone. I need to sleep. Twelve more hours would be good. Twenty-four would be better—

'What the fuck?' I groan, as Kirsty peels off the covers.

'Well, I'm awake now,' she says crossly.

'Well, I'm dying.'

'Come on. You'll feel better after a good fry-up. I make super good bacon and eggs.'

I should feel sick at the thought, but actually, I'm suddenly starving.

'Won't your boss mind me staying over?'

'Fran? Nah. She'd give you her own bed if I asked her to.'

'Dunno how you've got the balls. You treat her like you *own* her.'

Kirsty grabs a stained dressing gown from the hook behind the door. 'You need to remember who's got the power in the relationship, I keep telling you that. D'you have *any* idea how hard it is to find a decent nanny in London? One who speaks English and can drive, I mean. You could walk into a dozen jobs like *that*,' she says, snapping her fingers. 'She'd be totally screwed if you left.'

I'm not so sure, but I'm in no condition to argue.

I follow Kirsty downstairs in my borrowed T-shirt, which barely covers my knickers. If you can dignify a piece of lacy dental floss with the term 'knickers'.

'I know this great hangover remedy,' Kirsty says, far too loudly for my sensitive constitution. 'Hair of the dog. It's, like, vodka, raw eggs, tomato juice and—'

'Stop with the raw eggs, would you,' I beg. 'I don't think—'

'Jenna!'

Seriously. Is there no escaping this woman?

In fairness, Clare looks just as startled to see me as I am to see her. I yank my T-shirt down. 'What are you doing here?'

'Fran invited me for Sunday brunch. I thought you said you were going home this weekend?'

'Can't. Jamie put all my stuff in bin-bags and changed the locks.' I glance warily across at Fran. 'Kirsty said it was OK for me to stay over . . .?'

Fran waves a careless hand.

'You look awfully tired,' Clare presses anxiously. 'Are you sure you're not coming down with something?'

Kirsty snorts. 'Nah. It all came up last night.'

'Oh dear. You want to be careful, Jenna. Binge-drinking is very bad for you. You can do as much damage in one weekend session as—'

'I'm not very hungry after all,' I tell Kirsty. 'Actually, I think getting up was a mistake. I'm going back to bed.'

'I could bring you a cup of green tea,' Clare calls up the stairs.

I hide under the duvet before she offers me a dandelion smoothie or some hand-churned tofu. I'm relieved I don't have to leave Clare; I adore the twins, and I couldn't bear to have to say goodbye yet. But there's something about her earnest wholesomeness that makes me want to rush out and club baby seals for breakfast.

My body aches, as if I've been hit by a truck. Even my toes throb. I pull the covers over my head. I don't care what Kirsty says, I'm going on a detox tomorrow. I'm too bloody old for this.

I still feel one bulb short of a sunbed when I fall out of

bed again the next morning. I trudge down Cheyne Walk, trying to summon bright, Mary Poppins chirpiness as my liver waves a white flag. I hope Clare's out at the shop all day today. As soon as the twins go down for their nap, I'm joining them.

I pause to cross the road, and a piercing wolf whistle has me leaping out of my skin. For fuck's sake! In my fragile condition, any shock could be terminal.

'Jenna! Hold up!'

Xan crosses over, and looks me up and down. 'Good night, was it?'

'Since you ask.'

'I've seen better-looking corpses.'

'Fuck off,' I sigh. 'How come you're up this early, anyway?'

'Haven't been to bed yet,' he says cheerily. 'Came to pick up my car.'

'It's been sitting here a week. You're lucky it hasn't been towed.'

He points to the blue disabled sticker on his rear windscreen. 'I used the crip space.'

'Somebody in a wheelchair might have needed that,' I reprove him.

'My need was greater. Will you have dinner with me?'

'Will I what?'

He folds his arms and leans against Clare's gleaming black iron railings. 'You know. Dinner. Main meal of the day, usually eaten in the evening. From the French word *dîner*, the chief repast of the day, ultimately from the Latin *disiunare*, which means—'

'Yes, thank you. I know what dinner is. I just want to know why you want to have it with me.'

'Because my conscience fought a battle with my loins, and lust won out.'

My eyes slip involuntarily towards the bulge in his jeans. Xan snorts with laughter. I scowl. I can't help it, it's just one of those words. When someone says loins, you can't help but, well, *look*.

'Come on. A drink, then.'

'No drinks,' I say feelingly.

'OK. Evian all the way, I promise.'

I waver. His turquoise eyes goad me. Oh, shit. Xan is narcissistic, untrustworthy and arrogant; which, as every woman knows, is an irresistible combination. There's just something about a bastard. It's the combination of a Machiavellian ability to deceive and the thrill-seeking, callous behaviour of a psychopath. It's so . . . I don't know . . . so fucking *sexy*.

The front door opens. 'Xan!' Clare exclaims. 'What are you doing here?'

He jangles his car keys by way of answer.

'Jenna, if you wouldn't mind, Poppy just spilled Ribena all down herself.'

'Friday,' I hiss to Xan, 'Oriel at eight.'

'Thank heavens you're here early,' Clare says, slamming the door on her brother and hustling me into the kitchen. 'We've got to go to the hospital. I just had a call from the paediatrician.' Her voice is filled with hope for the first time in weeks. 'They think they might know what's wrong with Poppy.'

We're directed up to the NICU floor and shown into a small, windowless waiting room with boxes of tissues on every table. I hate it straight away. This must be where they tell parents their baby is going to die.

After a few minutes the door opens and a tall woman with spirals of red hair spilling down her shoulders like rusty bedsprings starts to back into the room. Her right foot is in plaster, and she's struggling with a pair of crutches. I leap up and hold the door for her. If she wasn't wearing a white coat with a stethoscope draped round her neck, I'd have thought she was a patient who'd got lost.

'Oh, thank you,' she pants, 'I still haven't quite got used to these.'

'I was expecting Dr Bryant,' Clare says warily.

'Yes, I'm not supposed to be back at work yet,' the woman says, sinking clumsily on to a chair and parking the crutches on the seat beside her, 'but when I heard about this case, I had to come in.'

Clare leans forward. 'You think you know what's wrong with Poppy?'

'There have been a couple of similar cases over the past few years. I don't know if you remember the Christian Blewitt case? Six or seven years ago, Angela and Ian Gay were accused of killing their foster-child by salt poisoning. They ended up in jail, but were eventually released and their convictions were quashed. When Cooper told me about what had happened to you—'

Clare looks nonplussed. 'Cooper?'

She laughs. 'I'm sorry, no wonder you're confused. I should explain. I'm Ella Stuart, paediatric consultant here at the Princess Eugenie.'

'*You're* Ella Stuart?'

'Quite recovered now, as you can see,' Ella says, 'and desperate to get back to work. It seems that, like most of my profession, I make a much better doctor than I do a patient. Your flowers are beautiful, by the way,' she adds. 'I've wanted to thank you for a long time.'

'You're welcome,' Clare says absently. I've never seen her look so thrown. 'But what does this have to do with your fiancé?'

'Cooper's not my fiancé! He's my brother-in-law.' Her smile fades. 'My husband died in February. Cooper came to England to collect some of his things.'

'I'm so sorry,' Clare says softly.

Ella collects herself with an effort. 'Jackson – my husband – wasn't the kind of man to stand by if he thought someone was being treated unfairly, and Cooper's the same. He asked me to look at the case again. He didn't want this haunting you for the next eighteen years.'

'That's ... that's so kind of him,' Clare whispers. She looks close to tears.

'In the case of little Christian Blewitt, it seems he had a rare medical condition which allows sodium to build up in the body,' Ella says. 'I think Poppy could have something similar.'

'Will she be OK?' Clare asks anxiously.

Her first instinct is to worry about Poppy, rather than be relieved she's off the hook herself. How can she think she's a bad mother? She's more committed to her children than any of the mothers I know.

'If she has what I think she does, then yes, it's perfectly treatable. I don't know if you've heard of diabetes insipidus?' Wincing, she straightens out her broken foot, and rubs her calf. 'It's sometimes known as water diabetes, but it has nothing to do with sugar diabetes, which I'm sure you're familiar with. DI is caused by the kidney's inability to concentrate urine properly, due to the deficiency of a hormone called vasopressin. It's quite rare, which is probably why it wasn't picked up when she was first brought in.'

'But you can treat it?' Clare says. 'She'll get better?'

'It can't be cured,' Ella says gently, 'but the symptoms can be almost eliminated. Poppy will need to take a modified form of vasopressin, and you'll have to stay very aware of her hydration levels. But if she does have DI, she should be fine.'

Shit, I feel terrible now. I knew Clare hadn't done anything to hurt Poppy; I kept telling Marc that. But other than call Davina, what have I done to help? Threaten to quit, and try to get off with her brother. Meanwhile, some guy who barely even knows her has gone off and got a top paediatrician to look into the case and find out what's *really* wrong with Poppy. Poor Clare. She must have been going through hell. Worried sick about Poppy, and then dragged off in the middle of the night and accused of trying to poison her own baby! What are a few credit-card debts and a crazy ex-boyfriend compared to what she's had to cope with?

Clare gulps out a half-laugh, half-sob. 'I kept telling them I didn't give her salt, but they wouldn't believe me.'

'You'd have had to force-feed her four spoons of salt to get the sodium levels in her body they recorded,' Ella says crisply. 'Trust me, even diluted in a pint of water, an adult would vomit that amount of salt, never mind a child. They should have had the good sense to check for an underlying medical cause, instead of jumping to sinister conclusions.'

Clare's eyes shine. 'Thank you,' she says.

As we leave, Ella murmurs something to Clare that I can't quite catch, but I notice it has the interesting effect of making her blush scarlet. I crane after the doctor curiously, wondering what I'm missing.

I load the baby carriers into the rear of the Range Rover. 'I'll drop you all at Baby Swim,' Clare says, starting the car. 'I have to go and sort out some problems at the Fulham shop. I'll pick you up afterwards.'

'Don't worry, we can walk back. It's a gorgeous day.'

Clare twists round in her seat, and smiles at the twins. 'I wish I could come with you. You're right, it's a beautiful day. It'll be lovely in that open-air pool.'

'Why don't you come too?'

She hesitates, clearly tempted. 'I can't. Craig and Molly are both sick. Someone has to be there when the delivery arrives.'

'I could wait for the delivery, and you could take the twins to Baby Swim,' I suggest.

'No, it's fine. I'll take them another time.'

'Take them now,' I press. 'Go on. You can borrow my cozzie. They'd really love it if you took them. And they'll be in the full-care class from next month, so you won't be able to stay.'

'I should get going. You'll be late—'

'Clare,' I say softly. 'You trust me with your children. Are you telling me you can't trust me for an hour or two with your flowers?'

She jerks, and for a moment I think I've gone too far.

'You really think you could manage?' she says finally.

'After dealing with these two horrors twenty-four/ seven? Walk in the park.'

'You'll need to check the stock against the delivery

inventory. Make sure you go through every tray; don't just assume that because the one on top is fine, the others will be. Anything even slightly damaged, you send back. *Don't* sign for it. And don't take any substitutes. That's one of the oldest tricks in the book.' She looks doubtful. 'Are you sure you can do this, Jenna? You don't know anything about flowers. Maybe I should just—'

'I know enough to figure out when someone's trying to pull a fast one,' I retort. 'I used to manage the stock at the sports club. I'll be fine.'

She's still reeling off instructions when she pulls up in front of the Fulham shop. I nod attentively, not listening to a word. Frankly, much as I love the twins, I can't wait for a couple of hours off from wiping snotty noses and changing nappies. How hard can it be to count tulips?

The metal shutters are still down; inside, the shop is cool and dim. I don't bother to switch on the lights, enjoying the green gloom. It smells *amazing*: like burying your head in the biggest bouquet of flowers you've ever seen. It must be fantastic to work in a place like this. Imagine going home smelling of roses and jasmine instead of puke and baby shit.

I plump down on the high stool behind the counter, spinning slightly to and fro. No wonder Clare loves her shops so much. It is kind of calm and peaceful here. It's not just the quiet of having no customers; it's the feeling that you're somehow grounded and connected with the real world. The living, growing world.

'You lucky bitch,' Kirsty sighs, when I call and tell her what I'm doing. 'It's Hector's birthday party this afternoon. Fran's invited eight little boys over, and guess who's got to entertain them?'

'Get your tits out,' I suggest. 'That should keep them quiet.'

'I might just do that,' she says thoughtfully. 'They've discovered their willies at ten, right?'

'Are you kidding? Rowan plays with his whenever I take his nappy off, and he's only six months.'

The bell rings as the door opens, and I quickly click my phone shut. A tall, grim-faced man in an ankle-length coat strides into the shop like he owns the place.

I come out from behind the counter and stop him in his tracks. 'Sorry, we're closed.'

'Where's Clare?'

'She's not here today—'

'Who're you?' he says rudely.

Bad-tempered American arse. 'I work for Clare. Can I take a message?'

'Unlikely.'

He doesn't leave. I glare pointedly at him, but he just glares back. He's got that mean, unshaven Clint Eastwood thing going on, but his eyes are gorgeous: a really piercing blue. He could be quite cute if he wasn't so fucking grumpy. And twenty years younger, of course.

'Can I help you?' I ask, making my tone as unhelpful as possible.

'Help?'

'Yes. Was there something you wanted?'

'Camellias,' he says suddenly. 'Give me some camellias.'

'I told you, we're closed—'

'You're here, aren't you?'

I wouldn't know a camellia if it jumped up and bit me. 'I really can't—'

'There,' he says, pointing to a bucket of red blooms surrounded by evergreen leaves. 'Just give them to me.'

'But—'

'You don't have to arrange the damn things. Just send them to . . . send them to Clare.'

'Who shall I say they're from?' I ask, with what I consider commendable patience given my insatiable curiosity.

'She'll know.'

I rummage through the paperwork my side of the counter, wondering what to charge him; even how to, for that matter.

'When you've figured it out,' he drawls, 'put it on my account. Cooper Garrett.'

Before I have a chance to process this crucial information, the shop phone rings. At the same time, a scrawny youth slouches through the door with a sheaf of paperwork in his hands. 'Delivery,' he grunts, wiping his nose on his sleeve.

When I look up, the American has gone.

I should never have let Clare talk me into this. It's like a zillion times more than I can afford, even when I'm not £16,000 in debt.

But this dress is so beautiful. And so sexy. And it makes me look so *thin*.

I twirl before the mirror. The pleated, gunmetal-grey Azzedine Alaïa flares gently from just below my bust, skimming my wobbles and rolls and ending flatteringly at mid-thigh. It looks classy, chic and expensive. Particularly expensive. I'm going to be in hock to Clare for the next twenty years.

What was I supposed to do, when she invited me to come to a private designer sale with her to thank me for holding the fort at the shop? Especially when she offered to loan me money to buy 'something special' to cheer me up. If I'd known breaking up with Jamie would earn me admission to Designer Heaven, I'd have dumped him years ago.

I slip on my new Manolos (I never thought I'd own a pair of Manolos; but like Clare said, in for a penny, in for three hundred and forty pounds) and skip downstairs, feeling like Carrie in *Sex and the City*. Only without the horse face and freaky hair.

'Oh! You look amazing!' Clare cries as I spin princessily into the sitting room. 'Marc, doesn't she look lovely?'

Marc doesn't bother to look up from his paper. 'Mmm.'

'Are you going out with Kirsty again?'

I flush. 'Actually, I've got a date.'

'A date? But how nice!' I can tell she's bursting to know who it is, but is far too polite to ask. 'I hope he's taking you somewhere wonderful.'

'I'm meeting him in town,' I mumble. Trying to distract her from any more tricky questions, I make a big deal of fiddling with my hair in the mirror over the fireplace. 'Do you think I should put my hair up? It's grown out a bit, and I'm not sure if it really suits me down.'

'Oh, up, definitely. I'll do it if you like.'

'It's OK, I've got a couple of clips somewhere—'

'Go on, I'm really good at it,' Clare pleads. 'Davina taught me. One of the few times,' she adds sadly, 'she ever took any interest in me.'

I don't have the heart to say no. I follow her upstairs, feeling like a total bitch as she brushes and pins. It's bad enough that I'm seeing Xan behind her back. All this shopping and sisterliness makes it a thousand times worse.

Clare pulls my hair in a soft, sexy chignon, leaving a few stray tendrils to frame my face in that hot, just-fallen-out-of-bed way. She picks up a make-up brush to touch up my inexpert application, and by the time she's finished I barely recognize myself. I look like a cover girl, with flawless foundation and huge, smoky eyes. It's a shame it'll all end up smeared on Xan's pillow.

She gives my shoulders a squeeze, and bends to meet my eyes in the mirror. 'I hope you have a wonderful time,' she smiles. 'You really deserve it.'

Seriously. Could she make me feel any worse?

Marc is champing at the bit by the time we get downstairs, anxious to get going on the drive to Davina's, where they're spending the weekend. He hustles Clare out of the door before she can offer me a lift. I breathe a sigh of relief. If this turns out to be anything more than a brief fling, I'm going to have to come clean with Clare. I can't stand all this sneaking around.

I'm just about to leave the house when Xan calls. 'Change of plan,' he says. 'Is the coast clear? Good. I'll be there in five.'

Three minutes later the doorbell rings. I glance in the hall mirror, blow myself a kiss for good luck and open the door.

A police car is waiting outside.

Xan sticks his head out of the rear window. 'Come on,' he grins. 'Hop in.'

'What's going on? Have you been arrested again?'

'Oh ye of little faith.' He climbs out of the car and holds the door for me. 'A friend owes me a favour. Meet Brendan and Lee. Ever been in a police chase?'

I fold my arms. 'Very funny.'

'Seriously. I'm on the side of the angels. Most of the time, anyway.' He runs his finger slowly down my bare arm, and I tingle. 'I lead a dissolute life, as Clare will tell you. Occasionally, I mix with characters even I deem too unsavoury for my tastes. I hear things. Sometimes I pass them on. Last month, when I was arrested? Bit of a mistake by the boys in blue. I got caught up in the wrong stake-out. Right hand didn't know what the left was doing. This is by way of an apology.'

I get in the car, wondering if Xan is a secret agent, a grass, an ex-con or all three. This is the weirdest first date I've ever had.

'Your bird's a bit overdressed,' Brendan grins, glancing in his rear-view mirror. 'She won't be tackling many villains in that get-up.'

'I'm undercover,' I retort.

Xan's hand slides up my bare leg. 'Now there's an idea.'

The police radio crackles, and we pull out into the road. I wait for the screaming tyres and sirens, but for the next two hours we schlep from one boring false alarm to another. Burst water mains, a 'domestic', two teens pelting rocks on to the road from a building under construction.

Finally, a call comes in alerting us to a shop robbery in progress.

'Fancy the blues and twos?' Brendan asks.

'Are you *kidding*?'

He switches on the lights and sirens. We tear down the King's Road, jumping red lights and ignoring zebra crossings. I cling to the seat for dear life as the car corners on what seems like two wheels. Xan's fingers slip beneath the edge of my knickers, and I nearly come with excitement.

The radio crackles again, telling us the thieves have fled the scene and run into an underground car park. We do an immediate 180, and turn sharply into the multi-storey we just passed, jolting over the speed hump at the entrance. Two figures are racing towards a low wall at the far side.

'Stay here!' Lee barks.

He doesn't have to tell me twice. I watch breathlessly as the two cops leap out of the police car and give chase, Xan's fingers stroking my clitoris with infuriating slowness. Almost immediately, they catch up with the fleeing figures. The cops slam them none too gently against the wall, yanking their hands behind their backs and cuffing them just like they do in the movies.

'Guess we'll have to make our own way home,' Xan says, releasing me and opening the car door. 'Brendan and Lee will need the back seat for the villains.'

For fuck's sake! *I so need to get laid*!

I sit up and straighten my skirt. 'Where the hell are we, anyway?'

'Darkest Fulham.' He grins at my expression. 'Don't worry, we're not far from my flat.'

Twenty minutes later, we fall through his front door. I fumble for his belt buckle, hampered by the impressive erection straining his zip. Buttons skitter noisily on the floor as I yank his shirt off his shoulders. He pulls my dress to my waist and slides the straps of my bra down my arms, freeing my breasts. Mindful of the lifetime it will take me to pay for the Alaïa, I quickly shimmy out of it before it becomes another casualty of lust.

Half-hopping with his jeans round his knees, he carries me into the sitting room, throwing me in a magnificent but slightly painful gesture on to the leather chesterfield. Winded, I squirm impatiently against the cold leather, spreading my legs ready. He shucks off the remainder of his clothes and slides between my thighs, his cock nudging my knickers.

At the last moment, he stops. 'Are you sure?'

'*Christ*,' I pant.

'I won't be around for long,' he warns. 'This isn't the start of something.'

I grab his buttocks with both hands and pull him towards me. 'Would you just fuck me already?'

He fumbles under the sofa. Seconds later, I hear the sound of a condom wrapper. Clearly the chesterfield has seen plenty of action. I don't care; actually, it's rather sexy. I've had enough of grown-up relationships to last me a while. I want some dirty, uncomplicated sex from a man who's been around enough to know exactly what he's doing.

Xan's turquoise eyes fasten on mine as he pulls my knickers off and thrusts into me in one seamless, practised movement. No need, now, for foreplay. The pulse of his cock inside me is all I want. I come moments later in thunderous waves, screaming my appreciation with scant regard for the neighbours.

'Now *that's* over,' Xan murmurs against my neck, 'the fun begins.'

On Sunday evening, I stagger up Clare's front steps like John Wayne. It wouldn't be accurate to say we haven't got out of bed all weekend. *Au contraire*: we've made full use of the kitchen table, the bathroom cabinet, the sofa (four times), the staircase, the fridge and (once) the bed. I have blisters, friction burns and a blossoming case of cystitis. I have never been so sated, sore, or hungry.

The house is cold and silent when I let myself in; Clare and Marc aren't yet back from Davina's. I offer up a silent prayer of thanks. The last thing I need is for her to recognize Xan's shirt and cut-offs.

I stumble down the hall, knocking my elbow on the under-stairs cupboard door. I yelp, hopping up and down and rubbing it as my funny-bone tingles painfully. Flicking on the lights, I try to shut the door, but it jams on something. I bend down and pull on the end of a leather holdall, trying to wedge it back in amongst the jumble of tennis rackets, umbrellas, wellies and baby crap. I succeed only in upending it into the chaos, spilling the contents.

You've got to be fucking kidding me.

I crouch down among the odd shoes and tennis balls and pick up the large, rectangular block of money in disbelief. I don't think I've ever seen this much cash in one place before. I run my fingers down the side of the brick, swiftly calculating the number of zeros I'm holding in my hands.

A hundred thousand US dollars. At least.

Why on earth would Marc have so much money in his gym bag?

FISHER · RAYMOND · LYON

8–12 ANDREW STREET · LONDON EC4A 3EA
TEL 020 7668 3100 · FAX 020 7668 3101
name@frl.co.uk

Mr M. Elias
97 Cheyne Walk
London SW3 5TS

Our Ref: TDR/1653-1/ea   15 June 2009

Dear Mr Elias,

Many thanks for your letter dated 11 June 2009. I am afraid
we are unable to represent you in your matrimonial proceedings
on this occasion.

If you wish us to refer you to an alternative family law firm,
please do not hesitate to contact our offices again.

Yours sincerely,

Nicholas Lyon

12

Marc

Maybe it'd be different if she hadn't cut off my balls over the money.

Shit, I know I screwed up. I wouldn't have blamed her if she'd freaked and gone off the deep end when she found out; I was ready for flying crockery, tears, a slap round the face. After months lying awake worrying about it, I was almost looking forward to having it out in the open. She'd yell, I'd apologize, hopefully she'd get over it, and that would be that.

But no. She had to be so fucking superior and *disappointed*.

I cling on to the strap as the subway rattles round a sharp corner. Must be nice and sunny up there on the moral high ground. Where the fuck does Clare get off? Telling me I can't 'handle' my job. Banning me from seeing Hamish and the boys. Christ! Who does she think she is, grounding me like a fucking eight-year-old?

Felix is right. I *am* pussy-whipped.

Back in the day, I kind of liked Clare's know-it-all confidence. Hell, I was used to it. It's what I grew up with. But having your ass handed to you by your mother is one thing. Having your wife rip you a new one every time you open your mouth is another.

When I was a kid, Mom took charge of all the household stuff. She picked out curtains and decided if we could afford a new sofa. She was the one who yelled three ways to Sunday if any of us came home with bad grades, not Dad. It was much easier to hit him up for cash, rather than Mom; it was him we went to when we were in trouble with her and needed someone to fight our corner.

But there was no doubt Dad called the shots when it really mattered. Mom might choose the colour scheme, but Dad picked the house. He let her win the small battles, because he knew damn well who'd come out on top in the war.

I realize women expect marriage to work differently these days. I never minded Clare working and building up her business till she was ready to have kids. I guess I just expected that when the babies came along, the flowers would take a back seat for once.

The subway train rattles into Sloane Square Station. I elbow my way through the crush of commuters up into the daylight, ignoring the newspaper guy as I pass through the ticket barrier. He ignores me right back. I love the British. You'd never know we spent Christmas Eve sharing a bird's-eye view of my wife's cunt.

It's a pleasant evening, with a mild summer chill in the air. I cut down a couple side streets and stroll along the Embankment, thankful I've survived another Friday cull. Four dealers on the trading floor had to clear out their desks today. Clare has no idea the pressure I'm under. Doesn't she read the bloody newspapers? It's carnage out there. Every Monday, a few more faces are missing from the trenches. Any one of us could be next.

As I mount the front steps and let myself into the house, I hear shouting from the kitchen. I drop my briefcase in the hall, and walk into total fucking chaos.

Clare, covered with some kind of chocolate Jell-O, is screaming at Rowan at the top of her lungs. The poor kid bursts into tears as Poppy cowers in a corner, terrified and bewildered. An upturned bowl drips more shit on the floor. Every surface is covered with dirty plates and cups. We could be on a sink estate in Peckham, rather than in a multi-million-pound house in one of the most expensive streets in London.

I snatch up my son before Clare does anything worse than scream. 'You don't have to shout at him. He's only a baby. He didn't mean to do it.'

Clare glares venomously. She's hated the poor bastard from the start. 'I've been dealing with them on my own for the past four hours!' she yells. 'I've put in a full day at work too, Marc! The last thing I need is to come home and clear up after these two monsters!'

'*Monsters?*'

'They've been absolute horrors! As soon as I get one settled, the other one starts. It's a total nightmare—'

Rowan hiccups miserably in my arms. There's something wrong with Clare if she can't see how helpless and vulnerable the kid is. 'Can't you control two small babies for five minutes?'

'It's not that easy—'

I'm sorry, but I really don't see the problem. Most

women would give their right arm to sit at home and look after the kids while someone else goes out and puts bread on the table. I don't know why the fuck Clare finds it so hard. She wants to be in charge, and then she expects me to be the main provider. She wanted babies, but she won't give an inch when it comes to her company. These damn career women want it all, and then blame *us* when they can't have it. It's a bloody con, and they've got away with it for far too long.

I wipe Rowan's snotty nose. 'My mother had six children under eight. *She* managed.'

'She didn't work!'

I could point out that when Clare didn't work, the situation at home was even worse, but I can't be bothered. 'Your choice.'

'If I didn't have the company, we'd be on the streets right now,' she sneers.

Change the fucking record, you ball-breaking bitch.

'Has it ever occurred to you,' I snarl, 'that you *drove* me to take chances? Flaunting how much more money you earn, how successful you are. Too successful to look after your own children—'

Clare throws the scrubber, with which she has been trying to sponge her ridiculously impractical white linen skirt, into the bowl of chocolate sauce and splatters it further round the kitchen.

'You try it!' she shrieks. 'It's impossible. *They're* impossible. They hate me. They've been fine all day with Jenna. It's *me* they can't stand. I'm a terrible mother.'

She bursts into noisy sobs, heedless of the children whimpering in confusion. I scoop Poppy up along with her brother, sheltering the two kids in my arms.

What does she want me to say? *Don't be ridiculous, darling, of course you're a good mother, of course your children love you. You've just had a bad day, it'll be better tomorrow.*

Like hell. She's been fucking shit from the start. First all the fuss over breastfeeding, then the near-hysteria when she had to cope with them on her own at home. She practically ignored Rowan; poor bastard was lucky he didn't starve to death. And the house looked like a bomb had hit it. Heaps of filthy laundry all over the place, dirty plates piled in the sink, stinking diapers in the bathroom, and nothing to eat in the damn cupboard. Clare bloody gave up. Most days, she was still wandering around the house in her crappy dressing gown when I got in from work. Hardly the kind of home a man wants to come back to.

Admittedly, Jenna knocked things back into shape, but Clare took her arrival as *carte blanche* to drop her mothering charade once and for all. Until the salt business with Poppy put her front-and-centre-stage again.

Call it Munchausen's, depression, neglect – I don't give a shit why she did it; I'm just damn sure it wasn't an accident. She can't be allowed to spend time on her own with them again. Jenna's a bolshy little cow, but I know she'd die for the twins. Much as I'd like to get rid of her, I need her to keep an eye on things when I'm not here. Until I come up with a better plan.

Poppy and Rowan bury their damp faces in my chest. I stare coldly at my wife over their heads. If Clare's waiting for reassurance, she's not going to get it from me. It's my children I care about now.

'I should never have had them,' Clare whines. 'They'd be better off without me.'

'Yes. Maybe we would.'

I leave her to stew in self-pity and take the kids into my study, settling them on the thick silk rug in front of the unlit fire. They immediately roll on to their tummies and start to trace the vibrant colours with fat fingers, burbling nonsense at each other. I watch them play happily for a few minutes, my anger at my wife building. *Christ, how hard is it, Clare? Change a few diapers, spoon in some apple sauce, sing 'Incy Wincy Spider' a couple times, and put them down for a nap. What the fuck's the damn problem?*

I pick up the phone. 'Hamish? Look, I'm sorry to bother you on a Friday night, but I need a favour.'

'I wish I could say it's a level playing field, but I'd be doing you a disservice,' Stephen Morton tells me. 'In this country, the woman still holds all the cards when it comes to custody.'

'But I've explained. Clare doesn't *want* the children—'

'Look, Marc,' the lawyer says, getting up from behind his vast mahogany desk and perching cosily on one corner, 'I don't want to rain on your parade. If your wife is as agreeable to your having full custody as you say she will be, we won't have a problem. I just want you to be fully cognizant of the situation should she prove less accommodating than we hope.'

Stephen Morton wasn't my first choice. He's smug, patronizing and smarmy. But Nicholas Lyon refused to represent me; his wife Malinche is an old schoolfriend of Clare's, though as far as I know they haven't seen each other for years. Lyon is also notoriously conservative, which could have made things a little sticky when it came to the business over the second mortgage and my borrowings from Clare's company. Morton didn't bat an eyelash. I just hope Lyon extends the same scruples if Clare approaches him. There's no question he's the best in the business; although, from what Hamish says, Morton comes a close, if less fastidious, second.

The lawyer returns to his side of the desk. 'We need to prepare for the worst, even if,' he adds, holding up one hand to forestall my protest, 'it turns out to be unnecessary. I take it your wife is financially able to support her children without your help?'

'Yes,' I say bitterly.

'The court will want to know you'd be prepared to give up your job and care for them full-time.'

I narrow my eyes. 'She'd have to pay me, then, wouldn't she?'

'If you were their primary caregiver, then yes, she would be required to pay you maintenance and child support.'

'And I'd get the house?'

'In all probability. It's helpful that she put the house in your name, not hers. She would be left with her company, of course, and enough funds to put a roof over her head.'

'The damn company's all that matters to her anyway,' I say sourly.

Morton pulls a pad of foolscap towards him. 'Marc, I'm sorry to be blunt, but right now this is all academic. Unless you have a very good reason, the court rarely gives custody to the father when the children are this young.'

'She tried to kill my daughter. Is that good enough?'

For a moment, Morton appears lost for words.

'Would you care to explain?' he manages finally.

His flashy gold fountain pen scratches as I talk. I

describe in detail the sudden dash to the hospital with Poppy, Clare being dragged out of bed by the police at midnight; and I tell him her latest wild claims of salt diabetes and miscarriages of justice and low levels of vaso-something. I don't believe a word of it, and I can tell from Morton's expression that neither does he. This is some bullshit Clare's cooked up to throw me off the scent.

When I've finished, he leans back, reads through his notes and taps his pen thoughtfully against his mouth.

'Was the post-natal depression ever formally diagnosed?'

'She was a basket case. Crying all the time, snapping at everyone, it was obvious—'

'But not medically diagnosed?' He puts his notes down and folds his hands on top of his pad like a doctor delivering a terminal diagnosis. 'Marc. I'll be honest with you. As far as the issue of your wife hiring the nanny goes, we'll have to tread very carefully. It'll depend entirely on which judge we draw. Some of them are very old-school on the subject of working mothers, but others . . . especially the women . . . I'm sure I don't have to tell you. We can play that by ear. But the salt business,' he adds, picking up his pad again and thoughtfully pulling on his lower lip. 'That could be very interesting. Obviously, from our point of view it's unfortunate no charges were brought, but we could make a lot of hay with the midnight arrest none the less. No smoke without fire, all that sort of thing.'

I find myself warming to the man. I'm certain Lyon would be far less enthusiastic about playing dirty. But I don't want a gentleman in my corner; I want a brawler who'll do whatever it takes to win.

'Let me do a little research into Munchausen's and this

salt diabetes,' he says briskly, scrawling in the margin. 'If there's any question about the children's safety, the judge will err on the side of caution, which in this case serves us well.'

'Will I be able to stop her seeing them altogether?'

'That's a little more difficult. Our case for custody is fundamentally circumstantial: if we can throw up enough doubt over the salt poisoning, together with the post-natal depression, and her clear reluctance to care for the children herself, as evidenced by the hiring of the nanny against your express wishes ... yes, it could be enough to swing custody in our favour. But unless we can prove the children are in immediate danger, we'd be unlikely to deprive your wife of access altogether. Let's take one step at a time for the moment.' He stops writing and looks me in the eye. 'One other thing. I need to know if there's a third party involved. I couldn't give a damn either way, but I don't want to be ambushed by the other side when we're trying to build a case based on your concern for your children—'

'There's no one else,' I snap.

'And what about your wife?'

I laugh harshly. 'Hardly. Not unless you count the bloody nanny.'

'It happens,' Morton says neutrally.

I glance at the flowers on his desk. Camellias. Like the ones Jenna brought home the other day for Clare.

There *is* something strange going on between them: an intimate, secret bond that excludes me. As soon as Jenna joined us, I was shoved out of the nursery, even though I was the one who'd looked after Poppy on my own for her first two weeks of life. The two women created a mysterious, feminine world full of secret smiles and laughter at my expense. Every time I tried to do anything with the twins, I was gently but firmly rebuffed. *This is our world. We don't need you.*

Clare would never cheat on me with another man: she's far too honest, too upright, to look at another guy. Plus she doesn't like sex much; never has.

But with a woman? With Jenna?

Slowly, the pieces start to slide into place. Clare putting a second pot of coffee on in the morning, just for Jenna; the nanny buttering a hot bagel for my wife when she comes down for breakfast. Clare leaving Jenna a surprise scarf to thank her for helping out at the shop; Jenna hand-washing Clare's cashmere sweater in return. Fixing Jenna's hair, going off on girly shopping trips, sharing confidences over a bottle of wine in front of the TV. No wonder my wife and I never sit down and talk any more. That fucking cuckoo has kicked me out of my own nest.

'You do realize that if we go down this route, things could get very dirty?' Morton asks, watching me carefully. 'If we have to go to court, she'll hire lawyers who'll fling plenty of their own mud your way. It could become very unpleasant for you.'

'I'll deal with it,' I say harshly. 'Do whatever you have to, Morton. Just make sure we win.'

I nurse my second Scotch as I wait for Clare to get home, buoyed by the alcohol and my conversation with the lawyer. If my dear wife refuses to play ball, I'm confident he'll be more than a match for anything her hired guns can throw at us.

Personally, I'm pretty sure Clare will agree to give me custody, especially as I'm willing to compromise and let her keep the house; it's mortgaged to the hilt anyway. It's not like she spends any time with the twins. She'll probably welcome the excuse not to have to bother with them. Regardless of my promise to Morton, I've no intention of giving up my job, so she'll only have to fork out for child support. I'll even give her reasonable access, as long as it's supervised; and not by Jenna. Thank Christ that lesbian bitch is out this evening. Last thing I need is her sticking her nose in.

I finish my drink. I'm almost looking forward to this.

The front door opens, and I hear Clare calling my name. I wait for her to find me.

'*Here* you are,' she says, pushing open the door to my study and switching on the light. 'What are you doing, sitting all alone in the dark? Where's Jenna?'

'She's out. Another date with her mystery man. It's lucky she was in whèn I got home – my key jammed in the bloody lock.'

Clare's lips tighten. 'I told her she couldn't take the night off.'

'I wanted to have the house to ourselves.' I force a warmer note into my tone. No need to start things off on the wrong foot. 'There's a couple of things we need to talk about, Clare. Why don't you come in and sit down?'

'I'd rather talk in the sitting room.'

Sure, Clare. Let's make sure you're *comfortable.*

She shrugs off her coat. 'I'm just going to get some tea. Would you like some?'

'Another Scotch, please.'

A few minutes later she joins me in the sitting room with my drink and a mug of that shit-awful green tea she drinks. *Way to go, sweetheart. Live dangerously, why don't you?*

As she hands me the glass, I notice she's wearing a short, clingy dress I haven't seen before. Makes a change to see her bloody legs; I hate women in pants. No mystery who she's getting all gussied up for.

'How was your day?' I ask as she settles in the armchair opposite.

'Busy. I spent most of it stuck in traffic.'

'Have you decided what to do when Wendy goes on maternity leave?'

She looks surprised. 'I told you about that? Jenna solved it for me. Remember Lucy Gardner?'

'Not really,' I shrug, irritated that once more Jenna is in the room with us.

'She retired from the Putney shop about six months ago. She got bored sitting at home, and came in to see about coming back to work the day Jenna was holding the fort in Fulham. Somehow, Jenna talked Wendy and Lucy into a job-share. It's the perfect solution. I don't know why I didn't think of it before.'

'Clare,' I say impatiently, 'there's something important we need to discuss.'

'Oh, Marc. *Please* don't,' she sighs, 'tell me you've lost more money.'

Jesus! Is she ever going to let me forget it?

'It's not about money.' I fight to keep my anger in check. 'Look, we both know things haven't been good between us recently. We're constantly at each other's throats. I'm miserable, and I'm sure you are too.'

Clare hesitates. 'All right. Yes. It's been difficult.'

'We can't go on like this. It's not good for either of us, or for Rowan and Poppy.'

'I can't remember the last time we sat down and really talked,' she sighs. 'We never seem to have a moment to ourselves.'

Whose fault's that?

'Marc, I know you don't like me working, but to be honest, sometimes it's the only way I get any peace. It's not that I mean to shut you out—'

'I'm not blaming you. I just want to find a way to work this out without fighting.'

Her eyes are suddenly wet. 'You've been so distant recently . . .'

'I talk to you,' I say, unable to keep the bitterness from my tone. 'You just don't listen.'

'Have you any idea how hard I've been working?' Clare exclaims. 'It was bad enough before you got us into debt, but now it's a thousand times worse. We could lose everything if I don't find a way out of this mess! I'm exhausted, Marc. I don't have time to listen to your problems.'

'You don't have time for anything except that damn company—'

'If it wasn't for that damn company, we'd be out on the street!'

'Oh, change the fucking record, Clare!'

I leap up and lean heavily on the mantelpiece. *Play the long game, Marc. This isn't the way to get her to agree.* I'll go to court if I have to, but it'd be so much easier if I can get her to sign off on things amicably.

'I don't want to argue with you,' I say wearily. 'I don't intend to end up one of those couples who still aren't talking when their children walk down the aisle. Let's sort this as quickly as possible so we can both move on. I've been talking to someone about the best way to—'

'So have I,' Clare says unexpectedly.

I swing round. 'You have?'

She blushes. I can't remember the last time I saw my wife disconcerted.

'I didn't want to go behind your back, but I thought one of us had to do something,' she stumbles. 'I hope you don't mind. I've made an appointment for us on the twenty-eighth—'

'Both of us?'

'Well, yes. You can't go to this sort of counselling on your own.'

'I'm not talking about counselling, Clare. Christ! I'm talking about *divorce*!'

I've never seen anyone turn grey before, but Clare does. The colour drains from her face, quite literally, like a cartoon. Unexpectedly, I find myself wanting to laugh, and struggle to hold myself in check.

'*Divorce?*' she whispers.

'Isn't that what we've been talking about?'

'Divorce,' she tries again, as if she doesn't understand the word.

'Come on, Clare. Don't tell me this is a surprise. We've barely spoken, let alone had sex, for months. How did you think this was going to end?'

'Is there . . . is there someone else?'

'Not as far as I'm concerned. What about you?'

She can't meet my eyes. 'Of course not.'

My anger flares again. *What about the flowers, you lying*

bitch? Never mind new dresses and sneaking around and the girly whispering in corners. You and that fucking mouthy dyke.

'I don't want this to get messy,' I say, dropping all pretence at friendliness. 'If we can agree everything ourselves, without getting lawyers involved—'

'But the twins are only six months old! They need us, they need a *family!*' She grabs at my arm in panic. 'Please, Marc. You don't mean this. I know things have been difficult recently, but it's just a rocky patch. It hasn't been much fun for me either, but we'll get through it. We can go for counselling, spend more time together. Jenna can take the twins one weekend, and—'

I shake her off. 'I'm doing this *for* Rowan and Poppy.'

'Think how they'll feel when they're older, shuttling between us, spending alternate Christmases . . . Oh, Marc, please, you *can't* want that—'

'It's better,' I say coldly, 'than being poisoned.'

'How can you say that?' she whispers, shocked. 'I didn't poison Poppy! You *know* I didn't! The doctor said she has salt diabetes, you can't blame me for that!'

'*One* doctor. *One* opinion. And I only have your word the woman even exists. For all I know, you invented the whole bloody thing.'

'But Jenna was *there*! She heard her!'

'She'd say anything if you paid her enough.'

'I would never do anything to hurt either one of my children!'

'Really? The thought's never even crossed your mind?'

She opens her mouth, then closes it again, guilt written all over her face.

My resolve hardens. However ugly this gets, however much she begs and pleads, I'm not letting her anywhere near my children. Not now, not ever.

'This discussion is going nowhere,' I tell her roughly. 'I'm sorry it all seems such a shock to you, Clare, but that's hardly my fault. If you'd paid the slightest attention to me, you'd have seen it coming. I suggest you go to bed and sleep on it. We can discuss your access to the children tomorrow, when we've both had a chance to calm down—'

'What do you mean, *my* access?'

'You can't possibly think I'm going to give you custody.'

'They're my *babies*!' Clare gasps. 'You can't take them away from me!'

'Oh, please,' I snarl. 'Don't pretend you want them. Ever since they were born, all you've done is dump them on someone else.'

'That's not true—'

I lean over her, experiencing a nasty thrill of satisfaction as she flinches away. 'Your company has always come first with you, hasn't it, Clare? For Christ's sake, what kind of woman waits till she's thirty-seven to start a family?'

'We said . . . we decided . . .'

'*You* decided. You always decide, don't you? Well, not this time. You think I'm going to let you keep the children so you can try to kill them again?'

'Don't be so ridiculous! I *love* them! I'd never do anything to harm them!' She sucks in a breath. 'This is the twenty-first century, Marc. Millions of women work, but it doesn't mean they don't love their children. You can't take the twins away just because I have a job.'

'You've made your choice. You can keep your damn company. But I'm keeping the kids.'

Clare springs out of the chair with such force, I take a step backwards. Her eyes burn like chips of blue ice in her pale face.

'You. Will. Not. Take. My. Children,' she hisses. 'I don't care if I have to give up every single shop. I won't let you take them away from me.'

For the first time, I realize this isn't going to be a slam-dunk after all.

I head towards the door. 'You're an unfit mother. You abandoned your children, and now, when it suits you, you think you can claim them back. Well, forget it. By the time I've finished with you, you won't be allowed in the same room as the twins, never mind get custody.'

'You'll never win! No court in the country will let you take two tiny babies from their mother!'

'Watch me,' I tell her, and slam the door behind me.

FISHER · RAYMOND · LYON

8–12 ANDREW STREET · LONDON EC4A 3EA
TEL 020 7668 3100 · FAX 020 7668 3101
name@frl.co.uk

Lady Davina Eastman
Long Meadow
Islip
Oxfordshire OX5 2RX

Our Ref: TDR/1708-1/ea   29 June 2009

Dear Lady Eastman,

Re: Elias v. Elias

Many thanks for your letter dated 27 June 2009, which made most interesting reading. Whilst it will have no direct bearing on the matrimonial proceedings between your daughter and son-in-law, it will certainly be given appropriate weight during the forthcoming custody hearing. I am most grateful to you for drawing it to my attention.

In line with your request, I will not make this information known to your daughter unless I fear we have no other option. I will, of course, alert you to this eventuality in time for you to have the option of breaking the news to her yourself.

Yours sincerely,

Nicholas Lyon

13

Clare

'It's the third time she's got me a parking ticket,' I fume. 'It's not like I needed her to renew her passport yesterday. We're not going to Montreal until October. She could have gone to the passport office any time. She certainly didn't need to park my car on a double-yellow to do it. Never mind the congestion charge during peak hours on a weekday—'

'I don't want to interrupt you mid-rant, but are you sure you don't want to come back to mine for a cup of tea?' Fran asks mildly. 'Or something stronger?'

I make room for her to sit down next to me on the front steps. 'I can't. We've got to wait for the wretched locksmith now, thanks to Jenna. I can't believe she's locked us all out. I *told* her the keys were on the hall table.'

'C'mon, Clare. Don't you remember what it felt like to be so mad about some bloke you wandered around with your head up your arse?'

'Frankly,' I snap, 'no.'

Tess Stimson

'Give me a break. You were crazy about Marc. You rang me up after every date to give me chapter and verse. "Oh, Fran, when he kisses me, I can feel it in my—"'

'OK, OK,' I shush crossly. 'We don't need the world to know.'

'What happens to all that?' Fran reflects sadly. 'Rod was nuts about me when we first met. We spent entire weekends in bed, and only got up to find more condoms or answer the door to the pizza guy. How did I end up stuck in Fulham on my own at forty with three kids, saggy tits, a roof that leaks and a back that goes out more often than I do?'

I smile ruefully. 'Tell me about it. I'm sorry to be such a pain in the rear, Fran. I'm just a bit fed up with Jenna at the moment, that's all. I really feel she held me hostage over the Olivia business—'

'That bitch! I hope you spread the word.'

'She won't be welcome in rather a lot of holiday homes in Provence this summer, certainly. Do you remember when we all avoided friends we thought might be after our husbands? Now it's the nanny poachers we worry about.'

'How much did you have to pay Jenna to stay?'

'More than I can afford.' I frown as Fran lights up a cigarette; she gives an apologetic smile, but doesn't stub it out. 'I wouldn't mind quite so much if she was a bit, well, grateful. But she's been really off with me all week. You know how she can get when she's in a mood.'

'She's Mother Teresa compared to bloody Kirsty,' Fran says darkly.

'It's my own fault. Davina warned me not to try to be her friend. I just didn't want to be one of those horrible uptight bosses that nannies complain about all the time.

Maybe I did blur the boundaries a bit. Perhaps I shouldn't have been *quite* so relaxed . . .'

Fran sucks hard on her cigarette. 'We all do it, darling. We're so terrified they'll leave. I give in to Kirsty far more than I ever did Rod. We're like battered wives. We should form a support group.'

'It's just got out of hand, Fran. I didn't mind at first, sitting down for a bit of a chat in the morning when the twins were napping. I thought it was good to build up some kind of rapport with her. But now, she thinks that if I'm home, that entitles her to stop pretending to work so we can both settle down for a cup of tea and a good natter. She even gets all narky when I ask her to do something, like take the twins on a play date.' Crossly, I bat cigarette smoke away. 'It's not like she's a guest. I am actually paying her to do a *job*.'

'Oh, dear. The honeymoon's really over, isn't it?'

'What do you mean?'

'Darling, next you'll be telling me she doesn't understand you.' She licks her thumb and finger and pinches out her cigarette. 'Look, the romance has worn off, that's all. If you were married, you'd be at the stage where you slump in front of the TV in your old dressing gown and have sex once a month. The magical aura of the heroine who rescued you from a lifetime of shit and nappies has faded. It happens to us all. Next you'll be bickering over cleaning up the kitchen or how much time she spends on the phone to her boyfriend.'

'So what am I supposed to do? Buy her chocolates?'

'That's up to you. The point is, now you have to decide if you want to stick with each other for better or worse, or get divorced.'

'I know which Marc would rather,' I sigh.

'Talking of which, why on earth didn't you ask him to come home and let you in? He's got his own keys, surely?'

I smooth my skirt over my knees. 'I tried to call him, but his secretary said he's gone to an important meeting and couldn't be reached. Anyway, I'd rather not drag him all the way back home on a fool's errand.' I hesitate. 'He's been rather . . . tricky . . . to deal with lately.'

Fran says nothing.

'I think we just need to spend a bit more time together,' I add defensively. 'What with the twins and work, we've barely seen each other for weeks. I can't remember the last time we sat down and *talked*.'

'Quite the domestic triangle you have there,' she says lightly. 'What with the stroppy nanny and tricky husband.'

'Scylla and Charybdis,' I sigh.

'As long as Jenna's the rock, and Marc's the hard place,' Fran quips.

'Don't even get me started on – oh! At *last*!' I leap up as the locksmith's van draws in to the kerb. 'I'll get a spare set cut for you, Fran, so we don't have to go through this again.'

'Just give me Marc's,' Fran mutters, scrambling to her feet.

I pretend not to hear.

'Of course I'm sure it was her,' I hiss into the phone. 'I know what my own nanny looks like!'

'What were they doing?'

'What do you think they were doing, Fran? I just told you, she was kissing him! She had her tongue down his throat. And no, I don't think she was giving him the kiss of life.'

I hear the click of her lighter. 'As long as he doesn't get her pregnant.'

'It's not funny! The twins were there!'

'I think they'll survive the trauma.'

'But she's my nanny!'

'And he's your brother. It's a bit complicated, I agree, but it's hardly the end of the world. It's not as if he's going to marry the girl. Xan's not the type to marry *any*one.'

This much, at least, is true. 'Well, at least I know now why she's been so stroppy recently,' I snap. 'As Davina would say, she's getting ideas above her station.'

'Clare Elias, don't tell me you think your mother's *right*?'

'Of course not,' I say uncomfortably.

I'm not a snob. I'm not! I've always thought of Jenna as my equal. In many respects, she's a lovely girl: honest, loyal, practical and organized. Just the sort of girl Xan needs, in fact. I wish he *would* meet someone and settle down; it'd be the making of him. It's just . . . not *Jenna*.

I can't help it: the thought makes my hackles rise. I'm ashamed to admit that I don't mind Jenna being my equal when it's my choice. But the idea of her as my sister-in-law . . . with as much right to walk into Long Meadow as me . . .

I grip the steering wheel. How *dare* she? I invite her into my home, I treat her as a friend, and she repays me by seducing my brother. What kind of message does she think this is sending the twins? Not to mention the fact that she went behind my back. I took her shopping, I lent her money for a new dress, I even did her hair and make-up! She must think I'm a complete fool. I thought I could *trust* her. How could she be so devious?

I turn into Kensington Church Street and begin the search for a parking space. For once, the gods are smiling on me: another Range Rover pulls out of a large space close to the restaurant and I nip quickly into it, to the annoyance of a virtuous hybrid coming the other way.

Spotting Jenna in a heavy clinch with my brother had one upside: it distracted me briefly from my nerves.

I stop walking. I don't know why I'm here. *What was I thinking?*

I look down at my unfamiliar high heels, the clingy wool dress that Jenna persuaded me into buying at the sale last week – 'body-con', she called it – the beaten-silver bangles on my wrists. It's not the kind of outfit I'd normally wear, though I have to admit it's younger and sexier than anything else I own. But I have no business looking young or sexy. I shouldn't have worn this dress, or these ridiculous heels. I shouldn't have spent an hour on my make-up this morning, or had my legs sugar-waxed specially at the salon.

I shouldn't have come.

I make up my mind to get back in the car and leave, to call him with some excuse about work or the children; but somehow, almost against my will, I find myself heading not back towards the car, but into the restaurant. I push open the glass door, and give my name to the painfully cool girl at the restaurant lectern, smoothing down my dress yet again as she leads me over to his table.

He stands as I approach, but to my immense relief makes no move to kiss my cheek, or even shake my hand.

'I thought you'd changed your mind,' he says.

'I did,' I admit. 'Several times.'

Cooper nods shortly, as if confirming my right to dither.

'I can't stay long,' I warn.

He glances around the restaurant, as if seeing his surroundings for the first time. 'Do you want to stay here?' he asks brusquely.

I chose this smart Kensington restaurant because it's vibrant and busy, a place to see and be seen in. There was to be no question of a small, discreet Italian restaurant in an unfamiliar part of town. Any number of my friends were likely to be lunching there. I had my explanation ready: I was meeting Cooper for lunch, to thank him for his help over Poppy, for persuading Ella to look at our case. There was nothing underhand or secretive about it.

But Cooper looks as out-of-place as a wolf in a cage of parakeets. He doesn't belong indoors, in this kind of gilt-and-gingerbread setting. There's something wild and elemental about him. In his plain, fine-knit grey sweater and jeans, he makes all the other men in the restaurant, dressed in their expensive suits and flashy watches and hand-stitched brogues, look somehow effete and immature.

I don't actually like it here, I realize. It's chic and stylish and the food is amazing. I've been here a thousand times. And I hate it.

'No,' I say, my heart lifting with the unfamiliar freedom of being honest and pleasing myself. 'I don't want to stay here. I want to go to the park.'

He pushes past the waitress, ignoring her outraged protests. I follow him outside, tripping in the stupid shoes, trying to keep up with his long stride.

Cooper stops suddenly. 'Take them off. They're not you.'

If Marc had said that, I'd bristle with indignation. Instead, I meekly slip off my heels and stand on the dusty, dirty pavement in my bare feet. Cooper isn't being arrogant. He's not telling me what to do. He's simply stating a fact. The heels *aren't* me. The fashionable restaurant isn't me. The designer clothes, London, Marc's shiny glittery rich friends, the expensive car, the nannies and cleaners and gardeners: none of it is me.

We turn into Kensington Gardens and I savour the whisper of cool grass between my bare toes. We walk across the park, past children shrieking with laughter, towards the Orangery and Kensington Palace. For perhaps ten minutes we stroll without speaking, my heels swinging in my hand, and I realize with a sense of mingled shock and relief that I barely know this man, but would follow him anywhere. It has nothing to do with love, or even lust. *Trust.* I trust him. For the first time in my life, I can relax my guard. I know this is someone I don't have to care for or worry over or look after; someone who will take care of *me*.

'You sent me camellias,' I say, as we reach the edge of the grass and rejoin the path. 'To the Victorians, that meant, "My destiny is in your hands."'

Cooper stops. He digs his hands in his pockets, ducking his head so that I can't see his face.

'I came to England,' he says, 'to see a woman. She . . . *possessed* me. I can't explain. I didn't know if I loved her, or hated her.'

Ella.

Abruptly he starts walking again. We veer left, towards the Round Pond, its brackish grey waters reflecting the overcast sky. Cooper is silent for so long, I think he's forgotten I'm even here.

He stops by a bench and sits down, leaning forward to

rest his elbows on his knees. I sit beside him, leaving a careful space of green slatted wood between us.

'I didn't realize it until I came here, but it wasn't really about her,' he says. 'A long time ago, I gave up something I cared a great deal about for my brother. I don't regret it. I'd do it again. But my brother was the sort of man who didn't care very much about anything.' He smiles wryly. 'In a good way. He was laid-back. *Live for today.* Everyone loved him. No one more than me.'

I think of my own brother, his reckless disregard for consequences, for the normal ties of love and friendship and family, his easy, careless attitude to life.

'People can only do that when someone else takes on their share of responsibility for them.'

Cooper glances at me in surprise. 'Yes.'

'I envy my brother that,' I sigh. 'I know I'm too uptight. I want to control everyone, everything. I didn't ask to be this way. But someone has to be the responsible one.'

'Have you ever let anyone else try?' Cooper asks.

I open my mouth, and close it again.

'I never let Jackson grow up,' Cooper says. 'I'd gotten so used to taking care of things. I never taught him how to take care of himself.'

'But – when he married—'

'If your brother got married, would you stop worrying about him?'

I shake my head.

'Ella was the one thing Jackson ever cared about. He gave up everything to be with her: his country, his job. Children, too: she refused to have any. And then she threw it back in his face.'

I pick up a scrap of stale bread on the ground, breaking

it into pieces and throwing them, one at a time, to the ducks.

'I thought I was angry with her, but it was Jackson I couldn't forgive.'

He lifts his head and looks directly at me for the first time. His cobalt eyes blaze with intensity. 'I didn't hate her. I think I knew that all along. And when I met you, I knew I hadn't ever loved her, either.'

My mouth is suddenly dry. My stomach swoops and soars, as if I'm riding a rollercoaster. The backs of my knees and neck prickle.

'I'm going back to the US tomorrow,' Cooper says, 'and then on to Afghanistan for a feature I'm writing. I don't know when I'll be back in the UK. I would never want you to . . . betray—'

'I couldn't,' I whisper; knowing in that second that, oh, I *could*.

I stay at work as long as I can, putting off the moment when I have to return to reality; to Marc. I won't leave him, of course. There was never really any question I would.

I shut myself in my office, and look up the number of a marriage counsellor my GP recommended, the last time I saw him for my headaches. I make an appointment for 28 June; a cancellation, the receptionist tells me. I don't ask if the couple reconciled, or divorced. I put the phone down wearily, feeling as if I've just had a capital sentence commuted to life imprisonment.

I've made the right decision, I think as I drive home. Marc and I have two young children whose happiness depends on us finding a way around our problems. We owe it to them to do everything in our power to succeed. *This is your life*, I tell myself. *For better or worse.*

I let myself into the cold, dark house a little after eight. For a moment, I wonder where everyone is, and then I spot a sliver of light beneath Marc's study door.

I push it open and switch on the light. '*Here* you are. What are you doing, sitting all alone in the dark? Where's Jenna?'

'She's out. Another date with her mystery man. It's lucky she was in when I got home – my key jammed in the bloody lock.'

I fight a surge of anger, knowing she's with Xan.

'I told her she couldn't take the night off.'

'I wanted to have the house to ourselves.' He smiles, but it doesn't reach his eyes. 'There's a couple of things we need to talk about, Clare. Why don't you come in and sit down?'

I don't want to sit and talk to you. I don't want to deal with your problems. I need to go away and think about what's happened to me today; I need to think about Cooper.

For better or worse.

I suppress a sigh, and unbutton my coat. 'I'd rather talk in the sitting room. I'm just going to get some tea. Would you like some?'

'Another Scotch, please.'

I fetch him his drink, and make myself a cup of peppermint tea. I'm tempted to add a slug of something stronger, but some sixth sense tells me I'm going to need my wits about me.

For a few minutes Marc makes nervous small-talk, clearly working himself up to tell me something. My nerves jangle as I sip my tea. Please God, not more financial losses.

I'm not sure how many more hits we can take before I have to go cap in hand to Davina.

He clears his throat portentously, and I steel myself. *Here it comes.*

'Look, we both know things haven't been good between us recently. We're constantly at each other's throats. I'm miserable, and I'm sure you are too.'

I hide my surprise. It's not like Marc to venture on to emotional territory. 'All right. Yes. It's been difficult.'

'We can't go on like this. It's not good for either of us, or for Rowan and Poppy.'

Maybe . . . maybe this is the moment I've been waiting for. If Marc and I are able to start communicating, perhaps we can begin to make up some of the ground we've lost since the twins were born.

'I can't remember the last time we sat down and really talked,' I say warily. 'We never seem to have a moment to ourselves.'

He scowls. Before I know it, we're back on the same old treadmill, covering the same old ground. *My company.* It's always about my company.

It'd be so easy to give up and slide towards divorce. I've seen so many women walk out of their marriages because things aren't perfect, like divorce is a lifestyle choice, rather than a last resort. I can't let that happen. I intend to fight for my marriage; for the twins, if for no other reason.

Nervously, I tell Marc about the counsellor. 'I didn't want to go behind your back, but I thought one of us had to do something. I hope you don't mind. I've made an appointment for us on the twenty-eighth—'

'Both of us?'

'Well, yes. You can't go to this sort of counselling on your own.'

'I'm not talking about counselling, Clare. Christ! I'm talking about *divorce*!'

My stomach goes into freefall. Divorce. Even though I've been thinking the word all day, hearing it said aloud, having it thrown at me when I'm least expecting it, disorientates me more than I would have thought possible. My head fills with a buzzing sound, like a saw or a hornet, and for a few minutes I can't take anything in.

'Come on, Clare,' Marc says impatiently. 'Don't tell me this is a surprise. We've barely spoken, let alone had sex, for months. How did you think this was going to end?'

'Is there . . . is there someone else?'

'Not as far as I'm concerned.' He leans on the mantel with studied casualness. 'What about you?'

Even though I know the question's rhetorical, that he cannot possibly know about Cooper, I blush. 'Of course not.'

His tone drops ten degrees colder. 'I don't want this to get messy. If we can agree everything ourselves, without getting lawyers involved—'

'But the twins are only six months old! They need us, they need a *family*!'

Marc shrugs me off. His stony expression doesn't change, even when I beg him to reconsider. How can he look at me with such dislike? How can he be so *cold*?

It starts to sink in that he's serious. He means it. *He's leaving me.* He's not even giving me a chance to defend myself, or state my case.

How can he do this to me? How can he do this to our children?

'Think how they'll feel when they're older,' I beseech, 'shuttling between us, spending alternate Christmases . . . Oh, Marc, please, you *can't* want that—'

He folds his arms. 'It's better than being poisoned.'

I don't understand him, this man I married. I don't even *know* him. Who is this stranger, who looks at me with such contempt and accuses me of the most heinous crime there is? Poison my own child? What kind of person does he think I am? Does he really believe I'm capable of that?

I fight back tears. 'I would never do anything to hurt either one of my children!'

'Really? The thought's never even crossed your mind?'

The memory flashes into my head, so vivid I can almost hear Rowan screaming and feel the cushion in my hands.

I close my eyes. One moment of weakness. That's all it was. I'd never have done anything. I swear. I love my babies. How much longer am I going to be punished for a split second of madness?

'. . . We can discuss your access to the children tomorrow, when we've both had a chance to calm down—'

Suddenly I focus on what Marc is saying. 'What do you mean, *my* access?'

'You can't possibly think I'm going to give you custody.'

He's just trying to upset me. He doesn't mean it. I'm their mother. They're only six months old; of course they'll stay with me. As if having a job makes you an unfit mother! Half the workforce would be in Bedlam if that were true!

What kind of parent does he think *he'll* make? What kind of example will he set his son? Pushing his face into mine, snarling and spitting, using his size and his sex to intimidate me. He doesn't really want full-time care of the twins; he'd go mad with boredom in a week. This is just posturing. Deep down he's a Sunday father, happy to play with them for an hour or two when they're clean and good-tempered and then hand them back when the real work starts. He has no idea what real parenting is, the commitment it takes. If he did, he wouldn't be doing this. He wouldn't be ripping all our lives apart.

'You've made your choice,' Marc snaps. 'You can keep your damn company. But I'm keeping the kids.'

No. No. *No.*

I jump up, my fists clenched at my sides, forcing him to step back. I will not let this bastard, this playground bully, dictate to me like this. I won't give him the satisfaction of seeing my fear.

'You. Will. Not. Take. My. Children.' I'm very, very clear about this. 'I don't care if I have to give up every single shop. I won't let you take them away from me.'

'You're an unfit mother,' Marc sneers, retreating towards the door. 'You abandoned your children, and now, when it suits you, you think you can claim them back.'

I stand petrified with shock as he slams his way out of the house. *He won't be able to get back in*, I think stupidly. *He hasn't got a set of the new keys.*

'Bloody good thing,' Fran says robustly, when she marches to the rescue twenty minutes later. She hands me a bottle of champagne. 'The man's an arse. About time you kicked him to the kerb.'

'Oh, Fran,' I sob, 'what on earth am I going to do now?'

'I'm afraid this isn't going to be very pleasant,' Nicholas Lyon says. 'Marc's hired Stephen Morton to represent him. That means things could get very messy.'

'What do you mean?' I ask warily.

'Morton's tactics tend towards the confrontational. I'm afraid he's not beneath using private detectives' – he says the words as if the occupation is on a par with muggers and rapists – 'to get what he wants.'

'Detectives?' I give a nervous laugh. 'I'm afraid I'm not nearly interesting enough to have any skeletons in the cupboard.'

Nicholas doesn't smile. 'I'm afraid that doesn't always matter. This isn't a criminal court of law, Clare; you don't have to prove your case beyond reasonable doubt. It's more a question of the balance of probabilities. No smoke without fire, that sort of thing. Family law doesn't deal with black and white, but with all those tricky shades of grey in between. There's no right and wrong. Whatever happens, everyone loses; especially the children.'

How did I end up here, in a divorce lawyer's office? The twins are barely six months old! What *happened* to us?

'I realize how hard this is, but we do have to move quite fast,' Nicholas says gently. 'The other side have already filed a petition, which means—'

'But he only left five days ago!'

'I understand that. However, I suspect your husband has been planning this for rather longer. He has done his homework, I'm afraid.'

Planning this? While I've been struggling to meet the bills and pay his debts, tearing myself into pieces and struggling to hold everything together, Marc has been consulting divorce lawyers and *planning* this?

I rub my eyes wearily. 'What does he want?'

'Considerably more than he's going to get. Morton should know better,' Nicholas snaps. 'He's plucking numbers from the air in the hope that when they finally name their real bottom line, you'll be so relieved you'll agree. Your husband is thirty years old and has a healthy income of his own. Maintenance is out of the question.'

I nod, as if any of this matters. Numbness envelops me like a shroud. If it hadn't been for Fran and Jenna – particularly Jenna, whose kindness has been almost painful – I don't know how I'd have got through the last few days. I keep waiting for Marc to call and tell me it's all been a terrible mistake. He can't mean this, surely? He can't really want to throw away the last seven years, destroy Poppy and Rowan's happiness, over . . . over *what*?

'It's just a misunderstanding,' I say suddenly. 'He's not going to go through with it. He wants to make a point, that's all.'

'Clare, I realize what a shock this must—'

'I know Marc; he's too proud to admit he's wrong. Well, I don't mind being the first to say sorry. If you—'

'Clare,' Nicholas says sharply, 'Marc is asking for a divorce on the grounds of your unreasonable behaviour. He's alleging that you are unstable and erratic, prone to violent outbursts of temper, and excessively antagonistic towards him. He also says you have refused him his conjugal rights for some months now, and that he came back one evening to find that you had changed the locks to prevent him accessing his own house.'

'That's ridiculous! Jenna locked us out of the house by mistake the other day, I had to call out the—'

'I haven't finished,' Nicholas warns. 'Marc is also seeking custody of the children on the grounds that you're an unfit mother and a danger to the twins.'

Even though I knew it was coming, it's still like a punch

to the stomach. *He's actually going to do it*. He wants to take my children.

'He can't do that,' I whisper. 'Nicholas, please. He can't take them, can he?'

'We'll fight him all the way,' Nicholas says.

'But they're just babies! I'm their *mother*! They need me!'

'Which is exactly what we're going to tell the judge.' He hesitates. 'Clare, I've got to be honest with you. Marc makes a plausible case. This salt poisoning—'

'But I've explained that! Poppy has a special type of diabetes—'

'Marc has produced witnesses who insist she was force-fed salt. He has copies of the police report, which is inconclusive, and a letter sent by a doctor at the Princess Eugenie Hospital referring the matter to Social Services. He claims he can produce a number of expert witnesses to back up his allegations. I'm not saying any of this is true,' he adds, holding up a hand, 'but I won't lie to you, Clare, we must take it very seriously.'

'You can't let him take them,' I plead. 'He can have everything. The house, the money. I just want my children.'

He pinches the bridge of his nose. 'Clare, I had hoped I wouldn't have to do this. I don't want to sink to Morton's level, but I'm afraid we have no choice. Marc has already thrown a lot of mud, and however we strive to explain it away, some of it is going to stick.'

'I can ask Ella Stuart if she'll testify for me. I'm sure she'd agree.'

'That would be helpful, yes, but it's not what I meant.'

He opens the folder on his desk and, taking out a letter,

hands it to me. 'I'm afraid we need to throw a little mud of our own.'

'What the *fuck* kind of game do you think you're playing?' Marc explodes in my ear.

Clearly he's received Nicholas's letter. I still can't quite believe Davina actually sent a private detective to Canada to investigate her future son-in-law, and then sat on the information for more than seven years; but for once in my life I'm grateful she's such a devious, suspicious bitch.

I hold the phone further away from my head. 'I think it's called tit-for-tat,' I say.

He's almost incoherent with rage. 'You lying bitch! How dare you brand me a fucking pervert! You want to drag the whole family through the dirt, is that it? Is this what you want for the children? You think it's good for them to grow up thinking their father is some kind of sex maniac?'

'No worse than growing up thinking their mother tried to poison them,' I retort.

'I was fucking twenty-one!' Marc yells. 'The girl looked a lot older than fourteen; she was knocking back shots in a fucking bar, for Christ's sake! How was I supposed to know?'

I cradle the phone between my shoulder and ear as I reverse into a space outside my house. As soon as the divorce is finalized, I'm getting rid of this vehicle. I want a cheap, ordinary car that doesn't require a twelve-point-turn to park.

'It can be upsetting when people take an innocent mis-understanding and turn it into something sinister, can't it?'

I say, climbing out of the car and locking it. 'You ask a pretty girl to dance, and the next thing you know you're a sex offender with a criminal record. People can be so narrow-minded. Especially judges in custody battles.'

'You're not going to win,' Marc snarls. 'I'll make sure everyone knows what kind of lying, conniving, psychotic mother you are.'

How could I have lived with this man, slept with him, had children with him, and never realized what kind of selfish, cruel person he was?

'If you do that,' I say, 'they'll have to know exactly what kind of father you are too. No court is ever going to—'

'Who said anything about going to court?'

'What are you talking about?'

'Have you checked the children lately?'

'Marc, what do you mean?' I demand urgently. 'Where are you?'

'Don't they have Baby Swim every Monday, Clare? At the Hurlingham?'

The blood starts pumping in my veins again. He's at the Hurlingham Club, in Fulham. Which means he isn't here, at the house, where the twins are, because they were both feverish this morning and I had to keep them home.

Thank God. *Thank God thank God thank God.*

I run up the front steps and unlock the door. 'I'm calling my lawyer,' I tell Marc. 'I'm letting him know you threatened to take the children. You'll be lucky to get supervised visits after this.'

I snap my phone shut. In the kitchen, I hear the twins' happy babble, and Jenna's voice as she chatters to them.

I sag against the wall. I don't know if Marc really would have tried to snatch the children, or if he was just taunting me. What would he have done with them, where would he have gone? With no money and nowhere to stay, he'd have run out of options very quickly. But Marc doesn't always think things through. He might have been tempted to do something stupid. It wouldn't be the first time. Thank God he didn't get the chance.

Straightening up, I go into the kitchen, where Poppy is happily splattering puréed parsnips over the table. I give her a deep hug, not caring that my suit will need to be dry-cleaned.

'Everything OK?' Jenna enquires.

'It is now.' I release Poppy, and brush crumbs from my jacket. 'Where's Rowan? Down for a nap?'

'Actually, after you left, he seemed much better. I don't think he had a temperature at all; it was normal when I took it, anyway.' She lifts Poppy out of her seat. 'I didn't want him to miss out, so I took him to Baby Swim after all.'

Shirebank

www.shirebank.co.uk

MS J E KEMENY

Current Account

69 BINFIELD ROAD

STOCKWELL SW9 9EA

Name: MS JENNA EMILY KEMENY
Number: 48760929

Branch: 469 Brixton Rd London SW9 8HH
Sort Code: 21-48-35

IBAN   GB73 SHIR 2148 3548 7609 29
SWIFTBC   SHIRGB22

Statement

19 Jul to 18 Aug 2009

At a glance

Start balance	4,129.55	*OD
Money in	27,500.00	
Money out	3,485.18	
End balance	19,885.27	

The Cradle Snatcher

Your transactions

Date	Description	Details	Money Out	Money In	Balance	
19 Jul	Start balance				- 4,129.55	*OD
21 Jul	Bill payment J Rowe	Online banking	2,000.00		- 6,129.55	*OD
22 Jul	Bill payment Visa	Online banking	100.00		- 6,229.55	*OD
22 Jul	Boots the Chemist	Debit	17.34		- 6,246.89	*OD
23 Jul	Bill payment Mastercard	Online banking	100.00		- 6,346.89	*OD
24 Jul	L K Bennett	Debit	189.94		- 6,536.83	*OD
26 Jul	Diesel	Debit	59.99		- 6,596.82	*OD
26 Jul	Jigsaw	Debit	149.99		- 6,746.81	*OD
27 Jul	WHSmith	Debit	6.99		- 6,753.80	*OD
29 Jul	Bill payment GE Credit	Online banking	100.00		- 6,853.80	*OD
29 Jul	Bill payment John Lewis	Online banking	50.00		- 6,903.80	*OD
29 Jul	Bill payment M&S FS	Online banking	50.00		- 6,953.80	*OD
30 Jul	Top Shop	Debit	29.99		- 6,983.79	*OD
30 Jul	Cash Withdrawal		50.00		- 7,033.79	*OD
1 Aug	Received C Elias	Bank Giro Credit		2,500	- 4,533.79	*OD
4 Aug	Boots the Chemist	Debit	24.99		- 4,558.78	*OD
4 Aug	Kate Kuba	Debit	149.99		- 4,708.77	*OD
4 Aug	Zara	Debit	64.98		- 4,773.75	*OD
4 Aug	Jo Malone	Debit	122.97		- 4,896.72	*OD
5 Aug	WHSmith	Debit	6.99		- 4,903.71	*OD
7 Aug	Bill payment O2	Debit	48.52		- 4,952.23	*OD
9 Aug	M.A.C.	Debit	75.00		- 5,027.23	*OD
13 Aug	Chelsea Brasserie	Debit	87.50		- 5,114.73	*OD
17 Aug	Received A Sterling	Bank Giro Credit		25,000	19,885.27	
18 Aug	End Balance				19,885.27	

14

Jenna

'What are you doing here?' I demand.

'Stalking you.'

'Seriously, Xan.'

'Seriously, Jenna.'

'Don't mess about. If Clare sees us, she'll go nuts.'

Xan snorts. 'If she sees us doing *what*? Chatting in broad daylight outside Marks and Sparks?'

He has a point.

'However,' he says, pulling me into his arms and giving me a knicker-wetting snog I can feel in my toes, 'if she saw us doing *this*, I could understand the problem.'

When I finally come up for air, I'm slightly surprised to see the twins gurgling happily in their double buggy beside me. It takes me a moment to realize I'm standing in the middle of Kensington High Street, not smouldering between the sheets at Xan's *pied-à-terre*.

He releases me, and pats down his pockets for a packet of cigarettes. 'Jenna, we need to talk.'

Four words you never want to hear: from your lover or your boss.

Shit. I knew it wasn't going to last, but I'd hoped it was going to last a bit *longer*.

'I can't talk now,' I say, as Rowan wails loudly. 'The twins need lunch.'

'Come over tonight. I'm ... going out of town tomorrow. I won't be back for a while.'

Clare's not going to like it, especially at such short notice. Marc's working late again, and she hates staying in on her own. Well, tough. I may work for her, but she's not the boss of me. I *am* entitled to go out in the evening if I want to. Even if it is just to get dumped.

'I'll see you at eight,' I tell Xan.

'Fine. Look, Jenna—'

I wait.

He shrugs negligently. 'Forget it.'

I turn the push-chair around and start to head back home, wondering if Xan really *did* follow me, or if meeting him was just coincidence. I wouldn't put anything past him.

Maybe he's decided to tell Clare about us, I think hopefully. We get on really well most of the time, though he can be a bit moody. He'll be laughing and joking around, and then suddenly he goes all weird and quiet, like his dog's just died. Five minutes later he's fine again. It's kind of hot, never knowing where you are with him, but it's exhausting, too. There are times you just want to have dinner and a movie and keep the drama on the screen.

I glance at the sky. It's overcast, but it doesn't look like it's going to rain. I think we've got time to nip into Kensington Gardens to feed the ducks.

Tess Stimson

I park the push-chair by the Round Pond and dig around in the basket beneath for the Ziploc bag of stale bread I brought with us. A bit further along, a couple are sitting on a park bench, deep in conversation. She drops her head, as if to hide tears, and as I watch he lifts her chin with his finger. He talks to her, straightening her collar as if she's a child, and the unexpected tenderness of the gesture takes my breath away. It takes me a full minute to register that the woman is Clare, and another few seconds to place the man as Cooper Garrett.

I fling the bread bag back in the buggy and quickly release the brake. I feel clumsy and embarrassed, as if I've walked in on her naked.

I can't believe it. *Clare*, of all people. Not that I blame her; Marc's a total wanker. But she's always been so serious and sensible and so . . . so *Julie Andrews*.

Flowers. Secret assignations in the park. Oh, Mrs Elias, what *are* you up to?

I smile to myself, startling a couple of old dears walking their dogs. *You go, girl.* I can kind of see why Clare might fancy Cooper: even though he's pretty old, he's still got this really cool, all-action-hero thing going on. It's quite sexy, in a way. You can imagine him in *The Poseidon Adventure*, leading everyone out of the ship. Marc's more like the rich loser on *The Titanic*, bribing the steward to let him escape with the women.

Clare's late home from work: getting her brains shagged out, if she's got any sense. Which she probably hasn't. She's just the type to fall madly in love, and then ruin it all by developing a conscience.

I put the twins to bed, and race to get ready for Xan. On

the off-chance he's *not* going to dump me, I want to look sensational.

I'm struggling into a bone-crushing, corset-style top and figure-hugging jeans when I finally hear the sound of a key in the lock. It's followed by a string of words I wouldn't want the twins to hear until they're at least twenty-one.

I yank my zip up and run down to open the front door.

'What the fuck is wrong with the lock?' Marc yells.

'It's my fault,' I pant. 'I shut us out, and Clare had to get the locksmith round. You've got one of those mega-security locks so he couldn't just cut new keys, he had to drill out the whole—'

Marc pushes past me. 'Whatever. Where is she?'

'She's not home yet.' I glance nervously at the hall clock. 'I'm supposed to be going out soon . . .'

'Don't worry. Go. I'll be here.' He smiles unpleasantly. 'I need to talk to my wife.'

I don't like the way he said that. I run upstairs, hoping he hasn't caught her out. Aside from the fact that she deserves a bit of fun, if they split, I'm the one who'll probably end up out of a job. The first casualty of marital warfare is always the nanny. The husband is convinced you're on the wife's side (which you are, of course; unless you're shagging him. Men are so bloody lazy. Why look for totty elsewhere when it's right there under your own roof?), and wives never believe you aren't shagging the husband (which you often are, of course. If he can afford to hire a nanny, he can afford serious jewellery). Either way, you're fucked.

I yank open my wardrobe. Never mind Clare's love life; right now I need to worry about mine. I'll be claiming my pension by the time Xan can get these jeans off. I need something more . . . accessible.

I finally settle on a short, sexy LBD, silver heels and no bra. Clare would say the outfit's tarty. Clare has far too high an opinion of men's taste, if you ask me.

'You look bloody sensational,' Xan says admiringly, when he answers his front door. 'Can I actually see your nipples through that top?'

'I put lipstick on them specially.'

'Bloody hell. I can't wait to get you into bed.'

I follow him into the lounge. He already has a bottle of champagne on ice; I can't help but notice the way his hands shake as he opens it. My stomach plunges. Marc's right. Xan must have a real drink problem to have the DTs like that. It might be better if he does give me the elbow. I don't want to break my heart trying to dry him out.

And he would. Break my heart, I mean.

He hands me a crystal flute. I stare at the tiny bubbles shooting skyward, the glass sweating in my hand. You don't open a bottle of champagne without a good reason.

At least he's got the guts to do it in person, rather than by answer-machine.

'You're dumping me, aren't you?' I say calmly.

Xan hesitates. 'Yes,' he says finally. 'I would have put it differently, but—'

'The result's the same.' I raise my glass. 'Cheers. Look, Xan, it's OK. I'm not going to make a scene.'

'Jenna, this has nothing to do with you. At least . . . of course it's to do with you, but not in the way you think.' He sighs. 'I don't expect you to understand now, but I'm doing this *for* you.' He sits on the leather chesterfield, and pats the sofa next to him for me to join him. I put my glass down and he pulls me into the crook of his shoulder, rubbing my back. 'I'm sorry, darling. I really wish I didn't have to do this. You know how much I like you, right?'

I shrug, ashamed to find tears clogging my throat.

'Oh, sweetheart. This sucks, doesn't it?' He turns my head and tilts my face up, in a gesture strangely reminiscent of Cooper in the park. I blink furiously. 'I'm crazy about you, Jenna. If things weren't such a bloody mess, I'd have probably ended up marrying you. If you'd have had me, of course.'

I summon a wan smile. 'Big "if".'

'Good girl.'

'Is this . . . is this because of Clare?'

'Clare?' He looks genuinely astonished. 'You think I'd throw away the best thing that's ever happened to me because my sister might get her knickers in a twist? I couldn't give a toss what anyone thinks, you should know that by now. She'd have come round, anyway. Clare's got a good heart. She might have been a bit sniffy for a while, but she'd have got over it.'

'Xan, you're not making any sense—'

'I know. I don't expect you to understand. I don't fucking understand myself. Trust me, self-sacrifice is not in my nature.' He picks up my glass and hands it back to me. 'Come on, darling. Drink up.'

'I realize this is a silly question,' I say, 'but I went to a lot of trouble to squeeze into this dress. I don't suppose you'd like to help me out of it?'

Xan nearly chokes on his champagne.

'Oh, come on.' I reach for his belt buckle. 'Didn't you know the condemned woman is entitled to a last shag?'

'You, my girl, are a total slut,' he whispers, pulling down my dress and fastening his mouth on my nipple.

I free his cock. 'Tart.'

'Tease.'

'Bastard.'

'I love you,' he sighs.

'I love you too,' I breathe.

I don't know which of you is worse,' Kirsty says. 'Clare, for not throwing that tosser out months ago when she found out he'd nicked millions off her, or you for letting her brother dump you and then shagging the arse off him anyway.'

'At least I got an orgasm out of it,' I say. 'Three, actually.'

'So, are you two back together?'

I prop myself up on my elbow and pick fretfully at her duvet cover. 'Not really. Friends with benefits, maybe. I don't know. I don't get it. I know he likes me. He made this big song and dance about not wanting to break up with me, but then he goes and does it anyway.'

'Maybe he's like Superman: too busy saving the world to have a girlfriend.'

'If he starts wearing his Y-fronts outside his trousers, I'll let you know.'

Kirsty settles herself cross-legged on her pillow. 'Seriously, Jen. Are you really OK about this?'

'I've had better days, but I'll get over it. I knew going in it was never going to be a long-term thing.' I sigh. 'To be honest, after Jamie, I'm kind of over the whole sexy-but-damaged routine. Right now I'd settle for a nice dull teacher or policeman who's kind to his mother and remembers my birthday.'

'The nice ones are the worst,' Kirsty warns.

'Looks like it's just going to be me and Clare, then. Isn't that going to be cosy? Two sad cows sitting at home with our cocoa. I might even take up knitting.'

'You just need to get back on the horse. Come out with me on Friday. There's a new club just opened off the King's Road. I know one of the bouncers, I bet I could get us in—'

'Not really in the mood. Sorry. Anyway, I don't want to leave Clare on her own yet. She's still really upset about Marc.'

'Why? I thought you said she was having a fling with that American?'

'I don't know if it's a fling,' I say quickly. 'They were only talking when I saw them.'

'Horny cow,' Kirsty giggles. 'Bet they're at it all the time.'

I shift uncomfortably. I should never have said anything to Kirsty. If she mentions it to Fran, Clare will die of embarrassment. She's got enough on her plate right now, I think protectively. She doesn't need the whole Gucci set gossiping about her love life.

I unfold myself from the bed. 'Actually, Kirsty, she's really cut up about Marc leaving. She hasn't stopped crying for a week. She keeps going on and on about not wanting the twins to come from a broken home. Davina made me promise to drag her by force if necessary to her divorce lawyer tomorrow. I think she's terrified Clare will take him back if he comes home.'

'You know, you've totally got Clare over a barrel. You should ask for another pay rise.'

'It's not always about money,' I say sharply. 'I *like* Clare. She can be a pain in the arse sometimes, but she's really nice. She doesn't look down her nose at me. She *needs* me.'

Kirsty grins unrepentantly. 'That's exactly why it's the time to ask.'

Our farewells are a little cool. Sometimes Kirsty can be a bit . . . *hard*. She's my best friend and everything, but I don't think I'd want her to look after my children. I know she'd take care of them, and look after them properly, but if I was a mother I'd want to know my kids were *loved*.

Clare's already in bed when I get home, even though it's not yet ten. I lie awake in the dark, listening to her muffled sobs next door. I'm a bit more upset about Xan than I let on to Kirsty, but what's happened to Clare makes my romantic upset look like a toddler's tantrum.

To my surprise, when I knock on her door at seven the next morning, she's already up and dressed. She looks like a corpse, but at least she's getting on with it.

'Are you sure you don't want me to come with you?' I ask. 'I can drop the twins at the Hurlingham—'

'I'll be fine. Nicholas Lyon is an old friend. Anyway,' she adds firmly, 'I'm sure this will be sorted out soon. It was just a silly row. Marc's probably nursing a hangover at Hamish's and wishing he could come back home. I wouldn't even be bothering Nicholas if Davina hadn't made such a fuss.'

She sweeps blusher feverishly across her cheeks.

'I could throw some spaghetti together tonight, if you

like,' I offer. 'It's about the only grown-up food I can do, apart from beans on toast.'

'Don't you have a date tonight?'

'Not any more,' I say casually.

Clare puts the brush down and turns to face me.

'Jenna,' she says carefully, 'I know I might not seem the best person to talk to about romance right now, but I do have eyes in my head. I can see how well you and Xan have been getting on. If you and he . . . if the two of you . . . well, I wouldn't mind if something happened. Not that I'd have any right to mind, of course,' she adds hastily. 'But please don't let me spoil anything. You don't get many chances to be happy. Hang on to them when they come along.'

'Never mind about me,' I say robustly. 'You've got enough to worry about. I'll be fine.'

She doesn't look fine as she leaves the house. She looks fragile and pale and very, very nervous. I hope this Nicholas Lyon has a big box of tissues. He'd better not let her roll over and give that wanker Marc everything he asks for. She's too bloody nice for her own good.

I'm in the kitchen drinking my tenth cup of coffee when the front door slams so hard I'm surprised it doesn't come off its hinges.

'The bastard!' Clare cries, throwing her bag on the table. 'He's been *planning* this! He's already filed for divorce on the grounds of *my* unreasonable behaviour! Mine!'

I nearly drop my mug in surprise. I've never seen her so furious.

'He says I'm an unfit mother! He claims I tried to poison Poppy; he's accused me of being violent and unstable and refusing to sleep with him. Well, that last bit's true, but the rest of it! It's ridiculous! He wouldn't even know which end to put the nappy on, and he's going for custody!'

'He'll never win. They're only six months old; no way will a judge give them to him.'

'I can't believe it,' she seethes. 'After everything he's done! I'm sorry, Jenna, but this is the last straw.'

'What are you going to do?'

Clare flips open her phone diary. 'I'll tell you what I'm going to do. I'm going to bloody bury him.'

Clare cancels every credit card, freezes their joint account, and even takes him off the car insurance. Legally, she can do nothing about the house (though at least she doesn't need to change the locks) or his repeated demands, through his lawyer, for access to the twins. But she has every stitch of his clothes couriered to the hotel in London where he's staying, along with the books and files from his study, and the hideous mounted boar's head she's always hated. As Dad says when Mum goes off on one about something, 'I don't know what effect she'll have on the enemy, but by God, she terrifies me.'

I watch her pack up his boxes, amazed at how tough she's being. Clare being Clare, she doesn't snoop through his private files first. I know I would.

It's as if she's boxing up their entire marriage, I think, as she tosses in a silver-framed photograph of the two of them on their honeymoon. She'd have forgiven him almost anything, except threatening to take her children. He crossed a line when he did that, and as far as she's concerned there's no going back.

A week later, a postcard arrives for me from San Francisco. I study the photograph on the front for a long time, picturing Xan standing on the Golden Gate Bridge, surrounded by gorgeous American girls flashing their perfect white American teeth and tossing their glossy American pony-tails. I imagine them begging him to say something for them in his sexy British accent. The photograph blurs, and I blink back tears.

'Shall we read it?' I ask Poppy.

She giggles, and knocks over her castle of empty yoghurt pots. I put her bowl of puréed parsnip in front of her, and step back out of range.

'"Missing you more than you know,"' I read. 'We miss Uncle Xan too, don't we? Especially at bedtime. "Look after Clare for me. Hope you enjoy your birthday present." Birthday present?' I lift Poppy's elbow out of her bowl, and wipe it. She puts it straight back in again. 'My birthday isn't till August. What's Uncle Xan up to?'

'Blah bup,' Poppy says.

'My thoughts exactly.'

She woke up with a bit of a fever this morning, but she seems fine now. I don't blame Clare for being a bit freaked out after our last medical drama, but she really didn't need to keep either of them home today. I'm glad I took Rowan to Baby Swim after all. It's nice to spend time alone with Poppy. I can give her a bit more attention than I'm able to when I've got both of them.

I hear the front door. 'Mummy's home early,' I tell Poppy. 'Isn't that nice?'

Clare comes into the kitchen and goes straight to hug Poppy, heedless of the puréed parsnip smeared all over her daughter. She wouldn't have done that a week or two ago.

'Everything OK?'

She gives Poppy a final squeeze and brushes crumbs from her jacket. 'It is now. Where's Rowan? Down for a nap?'

'Actually, after you left, he seemed much better.' I wipe Poppy's face and lift her out of the high chair. 'I don't think he had a temperature at all; it was normal when I took it, anyway. I didn't want him to miss out, so I took him to Baby Swim after all.'

'No!' Clare cries.

'He was fine, honestly. I wouldn't have let him go if I thought—'

'You don't understand. Marc's just called me. He said he was going to the Hurlingham – I didn't think it mattered, I thought they were safe here at home.' She collapses into a kitchen chair. 'Oh God, Jenna, what am I going to do?'

It takes me a moment to clue in.

'He's just trying to upset you. He's not going to do anything.'

'He will. You don't know how angry he is.' She leaps up again, searching her bag for her car keys. 'I have to get there first. I've got to stop him—'

'You don't have time. Call the club and tell them not to let Marc near Rowan.'

I soothe Poppy as Clare demands to be put through to the Baby Swim class. She explains three times, to three different people, that her son must not be allowed to go home with his father. 'No,' she snaps, 'I don't have a court order. Yes, I realize that – yes, Marc is his father. Look, can you please just go and *find my son*?'

She paces the kitchen, the phone clamped to her ear.

'It'll be OK,' I reassure her. 'Even if Marc's taken him,

he's not going to do anything. Where would he go? He'll bring him back once he's given you a good scare.'

'Supposing he doesn't? Supposing he takes him to Canada or— Yes, yes, I'm still here. Have you found him?'

I know the answer even before she drops her phone and turns to me, her eyes wide with shock.

'What am I going to do? Jenna, what should I do?'

I don't hesitate. 'We have to go to the police. I'm sure he's not going to try to leave the country or anything stupid, but they'll know what to do, just in case. At least it'll stop him pulling a stunt like this again.'

Sensible, law-abiding Clare makes me abandon the car on a double-yellow – 'Who cares about parking tickets *now*?' – and runs into the police station, Poppy in her arms.

'Please,' she cries, 'please, my husband's taken my baby!'

The receptionist picks up a telephone, a door opens, and we're suddenly surrounded by people and bombarded with questions. There is a moment or two of confusion over Poppy – 'I thought you said your husband had taken the baby?' 'Her *twin*! He took her *twin*!' – and then Clare is separated from me and ushered into a private room at the end of the hall.

As the crowd thins, I recognize Brendan, one of the two cops who gave Xan and me a ride in their police car. 'Jenna! What are you doing here?'

'Clare is Xan's sister. I'm her nanny.'

'I need you to give me some background,' he says, walking me briskly down a narrow corridor to an inter-view room. 'First, is there a restraining order against the father?'

'He and Clare only split up two weeks ago. They haven't even been to court yet.'

'So what makes her think he's taken the baby? For good, I mean.'

I explain about Marc, the threatening phone call, the sudden abduction of Rowan from his Baby Swim class.

'But he *is* the child's father?' Brendan says again.

'Well, obviously, but—'

'So there's no legal bar to his access? No reason he shouldn't pick his son up?'

'Look, Clare's not overreacting!' I cry indignantly. 'Marc said he was going to take him somewhere she'd never find them! He means it, he's got this whole bag filled with money hidden under the stairs—'

'What do you mean?' Brendan says sharply.

'I found a holdall under the stairs about a week before they split up,' I admit. 'It was filled with hundred-dollar bills. Maybe a hundred thousand dollars altogether?'

'Did you mention this to Clare?'

'I didn't think it was any of my business,' I say awkwardly. 'I didn't want her thinking I'd been poking around. And then Marc walked out, and after that I just . . . forgot.'

I suddenly realize the implications of what I've said. Oh, God. Marc planned this from the beginning. That cash was his fuck-you money. If I'd told Clare, none of this would have happened.

'It's OK,' Brendan says kindly. 'It's not your fault. This may have nothing to do with it. Let's just take one step at a time.'

We both know that's not true, but it's nice of him to say so.

He leaves me alone in the interview room for what seems like hours. Voices murmur outside, and at one point a secretary comes in to take down my name and address again. Fear makes me nervous and angry. Why are they wasting time? Marc could be getting on a plane to God knows where! Why don't they *do* something?

Finally, the door opens to admit a senior-looking officer with lots of gold buttons and a self-important expression. Behind him, Brendan can't quite meet my eye.

'What's going on?' I ask, looking from one to the other. 'Have you found him?'

'I think we need to take a step back,' the older cop says pompously. 'I'm sure they've just gone for an ice-cream and forgotten the time. Why don't you take the mother home and put the kettle on? I'm sure they'll be back before you know it—'

'Put the *kettle* on?'

'I understand the same lady was here a few months ago,' he says, glancing at Brendan for confirmation. 'She reported the two children missing, and it turned out they were safe and sound with the lady's brother and you, miss.'

'This is different!' I yell. 'He's *taken* Rowan. Why don't you get it?'

The arsehole cop presses his lips together. 'We've got the details, miss. If the little boy isn't back in twenty-four hours, we can issue an alert—'

'It'll be too late by then!'

The door opens again, and a policewoman ushers Clare in. She looks ten years older than she did this morning. Dark circles smudge her eyes, and her face is pinched and drawn.

'Clare, I'm so sorry I didn't tell you about the money!' I

burst out. 'I had no idea Marc was going to do something like this. I didn't think it mattered—'

She shrugs dully. 'Even if you'd told me, it wouldn't have made any difference.'

'But maybe you could have stopped him—'

'Let's go home,' she says tiredly. 'This is hopeless, Jenna. No one believes me. They probably think I've abducted him myself. We'll find Rowan ourselves. I'll call Davina. She'll know what to do.'

'I have a friend in the Canadian High Commission,' Davina says briskly. 'They'll have a watch on the airports by the time his plane lands. If that's where he's gone, of course, though I can't think where else he'd be. You need to go and see Nicholas Lyon again first thing in the morning, Clare. He'll deal with the legal end of things.' She sighs. 'The Canadians are a bit French, admittedly, but they're perfectly civilized. We'll soon have this all sorted out.'

Clare refuses to go to bed, spending a sleepless night fully clothed in an armchair downstairs, ready to leave at a moment's notice if Rowan is found. Upstairs, I pace the hallways with a fretful and miserable Poppy, who's clearly unsettled by the absence of her twin. I should have told Clare about the bag of money before. I just didn't think of it. How could I be so *stupid*?

The next morning, she insists I go with her to see the divorce lawyer, for moral support. We're ushered into Nicholas Lyon's conference room by a sympathetic secretary, who pours us coffee and offers us doughnuts and warm croissants. As if either of us could eat.

Nicholas comes in and gives Clare a warm hug. 'Don't

panic,' he tells her firmly. 'We're going to get Rowan back. I've already been in touch with the Canadian Consulate, and the moment Marc sets foot in the country he'll be brought before a Canadian court and ordered to return Rowan to the UK.'

'Suppose he refuses?' she asks anxiously.

'Canada is a signatory to the Hague Convention on Child Abduction. He'll be forced to bring Rowan back here so that the matter can be decided by a British court.'

Why is everyone so fixated on Canada? That's the first place everyone will look; and, if I were Marc, the last place I'd go.

'How are you going to force him?' I demand. 'I mean, all these conventions and stuff are fine, but haven't we actually got to *find* him first?'

'There's a port alert in place, Jenna,' Nicholas says. 'As soon as he arrives, they'll hold him. Don't worry, they're very much on the ball. One of the more helpful by-products of all the 9/11 security,' he adds wryly.

And if he's not in Canada? I think. *What then?*

When Rowan and Marc have been missing for twenty-four hours, the police finally take Clare seriously. An alert is issued, but it's as if Marc's vanished into thin air. He doesn't use his credit cards, an ATM or even his mobile phone. I start to wonder if Clare's right, and Marc *has* done something terrible.

For three days we don't leave the house, jumping every time the phone rings. If Clare loses any more weight, she'll snap. I wish I could get in touch with Xan. He's the only person I can think of who might help Clare through this.

On the fourth day, Nicholas calls.

'I've just heard: Marc and Rowan were on a British Airways flight to Lebanon three days ago,' he says wearily when I pick up the phone. 'I'm afraid we've lost him.'

I feel sick. This is my fault. I was the one who left Rowan at the swim class. I didn't tell Clare about the money. I let this happen.

Even Nicholas sounds defeated. He explains that Lebanon isn't a signatory to the Hague Convention. If Marc doesn't bring Rowan back of his own accord, Clare will never find him. She may never see her son again.

Davina hires a private investigator with contacts in Lebanon, but we have so little to go on. We have no idea which part of the country he's in, or even if he stayed there. It's like looking for a needle in a haystack full of needles.

In desperation, Clare calls Marc's parents in Montreal, but they either won't, or can't, help us. I wouldn't be surprised if his mother put him up to this. According to Clare, she's never approved of her career-oriented daughter-in-law.

With every day that passes, Clare gets quieter and more withdrawn. It's as if the life's being sucked out of her. She's lost all interest in her shops; desperate to distract her, I insist on driving the three of us to Fulham every morning, and we sit and watch Poppy playing at our feet in her baby gym, blissfully unaware of the drama going on around her. She misses Rowan, but she's only seven months old. She has no comprehension of what has happened. How could she?

For her sake, I try to stick to our old routine as much as possible. I take her to Baby Swim (Clare sits at the side of the pool, taut as a bowstring, constantly scanning the water) and to the park. Every night I bathe her and put her to bed, trying not to notice the empty space where her brother should be. Clare won't let me wash Rowan's sheets, or make up the cot properly. It's as if Rowan has died.

One night, four weeks after Rowan has vanished, I'm upstairs dressing Poppy in her pink pyjamas, trying to tame her dark curls with a soft teddy-bear hairbrush. A particularly wild tendril keeps getting in her eyes, so I reach for the nail scissors to trim it for her.

'What do you think you're doing?'

I jump. Clare stands in the doorway; Rowan's blanket, as ever these days, is in her hand. She watches me coldly for a few moments.

'I said, what do you think you're doing?'

'Her hair was getting in her eyes—'

'Did I say you could cut it?'

'No, but—'

She crosses the room and snatches the scissors out of my hand. 'I'll decide if I want my daughter's hair cut, thank you. I'm Poppy's mother, not you. You *work* for me. You're not her family. You have no right.'

'I just thought—'

'I don't pay you to think. I pay you to do your job.'

I pick up the hairbrush again. She can't help it. Given what she's going through, it's amazing she's still sane.

I read somewhere once that 90 per cent of parents split up after they lose a child. They're so consumed by their own grief, they don't have time for each other. They turn in on themselves, and instead of being drawn closer by their shared loss, they're driven further apart.

Clare doesn't seem to understand that I'm hurting too. She barely speaks to me; she's like a stranger these days.

She's always been self-controlled, but she's so tightly wound now, I'm terrified what might happen if the dam breaks.

She doesn't apologize for her outburst the next morning, or even ask if I mind working yet another Saturday; I haven't had a day off since Marc took Rowan. Instead, we go to the Fulham shop as usual. I flick on the computer in the corner of the shop and go through the staff rotas while Clare sits on the floor and plays with Poppy. After a while, I swivel and watch her. She doesn't have an ounce of patience to spare for anyone else these days, but she'll sit and thread flowers on a fine wire for her daughter as if she can think of nothing else she'd rather be doing. Two months ago, the idea of spending ten minutes entertaining Poppy would have scared the shit out of her.

I'm distracted by the doorbell, and look up.

Clare gets to her feet as Cooper Garrett walks in, still wearing his long leather coat, apparently heedless of the summer heat, as dusty and travel-stained as if he's just ridden across the desert with a vital message to save the world.

'I've found your son,' he says.

Juilliard

Dance Drama Music

60 Lincoln Center Plaza
New York
NY 10023-6588
(212) 799 5000

Mr. C. Garrett
Garrett Plantation
St James
NC 28777

August 21, 1978

Dear Mr Garrett,

It is with deepest sympathy we offer our condolences on the recent sad loss of your parents. We accept your withdrawal from our program for the upcoming semester with regret. We hope you and your family are able to draw comfort from one another at this time of such sorrow.

    Naturally we understand your decision to postpone your studies to care for your brother, particularly in light of his youth. It will doubtless be a great consolation to him to have you at home. However, you show great promise as a pianist, and we would like to assure you that a place will remain open here for you, should you decide to take it up at a later date.

    Once again, we extend our warmest sympathies to you and your family.

Yours sincerely,

Sarah Greene
Director of Admissions

15

Cooper

Lolly was right. She tends to be: the advantage of eighty-some years on this planet. She's taken care of me since the day I was born; if she says there's such a thing as love at first sight, I believe her.

I walk into Clare's flower shop on a bright May morning, my head filled with Ella. I've thought of nothing else since she pitched up two months ago in North Carolina, my brother's ashes in an urn tucked under her arm. Jackson's mysterious widow: the woman who was married to him for eleven years, and cheated on him for most of them.

I fucked her out of revenge, and then found I couldn't forget her. Trying not to think about Ella is like telling someone not to think of pink elephants: suddenly it's all you can imagine. I'm so eaten up with anger, I have nothing else left. Anger at Jackson, for dying at forty-two and making a mockery of everything I've given up; anger at Ella, for stealing my breath and robbing my soul.

Anger most of all at myself, for letting any of it matter a damn.

And then Clare looks up, her sad smile reaching her tired eyes, and my anger evaporates like it never was, and I realize: *Lolly was right.*

I'm forty-nine years old: cynical, battle-hardened, bitter and weary. I have no one, love no one, bar Lolly, an eighty-two-year-old black spinster who has nowhere else to go. I lost my parents in a fire at seventeen; I turned my back on music and Juilliard to look after my brother, and now I've lost him too. In my years as a journalist, I've seen human nature in all its forms; I've witnessed the best and worst it has to offer. I've grieved for the charred corpses of children bombed in Baghdad and interviewed a mother in New Orleans who gave birth to her baby in a tree during the floods. I've been there, done that, and I thought I'd lost my ability to be surprised.

'How can I help?' Clare asks pleasantly.

Words are my living. Every intelligent one deserts me.

'Flowers,' I blurt.

Flowers? Dear God, is that the best you can do? You're in a flower shop, for Chrissakes. Of course flowers! Flying carpets are next door.

Clare moves towards a bank of pink peonies; and suddenly I hear my mother's slow Southern drawl as she guides me, an itchy, impatient boy of nine, around her hothouse: 'The peony grants its recipient the power to keep a secret. Be careful who you give them to, Cooper.' Forty years later, and the memory is sharp enough to make me feel the punch of loss in my gut.

'Not those,' I say. 'She has enough secrets.'

Clare looks at me properly for the first time. Suddenly

it's important she doesn't see me as another customer, an ignorant American. It's important that she *sees* me. I almost forget why I'm buying flowers at all.

'Yellow tulips?' she suggests, with a dryness I only notice later.

'Hopeless love and devotion? Hardly. Nor,' I add, as she reaches for anemones, 'abandonment.'

Wedding ring on her finger. I'm ambushed by a blaze of disappointment.

A clerk babbles behind me. I still can't take my eyes off Clare, though of course I don't yet know that's her name. I only discover later that she has twin babies, a boy and a girl, whose existence amazes and terrifies her in equal measure, and a husband she talks of as if he's a third child. I don't know that she's the most honest, trustworthy person I will ever meet, that she's exhausted, bled dry, with the effort of trying to take care of everything and everyone, that her worst enemy is herself. All I know is that I've met the woman I was meant to marry; and she's married to someone else.

I only learn these details of her life later, but by then they don't matter; the bell has rung. I return to her flower shop two and three times a week, unable to keep away. I don't fail to appreciate the irony: in order to see Clare, I have to feign obsession with Ella. I turn down an important assignment from *Time* magazine. I spend a fortune on London taxis. I apologize to Jackson a thousand times in my head for not getting it: for not understanding what you would do for a woman, the right woman.

I know from the start it's pointless. A woman like Clare would never cheat on her husband. If she did, she wouldn't be the woman for me.

The Cradle Snatcher

I can't stay in London for ever, I tell myself, pushing open the door to Clare's shop and stepping into the damp gloom one afternoon in mid-June. Sooner or later, I'll have to pick up my life. I'm used to being alone. Jackson's dead, but he lived half a world away. Nothing's really changed. So why in hell do I feel so lonely?

Clare emerges from the back room, and I savour her smile of recognition. *The small things.*

'How's Ella this week?' she asks.

'Recovering at home.'

'Oh, I'm so pleased.'

Ella has just gotten engaged to William; to my surprise, I find myself wishing them well. I glance at a bucket of zinnias. Not my favourite flowers, but they're cheerful, and I imagine Ella's tired of lilies. The zinnias, bold and brash and colourful, seem appropriate.

I never know how to talk to Clare, and so I just watch as she bundles up the flowers with a twist of raffia wrapped around her wrist. She always works fast, not wanting to keep me waiting; but it's the waiting I come here for. She's lost more weight, I note with concern. I can count the knobs of her spine through the thin knit sweater.

I remember the irritating assistant telling me about Clare's daughter last time I came in. Jackson had meningitis at fourteen. Lolly and I thought we'd lose him; it was the longest forty-eight hours of my life. Even the doctors were amazed at the speed of his recovery.

I fumble over the words. 'How's your daughter? Poppy, isn't it?'

She smiles. I'd give my right arm for that smile to be for me. 'She's much better. How did you—'

'Your colleague. Craig.'

'How kind of you to remember. She had us terribly worried for a few days, but she seems over it now. She had so much salt in her body, they thought I must have given it to her.' Suddenly, her voice cracks. 'The police came . . . it was so dreadful—'

I don't know what to say. The police in this God-forsaken country must be fucking idiots. It has to be obvious to anyone with half a brain that this woman would never poison her own child.

She rubs at her eyes like a child and hands me Ella's zinnias. *Ella*. One of the top paediatricians in London. I can do something for Clare, I realize. Finally.

I bolt for the door, already dialling Ella's number on my cell. ('She's the one, isn't she, Cooper?' Ella says, surprising me. 'The one you've stayed here for?') It doesn't occur to me that I'm changing everything. I'm crossing the line, breaking my own cast-iron rule: never get involved.

'Lunch,' I suggest to Clare, seizing my chance when I come back a few days later. 'You can thank me then'.

I don't for one minute expect her to say yes.

I feel like a fox in a henhouse in that flashy restaurant. I take her instead to the park – or to what passes for green space in this miserable, overcrowded island – and she slips off her shoes and walks in her bare feet on the browned grass. I tell her I've been assigned to chase down a Taliban story in the North West Frontier Province; though I don't add that I called *Time* magazine that morning and volunteered. It's time to get my head straight. I can't sit around London for the rest of my life, mooning over Clare like a lovesick teenager.

I tell her, though not quite in so many words, that I love her.

I'm not made of fucking stone. I can't go off and risk my neck with Clare thinking I'm in love with Ella. I'll probably never get this chance again; I want to lay down my marker now, just in case. Life's uncertain. If nothing else, Jackson's death taught me that.

How did my brother bear it, knowing his wife was in love with another man? *I couldn't share*, I realize. If Clare was mine, I couldn't share her.

Through the next three brutal weeks in Afghanistan, I think of her, often. She gave me no encouragement, made no promises; I didn't expect it. But her image is like a talisman in my pocket, a stone to touch when I need to experience something honest and real. I don't bother to explore the implications for the future of my love for her. I don't overdramatize it, or make the mistake of thinking it means anything cataclysmic. It just *is*.

I return to London thinner, browner and calmer. In an hour's time, I'll be on a plane back to the US. Jackson's death is still raw, but the shock has passed; I'm no longer raging at the world. Ella has slid painlessly into the past. Clare ... Clare I will always carry with me. Surprisingly, the thought is comforting.

My plane has barely touched down at Heathrow before my phone starts buzzing with texts and messages that have floated around the ether, unread and unheard, while I've been skulking in damp caves. I listen to the first one, and don't bother with the rest.

Before Ella has finished explaining to me about Rowan, I'm collecting my bag from the luggage carousel at Terminal One, slinging it over my shoulder and taking the subway straight to Terminal Four. Screw *Time*. Their story can wait.

'Cooper, this is crazy,' Ella exclaims. 'You can't just get on a plane to Beirut!'

'Why? Think they'll be overbooked?'

'I left you a message because I thought you'd want to know about Clare and Marc, not so you could drop everything and disappear off on a wild-goose chase. Don't you think there are already people out there looking for Rowan? I've had the police interview *me* twice. No one even knows if Marc's still in Beirut. He could be anywhere with Rowan by now.'

I slap my credit card on the British Airways ticket desk. 'I'll find him.'

'You don't even know where to start!'

'I'll find him,' I repeat.

The plane to Beirut is empty. I stretch out on three seats, balling my coat under my head. I've worked the Lebanese story for twenty-five years: the pitiless civil war, the Western hostage-taking, and the fragile renaissance – before the car bombs and assassinations started again – of the last decade. I know how easy it is to disappear here. Ask Terry Anderson, held hostage in plain sight for seven years. To the West, it was as if he'd vanished off the face of the Earth. No one knew if he was dead or alive until he was released.

But I also know that if you ask questions in the right places, eventually answers find their way back. No one ever truly disappears. There are always ripples.

Marc Elias may have been born in Lebanon, but he's a foreigner by all but blood. The ripples he makes will be noticed more than he realizes. Sooner or later, I'll find him.

I refuse to allow myself to think of Clare, grief-stricken

and desperate for her child; Clare, newly separated from her husband. I can't afford any distractions. What matters now is finding Rowan. Everything else can wait.

It takes me six days.

Josef, my driver, comes to me. '*Habibi*,' he says, 'I have a friend.'

It works the way it always does. His friend, Mehdi, has a friend. Zahir has a brother, whose wife has a cousin. Cousin Antoine meets me at a seafront café for coffee and *man'oushi zaatar*. We smoke cigarettes and stare companionably over the Mediterranean. I have a friend, says Antoine, in perfect English, who lives in Jounieh, a few miles from here. More of an acquaintance, really. This acquaintance was recently asked to find a babysitter for an uncle. A widower, newly arrived from America. Or London. Perhaps Canada? His friend, or acquaintance, recommended his sixteen-year-old sister, who came home that night with stories of a sad baby with big blue eyes. Antoine shrugs. It could be nothing. It could be something. He'll arrange for me to meet the sister. It will be expensive, he warns.

I meet Rania the next day. Yes, she says, folding three hundred-dollar bills into her pocket. A blond, blue-eyed boy who cries all the time for his mother.

Rowan.

But we have to be sure. So Josef takes me to Jounieh, a high-rise sprawl across the slopes of a large bay north of Beirut. During the civil war, this was the Christian East. You took your life in your hands crossing the Green Line, the no man's land in downtown Beirut that divided it from the Muslim West. Josef risked his life for me a dozen times. I can count the number of men I trust on the fingers of one hand. Josef is among them.

A new American-style six-lane highway cuts through the mountains from Beirut to Jounieh. The Lebanese drive as if it's still a dirt free-for-all. Neon signs blink fitfully on all sides. Washing is draped between apartment buildings still pock-marked with bullet holes from the war. Somewhere, hidden in this concrete jungle, is Clare's son.

Josef takes me deep into an unfamiliar neighbourhood. We stop at a café on the corner of two narrow, gritty city streets with old movie posters peeling from the walls. We drink thick, burnt coffee, and we wait. An hour passes, then two. We smoke filterless cigarettes. Every now and then, a small man with gold teeth comes over to our table and mutters in Arabic to Josef. I'm patient. This is the way it is in the Middle East. We share more coffee, sweet pastries, cigarettes.

Suddenly there's a commotion outside. A silver car with a badly painted green passenger door pulls up. Two youths get out, and the gold-toothed café owner goes out to talk to them. After a few minutes, he beckons. As soon as we get outside, Josef and I are hustled towards the vehicle. I would never get into a strange car in Lebanon without Josef. Even so, I'm alert to the tension in his shoulders. I have a bad feeling about this.

After fifteen minutes' uphill drive, we arrive in front of an elegant, faded apartment building high over the bay. We sit in the hot car, waiting. A young woman comes out, glancing nervously at the car and twisting her hands. The two youths go over to her. There is gesticulating, shouting; one of the boys shoves the woman in the shoulder. I put my hand on the door handle, and Josef holds me back with a warning arm across my chest.

Without explanation, the youths climb back in and we're

driven back to the café. Josef huddles in a corner with the gold-toothed owner, who smiles at me and shrugs: *Shit happens.*

'The man with the child left,' Josef explains in low tones. 'Someone warned him an American was looking for him. He was there until twenty minutes before we arrived.'

Josef and I wait down the street in our own car until the youths have gone, and the café owner comes out alone. We follow him as he walks through the town, keeping well back, but he doesn't look round. He turns a corner and stops to hawk on the ground and scratch his ass. I grab Josef's jacket from the back seat and leap out of the car, throwing it over the man's head and bodily tossing him on to the back seat of the vehicle. He weighs perhaps a hundred pounds soaking wet. Josef guns the engine and races up into the hills. I pin the man, who's screaming in terror, flat against the seat. No one has even noticed us.

Josef doesn't stop till he reaches a deserted car park high over the city. I press my knee into the café owner's back, shoving his face into the leather seat.

'Now imagine you're seven months old,' I snarl.

'Please, *habibi*!' the man cries, his voice muffled. 'He said he'd kill me!'

'He's not here. I am.' I tighten my grip. '*Talk.*'

Ever since Ella broke the news, I've refused to permit myself to think about Clare in any other context than as Rowan's mother. I haven't dared to wonder what might happen now that she's free. She made no promises.

But now that I'm with her, separated by a few inches of charged, electrified air, it's impossible to maintain my resolve. We sit next to each other on the plane to Beirut, my second such journey in a week; almost, but not quite, touching. Occasionally, our elbows brush on the armrest, and we both jump as if burned. Neither of us can look the other in the eye.

Jenna leans across the aisle and taps my shoulder, breaking the spell. 'Are you *sure* it was Rowan?'

I nod curtly. Wissam Ghanour, the gold-toothed café owner, was surprisingly helpful once we persuaded him to our point of view. He took us to the 'safe house' Marc had pre-arranged with him, a two-storey building off the main road back to Beirut. The three of us waited in the car until it got dark, and we were able to see movement through the uncurtained windows. One blond baby looks much like another, especially one you've never seen in person; but I'd studied the photograph of Marc until it was burned on my retina. I recognized him the moment he walked into view. We had the right place.

Yesterday, Josef arranged a brief vacation for Ghanour in the Bekaa Valley with some of his relatives, while I flew back to Britain for Clare. I hated to involve her, but I had no choice. Besides, she's his mother. How much more involved could she be?

'How do you know Marc won't have vanished again since yesterday?' Jenna presses. 'Why didn't you just take Rowan when you had the chance?'

'I don't have his passport, in case you'd forgotten,' I say tersely. 'Even if I had, I'd never have got him back into Britain without Clare. An American man, travelling alone with a British child who has a different name? Alarm bells would've gone off in all directions.'

'So why didn't you go to the Lebanese police? They do *have* police here, right?'

'Don't be damn ridiculous—'

'Jenna, if Rowan gets caught up in the Lebanese legal system, I might never get him back,' Clare interrupts. She leans across me, her white shirt pulling tight across her breasts. 'Nicholas warned us: fathers nearly always get custody of children in Beirut, especially if they're boys. It could take years for an appeal to be heard, and even then I probably wouldn't win. It's too risky.'

'But you—'

'Please, Jenna,' Clare sighs. 'Listen to Cooper.'

Jenna shrugs, and picks up her magazine.

Clare sinks back into her seat, closing her eyes. I glare at Jenna. The girl's a real pill; I wouldn't have brought her, but we need to get close to Rowan, and a woman is less likely to attract attention. Clare's far too blonde and recognizable. She stands out like a sore thumb. With her dark hair, Jenna could pass for European Lebanese. She may be a pain in the ass, but the girl's our best shot.

We land at Beirut Airport, a vast new marble concourse very different from the crowded, sweltering concrete shoebox of the civil war days. Jenna and Clare collect their visas and we hurry outside. The humidity is smothering. Even this late at night, we're all sweating by the time Josef pulls up to the kerb to collect us.

He drops us at an anonymous small hotel in Hamra, the busy downtown shopping and commercial district of Beirut. It's full of tourists: an easy place to blend in. Plus, the manager owes me. Anyone starts asking about us, I'll be the first to know.

'I think I'll call Davina,' Clare says anxiously. 'I know it's late, but she's never looked after Poppy before. She's really not very good with babies—'

Jenna snorts. 'Mrs Lampard's the one who'll be changing the shitty nappies. Stop worrying. Poppy will be fine.'

'I know, but . . . honestly, I won't be long. I'll see you in a few minutes.'

'Don't get gung-ho on me,' I warn Jenna as we find a discreet corner in the bar. 'This isn't going to be easy. Clare's entitled to have access to her child. Whereas you—'

'Name, rank and serial number. I get it.'

'You need to understand what you're letting yourself in for.'

'You said. Forget it, Cooper. I'm in.'

She has balls, I'll give her that.

Clare returns downstairs. I notice other men in the bar watching her. Exhausted and sick with nerves, she still has an indefinable *something* that turns heads.

Her eyes flicker around the room, and then find mine. Her shoulders relax slightly. Or do I just imagine that?

'I'm going to bed,' Jenna yawns. 'I'll see you in the morning.'

Clare takes the seat she's just vacated. 'I'll be up in a minute, Jenna. Can you leave me the bed next to the phone?'

'How was Poppy?' I ask, as she picks fretfully at the arm of her chair.

'How was Davina, you mean,' Clare says tiredly. 'Jenna must have powers of persuasion I don't: Davina would never have agreed to mind Poppy if I'd asked. Anyway, they're all fine. Davina spoke to Nicholas this evening. He'll file a residence order as soon as we get home. That should make it much harder for Marc to leave the country if he tries to take Rowan again.'

Josef has already asked if I want Marc to be permanently taken out of the picture, an offer I reluctantly declined. He finds our Western reliance on the rule of law a strange way to do business.

'Clare, we *will* get Rowan back,' I reassure her. 'We know where he is. Someone's been watching the house since we found them. Marc's not going to get away again.'

She drops her gaze to her lap. 'But what about afterwards?' she whispers. 'What's to stop him doing this again? I can't play ping-pong with my children. Maybe next time Marc will take both of them. Maybe I . . . maybe I *should* let him keep Rowan. At least I'd still have Poppy.'

'Marc may be planning to come back for Poppy anyway,' I say gently. 'It was only luck she wasn't with Rowan. You can't think like that, Clare. Your son needs *you*.'

Her expression is anguished. 'I know I'm not a good mother, Cooper, but I don't deserve to lose my children, do I? First Poppy nearly died, and now Rowan's been taken from me. What do I have to do to show I'm sorry?'

'You have nothing to be sorry for,' I say forcefully. I take her hands in my own, forcing her to look up. 'Clare, listen to me. You *are* a good mother. But good doesn't mean perfect. Good doesn't mean you won't get tired and angry and make mistakes. No one gets it right all the time; or even most of it. You do your best, you fuck up, you figure out where you went wrong, and you fuck up again. You aren't perfect, and neither are your kids. But you're their mother, and you love them. In the end, that's all that counts.'

'Jenna's so patient and *organized*—'

'You think they give a damn how neat their closets are?'

'It's not just that—'

'You've got to get this idea that you've failed out of your head. This isn't a test. There aren't any perfect scores. What are you looking for, someone to tell you you've made class valedictorian?'

She blinks back tears. I fight not to pull her into my arms.

'Give yourself a break, Clare,' I say softly. 'So you're not Soccer Mom of the Year. You have a job. Sometimes your kids cry and you don't know what's wrong. Do you think any of that really matters?'

'Oh, Cooper. This isn't the kind of mother I ever intended to be . . .'

I thumb her tears away.

'None of us are the kind of parents we intended to be. If we even intended to be parents in the first place.' I think suddenly of Jackson, the closest I will ever get to a son. 'Clare, you're tearing yourself to pieces wondering if you're good enough. Don't you get it? The fact you even ask the question is your answer. Rowan and Poppy are lucky to have you.'

She catches my hand, and holds it against her cheek. 'What must you think of me? This is the second time you've rescued my children—'

'Next time,' I promise, 'it'll be you.'

'If we are to do this, *habibi*, we must do it soon,' Josef mutters. 'People are starting to ask questions about Wissam Ghanour.'

I glance back along the street. Josef and I have taken it

in turns to keep watch on the house for the past two days, while Jenna and Clare stay out of sight at various cafés and diners nearby. At night, I've made them return to the hotel, though not without a great deal of protest from Jenna.

So far, the only person to enter or leave is an old woman dressed in black, who arrives each day with a plastic bag of groceries and stays for a few hours. I figure she must be the new babysitter. I know Marc's still there; I've seen him moving about the house. But until he leaves Rowan alone with the sitter, we can't do anything. Josef is right; the longer we stay, the more risky this gets.

I leave him watching from a diner down the street, and drive back to the café where the girls are dragging out their fifth cups of coffee.

Clare looks up hopefully as I enter. Even though it's not my fault, I feel a bastard for letting her down yet again.

'He can't spend the rest of his life in there,' Jenna groans. 'Sooner or later he's going to drop his guard.'

'How has he managed to arrange all this?' Clare frets. 'He doesn't know anyone in Lebanon. How can he have rented a house and found a babysitter and done all this so fast?'

'It's not difficult. Money talks, and Marc had a lot of cash to throw around.'

Jenna looks at her feet.

'Sorry, kid.'

'I keep telling her it's not her fault,' Clare says. 'Even if I'd known Marc had so much cash, I'd never have thought he'd do something like this. I'd have assumed he was trying to steal my money, not my children.'

'Why don't we just bribe them more than he has?' Jenna suggests after a moment.

The thought has already occurred to me. Josef followed the old woman to a rundown tenement in the Armenian quarter the first day. I just don't know how likely she is to stay bought, by Marc or by me. If she double-crosses us, Marc could vanish again, and next time it might not be so easy to find him.

'We need to go,' I say, standing up. 'There's another—'

My phone rings.

'He's just left,' Josef says.

Clare's hand finds mine. Adrenalin that has nothing to do with the task in hand pumps round my body.

'Come on, Cooper,' Jenna snaps from the doorway.

The spell is broken. I have to let go of Clare's hand to drive, but every electron in my body zings with energy. I could move mountains. *Forty-nine years on the planet, and I never knew. Christ, what in hell have I been doing with my life?*

With a supreme effort, I force myself to concentrate.

'Are you sure about this, Jenna?' I ask for the final time as I park up a block away from the house. 'You know what to do?'

'Enough, already. Just keep your fucking phone switched on, all right?'

I hand her the temporary Lebanese cell. 'Hit nine on the speed-dial. I can be with you in two minutes.'

'You'd better be.'

We watch nervously as she walks towards the house. She's a tourist, we've decided; she's got lost, and wants to use the phone to call her friends. As soon as she sees Rowan, she's to grab him and bolt for the door. We don't have time for fancy cover stories, and anyway, none of us can think of one that'll seem halfway plausible. By the time

Marc finds out, we should be on our way to Syria. The plan is to fly out of Damascus, less than three hours' drive from here, rather than from Beirut: if Marc does give chase, he won't be expecting that.

Clare reaches for my fingers again, and squeezes so hard I lose all feeling in my hand.

'I don't know why you're doing this for me, but thank you,' she says quietly. 'I'll never be able to thank you enough.'

'You will,' I say. 'And you do know.'

The next ten minutes are the best and worst of my life. I feel as elated and confused as a teenager. I want to jump up and down on the hood of the car and scream her name; I want to flip down the seat and have her, here and now; I want to go down on one knee and ask her to marry me. More than anything, I want to make her smile again; to wipe that haunted, desperate expression from her eyes. Everything hangs in the balance. It all depends on Jenna.

The front door of the house opens again. Suddenly Jenna is running towards us, almost stumbling in her haste. She's holding something in her arms.

'Oh God,' Clare breathes, as I fling open the rear door.

Jenna throws herself into the car. 'I locked her in the loo, and pulled the sofa across the door,' she pants. 'It should give us another ten minutes.'

The bundle in her arms lets out a bewildered cry. Clare reaches between the seats for Rowan, tears streaming down her face as she pulls him into her arms. I can't stop smiling.

'Fucking hell, Cooper!' Jenna yells. 'Move it, would you!'

I throw the car into reverse, and pull a sharp 180. Clare buries her face in her child's hair, bracing herself against the dash with one hand. I glance in my rear-view as we pull out on to the main road, dirt spinning beneath our wheels. No one is following us. The street behind is empty.

I join the slip-road on to the highway, my eyes flicking constantly to the mirror. Another hundred yards, and we'll be free and clear.

Abruptly, we grind to a halt. I wind down the window and crane my head out. A few cars in front of us, two moped riders argue in the middle of the street, their scooters crumpled on the ground between them. A painted van covered with bells and harnesses noses out into the flow of traffic coming the other way. Within seconds the entire road is gridlocked. Bystanders gather round, adding their ten cents to the heated debate. I scan the side streets nearest to me, searching for a way around the chaos.

Clare moans softly and shrinks back in the front seat, clutching Rowan.

Threading his way through the traffic, a carton of cigarettes swinging from a clear plastic bag in his hand, is her husband.

Marc spots her seconds after she sees him. His astonished expression would be comical in any other circumstances.

For a moment, he seems frozen; then, with a howl of anger, he drops the cigarettes and launches himself towards us, ricocheting off the gridlocked traffic as he thrusts his way between cars. Vehicles are jammed ahead of and behind me, bumper to bumper: I have nowhere to go.

I reach across Clare, and open the passenger door. 'Get out. Double back and find Josef. I'll deal with Marc.'

'I can't just leave you—'

'Come on, Clare!' Jenna yells, tumbling out of the back seat and grabbing Clare's hand.

'Go on!' I urge. 'Josef will get you to Damascus. I'll meet you there. Please, Clare!'

She struggles out of the front seat. Rowan is screaming now, his face red and shiny with tears. Marc is just two cars away. Jenna reaches for Rowan, but Clare simply cradles him tighter against her chest.

I slam open my door, but a rust-bucket has crept up on my inside and blocked me in. With a snarl of frustration, I jam the door against the side of the ancient Mercedes and force myself through the gap. My coat snags, and I simply shrug it off.

Horns blare all around us. Marc puts his hand on the hood of a BMW and vaults across it, landing just feet from Jenna. She yanks Clare's hand and pulls her between two buses. I lose sight of them as I cut behind the painted van, flinging myself recklessly over cars and around motorcycles.

We've started to attract attention of our own. Volleys of Arabic fly from all directions. A Lebanese cop breaks off arguing with the two scooter riders to stare at us. His hand moves reflexively to the gun at his waist. My pulse quickens. The last thing we want is to involve the police.

Marc is the bigger and younger of the two of us, but he's clumsy and out of shape. I reach him just as the cop hitches up his belt and starts to head towards us.

With a loud laugh, I clap my arm round Marc's shoulder. '*Habibi!* My friend, I've missed you! It's good to see you! How are you? How's the wife?'

He tries to pull away, but my grip is steel.

'Who the hell are you?' Marc splutters.

'Your worst nightmare,' I hiss in his ear. I raise my voice, smiling broadly. 'It's been too long! I was starting to think you've been avoiding me!'

The cop hesitates, and turns back to the two riders. I shove Marc in the direction of the sidewalk, forcing him into the shadow of a bakery shop doorway. Behind me the traffic starts to move slowly around the scooters. Our vehicle, stationary in the middle of the street, is an island in the tide.

'I don't know who the fuck you are, you bastard,' Marc pants, freeing himself, 'but I'm going to break your fucking legs if you touch me again!'

'I don't think you're in any position to—'

'Wait.'

We both swing round. Clare is pale, but composed. In her arms, Rowan hiccups, and she drops a brief reassuring kiss on his forehead.

'I'm so sorry, Cooper,' she says, moving over to her husband, 'but I've changed my mind.'

MS SABRINA CHAGNON MD, MRCP, MRCOG
CONSULTANT OBSTETRICIAN AND GYNAECOLOGIST

The Portland Hospital
205 Great Portland Street
London W1N 6AH
Tel: 020 7390 8000
Fax: 020 7390 8888

The Homerton Hospital
Homerton Row
London E9 6SR
Tel: 020 8510 7300
Fax: 020 8510 7333

Mrs C Elias
97 Cheyne Walk
London
SW3 5TS

Monday, 14 December 2009

Dear Clare

Your booking investigations are all satisfactory. Your
haemoglobin was 12.8, your blood sugar is normal. You are
syphilis negative, HIV negative, hepatitis B negative and you are
immune to both German measles and chicken pox. Your blood
group is B positive with no abnormal antibodies. Your Down's
syndrome screening test gave a risk of 1 in 390. This in fact is
better than the risk due to your age alone (1 in 330).

I look forward to seeing you at your 20-week scan on
25 January 2010.

With best wishes
Yours sincerely

Sabrina Chagnon

16

Clare

'I'm so sorry, Cooper,' I say, moving over to Marc, 'but I've changed my mind.'

Jenna grabs my hand. 'Clare, come on! We don't have time for this!'

I don't move. We stare at one another, frozen in place like exhibits in a museum. Rowan presses his wet face into my neck, his tiny body heaving with silent sobs. Over his head I meet Cooper's eyes, willing him to understand: *I'll do anything for my children. Whatever it takes.*

Before I had the twins, I'd heard people talk about maternal love, of women who'd fight like a tigress for their child. I'd heard of it, but I didn't quite believe it. Now, I cannot imagine a world without Rowan and Poppy. To love a man is one thing, but to love a child is something else, something so consuming and all-encompassing, so *visceral*, it leaves room for nothing else.

Cooper was right. Being a good mother doesn't mean sewing in name-tapes and making potato-print paintings at the kitchen table. It has nothing to do with how many bedtime stories you read, the lavishness of the birthday parties, whether you work in an office or stay home to change nappies yourself. Nor is it even your willingness to throw yourself under a car for them, to take that speeding bullet. Being a good mother is a thousand, a hundred thousand, tiny sacrifices, a lifetime of putting someone else first. It's going without a new pair of shoes. It's never sleeping in on a Saturday morning.

It's putting up with a rotten marriage for twenty-five years because you have two children who need a family, a mother and a father, at home, together.

Cooper's words echo in my mind: *You are a good mother. But good doesn't mean perfect. Good doesn't mean you won't get tired and angry and make mistakes. You aren't perfect, and neither are your kids. But you're their mother, and you love them. In the end, that's all that counts.*

'I need to talk to Marc,' I say. 'Alone.'

'You can't be serious!' Jenna cries. 'Cooper, you can't let her do this! She's just scared, that's all. She doesn't mean it!'

For the first time, Marc seems to register what's going on. He steps forward, pushing his face into Cooper's. 'You heard my wife,' he snarls. 'Back off.'

Cooper doesn't flinch. 'Is this what you want?' he asks me curtly.

His expression is as cold and hard as granite. He could be a stranger. No trace, now, of the man who wiped my tears away with a touch so gentle and erotic that my body liquefied beneath it. I can still feel the electrifying brush of his skin against mine, and smell the clean, citrus smoke scent of his hair. I know exactly what I am giving up.

Whatever it takes.

'Yes,' I tell Cooper.

He turns away.

My heart thudding, I hand Rowan to Jenna. He clings to me in silent protest, fisting his small hands in my hair, too bewildered even to cry. Gently, I prise his fingers open. 'I won't be long, Jenna. You can wait in the car.'

Marc starts. 'Wait a minute—'

'Don't worry. I'm not going anywhere without my son.'

Two doors down, a small shop sells fizzy drinks and coffee. On the pavement in front of it are three iron tables emblazoned with faded brewery logos, and a couple of plastic chairs. I sit down at one of them while Marc buys two cans of cola. He puts one down in front of me with a grimy glass and a plastic straw in a paper wrap. I push the glass away and open the straw.

Despite his belligerent expression, Marc seems diminished somehow, less sure of himself. There are new lines around his eyes, and he's gained weight. For the first time, I wonder at the toll this has taken on him. He's lost his job, his home, his family. He's effectively on the run, living out of a suitcase with a diminishing pile of cash. I realize he may want to find a way out of this as much as I do.

I wait for him to speak, letting him take control of the conversation. We may have found Rowan, but he still holds all the cards.

'So,' he says, with an unpleasant over-confidence that tells me he's just as nervous as I am. 'Who's the American heavy?'

'A friend. How long are you planning to stay here?' I ask pleasantly.

'We were doing fine, if that's what you mean. We don't need you.'

I smile nicely. 'I can see that. Rowan looks wonderful. He's really grown. Poppy's been missing him terribly, of course. She's just cut another tooth, by the way. She kept us up for three nights while it came through.'

'You should have rubbed whisky on her gum. That always helps.'

I nod. 'Yes, of course. I should have thought of that.'

'Rowan's missed her too,' he adds, grudgingly. 'Especially at night.'

'Well. They're used to sleeping next to each other.'

Marc picks up his sweating can of cola, and studies the Arabic writing on its side like a biblical scholar presented with the Dead Sea Scrolls. I wait him out. I know my husband. He's a defiant child, bewildered at the way his small rebellion suddenly got out of hand. He wants nothing more than to come in from the cold, if only his pride will let him.

'You wouldn't listen,' he accuses me suddenly. 'I tried to talk to you, but you wouldn't listen.'

'Is that why you took Rowan?' I ask mildly. No rebukes. A simple question.

'I didn't think you wanted him. Either of them. You were always busy working, or else there was Jenna. I didn't think you'd even miss them. You said you wished you'd never had children. I thought I'd be doing you a favour.'

'I didn't mean it, Marc. I was just tired and overwhelmed. You knew that.'

He spreads his hands on the metal table and stares down at them.

'Clare, I've been thinking,' he says awkwardly. 'Things got a bit ... heated ... before I left. Maybe I said things I shouldn't have. These lawyers: they should know when you're just letting off steam. They twist things and make them sound so much worse than you mean.'

'Do you really think I poisoned Poppy, Marc?'

Startled at my bluntness, he looks up.

'No,' he says, after a long moment. 'No, I don't think that. Not any more.'

'I'm their mother,' I say quietly. 'I know I'm not perfect, but they need me. We can't snatch them back and forth like trophies. We have to put them first. They need me,' I repeat.

Marc stares in surprise. I realize I've never actually stepped forward and claimed my role as mother before.

'You never seemed interested in them. It was always the bloody shops—'

'And that made it OK to just *take* him?'

He scowls. 'I never meant things to go this far. Even when I borrowed the cash from Hamish, I didn't really mean to go through with it.' He glances at the chaotic street, the vendors selling soft pretzels, the women in black chadors, the unfamiliar shop signs in Arabic, as if seeing it all for the first time. 'It just ... it got out of hand. I've wanted to call you. Rowan was so much more upset than I thought he'd be. I tried to find him a babysitter, but—'

'Marc. Please. Let me take him home.'

For a long moment, he hesitates. And then he nods, once.

I close my eyes, sick with relief. Cooper has been wonderful, finding Rowan; but I couldn't have lived with the fear and uncertainty of never knowing when Marc would try to kidnap my children again. Stealing my son back from him would have meant depriving the twins of their father for ever. I couldn't do that to them. And, despite everything he's done, I couldn't do it to Marc either.

'They need you too,' I add.

His eyes blaze with sudden hope. My heart unexpectedly twists with pity.

'Do you – do you think we – not now, but maybe—'

I should despise him, for what he's done to me. The past four weeks have been unimaginable. I've missed Rowan so much, some days I haven't wanted to get out of bed. The only thing that made it even slightly bearable was the knowledge that at least my child was with his father; at least he was cared for and loved. I cannot begin to comprehend how the mothers of children who are abducted by strangers cope. Their lives must simply stop.

But I can't find it in me to hate him. He's the father of my children. He's been my partner for seven years, and I can't just switch off my feelings. It may not have been a passionate marriage, or a meeting of minds, but until recently it worked. I just dropped the ball, that's all. If I really try, maybe it's not too late to put things right.

Pity isn't love.

'I don't know,' I say honestly.

Marc nods again, satisfied for now.

A horn blares near us, making us both jump. Jenna beckons to me from car. In the driver's seat, Cooper is staring straight ahead, his eyes on the road.

'You should go,' Marc says.

'Yes.'

He puts his hand on my sleeve. 'Kiss Poppy for me.'

I climb into the car. Rowan is asleep in Jenna's arms, worn out with crying. I twist round in the back seat, watching Marc diminish through the rear window. His head is bowed as if in prayer, and I know without being able to see his face that he's crying.

Cooper doesn't fly back to London with us. Josef drops us at Beirut Airport, since we no longer need to flee to Damascus, and without a word Cooper books himself on a flight back to the US via Paris. I buy tickets to Heathrow for Rowan, Jenna and me, my heart aching. I can't blame Cooper. I know how he feels about me, and I know exactly what I've just done.

He doesn't even glance at me as we check in separately, much less say goodbye. I watch him pass through security, his back rigid, his long coat swirling angrily around his ankles. I can't bear to leave things like this. I never made any promises, but I have to explain. Somehow, I have to make him understand.

'I'm going to take Rowan to the bathroom,' Jenna says, watching Cooper. 'I'll see you at the gate.'

I find him hunched over a small cup of thick, black Arabic coffee at a bar to one end of the long marble concourse. The chrome stools on either side of him are free, but I hesitate to sit down. I can tell from the way his shoulders stiffen that he knows I'm there, but he doesn't look round.

'Cooper, I'm sorry,' I say nervously. The words sound hopelessly inadequate, even to me. 'You've been wonderful, and I couldn't bear—'

'We got Rowan back. He's safe with you. That's what we came for.'

'I know, but I wanted to explain what—'

'No need.'

'Cooper, could you at least turn round?' I say desperately.

He pushes himself away from the bar and turns, folding his arms. His navy eyes are hard and opaque.

'Can't we discuss this?'

'Why?'

I know this man can talk. I've read his prose, eloquent and moving. Yesterday he spoke to me as no one ever has before, making me feel normal and human and capable of this impossible feat, *motherhood*, for the first time since the twins were born. When he cares about something, he is passionate and fluent. And yet most of the time he communicates in terse Neanderthal monosyllables.

'Why are you making this so difficult?' I demand. 'What exactly have I done wrong? I persuaded Marc to let me take Rowan home. Isn't that what we wanted? Why are you treating me like I've just done a deal with Stalin?'

'Point made.'

He turns back to his coffee. I experience a blinding rush of anger. Does he think this is easy for me either? Does he think I don't *care*?

'If you want to wall yourself off from the rest of the human race, fine. I can't stop you,' I say furiously. 'You've been doing it for forty-nine years, so I guess you're used to it. But I can't. After everything that's happened, I'm not letting you pretend it meant nothing! You know how I feel about you! If it wasn't for the twins—'

'Do you think that helps?' Cooper snaps. 'You think it's some sort of consolation?'

'He's their father! I have to give him another chance!'

'So go. Do it.'

'I don't understand. What is it you want from me?' I cry helplessly.

His dark eyes blaze, and there is such raw heat in his expression that a fierce answering pulse of lust beats between my legs. My nipples tighten, and suddenly I can feel his warm mouth on them. His hands are skimming the surface of my skin, following the curve of my hips, sliding into the damp shadow beneath my breasts, exploring the warm, wet folds and crevices of my most intimate places. He hasn't touched me, and yet I can feel him in every cell of my body.

'I can't,' I whisper. 'The twins need their father. I can't just turn my back on Marc. He needs me—'

'I need you.'

'You're stronger than he is. You'll be fine without me. In a few weeks' time you won't even remember—'

'Your husband needs a wife. A housekeeper. Someone to look after him. I need *you*.' He pulls me into a tense embrace, his hands on my shoulders, his mouth inches from my ear. 'No one else sees you, Clare. No one else knows you the way I do. You don't need another child to look after. You need a man who can butt heads with you and win. It won't be easy. It'll be hard, and we'll have to work at it every single day. But it'll be worth it, because we'll have each other. Don't settle for second best. Don't take the easy way out.'

'What easy way? There is no easy way!'

'What do you want, Clare?'

'It's not that simple—'

'Stop thinking about what the twins need, what Marc needs! What about what *you* need? What is it you want, Clare?'

'I can't just—'

'Damn it, Clare! *What do you want?*'

I break away, panting as if I've just run a mile. Cooper drops his hands and opens his arms, letting me go.

'I can't. I'm sorry. I can't.'

I turn and run, as if the hounds of hell are behind me.

For four weeks, all I could think about was 'when Rowan comes home'. My entire being was focused on that one event, like a small child looking forward to Christmas, unable to imagine a day that might come afterwards. I should – I *do* – feel relieved, thankful, grateful and happy. I bathe my babies, savouring their laughter, revelling in the extraordinary resilience of childhood. They wake the next morning in bed beside me, squawking for breakfast, warm and soft and sweet-smelling, and my heart sings as I pull them into my arms. I feel lucky, blessed, as if I've been given a rare second chance.

I also feel bleak and empty, as if a Siberian wind has swept through me and hollowed me out. I want to crawl into a cold, dark place and hide.

Brendan, the young policeman who seemed more sympathetic than his colleagues when Rowan disappeared, and who stopped by almost every day even when there was no news, arrives shortly after our return with shiny blue helium balloons and a bottle of champagne.

'You're not pressing charges?' he asks, incredulous, as we open the champagne in the kitchen, even though it's barely nine-thirty in the morning.

'I keep telling her,' Jenna scowls.

'He agreed to let me bring Rowan back,' I say evenly.

'He has enough to worry about. He has no job, no money, nowhere to live. He's the twins' father. Sooner or later, we have to start mending bridges.'

Marc calls me a week later from a small flat he's rented in Clapham. 'I'm not ready,' I tell him. 'Just give me a little more time.'

I throw myself into work, but it doesn't have the same power of distraction it used to. Every time the doorbell in the shop rings, I look up, despising myself for my foolishness. *You made the right decision*, I tell myself firmly. *If Cooper can't understand that, it's just proof it would never have worked.*

Ten days after we return from Beirut, a bouquet of hyacinths arrives at home. Hyacinths: *You love me and destroy me.* Furiously I throw them into the dustbin, and then spend half an hour fishing them out and rearranging them in a glass vase.

'Those look pretty,' Jenna says when she comes in; and is then thrown into confusion when I burst into tears.

At Jenna's insistence I go to the doctor, who diagnoses post-traumatic stress and prescribes me Lexapro for depression and Xanax to calm me down. I throw the prescription in the rubbish bin on my way out of the surgery, and stop off at Patrick Cox on the way home for a new pair of shoes.

When I get back Jenna is sitting on the bottom stair, holding an opened letter. The twins have emptied her handbag and are playing with a box of Tampax while she sits, oblivious, staring at the paper in her hand.

I retrieve her mobile phone from sticky fingers, and put the top back on her new red lipstick, which is now drilled with tiny toothmarks.

She hands me the letter. 'My birthday present from Xan.'

It's a bank statement. I glance up, puzzled.

'Look at the bottom of the page,' she says dizzily.

Twenty-five thousand pounds. Even by Xan's standards, that's a little over the top.

'He's not coming back, is he?' Jenna says.

I sit on the stairs beside her. 'Not for a while,' I say carefully.

'Do you think it had anything to do with me?'

'I think you were the reason he stayed as long as he did.' I choose my words carefully. 'He's given up his flat and quit his job, Jenna. He said he needed to travel for a bit, to get his head straight. I don't know when, or even if, he'll come back. I think he'll end up in Italy; he's always loved it there.'

Jenna nods. I realize there will never be a better moment to tell her my decision.

When Marc walked out, Jenna promised she would never leave me. I was able to bury my fear and loneliness because she was there to pick up the pieces, to slide effortlessly into the role Marc had vacated. If she hadn't shored me up, I might have surrendered to the black terror that engulfed me whenever I stopped working or moving, whenever I gave myself a moment to think.

But things have changed. I'm not the same person I was six weeks ago. When the twins were born, I believed I lacked maternal instinct, that I was my mother's daughter; that I needed Jenna to do what I could not: to mother my children. In some ways, I know she is still more suited to the task than me: she's able to live in the moment, be in the present far better than I am. I'm always so busy worrying about the next problem, the next crisis. But I gave my mothering away for far too long, out of panic and fear. I was both lucky and unlucky to find Jenna; to employ a nanny so warm and competent that I felt I could never match up.

Beirut has changed that. Rowan and Poppy are my children. Only I will do.

'We need to talk,' I say.

'Oh God. That's never good,' Jenna sighs.

I pick up Poppy, and she scoops up Rowan. We sit side by side on the stairs, a child in each lap. I realize how foolish I was to worry about Jenna taking my place. In the end, this isn't about Jenna and the twins, or me and the twins; but about Jenna and me.

'I'll never be able to thank you enough,' I acknowledge, 'for what you did in Beirut. You were amazing. Not many girls would have had the guts.'

'Leap before you look, that's my motto.'

I smile. 'Jenna—'

'Am I being fired?'

'I don't think I'm going to need a full-time nanny any more,' I say softly. 'I want to do things with the twins myself. I know I'll never have the same knack as you, but I want to try. The thing is—'

'It's OK, Clare. I get it.' Efficiently, she rubs lipstick off Rowan's cheek with her thumb. 'You've been really good to me. I don't think I'd have had the balls to get away from Jamie if it hadn't been for you. You were really there for me. I'm going to miss you all terribly, but I understand.'

She's suddenly very busy brushing down her skirt.

I touch her arm. 'Jenna, I don't want you to leave—'

'No, it's fine, you don't have to explain.' She jumps up. 'So. I'll call the agency and tell them. Would you like me to work a couple of weeks' notice, or—'

'I don't want you to leave,' I repeat. 'Jenna, I don't need a nanny any more. That doesn't mean I don't need *you*.'

She looks understandably confused.

'I want you to work for me at PetalPushers. As a manager.'

I lead her into the sitting room. We put the twins into their playpen, and sit opposite one another on the same sofa where I interviewed her all those months ago.

'You're a wonderful nanny, but sooner or later you're going to want children of your own,' I tell her. 'You need a break from babies before that happens, trust me. You're so good at organizing things. You're a natural manager.'

'I – I don't know—'

'Craig will be there to look after the business, but you'll be in charge of the Fulham shop. Molly wants to move to the Camden branch to be nearer to her family. You can take over from her.'

'I've never done anything like that before. I'm not sure if I could.'

'I've watched you for the past few weeks at the shop. You're a fast learner, and you're good with people. Anyway, it wouldn't be full-time; not yet, anyway. I thought, if you agree, of course, we could sort of . . . job-share. Just until the twins go to nursery. We'll have to work out the details, but it would mean I could spend more time with the twins, and still run my company. And you'd get the chance to stretch your wings and learn something new.'

Unexpectedly, she bursts into tears. I can't remember ever seeing her cry before. 'Oh, Clare. Yes, please,' she sniffs. 'I'm sorry, I was just – I couldn't bear to leave – I'd miss you all so much—'

My own throat is suddenly clogged. We've come a long way in the past six months, I realize. At the start of any relationship, romantic or otherwise, you never know quite how or where it will end. That first, giddy honeymoon stage never lasts. If you're lucky it gives way to a deeper, less intoxicating but ultimately more fulfilling relationship built on love and trust and mutual respect. Or it will fail; all that promise and hope ground down by neglect, until nothing is left but recrimination and regret. In the end, like so many things, so much of it comes down to luck.

Jenna and I have come from very different places, and been dealt very different cards. But in the end, I think, as we get up and go into the kitchen and start the familiar routine of making tea, we are just two women who know without words how hard and terrifying and amazing motherhood can be, regardless of whose hand rocks the cradle; and who understand that, from the moment you learn to love, you must also learn to let go.

Two days later, Marc is sitting on the front steps when I return home late from work.

'I didn't ring the doorbell,' he says, standing. 'I didn't want to put Jenna on the spot.'

'She's not here this evening. She went to a policeman's ball, of all things.'

Brendan still seems to find himself 'just passing', even though the case has been formally closed for weeks. I'm glad, for Jenna's sake. Xan was never going to settle down.

'Can I come in?'

I hesitate. 'The twins aren't here. Davina has them for the weekend. She seems to be taking to grandmotherhood rather well, actually, though she'll kill anyone who calls her that. She's left Guy, did you know? It appears she found him with a fourteen-year-old stable-girl and called the police. He's out on bail, but Davina's already changed the locks.'

I'm aware I'm babbling. I knew Marc would come back home, sooner or later. I've been through this in my head a thousand times. I can make it work. The twins deserve a proper family. It'll be different this time.

I'm not ready.

Pity isn't love.

'I'm sorry I've missed them,' Marc says, 'but it was you I wanted to talk to.'

He follows me into the kitchen. It seems odd to see him here: at once familiar and strange. I pour him his usual Scotch; he nurses the glass, but doesn't really drink. We stand awkwardly on opposite sides of the kitchen island, and I look at my husband and try, very hard, to remember why I married him.

'I'm going back to Canada,' Marc says abruptly. 'I wanted you to know.'

For a moment, I'm too stunned to speak.

'Canada?'

He shrugs. 'I can't get another job here, not with the financial markets in the mess they're in. And to be honest, I'm not sure I still want to do this kind of work. I want something a bit more . . . real.'

'But why not stay in England?'

'My family are in Canada. I need to be around them right now.'

'I thought – you said you wanted—'

Marc puts down his untouched glass. He moves around the counter and gently wraps his arms around me. To my surprise, it's strangely comforting. 'It was never going to work, Clare,' he murmurs into my hair. 'Not after everything that's happened. We both know that.'

'We could try. We've both made mistakes, but—'

'Clare, even you can't fix everything.'

'Are you sure this is what you want?'

He pulls back, his gaze searching. 'Can you honestly tell me you're disappointed?'

I'm swept with sadness. We started out with so much hope and faith. I was so sure we'd make it, if I just kept *trying*.

'The thing is,' he adds, suddenly awkward, 'I've met someone. It's early days yet,' he adds hastily. 'We sat next to each other on the flight back from Lebanon. She's twenty-three. She lives in Montreal too; our parents even know each other. It seems they're third cousins or something. You know how it is with the Lebanese.'

I don't, but I nod politely.

'I won't see as much of the twins as I'd like. But I'll be back and forth to London every couple of months. And maybe, when they're older, they can come visit.'

'Maybe,' I say.

I kiss him goodbye, relieved but also strangely bereft. It's not just Marc I've lost. I had a vision of the future, a life that included a husband and family. I feel as if I've somehow lost my innocence. The page is no longer fresh, but blotted with mistakes and crossings-out. Life will go on, but nothing will ever be quite the same.

Worst of all, of course, is the knowledge that I have lost Cooper for nothing.

Only for my children. I would have given him up for nothing and no one but them.

'Call him,' Jenna urges, one night when we have both stayed up too late and drunk too much wine. 'What have you got to lose?'

'I made a choice,' I tell her. 'No matter what happened between us, he'd always remember that.'

I take heart, instead, from her blossoming romance with Brendan. Jenna has been through the romantic mill: first with Jamie, and then Xan. I know my brother came very close to breaking her heart. Brendan Kelly is the sort of man she wouldn't have looked at twice a year ago: respectable, thoughtful, quite handsome in a conventional way, but lacking that devilish spark, that certain something, that sets girls' hearts pounding. He's too *nice*, I decide, the second time he comes round to take Jenna out, as I put his flowers – coals to Newcastle, but it's the thought that counts – into a vase. Women like the bastards, heaven only knows why. You don't appreciate a decent man until you've been hurt a few times. Perhaps Jenna wasn't ready for Brendan until now. Maybe, somewhere out there, someone is waiting for me to be ready too.

The first Saturday in September, at Davina's suggestion, I take the twins to Long Meadow for the weekend. She hustles me unceremoniously back out to the car. 'I'm sure you have work to do at the shop,' she says, 'and I don't want to be inhospitable, darling, but I have a gentleman friend visiting this afternoon. The twins will be a charming addition, but one really doesn't need one's *adult* daughter broadcasting one's age.'

Slightly put out, I drive back to Fulham. Jenna made me promise to go in and sort out the accounts this weekend, so I might as well get on with it. Finances will clearly never be her forte, and the last thing I need is to play gooseberry to my own mother.

I notice with annoyance that Anna, the Saturday temp, has filled every single bucket outside the shop with yellow tulips. They look wonderful, of course, but the sun will wilt them in a matter of hours.

I storm in, ready to haul her over the coals, and find my way barricaded by another magnificent bank of yellow tulips. Clearly there's a problem with the suppliers. We seem to have half the fields of Amsterdam filling our floor space.

'Anna!' I move a large box of orchids and red heather out of my way. 'Anna, I can hardly move in here! We need to call—'

A shadow moves in the back of the shop.

I gasp, and drop the box of orchids.

Cooper carelessly pushes aside the heaps of flowers blocking his way, and picks up the orchids, lifting the cellophane lid. 'There are over twenty-five thousand species of orchid,' he says conversationally, 'more than any other flower. In the wild, they grow in the rainforests of the tropics, strange and brilliant, their intense scent almost too much to bear. The Victorians believed they stood for ecstasy.'

Davina, Jenna: they must have been in on this.

'Red heather,' Cooper says, handing me a spray, 'promised passion. Lavender' – he adds it to the heap in my arms – 'signified devotion. Orange blossom, eternal love. Red roses, of course, need no explanation.'

My arms are full.

'Cooper—'

'You made the right choice. The only choice. I promised you the next time I rescued anyone, it would be you.'

'Cooper,' I whisper.

'Yellow tulips,' he says, drawing me towards him, down into a dizzying kiss, crushing the flowers in my arms between us, drowning us both in their heady, glorious, intoxicating scent.

Hopeless devotion.

'Yellow tulips,' I say.

Acknowledgements

As always, my deepest thanks to my wonderful friend and agent, Carole Blake, and to my talented (and patient!) editor, Imogen Taylor. I am the luckiest of writers to have both of you. Every conversation is a pleasure.

All those at Blake Friedmann and Pan Macmillan – Oli Munson, Trisha Jackson, my smart, eagle-eyed copy editor Vicki Harris – you are amazing. How you manage to do what you do, in the time that you do it, never fails to astonish me.

In researching the background to this novel, I found one book, *The Meaning of Flowers: Myth, Language & Lore* by Gretchen Scoble and Ann Field, particularly helpful. I recommend it to any readers looking to pursue this avenue of interest.

For the girls: Michèle, Georgie, Danusia and Sarah: what would I do without you? The next book is specially for you . . . I love you all.

Kisses, too, to my father Michael and WSM Barbi, to my out-laws, Sharon and Harry, to Charles and Rachel, to Brent and especially to my WIL Jelena: thank you all for providing me with never a dull moment. I'm truly blessed in having a family like mine.

Henry, Matthew and Lily: you're the reason I get up in the morning. Quite literally, thank you very much. I adore you.

To my wonderful, amazing mother, Jane, whose love, wit and wisdom I miss still.

Above all, to my husband, Erik. For tea in the morning, for 3 a.m. editing sessions, and for quite simply being the sexiest, funniest, most wonderful man alive.

TESS STIMSON
Vermont, September 2008
www.tessstimson.com